R.W.W. Greene

EARTH RETROGRADE

THE FIRST PLANETS, BOOK II

ANGRY ROBOT
An imprint of Watkins Media Ltd

Unit 11, Shepperton House
89 Shepperton Road
London N1 3DF
UK

angryrobotbooks.com
twitter.com/angryrobotbooks
Guess Who's Back

An Angry Robot paperback original, 2023

Cover by Kieryn Tyler
Edited by Eleanor Teasddale, Paul Simpson and Andrew Hook
Set in Meridien

ISBN 978 1 91520 248 2
Ebook ISBN 978 1 91520 247 5

Printed and bound in the United Kingdom by TJ Books Ltd.

9 8 7 6 5 4 3 2 1

To Jack the Cat who woke me every day at 3:15am, and/or 4:23am, and/or 5am so I could finish this book. He's the real hero here.

Excerpt from the First Prime Ambassador's televised speech to the United Nations, Oct. 1, 1979.

I regret...

...the need to interrupt this period of mourning. Millions of your brothers, sisters, parents, lovers, children, and friends died over the past year because your leaders chose to ignore the First's rightful claim to this planet and resist their directives. I will restate the latter so they cannot be misinterpreted by those who would mislead you regarding their content.

Directive One: Effective 11:59pm, Greenwich Standard Time, Aug. 13, 2036, any humans remaining on Earth will be euthanized and disintegrated without appeal.

Directive Two: Prior to that deadline, humanity will mitigate the damage it has done to this world, its moon, and its gravity well to the furthest extent possible. Your settlements, infrastructure, and monuments, with very few exceptions, will be rendered to raw materials and returned to the earth.

It is the responsibility of your governments and corporations to create the means of planetary evacuation. Limited technological and organizational assistance will be made available to this end. Questions may be communicated via the numerous embassies we have established.

We have prepared a sanctuary beneath the surface of the planet you know as Venus. It is the native world of the First, but humanity may make use of it until the First have need of it again.

Regarding the planet Mars, the planet's native species was well established when the First traveled there four billion years ago, but it has since departed. We have no indication when or if it will return but see no reason why you should not make use of the planet until that time.

Humanity may make proportional use of the resources of the asteroid belts as well as those of Jupiter, Uranus, Neptune, Saturn, and Pluto.

People of Earth, you have seen our evidence, and you have experienced a measure of First capabilities. This planet belongs to the First by right of a claim made millions of years before your species evolved. You cannot remain here, and you would be wise to come to terms with that reality sooner rather than later. To put it simply, we were here first.

TIMELINE

- 1945 – Robert Oppenheimer invents the Atomic Engine.
- 1950 – Humanity walks on the Moon.
- 1951 – Brooklyn Lamontagne is born.
- 1956 – Brooklyn, age five, listens to coverage of Chuck Yeager's landing on Mars.
- 1961 – Topeka, Kansas and Ufa, Russia are destroyed by meteorites. Jet Carson and the Freedom 7 face off against the so-called Mercurian Menace.
- 1967 – John F. Kennedy, saved from assassination by an alien agent, begins his second term.
- 1972 – Cleveland, Ohio is wiped out by a meteorite. George McGovern, a pacifist – and secretly an alien, loses campaign momentum, and hawkish Richard Nixon wins election to the U.S. presidency.
- Fall of 1976 – Brooklyn enlists in the Earth Orbital Forces to avoid a prison sentence. Jimmy Carter and Jessie Jackson are elected to the White House.
- July 1978 – Brooklyn and Designed Ambassador "Andy" Andromeda fly from Venus in an antique spaceship to save New York City from a meteorite and the Earth from a suicidal war against the returning First. Brooklyn sacrifices his life so the mission will succeed.
- October 1978 – Responding to First demands, Earth forces attack the Designed ambassadors. Using First Tech, the Designed shut down all electrical power on the planet for several months.

- November 1978 – Andy leads an unsuccessful attack against the Prime Ambassador's ship in an attempt to get the power back on. She flees into space.
- November 1980 – Bob Dole is elected President of the U.S.
- Spring 1981 – Salvagers recover Brooklyn's frozen body from high-Earth orbit, and thanks to treatments he received from the mysterious Dr Paul Carruthers, he returns to life. The EOF discharges Brooklyn with prejudice because of his alleged collaboration with the enemy, and his Earth citizenship is revoked.
- 1983 – Designed scientists create an airborne AIDS vaccine and release it worldwide.
- 1984 – Dole rides his 'wartime' presidency status to a second term.
- 1985 – The first of the United Nations evacuation flights heads to Venus.
- Fall 1987 – Designed scientists unleash an airborne virus that destroys the fertility of fifty percent of humans who contract it. Andy and the Designed outlaws liberate a vaccine for the contagion and give it to the United Nations.
- Oct. 14, 1987 – Baby Jessica falls down a well. She is saved within two hours by Designed engineers.
- Spring 1988 – The original Designed are replaced by the so-called Angels and the First Cathedral of the Cosmos. The Cardinal of the Cosmos becomes the First's representative on Earth.
- 1988 – Donald Rumsfeld is elected president of the United States.
- 1990 – The U.S. and U.S.S.R. announce they will evacuate their citizens to Mars instead of Venus.
- 1992 – Pat Buchanan, with support of the First Church of the Cosmos, wins election to the U.S. Presidency. The presidential term limit is revoked.
- 1995 – The third U.N. evacuation flight leaves for Venus.
- Fall 1999 – Brooklyn gets a message.

PART ONE
Fall 1999

ONE

The old ship rocked, the forces of re-entry buffeting and scorching. A lot of the tell-tale lights on the control surfaces blinked to yellow or red. Too many stayed that way. The pilot tapped one of the more important ones, and it flickered reluctantly back to green. He wished he could set himself straight so easily. *Fifteen words. Fifteen fucking words that change everything.*

Overhead, a conifer-shaped air freshener danced on the end of a string and lost ground to hot circuits, baked dust, and the salty, clam-flat miasma of the copilot's breath.

"You check the thing?" the pilot said.

"Did." The copilot was wearing a bulky exosuit. Inside it, her mouth, arms, and tentacles moved languidly through a chilly, fishy brine that mimicked her natural environment.

"You check it, check it, or just look at the lights?"

"Jelly Tech doesn't break."

Do you know anythin"bout this? The pilot's attention leapt back to the coded message he'd received moments before initiating reentry. *Fifteen words.* Two decades living under a sword, millions dead, millions more displaced, billions terrified. *And the fuckin' sword decides to split*! The First Cathedral of the Cosmos still loomed over the planet. Jury-rigged scavenger ships labored daily to sweep human garbage from orbital space. Construction crews lived and died in the vacuum, piecing together the latest evacuation fleet.... There was a large, glaring absence of proof, but the messenger was generally reliable.

He rubbed his face. Present tense. Stay in the moment. "Ain't the Jelly Tech I'm worried about. What does Bugs say?"

"Your toy computer has crashed. Again. Shall I reboot it and ask more politely?"

"Don't understand why you ain't freaking out about any-a this," he said.

"Jellies don't break, either."

Something in the ship's living section fell over with a bangclatter. "Nice work locking things down back there."

The copilot gurgled. "It was your turn to secure the–"

An explosion off to port rocked the ship. The radio crackled. "Unknown vessel, this is Earth Emigration & Customs, identify yourself immediately."

"They talking to us?"

The copilot manipulated the radio with one metal hand. "It appears so. The camouflage may not be functioning correctly."

The radio again. "Unknown vessel, identify yourself." A second explosion, this time from starboard. E&C picket ships bracketing the target, showing off, or just aiming badly. The pilot had made hundreds of successful clandestine landings on Earth over the years – from Venus, from Mars, from the Belt, from the Moon – but today of all days...

"You said you checked it!"

"Our tech doesn't break."

"Something fucking did!"

"Unknown vessel, identify yourself or number three is going right up your ass." The voice on the radio was not pitched to amuse.

The copilot folded her arms across her broad chest. "We should have armed the ship."

"The hell would a few guns do?"

"Far more than your panic. Earth ships are not insuperable."

"Unknown vessel, this is your final warning."

The pilot jammed his finger at the radio, triggering its transmission function. "This is the *Sweet & Low* out of De Milo." He rattled off a string of numbers; counterfeit, but they'd worked a decade before. "See, nice and friendly."

A projectile hit the ship somewhere, creating a spin the pilot barely recovered from. Then another, nearly worse. "That ID doesn't wash. Next shot's gonna coun–"

The pilot stabbed the radio again. "It's Brooklyn Lamontagne, damn it! Brooklyn Fucking Lamontagne! On board the *Victory*!"

They were escorted to a porta-office. It was like a semi-trailer with one end tapered to an acute angle, made to be easily transportable and one day packed into an evacuation ship to serve as housing on Venus.

The E&C official was middle management, human and sour. He failed to introduce himself, but a nameplate ratted him out as 'Special Agent Peter Cramm'. The distaste showed in his face as he pointed out an object on his cheap, foldable desk. "What's this?"

"A rock," Brooklyn said.

"I see it's a fucking rock." It was gray, veined with crystal. "Why do you have half-a-ton of them boxed up in your hold?"

"Ballast. Keeps the ship from rolling in rough weather."

"Bullshit."

Brooklyn leaned back in the chair. "Old ship. Doesn't handle like the new ones."

Cramm directed his attention to the copilot. "And who are you?"

"That's Float," Brooklyn said.

"That is not my name," the medusozoa said. "Brooklyn tends to abbreviate the names of those familiar to him."

"What's your real name, then?"

Float helped him with the spelling so he could type it into the desk computer.

The guy's eyes flicked back and forth, scanning the records. "Says here you have diplomatic immunity." His eyes landed on Brooklyn. "But you don't. In fact, you weren't ever supposed to come back to Earth. Any reason I shouldn't seize your ship and turn you over to the judge?"

"Saved the world a while back." Brooklyn stroked the patchy stubble on his jaw. "That count for anything?'

Cramm tented his hands on his desk. "Computer says you were discharged with prejudice from the Earth Orbital Forces and nearly got your ass jailed for treason."

"Working with the enemy." Brooklyn smirked. "An' here you are working *for* them. How's that going? Sleepin' okay? How're the job prospects?"

Not a nervous swallow, not a nostril flare, not a dilated pupil. Cramm wasn't in the know, or he was hell at the poker table. "You're also a known associate of the leader of the Designed Liberation Front."

"Dated a while in the '70s. Haven't seen her since before she went all Pancho Villa on you."

Cramm tapped the computer monitor. "Record says you were born in 1951."

"Sounds right."

"You don't look forty-eight. Had to guess, I'd say you haven't cleared thirty yet."

"Atkins Diet. Keeps me lean and mean." Brooklyn let the front legs of the chair touch down. "Look, take my prints if you want. They'll check out. I'm the one and only, and ain't no warrants out on me."

"What are you doing back here?"

Brooklyn pulled a lazily folded piece of paper out of his jacket pocket and dropped it on the desk. His get out-of-jail-free card for this trip. Better than some he'd had, weaker than others."Class reunion. Big three-oh."

Cramm looked the paper over. "Says here you're a day early and twenty thousand miles too low. Reunion's on *Eisenhower*. You were in a landing approach."

"The navigation system crashed, and I lost track o' where I was. Then some asshole shot at us. You gonna pay for the repairs?"

Cramm reddened. "You got twelve hours down here to arrange for ship repairs and get back into orbit." He stamped the visa. "Next time we see your ass down here, we shoot to kill."

The Emigration & Customs inspectors hadn't limited themselves to the cargo hold. The team was finishing up in the engineering section. Float excused herself to check the 'ballast', and left Brooklyn to negotiate.

"Damned antique is what we got here," said the team's boss, a cigar-chomping woman of about fifty. She wiped her hands with a greasy rag that she stuffed into her pocket. "Didn't know any of these were still flying."

"Might be the only one," Brooklyn said. "Got it as salvage in the early '80s."

Her cigar bobbed. "EOF the only ones who made fuel for the Type Threes. Got an old depot you been raiding or somethin'?"

"Stealing from depots is illegal, ma'am," Brooklyn said. "We get our fuel in the Belt, mostly."

"In the Belt." She pulled the rag back out and blew her nose in it. "You can get anything in the Belt. That's what they say. Right, Paul?"

The guy she called Paul was about her age, balding. He whistled. "Never heard that about the Belt, boss. That's where the Reds send their political prisoners, right? I don't remember reading anything about them being well-provisioned."

"They're doin' a lot better now," Brooklyn said. "Ought to go out and see."

"Maybe I will." She beckoned her flunky. "Paul, show the man what we found on his ship."

"You did some nice modifications on this thing." Paul led the way to something Brooklyn had hoped they wouldn't spot. "Used to be you couldn't get one of these off the ground without a launch sled."

"Put a set of First Tech lifters in as soon as I could. Cleaner, quicker, a lot less fuel."

"Saw the field generator, too. Lets you get up to speed helluva a lot quicker, I bet."

"Fuck physics, right?" Brooklyn said. *Fucking things is what the First do best.*

Paul stopped and rested his hands on a metal box wired into the power systems. "This appears to be Jelly Tech, though. If I ain't mistaking," he tapped the box, "this is one of those gadgets lets the Jellies hide from First Tech. Couple of tweaks, an' it works real good on our stuff, too."

And shit. Brooklyn rubbed his jaw. "All I know is the guy put it in for me said it would make the HVAC work better."

"Did it?" Paul smiled.

"I'm still breathing."

"Lucky," the boss lady said. "And you're damned lucky this little sneak box ain't working. Level One contraband. We'd have to run you in for it."

Brooklyn whistled. "How much would it cost to have you rip that horrible thing out of my ship and run it through a crusher?"

"Be safer for all concerned that way." She pretended to do some math and offered a number.

Brooklyn reached for his wallet.

"An' don't forget Paul."

Float flexed her exosuit's fingers. "The ship was holed twice. One of the projectiles passed through a rib on the starboard side. In addition, several systems were damaged during the search. It would not be wise to fly without repairs."

Brooklyn avoided looking at the severed power cables that had led to his Jelly Tech camouflage unit. Paul had not been gentle or tidy. "We know anyone local?"

"The Konduz brothers aren't far, but it will be more expensive if they have to come to us."

"Had to pay four days of parking fees as part of the impound. Don't see E&C giving us a refund if we leave early."

"You should have used one of the fake IDs that still worked."

"Demarco's message threw me." The printout was still in his pocket, decoded right before re-entry. *Have it on good authority OAO have pulled out. Keep it under wraps. More later.* Demarco often referred to the First as 'OAO', short for 'Our Alien Overlords'. "You think he's right?"

The exosuit's right arm rose to chest level, and it twisted its wrist back and forth – Float's version of a noncommittal shrug. "The First are achieving their goal. Leaving would be against the tide."

Brooklyn pinched the muscles in the back of his neck. "Fixup's all you. You know where the cash is stashed. I'll make the delivery, but if an exit ticket with my name on it don't ping on their systems soon, Emigration's gonna be on my ass."

"Diplomatic immunity." The jelly's laugh sounded like a bad head cold. She might have been laughing at Brooklyn's inconvenience, the rules of diplomacy, or the number of syllables in the phrase 'diplomatic immunity'. Hard to tell with Jellies.

"I'll take your word for it." Brooklyn slung his go-bag over his shoulder. "Call you as soon as I can."

TWO

Brooklyn punched the next preset on the van radio and caught the back half of a Zeppelin tune on New Jersey's WKXW. FM radio was getting weird, and it didn't help that there wasn't much new to play. Established artists only, the cash cows. Broadcasters padded the thin air with blocks of the old stuff and increasingly paranoid talk shows. AM was where the action was – lots of live recordings from local clubs and basement studios. Pirate shit, mostly, now that the Feds had more important things to worry about. Too bad the rental van's radio wouldn't switch over. Too bad the cassette deck was busted.

A right turn at the Nity Nite Motel – where particolored block lettering promised color TV's, adult movies, and water beds – and past the strip club. Park beside the next warehouse on the left. On the side of the warehouse were the words "GIVE US BACK THE POWER YOUR KILLING US!", an appeal not addressed to anyone local.

The rental van squeaked to a stop. Piles of pallets and dented trash bins warred with blanket squats for indifference, half-shadowed and half-jaundiced by the shitty lighting. Brooklyn twisted the key back in millimeter increments and killed the engine. It ticked, cooling after the long drive from LaGuardia. If Demarco was right, this might be the last delivery, the final exchange of relics from the archeological dig on Venus for cash. *It figures that peace, or whatever the hell this is, would hit me right in the wallet.*

The key went into his pocket, the van door locked behind him. The air was warm and thick but cleaner than it had any right to be. The regulations and tech the First had deployed against the human stain were doing their jobs.

Maybe a little too well. *Where the hell is everyone?* He straightened the collar of his jacket. "Whack?"

The only sounds were from traffic and whatever bassy pop was playing at the strip club next door. Brooklyn's head got swimmy for a couple of seconds while his eyes, ears, and nose tuned up, the shit he'd been laced with in the service reacting to stress chemicals. It was a new trick. He'd been stronger and faster since the beginning; the super senses had only shown up after a bender a couple of months before.

Seeing and hearing better than the average bear didn't make Whack-Whack appear, but the parking spot looked a hell of a lot worse. Smelled worse, too. Heinz-level varieties of piss and rot. Brooklyn rapped at the side door where Whack usually met him. It swung open on its own.

Shit. He'd been making drop offs at the warehouse for more than seven years, and that had never happened. The security camera whined overhead, its autofocus doing its best to keep up.

"Whack?" He pushed the door open more. The lighting was better inside, but there were still plenty of ambush-friendly shadows. "Tony? It's Donato." Brooklyn's ma, Lola, had been Lolita Villalobos before she married Arnaud "Al" Lamontagne in '49. It hadn't been too hard to pass as "Donato Diaz" in the New Jersey underworld. "Hello?"

Whack-Whack was a wiry little guy, skinny as a shadow, but Big Tony would have been hard to miss in the grayscale Brooklyn's enhanced vision turned the scene into. *Darlin', you got to let me know...* He hummed some more of the song as he slid through the door, his back against the wall. There was a greasy, burnt smell – copper, and a hint of ozone. Somebody's lunch left too long in the microwave, maybe. Up the stairs.

The light was still on in the office, but that room was empty as well. No sign of a struggle or quick exit. Worse, no envelope of cash for the Venus-to-New Jersey delivery. "Whack?" The coffeepot on the folding table was cool to the touch.

An angry vibration sent Brooklyn's heart rate through the roof. He fumbled the burner phone out of his pocket. He'd picked it up at a convenience store outside the city and texted the number to Float and… "Whack?"

"It's Henry."

The quiet, twitchy one who never offered to help unload the fucking rocks. "The hell is everyone?"

"We got a problem."

"Only problem is if you don't have my money," Brooklyn said.

"Got your money," Henry said. "Meet me at the titty bar next door. Ten minutes."

Brooklyn grumped at the ice in his highboy glass. He'd left the van, walked right past the strip club, and caught a cab downtown. Henry had been pissy about the change of venue, but Brooklyn wasn't about to meet him someplace he hadn't picked himself. The paperwork on the rental van led to a fake ID and a hacked cashcart.

The bar bustled around him. Humanity in all its colors and flavors getting high off sexual tension, ego, desperation, and any number of complicated chemical chains. He sipped at his Old Fashioned. Henry was at the door. Brooklyn waved him over.

"You know Sinatra played this place once?" Henry was a nervous-looking guy in a pair of knock-off Oakleys and a Yankees cap. He pulled a mirror out of his breast pocket and laid it on the bar. "You mind?"

"Your town, man," Brooklyn said. "Know what you can get away with better than me."

"Radical." Henry powdered the mirror with a small vial and used a razor blade to sculpt three lines on its surface. "Guess they don't say that anymore. Now it's 'phat' or 'skillet' or something." He rolled a fifty-dollar bill into a straw. "Want some?"

Brooklyn shook his head. "Don't let me stop you."

"I won't." He snorted one of the lines. "Where are the rocks?"

"Left 'em at the warehouse. Where's my delivery fee?"

Henry made a 'wait' gesture with his left hand and used his right to hold the fifty. He snorted another line. "Too uptight, dude. Gotta take a chill pill." He cleaned the mirror with his finger and rubbed the powder into his gums. "Look at these assholes. All the shit goin' on, and they make like it's another excuse to party. You got kids?"

Brooklyn shook his head.

"I got two. Teenagers. Live with their mother." He slid the mirror back in his pocket. "They really talk like that, you know. 'Phat' and all that shit. All a sudden, like they learned it in school."

"Your tax dollars at work," Brooklyn said. "Let's get this over with, man. Places to be, people to see."

"Donato Diaz, Donny D." He dabbed at his nose. "Not your real name, right? We got a problem, see. And this," he patted his coat, "is the last money you and me are gonna see for a while."

Brooklyn tensed. "What'd you hear?"

"Didn't hear a fucking thing. Saw it." Henry rapped his knuckles on the bar and ordered a double Jack straight. "Everyone in the crew is dead." He snapped his fingers. "Just like that. Burned down where they stood. Tony, Whack, all of them. Little piles-a ash."

"Ash." The Old-Fashioned glass was empty when he put it

back down, lonely ice cubes kissing in the bottom. "Could be Designed, or Jellies. Could be people using alien tech. How'd they miss you?"

"I was a few minutes late. Dropping the kids off at their mother's. Got there after it was over." Henry downed the Jack in one go and ordered another. His voice was cracking on the edges, and he cleared his throat. "Could be the rocks."

"Why now? We been doin' this for years." The rocks were curiosities, barely that, from De Milo, the human city deep beneath the surface of Venus. Even the geologists there were barely interested in them, noting only that the crystals inside them seemed artificial. "What else was Big Tony into?"

"The usual redistribution of wealth." He sniffed. "Moved some drugs, coffee when it started getting scarce. Loaned money." He flattened his hands on the bar. "Those type-a guys use bullets, though."

"Tellin' you the rocks are trash."

Henry eyed him. "Lot of money for trash, man."

"What the buyer wanted." Brooklyn's pals in De Milo had been careful not to send anything too interesting to the mystery man who'd offered to trade his extra First Tech for alien artifacts back in the '80s. Pottery, mosaic tiles, couple of hand tools... The rocks had really piqued the collector's interest, and Brooklyn kept supplying them even when the original deal expired. Big Tony had been happy to keep playing middleman. "Speakin' of which, you owe me."

"Finish your drink." Henry looked right and left. "We'll go 'round back the building, finish this out there."

"Don't see why we gotta do it on the sly, man," Brooklyn said. "Just watched you do coke at the bar. Let's just do it here."

Henry's face was red either from anger, booze, or cocaine. "We do it my way, or you won't see a fucking penny."

Brooklyn raised his hands in mock surrender. "Your town, your rules. Lead the way."

They paid, and Brooklyn followed the crook to the back of

the joint and through a door that led to the alley outside. It was deserted, trash strewn, and filled with dumpsters. *Great place for a murder.* His head did the swimmy thing again, and an extra big pump of adrenaline turned him hot and jittery. For once, he and his weird body were in agreement: Henry wasn't going to play nice.

"They find you, you'll give me up?" Brooklyn said.

"I'll sing Donny D so loud you'll hear me in space," Henry said. "But they ain't gonna find me. Plans on plans, amigo."

"You're leavin' town."

"Me an' my nest egg, which could be a little bigger, so..." Light glinted off the butterfly knife that flicked into Henry's hand. He swept it toward Brooklyn's throat, catching his chest instead when Brooklyn slapped the blade down.

Henry pulled the knife back in, holding it at waist level, ready to lick it out again, cut little pieces off at any opportunity.

Brooklyn took a long step back and made a pistol shape with his right hand, dropped his thumb like a hammer. ZEEK! Blue light flashed from his watch, running along the back of his hand to the end of his pointer finger. The zap hit Henry in the neck, and he collapsed like a felled tree, top and bottom teeth coming together with a crack.

"Fuck!" Brooklyn flailed at the watch's catch until he got it unfastened and let the thing drop to the ground. It burst into flames, and he didn't bother to stamp them out. It was never meant to be anything but a one-shot holdout.

He lifted his shirt to get a look at the knife wound in the rum light of the alley. It was long but not too deep, neck and neck with the burns on his hand and wrist for the evening's Gold Medal of Pain. Brooklyn fought back the adrenaline shudders and squatted to check Henry's pulse. The neural disruptor in the watch was Jelly Tech and sometimes had unexpected effects. The crook was breathing smooth and slow, and he'd pissed himself. Brooklyn grimaced and went through his pockets. He found an envelope of cash, along with the rest of the cocaine.

The coke made the pain a distant thing. A nearby dumpster was plenty big enough to hide an unconscious thug in, so Brooklyn grabbed him by collar and belt and hoisted him up. *Gotta find another way to pad that college fund, asshole*. The burner phone, minus its battery, followed.

Goodbye, Donato Diaz. He zipped his jacket up over the ruined shirt.

Time for Plan C.

There were a lot of bars in Jersey. Brooklyn found another one and switched to Jack & Cokes while he called Float on the house phone.

"This is not a good time," the jelly said.

"Sorry to interrupt." Brooklyn's snort attracted the attention of the bartender who'd been none too happy to let him use the phone to begin with. If Float was running true to form, she was at the Aquarium, the biggest Jelly sex club in New York, not that he blamed her. No doubt it got cramped and lonely quick in the exosuit's tiny living space. He dropped to a whisper. "Somebody killed all Big Tony's guys."

"Who?"

"Hen– One who survived thinks it's got something to do with the delivery." His mouth firmed. "I got the cash."

"Did you kill him?"

"All he knows me as is Donato. Got fresh about the money, an' I zapped him. Sleepin' it off in the garbage."

"You should have killed him." The phone line hummed. "If you aren't off Earth in seven hours, Emigration will come for you."

"I'll keep 'em happy and leave early." The line hummed. "You ask anyone about the thing?"

"I gathered passing fish," Float said, "to no avail. Could your new problem have anything to with it?"

"Can't imagine Demarco's the only one with the skinny."

Brooklyn slid another twenty across the bar and signaled for the backpack he'd asked the guy to stash for him. "I'm in the wind. Call you from the space station once I figure out the next step."

THREE

Taking public transportation back to the city and into Queens wasn't the smartest idea, but he had a hunch it might be a while before he got a chance to get back. He compromised and walked from the train instead of taking a bus or taxi. No one offered to shoot him during the trip, and by the time he passed through the gates at Calvary Cemetery in Woodside, he figured he was safe.

Lolita Lamontagne had got in just under the wire, before burials were banned in favor of cremation. Her second husband, Mike, hadn't been so timely, but Brooklyn had dug the hole for his urn – right next to her stone – himself.

It was a big cemetery, and it took him a while to find the site. He amused himself by trying to guess where Giuseppe "the Clutch Hand" Morello had been planted. Ol' Giuseppe had been the boss of bosses back in early century, the inventor of the protection racket. He liked to dismember his enemies and ship their bodies to other cities in wooden barrels. There were a lot of gangsters buried in Calvary, but the Clutch Hand's grave was unmarked.

Ma was buried in so-called New Calvary. A nice spot with a bench, next to Brooklyn's old man, and not too far from his pal, David.

"Hey, Ma." He knelt to pull some weeds and brush some mulch off the stone. Sixty-seven years old. She'd made it through a lot of shit only to catch cancer. Mike had died of the sads about a year later. Seeing them together over the last decades of her life had made Brooklyn less forgiving of his father. The old man, in retrospect, had been kind of a dick. "Saw on the signs comin' in that they'll be pulling the stones out soon. Be a real pain in the ass ta find you after that."

The headstones and monuments would be crushed to gravel and spread over the ground to prepare for a new layer of topsoil in a couple of years. City officials and the Designed had gone back and forth on the plan, arguing whether leaving the bodies in place or digging them up and burning them would have less impact on the environment. Eventually, they'd change the name to Calvary Meadow. Or not. *Whole new ballgame, maybe.* "You and Mike held out a couple more years, well... things mighta been different."

The majority of graves in New Calvary were from 1978, and most of the stones from that year weighted down empty boxes. All the stiffs had been tossed into mass graves or flung on bonfires during the bad time. Splitsville or not, the First had a river of blood on their hands.

Brooklyn poked around until he found David's monument. Cold, gray stone, level with the ground to make it easier to mow the grass. October 16, 1975. His hand floated to his mouth. If the Jellies hadn't been stealing military secrets in advance of their invasion. If Galvano hadn't agreed to act as the middleman. If Brooklyn hadn't been working for Duke Carlotta. If he hadn't agreed to hang onto the tapes. If Prick hadn't ratted him out. If David hadn't tried to play hero.

The stream of ifs had worn away the guilt some. Brooklyn had made some bad moves, certainly he'd contributed to the events of that night, but he didn't own the whole thing. Not off the hook, but he had come to see he had plenty of company there. Most of what he felt now was a twenty-four-year-old sadness that a pal had died young. He took another look at the Calvary Cemetery class of '78. *Lot o' that goin' 'round.*

Ma. Mike. David… the First hadn't had anything to do with those deaths, but only karma would hold them to the rest.

PART TWO
Jigsaw Youth

FOUR

He rented a so-called "suicide booth" for the ride up to *Eisenhower*. It had started its life with Ma Bell in the '70s but found new purpose as a one-person spacecraft via First Tech. The lifter unit it used was smaller than a cigar box, but it was enough for a ride into orbit. The blue glow of the First Field kept the air in, the cold out, and would stand up to any micro debris that whammed into it during the ride.

At least, that was the idea. Enough people had pushed the envelope with the things, deliberately or otherwise – or forgotten to check the batteries – that they'd earned their nickname. Take a ride up, look at the sights, and just step out. End of story.

Brooklyn tried to get comfortable as the lifter did its job, grabbing gravity and pushing against it, sending the booth into a steady climb into orbit. He hated the fucking things, and the rudimentary gauges that volunteered speed, altitude, and air pressure – none of which he had any control over – failed to make him feel any better. He gritted his teeth and hung on as the booth followed its preprogrammed route to *Eisenhower Space Station*.

The station had grown wildly in the years since the Earth Orbital Forces dissolved and U.N.'s focus changed from defense to evacuation. Hasty add-ons jutted from the aging superstructure. Thousands of inflatables clung like leeches to the station's skin, temporarily housing workers or refugees waiting for the next boat to Venus.

The world spun outside the booth's thin windows until it was given permission to land in one of the public hangers. The woman at the rental-agency desk inside returned his deposit, and he walked to the center of the station and the memorial wall there. *Second depressing spot o' the day. If I still had a shrink, they'd have some questions for me.*

After the Designed stopped the meteorite the Jellies had chucked at Manhattan, they offered proof of the First claim to Earth. The eviction order followed. Earth Orbital Forces, primed to fight an alien invasion since the '50s, attacked the Prime Ambassador's ship with everything they had in range.

The Designed never fired a shot. They just cut the power. From flashlights to cities to airplanes to emergency life support to HVAC to transistor radios to atomic engines. Airplanes fell from the sky. Scrambling EOF fighters plowed into buildings and people. Two of the big capital ships – including the Admiral's flagship, the *Wapakoneta* – crashed into Hong Kong, unable to deviate from the attack run they'd started. Hundreds of Earth ships just drifted into the darkness, never to be seen again.

Six months later, the Designed flipped the juice back on and calmly restated their sponsor's demands. This time there was no argument. Millions were dead on the surface, and near-Earth orbit was a charnel house. The resistance was over.

Brooklyn checked the memorial wall for new names. There were always a few. Cleanup and salvage efforts were ongoing. He traced a couple of the fresh-cut ones. *And after all that, the fuckers just left. Got clean away*. Getting away with it was the best part of any plan; he just couldn't figure out what the First had *gained* from all of it.

"Friends of yours?" The Emigration & Customs guy, Cramm, came up behind him. He bounced on his heels, comfy in the lower gravity of the station. Point-seven-five of Earth's. Goldilocks would have no reason for complaint.

"Some of them," Brooklyn said. "You?"

"An aunt on my mother's side. I was too young."

"Lot of them were." He let his hand drop. "Sweet-a you to make sure I got up here okay. Must be nice to get a break from rounding up bums an' chucking them into space." Emigration had been having a hard time convincing the world's middle- and upper-classes to leave the planet and were not above conscription from homeless shelters and emptying prisons to fill the evacuation ships.

The guy chuckled. "Keeping bums like you out here is part of the job too."

Brooklyn slid his hands in his pockets. They were easier to control there. "Well, I got a party to get to, so you can just go back down. Job done."

"I'll walk you." The guy's smirk got bigger. He was really feeling it. "We're the ones hosting the thing. Drop by the information table, and I'll give you a pamphlet about the joys of getting the fuck out."

"Welcome, classmate!" The woman at the entryway table was wearing blue and had teased her hair so big it would never have fit in a vacsuit. He spotted the nametag. Cindy Lehman. *Cheerleader, Bay Side resident, dater of football players, the "Fox of Rockaway Beach"*. She wouldn't have shared an emergency oxygen pack with him back in 1969. Now her famous smile was framed with cigarette-smoker's wrinkles and a softening chin.

Brooklyn had grown out his facial hair and added some streaks of gray to the resulting patchiness, as well as to the mop of hair on his head. It maybe hid that he'd stopped aging in the late '70s. He avoided things like class reunions because he didn't enjoy trying to explain that.

Cindy scanned the table in front of her where a few dozen nametags were laid out in neat rows and columns. "It's so good to see you..." The unspoken question hung for a beat too long, and her smile faltered.

"Brooklyn," he said.

"Brook!" she squealed. "Of course!"

The smile showed itself again, but the wattage had waned. *Saving her energy for people she actually remembers.* She pointed. "You can grab your nametag right there. Everything's paid for courtesy of Emigration & Customs."

"Heard that. What's the angle?"

"They're encouraging all the Baby Boom classes to have reunions up here." She leaned closer and lowered her voice. "They think it will encourage us to emigrate faster, but there's no way I'm leaving Earth!"

Them who drags their feet wins, as Demarco might say. Brooklyn picked up his nametag, his yearbook photo and first name printed on it. He begged off adding his information to the "classmate contact" list. He also refused a VHS tape provided by the sponsor.

"What have you been doing since graduation?" Cindy's eyes drifted to the door he'd come through.

She'd never been much interested in current events. *Accessory to murder and treason. Smuggling and identity fraud. Usual shit, Cindy. How 'bout you?* He slipped a look at her left hand. A pale stripe showed where a wedding or engagement ring usually hung out. "Waitin' on someone special?"

She flushed. "Better get inside before all the mixers are gone!"

Brooklyn peeled the backing paper off the nametag and followed her advice. He ordered a margarita with an unsalted rim and looked around the room for familiar faces. One found him first.

"Jesus, Brook! You haven't changed a bit! The fuck's your secret?"

"Clean living and low gravity." He clapped his old pal Chris on the shoulder. "What's yours?"

If Chris had one, it had nothing to do with eternal youth. Rangy adolescence had given way to paunchy baldness and pleated chinos. "I ain't seen you since… I guess since you were in jail that time. Meant to come visit when you got back home, but… You know how it is."

"Got some idea. Thanks for taking care of Ma."

"I was real sorry to hear she'd passed. She was a good lady." He squinted at Brooklyn's face. "For serious, man. You ain't aged a day."

He waved it off. "Whatcha doin' with yourself?"

"Working at the dealership an' waiting for my old man to croak. You?"

"Computers, mostly." Brooklyn signaled the bartender. "Lemme get you a drink. Beer?"

"Gives me gas. Scotch and soda."

"That's your dad's drink."

Chris got squirmy-eyed. "Bastard spends half the year in Florida and still doesn't trust me to run things."

"Sure, sure." Brooklyn ordered a second margarita and a Cutty Sark and soda for Chris. "Tell me what's been going on in the neighborhood."

Brooklyn listened to Chris complain about his old man and his wife for twenty minutes over their drinks before pretending to need a restroom. He clapped Chris on the shoulder again. "Nice ta catch up, man. Spot you next time I'm in town."

Chris raised a new drink. "Good seein' ya, Brook. Drop by the yard, and I'll get you a good deal. Put you in something real nice."

Brooklyn avoided the main bar in favor of a smaller one near the back of the room. There was beer there, along with a guest book to sign, a display of senior superlatives *(Most Likely to End Up Exiled ta Venus)*, and an in-memoriam table. He grabbed a beer and surveyed the names and photos to see how many he recognized. A lot of members of the Class of '69 had bitten it in '78. David had graduated in '68, so his picture wasn't there. A neighboring display showed classmates who'd emigrated off Earth, a far smaller number. He scanned that, too, telling himself he wasn't looking for anyone in particular.

It was a night for being found first. "I thought that was you," she said.

Carmen's voice hadn't changed. A rich alto that pulled goosebumps out of his skin. Thirty years of work, marriage, kids, and Earth gravity made her look more like his memories of her mother than the occasional nostalgic fantasies his mind fielded. At one time, she'd been the love of his– Anyway, she was another big reason he hadn't wanted to go to the reunion.

"Bet it was your idea to set this up." Brooklyn drank some beer. "Get 'em over here with the suds, hook 'em with the sads."

"Totally guilty." They stood side by side, eyes firmly on the memorial display, a nervous bubble between them. She reached out to touch a photo of a smiling young woman. "You remember Snookie, right? My cousin."

"Sure. We went out with her enough. Her and whatshisname. Older guy."

"Chad Long. NYU student. They got married right after she graduated."

Brooklyn nodded. "What happened?"

"That big food riot," Carmen said. "Lot of them died then."

Another thing Brooklyn had missed while playing popsicle. By the time he'd thawed out, humanity was adjusting to the new order and arguing about gas prices again. As a species, people had short memories. "I was… somewhere else."

The bubble burst in a sharp laugh. "Your mother told me." Their eyes met. "I barely knew you were dead before you were alive again. You could have been one of these pictures."

"Lot of that shit was classified. Couldn't even tell Ma everything. Made her sign a bunch of paper when she came to see me."

Her hand found his arm. Underneath the years and trauma… Carmen. His throat got tight.

"What happened to you out there, Brook?" she said.

"Buy me a real drink, and I'll tell ya."

The naked emotion on her face would have brought his to the surface, so he couldn't look at her. The bar top, the drink sitting on it, his boots, anything was safer.

"The biggest thing of your life, and you can't remember it?"

"Not a bit. Not what I did, what I felt." He rubbed his forehead. "Lost most of that whole time. It's just empty space." The signs had been there, but there'd been little time to read them. He'd come back from death thrice, but not all of him had made it. A few hours gone, a day, then months. "And… I mean, you know me, Carm. Can you imagine me doin' somethin' like that? I sure as hell can't."

"I think we don't really know what we're capable of until we're confronted with it."

"Sure." He picked up his drink. "Or the whole thing is bullshit. A big scam. Not like I can remember either way."

"What about the ambassador… Andy?"

"I met her. I remember that much. Talked to her." He drummed his fingers on the bar. "Stupid thing to get fucked up about."

"No, Brook. Meeting her, those things you did, changed everything." She paused. "What do you remember about… about waking up?"

"I only remember the guys who found me because I met them on the *Dick Cavett* show. I remember the hospital. A nurse there filled me in on some of what I missed." His hand rose to his mouth, smoothed his immature moustache. "How we saved Manhattan, but all those people died anyway. Mighta got a little crazy then. Wanted to know about Ma… and you. People I served with. People I met in De Milo."

The First had been in charge more than two years by then. A new status quo in place and never to be normal again. Trains running, bodies buried. His lawyers got him in front of the cameras as soon as possible, hoping the court of public opinion would head off the charges of treason and a court martial.

Andy and some of the other Designed had gone rogue in the meantime. They'd tried to get the power back on early and were forced to flee in defeat.

"Andy went to see Ma as soon as the meteorite had been taken care of," he said. "Told her what had happened and that someone would go back to get me. Then it all went to shit."

Andy and her pals had surfaced again in the mid '80s, invading the Designed Artiplanet to get a vaccine for a contraceptive virus unleashed on Earth. He'd seen her briefly in a news clip then and not since.

"Don't usually talk about this," he said. "Float knows most-a it. Ma knew a little."

"I was really sorry to lose your mother."

"Saw her when I could. Every couple of months, at least. Called. Wasn't enough. She deserved better."

"You never visited me." She offered an eyebrow commentary.

"Yeah, well, didn't want to cramp your style. Got enough on my conscience without bein' a home wrecker."

"Same old Brook." Carmen set her drink on a souvenir 'Class of 1969' coaster. She was three-quarters of the way through her second Blue Lagoon. She hadn't been much of a drinker back in the day. Maybe motherhood changed that. "You've met aliens. What are they like?"

"Jellies are like, I dunno, pissed off boogers in a can," he said. "They like starting fights and got their asses handed to them a few too many times. They're here because they don't have anywhere else to go. The First… they're a fucked up mix of god, grumpy old lady, and spoiled six-year-old. No one can tell them 'no'." Brooklyn ran his fingers over his jaw. Carmen said she liked the beard attempt. "Only met a few Designed, the green ones and the new guys the First came out with after the originals got squirrelly. The Angels. Mostly assholes. Splinters are just like you an' me until they're not."

"How'd you hook up with Float?"

"Found her in the desert, believe it or not. Out in New Mexico. Her suit'd locked up on her, and she was jus' standing there getting' loopy in the heat. Hauled her back in my truck."

"Weird."

"She's just a kid, in Jelly terms. Something like two hundred years old." He put his elbows on the bar. "An exile. Lot of the younger ones ain't happy with the way things are goin'. They pitched a fit when the Smack sank its battle fleet in the Marianas Trench so they could go back to the old ways. Float and some of her pals got themselves kicked out of 'all the seas and oceans of the world' for putting up a fuss."

Carmen picked up her drink again. "I still have a hard time getting my head around it all."

"You and what's his name – Steve – what're you gonna do about the deadline?"

"We have money set aside, but we're not sure what to do with it. Steve wants to stay here and keep saving until our grandkids can emigrate to Mars in style. He figures they'll have worked all the bugs out of the colony infrastructure by then."

"Carm, I..." The words stopped. Demarco had ordered discretion, and the old man generally had good reasons for such things. "That sounds like a good plan. Take it slow."

"Carmen," Cindy, the former Fox of Rockaway Beach, broke in, "we have a problem." She pointed toward the distant dance floor where a man without pants was dancing wildly to the Rolling Stones' "Honky Tonk Woman".

"Who is that?" Carmen said.

"Brian Fenmaster. He guzzled a half bottle of tequila and did a line of coke right in front of Mrs O'Neil."

Brooklyn focused on the face above the whirling dress shirt. "Brian and I were in shop class together. He was never a doughy white guy. You got a crasher."

"How was I supposed to know that?" Cindy said.

"His yearbook picture is right on his nametag!" Carmen rose from her seat.

The gatecrasher whirled into a group of dancers. He shook his dick at Chris and forced a kiss on the woman next to him. Chris roared and aimed an awkward haymaker at the interloper.

"Ah, shit." Brooklyn rose to his feet as Chris's backswing caught one of the other dancers in the face and sent her reeling backward. The pants-less man leapt on Chris's back, and they both fell to the ground. Brooklyn followed Carmen into the scrum and grabbed the collars of both men, hauling them to their feet.

"What the fuck, man! What the fuck!" Chris's face was alarmingly red. He struggled against Brooklyn's grip, straining to grapple with his ersatz classmate.

"Who the hell are you?" Carmen stabbed her finger at Not Brian.

"Call station security, they'll take care of him," Brooklyn said.

Not Brian aimed his dick at Chris's legs and released a hot stream of piss.

"I'll make the call," Carmen said.

The crasher heralded the unofficial end of the reunion. Carmen and the other organizers had booked the room until 2 a.m., but there weren't enough people left for a decent softball team once security escorted Not Brian away. Brooklyn and Carmen had another drink as the wait staff cleaned piss off the dance floor. Cindy left with an ex-boyfriend soon after.

"Split a piece of cake?" Brooklyn said. "I'd say we could go back to my place for a nightcap, but just remembered I don't have a place."

Carmen sighed. "I should get back. We have a new dog. Rosa. Steve's good with her, but I'm better."

"I bet." Brooklyn swirled melting ice in the bottom of his glass.

"Never figured you for a spaceman, Brook, but it suits you." She smiled. "You've grown up."

It was the eyes. A woman's compassion could look a lot like love to the hopeful and stupid. Brooklyn was no longer one of those. "Still twenty-eight."

"On the outside maybe, but you were always sort of an old soul."

"Crossed with a toddler."

"Yeah."

He walked her to the shuttle terminal. The E&C info table was empty, Cramm and his swag gone to his hotel room or back to Earth to spend his overtime pay. Some of their classmates were waiting at the terminal in various states of sobriety. Many were opting to spend the night on the station on the E&C dime. *Low-grav, middle-aged drunken nookie and a breakfast buffet. Good times.*

Carmen went to get her ticket while Brooklyn checked out the view. *Eisenhower* was in a geostationary orbit, and the big terminal window always looked out on North America. It was night there, the lights of the cities like frozen fireworks on the surface.

Brooklyn rolled his shoulders. A bed would feel nice. Clean sheets instead of a sleeping bag and his acceleration couch in the *Victory*'s cockpit. *Close the door on the universe a while.* His reunion nametag was good for a night at the station hotel, and after that...

Some hot, hard emotion had changed Carmen's gait, her arms were wrapped around her body like she was trying to hold it together. "They won't let us leave." Behind her, at the gate, other passengers were gathering in growing concern.

"For how long?"

"Ever." Her eyes were bright. "They won't let me go home, Brook!"

PART THREE
Gangster Glam

FIVE

Carmen checked into the hotel, and Brooklyn stood by while she called her husband. He thanked Brooklyn for his concern and claimed he "had it from here". Carmen agreed. She gave Brooklyn a goodbye hug.

"It's probably nothing. An administrative error," she said. "I'll let you know how it goes."

Brooklyn lingered in the hotel bar longer than he should have in case she changed her mind and went to his room around 2:30 a.m. The sheets were clean, and the shower beat the one on the *Victory* by low-g leaps.

The rest of the displaced members of the Class of '69 were working their cell phones for news and answers at the terminal when he returned there after checkout. Every return ticket to Earth had been canceled.

He watched the chaos and left a message for Float. A group of station punks had crawled out of whatever crevice they'd spent the night in to bum money out of passersby. "Know anyone headed to Tycho in the next few?" he asked them.

The tallest kid, maybe seventeen and twitchy as hell, looked at his pals. "You a cop?"

"Relax, pal. Just looking for a ride. A safe one."

"A long-lifer." The kid's derision drew a round of guffaws from his pals. He had stick-and-poke tattoos on his forearms – a skull, and one that sort of spelled out "better living through chemistry". His face and hands were a study in withdrawal tics. Probably something Jelly-made. "Whatcha got worth hanging around for, man? World's coming to an end."

"Always something new on TV," Brooklyn said. *"Love in the Belt* is looking pretty good this season."

"Word!" the shortest kid, a tween, said. She had a guitar slung around her neck and a hat for change on the ground in front of her. "That ep where Janice and Charley get trapped in that mining robot an–"

The tall one held up a shush hand. "Might know someone. What's it worth to me?"

"I'll figure it out. Just wanted you to feel useful." Brooklyn leaned closer and took a sniff. Neurotoxic peptides. The kid reeked of them. "Gonna die ugly, pal."

The kid blanched.

"The rest of you on that shit too?" *One species' enema was another's high.* Brooklyn inspected the other punks' faces, stopping at the guitar player. "Jellies use it to kill parasites. It'll melt your brain, but no skin off my ass if that's what you're looking for."

The girl with the guitar clamped her lips. She was a runaway, probably. Most of the station punks were, either fleeing a shitty home life or trying to escape themselves. There were plenty of weird little spaces inside the station to squat and hide.

Brooklyn shot a glance at his wrist, forgetting for a second he'd left his watch in Jersey. "Any-a you dinks wanna do something useful with your life, keep an eye out for a boat called *Super Freak*. Due here in a few days. Tell the guy running it Demarco sent you. If you're not an asshole, might give you a ride to Venus." He dropped some bills in the girl's hat and nodded to the tall kid. "Probably too late for you, but the rest of 'em might have somethin' to live for."

The first dude to fly from Earth orbit to the Moon's back in 1950, a quarter-million miles, did it in a single-occupancy tin can with less computing power than a digital watch. Getting up and down the gravity wells were the hard parts; the trip between was cake. As a result, there was a wide array of orbit-to-orbit transportation available on the station, some of it even licensed.

Brooklyn bought a ticket on the *Magic Bus,* a bright yellow flying party that traveled between *Eisenhower* and *Dragon,* the Moon space station, a couple of times daily, a six-hour trip, drinks and drugs included. He spent most of the ride up front with the pilot, an aging rave queen who'd decided to take the party with her when she emigrated. She'd given up the hard drugs after an overdose four years before and now had three drivers and two buses working for her. She tapped the large first-aid kit strapped to the cockpit wall. "Got my EMT cert just in case. All my drivers do."

The low-budget docking section of *Dragon* – formerly *Red Star Station,* pride of the Chinese Space Service – was a wreck, all flashing alerts and muted alarms, joins and seams sprayed thick with emergency sealant. The only lucid conversation available was with the guy who rented him a booth for the ride down. Brooklyn pulled his vacsuit out of his go-bag and donned it so he wouldn't have to struggle into it inside the vessel.

On the way down, he worked the radio using one of the emergency aliases stowed in the bag. "Hello, Tycho. Landin' in about thirty minutes an' need someone to open the door for me."

He repeated the message six times before someone answered.

"What do you have?" The voice was low, the accent East European.

"Got a box of Little Debbie's. Kind-a squashed but sealed. All yours if you get the door."

"What kind?"

"Swiss Rolls."

"Look for red-green-yellow-green. South quadrant. Thirty minutes."

* * *

The booth glowed blue and lifted off for the return trip as Brooklyn sucked canned air and eyeballed the airlock doors and hatches on the south side of the city. Most of them were flashing out-of-service lights, dire, stay-the-fuck-out red, but one was going red to green to yellow to green to red again. He covered the distance with a smooth lunar skip. *Like ridin' a damn bike.*

He passed through the airlock and opened his helmet. "Got your snacks an–"

The doorman was ugly and rail-thin, the perfect storm of low gravity and poor diet. He brandished a handgun. "Fuck Little Debbie. Gimme your money."

"Bullets and pressure don't get along too good." Brooklyn raised his hands. "Might put a hole in something needs to stay intact."

"Won't be breathing much longer anyway I don't get some cash."

He faked some sympathy. "How far you behind?"

"How far do I need to be?" The man smacked his lips. "Enough to trigger a bounty."

"Got credit not cash," Brooklyn lied. "S'pose, I renew your license?"

The crook waggled the gun. "Suppose you give me everything you have."

"All I got on me that you could use are extra underwear and snack cakes. Won't get you too far."

"Could just kill you. Pawn your suit."

"Hole me, hole the suit, babe. Boots fill up with blood and shit." Brooklyn sighed. "Where'd ya be then?"

The barrel of the gun lifted. "Shoot you in the face."

The helmet slid closed. "I can stay in here all day." Brooklyn folded his arms and leaned against the airlock door. "Look, pal, let's you an' me walk over to the Air Office, an' I'll pay off your bounty. Thirty-day tickets for both-a us. No one gets shot, an' we both walk away breathin'."

The gun lowered some.

"Forty-five days. Best I can do right now."

Yeah, getting to the Moon was a cinch. Even a suicide box could get there with some kind of propulsion system tacked on and a pilot who didn't mind breathing shallow and pissing in a jar for a couple of days. Land in the north quadrant hospitality area with a pocket full of cash, get met with a smile at the Visitor's Center.

But the smile only lasted till the money ran out. Then the bed went, the food, water, and, finally, the air. Get to that point, a bounty popped up. Anyone could claim it, earn enough scratch for a few weeks of love, rent, or to keep their own bounty at bay. The airlock awaited anyone who couldn't get square within seven days of their arrest.

Lots of motivation for bad behavior. "What's your name?" Brooklyn eyeballed his captor. "Hafta say for the license anyway."

"Gregor Begonovic."

"Long you been on the Moon?"

Begonovic wiped his nose with the back of his hand. "Three, four years."

The south side of Tycho, once an amusement park the size of Disneyland, was full of desperate people sleeping behind the carbon-dioxide scrubbers, eating trash, and strangling each other for a few more days of air. *And Greg got himself a gun somewhere.* Brooklyn grunted. *Big Tony woulda eaten this guy for breakfast.* "Surprised you got to answer the phone. Used to be rules 'bout that. Seniority."

"I cut the line." Begonovic popped his lips. "Offed the two in front of me. I don't breathe, no one does."

They walked-skipped some more in the low gravity. "This is the right one." Brooklyn led the way through the door, past the guards posted there, and flashed the dour clerk a smile. "Dick

Clarke's the name. Here for an air license," he pointed with his thumb, "an' ta claim the bounty on this asshole. Watch it, he's got a gun."

– From Tycho on $15 a Day, Lonely Planet (1992)

West Coast mob boss Micky Cohen and a pantheon of pals opened the Moon Dust Casino & Hotel here in the Fifties, the early days of the gee-whiz space race. Grace Kelly and the Prince of Monaco were married at the Moon Dust in '56, Marilyn Monroe and Arthur Miller just a month later. Elizabeth Taylor built a mansion nearby in a part of the city she named "Millionaire's Row" and set off a firecracker-string of celebrity one-upmanship.

Nowadays, this "Adult Disneyland" has more in common with the seedy side of Atlantic City than Hollywood. The millionaires have all gone on to God (or Mars), but it's worth a stroll down the Row to see what's left. Anything useful was scavenged from the old buildings long ago, but the ruins are testament to a Golden Age gone by. Note: Bring a pressure suit! This part of town is not well-maintained and any emergency shelters are probably out of order.

For a safer (more expensive) night out, stick with Uptown or the Strip, but keep your hand on your purse and your eyes on your drink.

SIX

"*Knight Rider*?" the bouncer said. "Never heard of it."

Air license in hand, 'Dick Clarke' had used Begonovic's bounty to pay a week's rent on a capsule hostel a few blocks off the Strip and stowed his gear inside. He bribed the hostel guard not to steal anything and went looking for a bar.

Evelyn, the bouncer, said she didn't drink while working, and he was sticking to beer.

"I was in a two-parter. Background thug. Guy I knew knew a guy, an' I needed money. Really wanted to be a consultant, but I don't have a degree. Turned out all the computer shit was faked anyway."

The talking car was where he got the idea for Bugs the Barely Functional Navigation Computer. He didn't share that with Evelyn, who was in her late 30s, looked like Patti Smith, and was not falling for his shtick.

Evelyn got up to roust a handsy drunk. The dude towered over her, but she put him in an arm lock and marched him to the door.

"Nicely done." He saluted with his glass when she returned.

"Worked in Vegas before this. Wasn't much harder in Earth gravity." She looked at the wall clock. "Well, Dick..." she said the name like she knew it wasn't real "...it's the end of my shift. You gonna say goodnight or follow me to a cheaper bar and try more of your bullshit on me there?"

Evelyn asleep looked even more like Patti Smith. Brooklyn got up before she did and met her roommates outside the bathroom. After some eye-rolling and snide comments about her choice of sleepover guests, they left for work or whatever, and he made breakfast.

She woke while he was searching the cabinets for plates and silverware. "Robbing the place?" she said.

"Stealing your tea one bag at a time." He pointed at a mug on the table. "That's your cut."

She held the mug with both hands, breathing the steam. Two mismatched plates beat her to the table, and he divided the eggs between them.

"Where'd the eggs come from?" she said.

"Your roommate, the tall one, told me where the store was. Got some real cheese, too." He grinned. "Saved money on a hotel last night, figured I'd splurge."

"Probably should've found out if I like eggs first."

His face fell. "Do you?"

"Guess you got lucky twice, cowboy. Don't push it."

He sat across from her. "You need ketchup or anything?"

She shook her head. "When are you leaving?"

"Your apartment or the Moon?"

"Cute and lucky have a lot in common, Dick."

"That's not my real name." A risk, maybe, but it had been a while since he'd met someone he liked. "It's Brooklyn. Friends call me Brook."

"I'll stick with 'Dick' until I'm proved wrong."

"Might take a bit," Brooklyn folded his arms, "an' I'm only in town a couple weeks."

"Better work fast, then."

"All right." He considered. "What's a nice lady from Vegas doin' on the Moon?"

"That the best you can do? Gonna ask about my major next or what rock bands I like?"

"Not anymore."

"Sixteen months ago, I had a heated disagreement with the manager of the casino where I was working. Had to make myself scarce. It blew over, but I overstayed my ticket."

"An' you're stuck here."

"Lost everything but my emotional baggage."

"Breath of fresh air in the morning, ain't you?"

Evelyn blew on her tea. "I was in college when the First showed up. Lost a sister while the power was out. Probably more of a glass-half-full girl before that."

"I was off planet, but I've heard it was bad."

She moved the plate of eggs away a few inches. "For a few days it was almost fun. Bundling up, reading and playing cards by candlelight… Then it was a week. Two weeks. Three. Fucking forever."

"I'm sorr–"

She raised her hand to cut him off. "Save it."

Brooklyn took his plate and silverware to the countertop and let Evelyn be quiet for a bit. He washed the dishes and the pan he'd used for the eggs. "More hot water?" He refilled the mugs. "I can't go back to Earth either. Least not as myself."

She sipped her tea. "Well, aren't we a pair, Dick."

– Long Distance to Earth

"It'll be at least two weeks," Float said, her voice clear despite dubious quality of the public comm. "Konduz has been calling around to junkyards for parts."

"Fuck me." A quarter million miles of silence shot back and forth on the line. "Any blowback from the delivery?"

"Nothing so far from your loose end."

"He's got his own problems." Brooklyn ran his hand over the back of his head. Henry might have sussed out that Donato was a fake, but unless he spent a lot of time looking at old newspapers, there wasn't much reason to put Donato's face with Brooklyn's name.

Meantime, they were hemorrhaging money.

"I'll try to get some passengers," he said. "When the ship's ready, you can pick us up on the nice side of Tycho, and we'll head to Venus. Gotta let the professor know we're outta business, anyway."

"Suits me."

"Any new fish in the net?"

"You'll be the first to know."

SEVEN

They were watching TV in bed – some loud morning talk show. Evelyn's head was on his shoulder and a mason jar of bourbon balanced on his stomach. On screen, a woman with big hair was insisting Elvis had been a splinter – an embodied First – and that she'd given birth to his son a few months after he died. The kid was the right age but didn't look much like the King beyond the shiny duck's ass he'd combed his hair into. Didn't sing like him, either.

"You believe any of this?" Evelyn said.

"Never liked Elvis much. Kind of a sellout, you ask me."

"My mother saw his very last concert." She sat up to swig from the jar. "There's something like this on just about every day."

"If you were a disembodied brain that hadn't had its ashes hauled in a zillion years, who'd you wanna be?"

"Not Elvis. Not a lot of laughs in dying on the toilet." Evelyn squirmed until she found a more comfortable position against him. "Might be fun being a rockstar, though."

"If Elvis was a splinter, his patron could-a let him burn up just to record the experience."

"Maybe the Colonel was the splinter. Got Elvis hooked on drugs so the First could enjoy the show."

Brooklyn took his own swallow from the jar. "Maybe you're a splinter."

"Maybe I should beat you to death so the First don't get bored and make me do something even stupider."

"What's more stupid than killing me?"

"Letting you live." Evelyn picked up the TV remote to turn the sound down. "I don't see Elvis doing much to prepare humanity for an alien invasion." She settled back into the pillows. "Maybe Bowie. Or Gary Glitter."

"Not every splinter has a job to do. Most are just supposed to live and do life things. But maybe the First needed that little fucker," he jabbed his finger at the screen, "to be born and become the new alien messiah."

"Or splinter-Elvis died on toilet after fathering that woman's love child."

"Or Mama's just trying to make money off a kid who looks a little like the King." Brooklyn lifted the jar. "To the asshole who knows, 'cause I sure don't."

Evelyn claimed the jar and put it on the rickety chair beside the bed. "I'm not working tonight. You wanna do something?"

"Like what?"

"Pearl Jam is playing the Crater Lounge. Maybe we can get tickets."

"Yeah, I'm game. I'll make some calls."

"Think he's a First?"

"Eddie?" Pearl Jam had moved to Tycho in 1994, claiming the music scene on Earth was too corporate. "Yeah, if I was a First, I might want to be Eddie Vedder."

Evelyn cleaned up good, and Brooklyn didn't look too bad himself by the time they were ready to go. They walked arm in arm to the mono-rail that ran most of the way uptown. Evelyn did a fair Gilda Radner impression, and Brooklyn's stomach was aching from laughter by the time they met the scalper.

"Ever seen these guys before?" Evelyn said after Brooklyn had forked over twice the original price.

"Few times. Once here. First time when they were Temple of the Dog."

"I lived in a squat for three months with Andy Wood."

He smiled. "Always gotta out-cool me."

"Can't help you're so boring." She shoulder-bumped him.

"Give you a lift when I leave," Brooklyn said. "You could take the money you've saved up and start fresh on Venus."

"You ready to settle down with me, Lamontagne?" She grinned.

Brooklyn took a couple of steps and leaned against a lamppost. "Not too good at stayin' in one place. It gets… I don't know. Stay someplace long enough, people think they know you. Hold up this idea of what you are an' you gotta live up to it. It's complicated."

It was past eight, and street heaters were running on low to save power. Evelyn pulled her jacket collar up around her neck. "Not a big fan of complicated."

"Don't blame you."

"Not a fan of how much you drink, either. More you drink, more I drink, and I don't want to go back there."

He nodded.

"Not sure I'm ready to leave. I can still see Earth from here, you know? All my shit is there."

"Gotta lot of shit there myself."

She drew herself up. "You still stayin' over after the show?"

"Complications and all?"

She smiled. "As long as the complications stay on your side of the bed."

"Appears I will, then."

PART FOUR
Nothingman

– Long-Distance to Eisenhower Station

"Chris is dead," Carmen said. "He had his own vehicle up here and tried to sneak back. They shot him down. Three others in the car with him."

Brooklyn felt nothing. It worked that way, sometimes. Whatever Dr Carruthers did to him all those years ago sometimes clamped down the big feelings. Sadness and anxiety were fine, murderous rage and anguish not so much. Or maybe that was just wishful thinking. Maybe he really did, as a former lover had suggested, possess the emotional depth of a shot glass.

"Steve's pulling all the strings he has, but he's not getting anywhere," she said. The signal bounced back and forth between Tycho and *Eisenhower*. "You still there?"

"Yeah. Just don't make any sense. We're talking a few thousand people at most, and it's a one-time trick. No one's gonna travel under those rules. It's like they were trying to hit a quota or something. Like cops putting up speed traps at the end of the month." *And there might not be anyone higher up to impress anymore*. "Feels desperate."

"Maybe they just don't like the Class of '69." There was a note of panic in her voice. "Emigration is acting like they knew all about it, but Steve's contacts say it was total surprise. Orders right from the Cardinal. We have nine days before we have to leave the station."

Brooklyn plucked his lips. The original Designed, Andy's

crechemates, had been phased out and replaced in the late '80s by the so-called "Cathedral of the Cosmos". The Cardinal had recast the First takeover as a holy crusade, preserving the righteous humans on Venus while the Angels fought the forces of evil on Earth and built a new Eden there. "What's your backup plan?"

"Steve liquidates everything we own, and we emigrate now. Friend of mine says nice things about Venus. I trust him."

The thing about trust was that everyone was worthy of it to a certain degree. Some people could be trusted with rocket launchers. Others..."Maybe hold off on selling it all," Brooklyn said. "Money you have will go a long way in De Milo. If you want, meet me in Tycho next week. Got room for four if you see anyone around you like. I'll give you the friends-and-family discount."

"It feels like we're giving up."

"Call it a work around." He gave her a phone number. "She'll set you up with fake IDs to travel on, keep your real names out of the system." *Steve ain't the only one with a few strings to pull.* "We can sneak you back in later if we need to."

EIGHT

"Ow."

Brooklyn's hands had hit a sensitive spot. Evelyn liked him to rub her feet after she got off shift, massaging her long toes and graceful arches with baby oil. She was lying on her stomach, her head at the bottom of the bed while he worked. They were naked and comfortably post-coital.

"How's it gonna feel cooped up with your ex and her husband all the way to Venus?" she said.

"At least I'll get a little money out of it." He interlaced his fingers with her toes. "Carried a family of seven there once. Grandma, too. All I got was empanadas."

She smiled at him over her shoulder. "A real hero of the proletariat."

"Folks like that need to move in quick and get theirs before the Steves of the world buy up the good bits."

She rolled over and sat up to face him. "Sometimes it sounds like you're happy the First came."

"Don't like the way it happened, but what came out of it ain't all bad. Look at Tycho. First time I came here it was a playground for assholes. Now," he sucked his teeth, "now it's like there's room to breathe."

She popped an eyebrow at him.

"I know how it sounds. Yeah, you can get killed for not paying for air, but you can also make your own way. Find a corner to claim 'stead of working for some prick in a factory somewhere. Venus is even better. There's a chance to build something new."

She knew a little bit about him now. The EOF and De Milo. Float and the *Victory*. He'd have told her about dying and coming back, but he was a little afraid she'd want a demonstration.

"New sounds nice," she said.

"That mean you thinkin' 'bout coming up with me after all?"

"No." She rolled onto her stomach and gave him her feet again. "Just thinking."

She woke screaming that night. Nightmares about the past.

"The sky turned orange." Brooklyn held her as she talked it out of her system. "And stayed that way the whole time. Something about how what they were doing affected the light."

The sky in the pictures he'd seen looked more like blood, but he didn't say that. There might have been geographical differences in how the energy the First wrapped around the planet changed the view.

"The clock on the classroom wall stopped right at 11:13 a.m. They let us out of school a couple hours later when it didn't come back on. Broke us up into neighborhood groups so we wouldn't walk home alone. Had to go by this plane that crashed downtown. Right into the hardware store. They were trying to put the fire out with fucking hand pumps."

She was starting to run down. It wasn't the first time she'd woken them up in her panic, and he was learning the ebb and flow of it."

Brooklyn listened and stroked her hair until she fell asleep.

Carmen, Steve, the Fox of Rockaway Beach, and her old quarterback boyfriend Gooch walked into the bar. Brooklyn introduced them to Evelyn.

"Any problem finding the place?" he said.

"We've been to Tycho before, years ago," Carmen said. "Fifth wedding anniversary."

Steve offered a firm handshake. Gooch wanted to play the grip game, and Brooklyn tried not to embarrass him too much. The Fox offered a smile that failed to escape the lower half of her face. When the waiter showed them to their table, Evelyn sat beside her.

"Is this your first trip to the Moon?" she said.

Cindy nodded, her eyes somewhere between headlights and deer eyes. She'd left her husband and teenage kids behind in favor of Gooch, and seemed a little stunned by her own audacity.

Gooch sat next to Brooklyn. "How much can you bench?" he said.

"Lot more on the Moon than on Earth." *Thousand pounds on Venus – call it nine hundred on Earth – but it was for science and because Milk paid off my bar tab.*

Carmen smiled at Evelyn. "Are you going to Venus with us?"

"Brook's pretty," Evelyn ruffled the back of his hair, "but I don't know that he's moving-across-the-solar-system material."

"You should have seen him in high school," Carmen said. "If there was any way to end a nice day by jumping out a window, he'd find it."

"Sounds familiar," Evelyn laughed. "Between Brook and the news, I've tried to keep up, but I'm still not sure what's going on. You're being forced to leave?"

Steve put his hand atop Carmen's on the table. "It's called an 'enhanced-emigration protocol'. It was written into the agreement the UN signed with the First, but it's never been used before. Essentially, anyone beyond low-Earth orbit on a visitor's ticket when it was declared was not allowed to return."

"The Moon, Mars, Venus, the Belt, and all points between," Carmen said.

"What about the private space stations?" Brooklyn said. "There are a couple of dozen of 'em. Don't imagine Emigration showing Sam Walton the door."

"If Sam had hosted your reunion party, I doubt we'd be here right now," Steve said. "Maybe I should have donated to the president's campaign instead of the other guy."

Carmen glanced at her husband. "If Emigration is ready to play those cards, I don't want to know what comes next."

"Best thing that happened to me in a while." Gooch laced his thick fingers through Cindy's. "Debt gone. Alimony gone. Prettiest girl in Queens right here. Find some work, and it's all gold ahead. Right, babe?"

Cindy smiled weakly.

"Brooklyn said something about a dog," Evelyn said.

"Rosa." Carmen's eyes sparkled. "She's back at the hotel seeing how far she can jump."

"I'd love to meet her," Evelyn said. "It's been a long time since I saw one."

"I'm sure that can be arranged after dinner." Steve leaned in. "As long as you agree to walk her around the block a few times."

Rosa was some kind of spaniel thing, and she wasn't good on a leash. Brooklyn and Evelyn took her up to Millionaire's Row to let her run in Zsa Zsa Gabor's desiccated front garden.

"Keep an eye on her," Evelyn said. "She might look appetizing to somebody."

"We won't let her get too far," Brooklyn said. His eyes had tuned up, and he could see into the garden's shadows well enough. Not a pooch eater in sight. "You have a dog as a kid?"

"Couple. You?"

"My dad never let me have one. Always said our apartment was too small. Ma had a cat."

"We ate the last dog we had. Bonnie."

His head jerked.

"Beat the hell out of starving. I like to think she would have volunteered." She coiled the leash around her wrist. "You don't have the monopoly on demons."

"I know, but, Jes–"

"Call her. Let's get her home to Mom and Dad."

The next day, outside an uptown hotel with a queen-sized bed, room service, and a late checkout. "What if I told you things are gonna change?" Brooklyn said.

Evelyn put her hands in the pockets of her jacket. "Change how?"

"Like," he looked side to side, "like the First are gone. I mean it. They just fuckin' took off."

"Guess I'd want proof before I opened the champagne."

"I get that. I really do." He worked his mouth.

"Is it true?"

"Maybe. Someone I trust says so."

"You don't even trust yourself, Dick."

"There's that." He kissed her. "Look you up next time around?"

"Sure." Evelyn smiled, maybe looked a little sad. "It's been fun."

NINE

The multi-ton ship rumbled down with precision and care and alighted on the landing pad in front of them. The repairs had been fast and cheap, and little time had been spent on making the new sections of hull blend with the original.

Important part is that they hold.

Cindy wrung her hands, her puffy eyes on the ship. "I thought it would be… better."

"Ain't lying, babe." Gooch slid his arm around her waist. "Looks like it's been hauling garbage for twenty years."

"Gooch!" Carmen slapped his thick arm. "A little gratitude. It's a piece of history."

Gooch guffawed. "Piece of something. I get a refund?"

The airlock door slid open to reveal an alien warrior clad in her shining battle suit.

"That's Float, copilot and head of the complaints department. She can bench about two thousand." Brooklyn waved to her. "Got anything else to say, Gooch, take it up with her. Or stay here until they toss you out. Your choice."

"Just joking, man. Tryin' to keep it light for Baby Girl." He offered a chicks-are-crazy smile/shrug combo. It looked well-practiced. "One-way trip like this. It's tough."

Four pallets were waiting to be stuffed into the *Victory*'s tiny cargo hold. The ship had started life as a long-range multi-purpose platform in the early '50s, and her designers hadn't had cargo in mind. Forty-plus years of refits and overhauls hadn't changed that much. Most of the space Brooklyn had carved out had once belonged to ammunition and rescue gear.

"How many times did Bugs crash on the way?" he asked Float.

"Three and a freeze. Call it four."

"Getting better."

Steve put his hand on Brooklyn's shoulder. "Appreciate like hell you doing this for us, Brook." He looked like an L.L.Bean model, a stylish refugee in a lined barn coat and thick boots, a blaze-red backpack over one shoulder. "You could have made some real money and chose friendship instead." His gray eyes whispered 'sucker.'

Brooklyn cleared his throat. "Float will show you around while I get the cargo stowed. Probably be ready to leave in ten–fifteen minutes."

Three of them followed the exo into the ship. Carmen lingered to look up at the quarter Earth hanging overhead. "There's no way we can get everyone off that thing is there?"

Might not need to. "Five billion's a big number, Carm. Maybe two million have emigrated so far, Mars and Venus combined. What is that? Half a percent?"

"Less." Her forehead furrowed. "Point-oh-four percent."

He grinned. "Look at you. Who needs a working nav computer when I got Math Club Carmen on my side?"

"What's wrong with the computer?" He'd once burned down their apartment with an attempt at technical acumen.

"Not a damned thing."

"Brooklyn!"

Gooch failed to offer help while Brooklyn jockeyed the pallets into the cargo hold.

"What's this other stuff?" the former football star said. He toed a stack of cardboard boxes bungeed to the wall.

"Mostly junk food. You wouldn't believe what you can get for a bag of pretzels and a six-pack of soda out here." He gestured toward the stairs. "Let's get you stowed."

The passenger berth was a narrow room with two bunks on either side and space below them for storage. "Push the bunks together if you want to get freaky." Brooklyn pointed up the corridor. "The cockpit. That's where I sleep and where you are not allowed. Stay out of engineering, too. Float stays in there. Galley, bunk, 'fresher… water-processing works well enough that you can probably get a shower apiece every couple of days. No laundry. Plenty of books for the 'fiche reader. Board games in the bunk."

Brooklyn headed to the cockpit and fell into his seat. Lights were mostly green all around, and he tapped the key that turned on the microphone. "Good morning, Bugs!"

It took a second, but the computer grated out something that might have been "Good morning, Captain." He'd been working on the thing for years. Float, out of sheer perversity, refused to help.

"Plot me a course to Venus, pal."

The screen turned blue with an error message.

Brooklyn swore. While he waited for the thing to reboot, he coded a message to Demarco on the secure set. *Anything new on the OAO? Inquiring minds wanna know*. It was a separate system, thank the gods, and not prone to the failures of his more recent work. When the navigation computer announced it was ready, he forwent the voice input and keyed in the coordinates. There were better times to go to Venus. When the orbits lined up right, the weird little planet was only twenty-four million miles away. At worst, it was about a hundred and sixty-two million miles. They were well past the sweet spot and headed into fuck-that's-a-long-trip territory.

Bugs spat out the requested information. Brooklyn printed out a copy and taped it to the wall. *Little over two weeks*. He rubbed his eyes. Flying alone, or just with Float, was far preferable to hauling passengers. He and the jelly knew each other well enough to stay out of each other's way, maybe coming together a couple of times a day to check in. Cramming six into the space of a big Winnebago with no pit stops… At least Float could hang out in her tank and ignore everyone.

He tapped the intercom. "Find some place comfy to sit and strap in. We're launching in ten minutes."

PART FIVE
Given to Fly

TEN

It was the day after the first big fight over bunk and bathroom cleanliness, and the four travelers had been keeping to neutral corners ever since. Steve was reading tech manuals in the hallway outside engineering. Carmen was napping in the bunk room with the dog. Gooch was in the galley, and Cindy had parked herself at the cockpit entrance, which is why she was the second one aboard to see the derelict on the monitor.

"What was it?" she said.

Brooklyn squinted at the screen. "Looks like it might have been a boat. Just about make it out."

First Tech could get just about anything that worked as a Faraday cage into orbit. After that, travel between the spheres was a matter of propulsion, consumables, and orbital mechanics. Rocket science. Commuter and low-Earth-orbit conversions like the suicide booths were common, but every once in a while someone got the idea to seal up something big, outfit it cheap, point it at Venus or Mars, and go. *In space, no one can hear your 'oh, shit!'.*

"Come in and take a look if you want," he said. "Radar imaging ain't the best."

She twisted into the space and sat on the edge of the reclined copilot couch Brooklyn was using as a bed. "It doesn't look like much of anything."

"It's tumbling slow. You gotta watch it a while."

"You must have good eyes," she said after a minute. "Is it dead?"

"Hope so." Brooklyn unlocked the control panel. "Can't be a ghoul without a grave."

It took several hours to get close enough to see the derelict out the window. It had started out as a fishing trawler, its name still painted in hanji on the hull.

"First one like this I found was a Miami city bus," Brooklyn said. "Saw an old submarine last year. That one just about made it."

"Do any of them get to Venus?" Carmen said.

"Try to do it like this, on the cheap, you gotta be real lucky. Lot can go wrong." He tapped the window.

"What do you think happened to them?" Cindy pointed to the tumbling tomb with a thrust of her chin. Her arms were folded as if she were cold, although it was T-shirt temperature on the *Victory*.

"Power died, maybe. Or they figured their air needs wrong and suffocated. Or their heat exchanger failed, and they cooked to death." Brooklyn frowned. "One of them. Maybe all of them."

"No chance anyone is alive over there?" Carmen said.

"Nah. It's cold. Windows frosted over. Takes a while for shit to cool down out here."

"What's the point of getting this close?" Without regular applications of product, Steve's hair had fled under a Detroit Tigers cap from the ship's small lost-and-found locker.

"Money," Brooklyn said. "I'm going to make some. Cut you in if you give me a hand.

Float didn't sleep often, but she went down hard when she did. Brooklyn rapped on the glass of the sixty-gallon tank she used as a bedroom on board the *Victory*. Not a quiver. There were ways to wake her, but they seldom resulted in a good mood. She spent a lot of the time between planets stretched out and floating free in her tank. Brooklyn took a quick inventory of the telltales and status readings in the engineering section and went back to the airlock.

Cindy was inspecting the inside of a vacsuit helmet. "I heard this is a lot like SCUBA diving."

"Never been," Brooklyn said. "Not too late to change your mind, if you're nervous."

"ER nurse." She'd put her hair in braids, and they tumbled around her face. Cindy was starting to get used to the idea of leaving Earth, but Brooklyn wouldn't put money on her relationship with the quarterback. The last thirty years had given her some steel. "When it comes to blood and stuff, I'm the best choice."

Brooklyn closed and dogged the inside door of the airlock. "I take care of my gear. It'll take care of you. Just keep your breathing steady and try not to freak out if you get in trouble."

Cindy put the helmet on, and he showed her how to check and recheck her seals. "We should be good," he said. "Ready?"

Silence.

"Can't see if you're nodding," Brooklyn said.

"I'm ready."

He worked the airlock controls, pulling the air out of the small space, and undogged the outer door. "It's like mountain climbing. Probably. Never done that before either. We're tethered to the ship and to each other. You can't go anywhere unless I do too, and I can't go unless I unclip from the ship."

Cindy tugged at the fabric of her suit. "I thought these would be thicker. All the shows I've–"

"Different gear for different purposes. If we were on the Moon, we'd add a few layers to counter the regolith. Shit scours through everything. Out here, though, we're just fighting vacuum and radiation. These are fine for that."

Brooklyn didn't scrimp on suits. His gear could keep the air fresh for twenty-four hours, and the low-watt First field running over it kept the radiation at bay.

The trawler was twisting slowly on its long axis.

"Weird to see a boat out here," she said.

"Steel hull. Lotsa compartments. Probably got a big cargo space right in the middle. Makes sense for a conversion."

The conversion had robbed the trawler of its superstructure and rigging. What was left was a sixty-foot shell with solid-fuel rocket engines crudely mounted into the stern. The conversion crew had painted the whole thing high-visibility white and added Buck Rogers-style racing stripes to hide the rust and make it look 'spacey'.

Brooklyn used his thumb to trigger the comm switch on his glove. "Pan the flood to the left, willya?"

Gooch was probably better with machinery, but Brooklyn didn't trust him in the cockpit. He might be dumb and arrogant enough to try something that would leave everyone floating.

"Ten-four," Carmen sent back. The eight-shape the Victory's floodlights projected moved down the hull of the trawler from bow to stern.

"There's the front door." Brooklyn pointed. "Freeze the lights." The eight stabilized on a boxy airlock welded onto the deck.

"You think there'll be kids in there?" Cindy said.

"Refugees usually bring their families with them." He unclipped the tether from the *Victory* and activated his thruster pack. He took hold of the ring on the back of Cindy's suit and pushed off from the hull. "Let's go."

The trawler's airlock rotated to the dark side of the ship before they got close, and he shed *v* so they could catch it when it came 'round again.

"What's it like out there?" Steve's voice crackled.

"Kind of like diving, I guess," Cindy said. "We spent our

honeymoon diving wrecks in the Keys. The boat is giving me serious deja vu."

Steve laughed.

"We used to talk about opening a dive shop down there. Ride out the deadline swimming and eating mangoes," Cindy said only to Brooklyn.

"Doesn't sound too bad." The airlock door edged into view at the top of the eight. Brooklyn used the thruster pack to put them at the threshold. His boots made contact with the deck, and the electromagnets in the soles activated. He undogged the outer door of the airlock and pulled it open. "After you."

The headlamp on Cindy's helmet moved with her, illuminating a new horror with nearly every step.

The trip's organizers had crammed at least six families into the space. Chinese, probably, although it was hard to see faces through the ice, and signage in one Asian language looked a lot like another to Brooklyn. Their deaths hadn't been violent, at least. Most of the bodies were snugly tethered to their bunks, sleeping bags and Velcro holding them in place.

"I bet the air mix went bad." Brooklyn rounded his shoulders repeatedly trying to reach an itch that would have to wait until he was out of the vacsuit. "Alarms didn't go off. Must have happened right after they left orbit. Looks like they've barely touched their consumables."

"Great score for Lamontagne Salvage," Cindy said.

"I'll do it, but I won't feel great about it." Ten or twelve kids. Various ages. Six sets of parents. A couple of grandparents, maybe. Aunts and uncles. *Yearning to breathe free. Or just fucking breathe.*

"Lucky thing they froze. This could have been way worse."

"Yeah, lucky." He cleared his throat. "Looks like a couple power breakers popped, and no one was alive to reset 'em."

"Now we just move everything over to your ship?" Her

helmet light chased shadows as she looked around again. "Do you have the room?"

"New plan," Brooklyn said. "We'll put a claim beacon on this heap and follow it the rest of the way to Venus. Add a week or two to our flight time, but once we get it there, we can sell the whole thing."

"Bodies and all?"

"Doesn't make much sense to toss them out here. Get to Venus we can make it so they burn up in the atmosphere together."

The salvage claim would hold up unless the refugees had family in De Milo. Then the new civilian courts would get involved and split the value. Refugees severed any legal ties to Earth once they left the atmosphere. "You folks could make back your transit costs plus."

"Is it worth that much?"

Brooklyn's helmet lamp flitted around as he considered the question. "Seen worse. Hull's okay. Good size. If they can make out what fucked up the air, someone could trick this thing out as a freighter. Earth to Venus. Venus to Mars. Real slow with the engine it has, but it'll get there." He hummed. "We'll set up the beacon and head back. Radio in the claim. If these folks went through channels, E&C will try to let their relatives back on Earth know they didn't make it."

"It's not much," Cindy said.

"Better than a lot of people get."

They moved the few floaters into empty beds and couches and strapped them down. While Brooklyn restored power to the communications system and linked it to the salvage beacon, Cindy combed the galley for supplies. "Will we have enough air for a longer trip?"

"Had new scrubbers put in before we left Earth, and I *know* my alarms work. Food's the only thing not a closed system. You done?"

"Just." She pointed. "Everything is in those two bags."

Small bags. Reason warred with convenience warred with a desire not to carry passengers any longer than necessary. Setting up a tow wouldn't be easy, but he liked the idea a lot better than spending extra time with Gooch.

"You think Steve or Carmen are better to wake up to?"

"What does that mean?" Cindy said

"Need one o' them to roust an angry jellyfish and tell her to get dressed."

ELEVEN

"*Victory* to *Unfunky UFO*, coming in with salvage and citizenry."

"Hey, *Victory*." The radio crackled. "Whatcha got for us?"

Towing the trawler had added several days to the trip, plus an additional spacewalk when Brooklyn went back to make sure the thing would slow down when it needed to. Steve had come along to see how it was done, and together they'd jockeyed the boat into temporary orbit nearby.

"Refugee ship," Brooklyn radioed back. "Make someone a decent work truck."

"You need docking space?"

"Just for *Vicky*, right now. Couple o' things to take care of before we're ready for an open house."

The voice on the radio relayed docking instructions. "Happy landings, *Victory*. Good to have you back."

"*Unfunky UFO*?" Cindy said from the doorway. She'd spent a lot of time there since they found the trawler. She and Gooch weren't talking much.

"Parliament song." He'd won station-naming rights in the lottery Demarco held. "I was high as hell on mushroom tea when I picked it. The UN has a station up here too, but this one's better."

He moved the *Victory* into docking range. *Unfunky* wasn't much more than salvage itself – shipping containers and assorted scrap hulls welded and braced together. First Tech played a role in keeping it that way, but Colony Director Yuri Kasperov had taken pains to make sure she could do without. The former Soviet space officer didn't have much faith in the kindness of strange visitors from other planets, and his attitude was contagious. *And correct.* What the First gave, they could easily retake.

The old ship rocked as it made contact with the station, and the docking telltales flashed from red to yellow to green. A couple of them flickered uncertainly back to yellow, warmed up green again, and vacillated between. Brooklyn put the reactor on standby and headed to the galley for a tea refill and a sandwich.

"We'll be here a couple of days," he said. "You can sleep on the ship or get a room on the station. Give you a chance to get your legs under you and make some decisions."

"You hear anything new about work?" Steve said.

"Channel 53 is all jobs all the time. Right now, there's a captured asteroid in low orbit. Tidal forces are ripping it into little pieces, and they're putting together a crew to catch the good parts before they de-orbit." Brooklyn blew across the surface of his tea. "Not much work on the station itself, but you might get lucky."

"Or we take our chances in the caves," Carmen said.

"Free heat, light, air, and plenty o' space. Food's cheap if you're not picky. Lots of new construction going on." Brooklyn hefted the milk crate of records he'd grabbed from the cargo section. "Get yourself some of these and open a dance club."

"What about our cut of the salvage?" Gooch said.

"I'll have the cash for you before I head down." He considered. "There's a bulletin board in the hub outside. Look it over and pick a couple of chores. Write your name next to them. It's how you pay to use the station. If you got the know-how, you could do station maintenance. If you don't, there's always a bathroom to clean. No one'll bug you if you don't pitch in, but you might get a cold shoulder the next time you're here.

"There's something similar down below. Four outta five days a week you can work for yourself, but the fifth day you gotta do community chores."

The *Victory*'s low ceilings and re-re-recycled atmosphere were weighing heavy, but Brooklyn ate lunch and washed the dishes before grabbing his jacket and heading out. Even at a looky-loo's pace, the quartet from Earth should have had enough time to get out ahead of him.

Be nice not to see them for a while. Never thought I'd say that about Carmen, but she's gotten… something… in her middle age. Old? Settled. She's a different person around Steve.

Brooklyn and Float stopped at the bulletin board and claimed a couple of jobs each. The station's full-time crew had all it could handle with daily operations and taking care of the odd emergency, so the extra help mattered.

"I'll meet you at *Turk's*." Float made a beeline for the currency exchange.

Brooklyn fixed his collar and went on ahead.

Turk's was the station's original bar, built out of an Airstream trailer the proprietor flew into orbit in '83. More rooms followed, and now the venerable establishment was a maze of corridors and abandoned ideas. Interesting in concept, but hell to find the bathroom in. The proprietor was a former London punk, missing a leg, with a record collection that had its own room. He'd given up his shop in De Milo and moved into orbit because the lower gravity of the station was easier on his remaining limbs.

"Oy, ya foocker!" Turk reached without looking for a bottle of Brooklyn's favorite.

Brooklyn put the milk crate of records he'd carried from the *Victory* on the bar top. "Former owner was a deejay. Might be something in there you like."

Turk made a sucking-lemons face. "Probably all Top-of-the-

Pops shite." He poked the crate with one finger. "Whadaya want for them?"

"A hangover and the use of your tug for a few hours tomorrow."

The barkeep pulled at his lip. "I've seen how much you can drink. How 'bout the tug and a good buzz?"

Brooklyn leaned his elbows onto the bar. "Booze me."

Turk pawed skeptically through the box of records. "Who the 'ell is Matthew Wilder?" He broke off to give a hairy eyeball to Float who'd just come in. The jelly put a stack of glass coins, about two thousand nola if Brooklyn was counting right, on the bar.

"That should square us," she said.

The barkeep made a show of counting them and nodded. "Drink?" He busied himself with Jelly mixers behind the bar. The brief cold war between the bartender and Float, which had started because of a jovial fistfight between a couple of rival Jelly blooms, was over.

"Turk says I can use his tug tomorrow. Go over to the wreck. Care to join me?"

"I have plans."

Turk put Float's drink, mostly liquefied brine shrimp and neurotoxins, in front of her. "Jelly boat parked on the other side of the station. The lady's probably sick of your mug and wants to see some prettier faces."

"Agemates?" he asked her.

"Yes. A well-established bloom."

"That mean I gotta worry about finding a new partner?"

Float twisted the wrist of her exosuit. A noncommittal gesture. Jellies were naturally social and tactile, and it wasn't easy for her to spend all her time with someone she couldn't touch without killing. "We'll see."

Turk's tug was open to vacuum, a space tractor, but Brooklyn was happy working in a vacsuit. Almost preferred it. It was quiet, for one thing, and safe, as long as he didn't make a stupid mistake or karma came 'round with a raging hard-on. Shit could go wrong, but there were steps to take in response. *Maintain the gear, follow the checklist. Find the hole, patch the hole. Good to go.*

Brooklyn strapped into the tug's seat and tuned into his salvage beacon. The signal led him right to the trawler. He brought the tug in close and set the grapplers.

The first job was that of an undertaker, moving all the bodies out of the ship and tying them together. The family that was roped together, stayed together – assuming the knots were good. He finished the bundle off with a cheap chemical rocket he'd picked up at the station, aimed the whole thing at the planet, and fired. The rocket had just enough fuel to put the corpses into a re-entry orbit. Gravity and friction would sink their claws in, and the bodies would be gone in no time. *Shooting stars, ashes to ashes and all that shit.* More victims of the First and opportunity's knock.

A moment to drift and breathe. The locals had done a good job cleaning up the wreckage left behind by the Jellies' blockade two decades before. A lot of the bigger pieces had gone into the construction of the space station. Small technical stuff went downstairs to the Boneyard or to people like Brooklyn who tried to sell it at a profit elsewhere.

He towed the trawler to a docking collar on *Unfunky UFO* and hooked the derelict up to shore power for an overnight warm up and recharge. A few interested parties had come knocking already. Selling the boat off in pieces might have been more profitable, but it would take longer, and he was all ready tired of the whole thing.

He rubbed his eyes, and the brief darkness filled with flashes of faces. *Knew better than to look too closely*. Seven girls, five boys. The oldest barely a teenager, the youngest still in diapers, bare to vacuum. No suits for them.

Brooklyn brought the keys to the tug back to *Turk's*, accepted his buzz and paid extra for a hangover.

* * *

Waking up was the opposite of tubular or whatever it was the kids were saying these days. Whatever Carruthers had injected him with all those years ago didn't do shit for dehydration or pain, and he'd consumed enough booze and other recreational chemicals to leave him with a good headache. Brooklyn stumbled from the *Victory*'s cockpit in search of water and aspirin.

Steve met him in the corridor and kept him from both. "Got a minute?"

The smell of cheap alcohol oozed from Brooklyn's skin and clothing. There was blood, origin unknown, on the front of his coveralls. He raised his hand to probe his mouth and nose. Bar fights were nearly recreational at *Turk's*. He studied the hand he'd lifted to his face. Fading bruises or dirt on the knuckles, it was hard to tell in the dim light of the hallway.

He blinked. He'd forgotten something. Steve. *Do I have what?*

The slick handed him a cup of tea and gestured to the table visible through the narrow galley door. Carmen was already seated there. "We have a proposition for you."

"You guys are sweet, but I feel like shit and I'm not really into threesomes." *Usually.*

"A financial proposition, Brook." Carmen rolled her eyes. "M.O.N.E.Y."

"Better." Brooklyn struggled with the catch on the wall-mounted first-aid box and tore open a paper packet of aspirin. He washed the pills down with a swallow of hot, bitter tea and grimaced. "Thrill me."

"We want to buy the trawler."

"Who's we?"

Steve leaned against the counter. "Met a guy last night says we can make money running supplies back and forth to the new asteroid and elsewhere. He'll put up a quarter of the cost."

"Leaving you on the hook for seventy-five percent," Brooklyn said. "You got that?"

Carmen glanced at her husband. "We figure you owe us a cut already, plus what we brought with us. Cindy and her husband will pitch in too."

"Husband?"

"She broomed Gooch. Hubby's coming out with the boys in a few weeks to join her."

Brooklyn put his hands on the table. "Sure you want to go in with her?"

Steve folded his arms. "We don't know anyone else."

"She's a nurse," Carmen said. "He's a heavy-equipment operator. Good things to bring to the table."

"Who's your silent partner?"

"Guy named Grisha. Russian. Says he knows you."

"Last I knew, he had his own boat to worry about. Calls it *SuperFreak.*"

"It passed through a micrometeor swarm a couple of weeks ago. He sold it for scrap," Carmen said. "He'll boss the refit for us, and we'll be dumb labor. He figures there's enough room on the trawler for us all to live and work."

An' you'll have somethin' to get back to Earth in when the news about the First hits, and an off-world investment to offer your friends at the golf course. Brooklyn rubbed his eyes with the heels of his hands. *Money always does OK*. "Alright. Let me get a shower and make some calls. Got some people to disappoint."

He scrawled his name on the third sheaf of documents, this time above the word "witness". On paper, he was $57,000 ahead, and the newly incorporated Space Dog, LLC was the proud owner of a ninety-foot fishing trawler rechristened the *Foundling*. Steve had found some champagne somewhere, and he flourish-popped the cork.

Gonna wish they'd celebrated with something cheaper 'fore too long.

Grisha had grown his hair out since last Brooklyn saw him, and his empty shirt sleeve had filled up with a prosthetic more tentacle than arm. He'd lost the meat fighting the Jellies a few hours before Brooklyn died the second time.

"Nice flipper," Brooklyn said.

"Got it in the Belt." Grisha grinned through his thick beard. He was sticking to the local mushroom vodka, a bottle of the clear liquid clutched in the coils of his prosthetic. "But the doctor has moved on and said I need to keep better track of the rest."

"How are things?" Brooklyn said.

Grisha see-sawed his remaining hand. His left. "Too many people below, and work is only slowly coming to balance. The local vodka is good and cheap. Kasperov needs vacation. The Trolls are gone again."

The Trolls were Designed, engineered and bred by the First as technicians, builders, and grunt labor. They'd spent most of the last century readying the Venus caves for human occupancy. "Whaddaya mean 'gone'?"

"Four or five weeks ago, they just," he made a flying motion with the bottle, "gone."

"Where'd they go?"

"They didn't say." Grisha waggled his bushy eyebrows. The Trolls' silent hand-language wasn't widely known. Brooklyn only knew a few dozen words of it. "No one knows."

"Somebody does," Brooklyn said. "Last time they left, they built the Cathedral. Bet the Angels know where they are."

Grisha lifted the bottle to his lips. "They are not talking either."

Brooklyn flipped the socket wrench in his hand and passed it back to the chipper preteen who was serving as his helper. Her parents were station keepers, and she had the long, lean look of a childhood in low gravity. If she'd been born on Earth, she might-a had a future on the basketball court. As it was, she tagged along as Brooklyn did his station chores and learned a little about the HVAC systems.

"Different from the ones we did yesterday." She ran greasy fingers through her knuckle-length shock of bright blue hair, standing it on end. From the looks of things, machine oil and smudges were her favorite accessories.

"Station came together at different times, pieces of scrap refitted and bolted on," Brooklyn said. "Lucky if you find two filter housings alike in the whole thing, much less on this side o' things." He shook the plastic bin they'd been dragging around the station for the past six hours. "Filter material comes from De Milo. It's cut and fitted into recycled housings up here."

She hummed. "You're from Earth, right? Is it true, what they say?"

"'Swhat true?"

"My dad says you can go outside and stand right under the sky without a vacsuit."

"Don't need Earth for that," Brooklyn said. "You can do that in De Milo."

The girl scoffed. "'Snot a real sky. The sun's a fake, and there's a roof over all of it."

The shittiest end of the many shitty-ended stick humanity had been handed. Earth was the only place where they could walk out their front door, dig their dirty toes in the grass, look up at the stars, and take a deep breath of fresh air without being under a dome or something. "If you were on Earth, you'd be in school now instead of learning something useful. And there's snow. Comes right out of the sky and gets all over the damned place. Freeze your ass off."

"I'll be in school soon," she said. "Mama's rotation is over at the end of the season, and we're going down to De Milo."

"Nervous?"

She shrugged. "I know it will take me a while to get used to the gravity. Mama said I might have some agoraphobia, too. But I want to go. It's time."

"Just don't get so wrapped up in school and sh– stuff like that you forget to–" he faked a cough to cover that he'd been about to say 'see the world' "–that you forget to live a little."

"What does that mean?" she said.

"Ya know, raise a little hell, maybe steal a car, kiss boys, punch cops…"

She looked at him blankly.

"Or maybe just do your homework and eat all your mushrooms like a good kid." He flipped the top of the bin closed and held it under his arm. "Job's done. We'll report to your mom and call it good. Okay?"

She nodded. "I like kissing girls better."

"Don't blame you a bit."

Brooklyn and Float spent their last day on station in the market, filling up space left by their passengers' luggage. *Never fly empty*. Necessities and luxuries were easier to get in De Milo than they used to be, but it was still a pain in the ass to dash into orbit every time the sugar ran out or someone wanted a drink of something that didn't taste like mushrooms. They cleaned the *Victory*'s 'fresher, the bunk area, and galley, and returned to the airlock where their next job was waiting. Six people looking for a ride down the well to De Milo. Float showed them to their places and collected their fares.

Brooklyn returned to the cockpit and took the reactors off standby. The various telltales flickered to yellows and greens, and Bugs rasped its infuriatingly unsexy greeting before freezing and requiring a reboot. *Being a spaceman always seemed cool on the shows. Brooklyn Lamontagne, bus driver. Ma would be so proud. Actually, she probably would.*

He clicked the intercom. "If you need to piss, do it now. Upper atmosphere gets kind of choppy this time of year, and I don't need you smearing blood and broken noses all over my boat. Launch in five."

PART SIX
Resist Psychic Death

TWELVE

Human scientists had a lot of theories about First Tech – natural forces, strange matter, gluons, fuck-it-trons, gravity-wave manipulation, cosmic voodoo – but nothing that panned out in the lab. It was generally agreed the conquerors had held back most of the good shit. They wanted humanity out of their hair, not uplifted to a new level of galactic annoyance. The lifters and field generators they'd allowed access to couldn't begin to explain how to create a stable energy tunnel down through the atmosphere of Venus, but it worked.

Brooklyn steered his ship toward the coordinates of the tunnel mouth. "I hate this damned thing."

In a perfect world, Bugs would have responded with a quip or a surly "does not compute", but despite a lot of work during the Moon-to-Venus trip, the thing was still dumber than a spark plug. It stayed quiet, but it at least it didn't crash again.

Float found her partner's anxiety amusing but kept her gurgles to herself.

The blue glow of the tunnel flashed into being, and the *Victory* went down its throat. Somehow, the glow protected the ship from the storms and turbulence of the upper atmosphere. Somehow, it held back the massive pressure and metal-melting heat of the lower levels. Brooklyn's testicles shrank as they always did in the tunnel. *One hiccup, one glitch and we're paste. No coming back from that.*

Probably. Anyway, he wasn't eager to try.

He flicked on the radio. "*Victory* to De Milo ground. We're just about through."

A response jittered out of the static. "Ten-four, Captain Lamontagne. We got Pad Six waiting for ya. Just lit the beacon."

Pad Six. The first time the *Victory* took off from De Milo, it had been all junk piles and work sites. Not a proper landing pad to be seen. "How close is that to the market?"

"Right next door," the flight controller said. "Guessed you were coming in loaded for bear."

Yeah, Yogi Bear. This boat is one big pic-a-nic basket. "Just for that, I got a box of Pop-Tarts with your name on it. Drop by *The Toad Stool* when you want to collect. I'll leave it for you."

"Will do." Static crackled. "Happy landings."

Leaving the glowing blue tunnel behind, the *Victory* slid through the relatively short passage through the planet's crust. It ended in an iris gate, which sphinctered shut behind. That part was seldom commented upon, marvel of engineering though it was. The next bit, the shock of dropping into a mid-summer snow globe with a 1,239-mile radius got all the attention. The First had dug twelve of the things, each with an area of four-point-eight million square miles. Total land was barely a thirtieth of Earth's surface area, but seventy percent of the home planet was covered by water anyway. There was plenty of room in the caves for five billion people, provided the power stayed on, the air stayed fresh, and the water kept running. *Wonder how many will stay once they learn they can go home.*

Brooklyn took the *Victory* into a wide figure-eight over the city. Patches of green were spreading slowly over the gray sand, enough water in the air for a wispy layer of clouds about half a mile up. Rain was still decades away, so irrigation was standard practice, electric pumps pulling water out of reservoirs buried even more deeply in the ground.

The UN evacuation ships were one-shots. Their wide bodies

went through the tunnel and landed in preordained spots, serving as housing for the new arrivals at first, then scavenged building materials. Their propulsion systems went back to Earth for the next trip.

De Milo population was approaching a million, a democratic-socialist utopia for now, likely to change once the shock wore off and people stopped playing nice. Or Wal-Mart opened a store and chased all the mom-and-pops out.

The figure-eight ended at the assigned landing site, and the *Victory* rocked gently into place. Brooklyn put the ship to sleep and got up to stretch. It took a minute to recognize the feelings he was having. Relief. Relaxation. Henry and Emigration officials might have been top dogs in their own neighborhoods, but they'd have a helluva job reaching across space to fuck with him in De Milo.

Float lost at rock-paper-scissors, so she chased the passengers out of the ship and turned to the cargo while Brooklyn filled a few shopping bags with bribes. He slipped the launch-pad mechanic a box of Hostess cupcakes and an IOU in return for a reactor inspection and a consumables top-off. It never hurt to be ready for a quick getaway.

A dozen kids were parked outside the fence, watching the ships come down. Brooklyn gave them a candy bar each. Their joy was infectious, sure, but the gossip he got from them was part of the calculation. Most of the kids ate only a few bites before tucking the rest of the candy away somewhere. Earth treats were hard to come by a hundred sixty million miles from the nearest Hershey factory, and they'd learned to make things last.

"Shouldn't you guys be in school?" Brooklyn said.

One girl, her mouth ringed in chocolate – her family might have been one of his fares a few years before – laughed. "It's Saturday!" Another kid, probably her brother, was using the fence as a jungle gym.

Brooklyn made a mental note. The counting of days and

weeks between the planets could get a little slippery. The *Victory*'s computer insisted it was Friday – if nothing else, it was good at counting – but when on Venus, do as the Venusians do. "This is what you're gonna do all day? Can't be that many people coming down for you to harass."

The eldest girl, maybe eleven, spoke for the group. "We're going over to the farm later. See the baby goats."

"Luwanda's place?" Brooklyn said.

The girl nodded.

"Tell 'er I got a case of that tequila she likes. She can get it wholesale if she talks to me before I take it to market."

Goats were small enough to fit on a ship, ate just about anything, and provided plenty of milk and manure. Luwanda's farm was one of the oldest.

"Have you seen these?" the eldest boy in the group held up a metal circlet.

"Marco," a girl, his sister, chided. "You aren't supposed to have that."

Marco flushed. "I'm not gonna use it!"

Brooklyn took it. The metal was springy and flexible, light. The ends tapered to rounded points at six o'clock, and it felt maybe a millimeter thicker between eleven and one. It was silk smooth and felt good in his hands. "What is it?"

"You put it on your head," the eldest girl said. "It's like TV."

He held the thing up to the light and looked through it. "You watch shows on it?"

"Nah. It's–" she hesitated. "It's like you put it on and you're a different person. The Angels are giving them out."

Brook flexed the circlet. "You just put it on?"

"They all have different people on them."

"So, it's like a game."

"Just put it on. But sit down first."

Brooklyn sat cross-legged on the ground and fitted the band around his head.

"Close your eyes," the kid said.

Who do you want to be? *The question was unvoiced but not unheard. It arose from somewhere in Brooklyn's own mind, soft but insistent. What are my options?*

Clean hot water pounded and caressed her bare skin. The New York Ritz Carlton had amazing water pressure, and she was always happy when the agency paid to put her up there. It was past its prime, surely, but the war had aged everything and everyone. Working in New York for a couple of weeks meant she could squeeze in a day or two in Queens to see the family, although Mama would no doubt chastise her about her lifestyle, and the cousins would pester like pigeons for details of her latest love affairs. She shaved her legs. Showering alone was a relief after weeks of Alphonse following her under the water and "helping" her wash. Her breasts had never been so clean! She rinsed her dark bob of hair and turned off the water. The hotel had lovely towels, white, thick and soft as clouds. She wound one around her head, wrapped another around her body, and exited the bathroom to see what room service had brought. Eggs, bacon, a pitcher of orange juice and a tall bottle of good vodka. She mixed a drink and carried it to the window. Forty-Seventh Street snaked far below, traffic like ants on a log. She sipped her drink. Hours to go before the shoot with Irving. "Let's see that long neck of yours, Doe!" It was good to be Dovima, so much better than being Dorothy had been.

He nearly fell over in his scramble to pull the band off his head. "I was a chick!"

Marco nodded. "Dorothy. She's boring."

Brooklyn examined the band again. "The hell you get this?"

"The Angels started giving them out a few weeks ago. Everyone has them."

"Not everyone!" Marco's little sister said. "Only some people."

"People who go to the church," the eldest girl said.

Brooklyn gave the band back to Marco. "Better give that

back to your mom, bud." He twisted his way out of the sticky horde and walked to the edge of the launch field to find a cab, or a scooter to rent. Kasperov had put five miles of road between the new-and-improved field and the edge of town. Better in the face of a crash or a lift-off explosion, but a pain to walk even in Venus gravity. While Brooklyn waited in the queue, he tried to find the feeling of respite again. He took a deep breath. Even the sulfur dioxide in the air seemed to be giving him a pass. Money in his pocket, several pallets of trade goods–

The circlet reminded him of something, but he couldn't put his finger on it. Too many changes too fast. The message, Big Tony, enhanced emigration protocols, the circlets…

The guy at the rental counter put up a sign. "I'm out," he announced. "'Til someone comes back this way, I got nothing to ride."

Brooklyn was still three deep in line, juggling his shopping bags. Odds were good something would be heading back soon, but three somethings…

He raised his voice. "Not even a bike?"

The guy spread his hands. "Everything's out, man. Gettin' hard to keep up."

Brooklyn swore. "Guess I'm walking, then."

His house was where he'd left it, which was no longer a guarantee in the growing city. The first couple of times he'd lost track of it, there'd been a note, but the last relocation required a trip to city hall and a thorough survey of the latest zoning maps.

He unlocked the battered shipping container and stuck his head through the door. Bare walls, a simple bed, a rough kitchenette, a lamp, a crate with some books on it, a compost commode, and a vintage Snoopy astronaut doll. No squatters. He tossed the go-bag on the bed and checked under the mattress for his spare plasma blaster and cash stash. He left the weapon and added a few layers to the roll of cash.

The narrow mattress was tempting, despite its meanness and coating of dust. A nap would take the edge off his post-flight weariness and post-hike crankiness. But so would a drink. He relocked the door and pointed himself at the medical center.

Most of the adhoc buildings bore a mural or two, and Brooklyn stopped to consider defacing one of the new ones. A purple woman, framed in a "holy" light and stars, a cosmic Madonna. The image had been inspired by the one he'd drawn in the *Victory*'s cockpit in the days before his third death twenty years before. His rescuers – neighbors and friends from Mexico – had taken a picture of the image and brought it with them when they emigrated to Venus after their lucrative press tour. The drawing and the rescuers' story, Brooklyn's Lazarus-like return, had taken on a life of its own. A church was born, and, for a time, parishioners had sought Brooklyn out to bless babies and weddings. Surliness had put an end to the petitions, but the weird little faith had refused to die. *Bet you think that's pretty damned funny.*

He stomped on. The doctor was with a patient when he arrived at the clinic, so he put his feet on the coffee table in the expanded waiting room, ignoring the receptionist's carefully directed glare. Something funky was playing on the stereo, probably Demarco's influence. The Drs Jillian Milk were many things, but they had a tin ear when it came to music, and their tastes were stuck firmly in the early '60s.

The door to the examination room swung open. "If it doesn't feel any better in a couple of days, come back in," the doctor said.

The patient with her frowned when she saw Brooklyn and beat feet out of the clinic with her head down. *Another fan.*

"Where's your big sister?" he said.

The doctor took off her white-ish coat and hung it on the

door. "Day off. Leon's out of town with Kas for a few." She rubbed her unscarred face. "Bar?"

"Bar."

The Toad Stool had changed its name to *The Mush Room*, but the words on the sign were the only difference Brooklyn could spot. He traded a bottle of middle-shelf rum for an all-you-can-eat lunch.

"I can't believe you actually chose to eat that." The Jillian Milk who sat beside him was in her mid-thirties and had none of the scarring and only a little of the weariness that defined the other's face. His friend's face, although this Milk had become a pal, too.

Brooklyn grunted, his mouth too full to respond otherwise. He washed the over-sized bite of fungus-and-alien-grain burger down with a long slug of mushroom beer. "De Milo's the only place I can get it."

This Jillian Milk had come to Venus in 1987, dropped off by Andy and her outlaws after their successful assault on the Artiplanet virus lab. She was one of several humans rescued from cold storage during the raid, and there was no way of knowing whether she or her doppelganger – older, scarred, and married to Director Kasperov – was the original. Demarco had taken to calling her "Skim," and of course it had stuck.

She ordered a Reuben with fries, a mix of imported and homegrown ingredients at least four times as expensive as Brooklyn's burger. The fun part of her vodka tonic was locally sourced, a pirate of Brooklyn's own retired label, but the tonic was Earth made.

"You look like you need that," he said.

A fry moved lethargically into her mouth. "Busy days. Kas recruited old me to run the De Milo Medical Association. She gets to decide who can hang up a shingle and play doctor, and I get to run her clinic."

"Funny, considerin' neither of you went to med school."

"Don't tell anyone, and I won't remind everyone in here what an asshole you are."

Brooklyn wiped his mouth with a cloth napkin and looked around the room. "Wouldn't hurt my feelings much. Don't recognize a quarter of 'em."

"Progress." She sipped her drink. "There are more than a hundred and twelve different languages spoken in De Milo now."

"Surprised Kas hasn't tried to make Russian the official one."

"Esperanto, apparently. They'll start teaching it in the primary schools in the fall."

"Brought four more in with me from Tycho, but they decided to stay outside."

"Any useful skills?"

"Nurse and a construction worker. Do-gooder and an accountant. A dog."

"We'll take the nurse, the construction guy, and the dog." De Milo needed infrastructure – transportation, water, sewage, food production and distribution, schools, fire departments, and hospitals – and none of that could be built without know-how and materials. "Once the middle-class starts coming in we'll have one farm to a thousand accountants and lawyers."

Brooklyn grinned. "Jack and Jill Suburb don't like coming a zillion miles to find a shovel waiting for them."

"My family sure wouldn't." She made a face. "I don't see you with a shovel, Mr Lamontagne."

He put his hands behind his head. "Done my share of digging, babe. Potatoes, ditches, foundations. Moved your clinic twice already. Not my fault I got more marketable skills."

She snorted. "You could do a lot more than flying that bucket around committing identity fraud."

"True," he held up one index finger, "but, see, I don't want to." He leaned in. "Speaking of identity fraud, you tried one of those head things the Angels are handing out?"

The circlets weren't ubiquitous, but now that he knew what to look for, Brooklyn had spotted several people under their influence or talking about their experiences. "Beats the hell outta living in a cave," one guy said. The band had left a clean spot in the dirt accumulated on his forehead.

"It's only the churchgoers, so far," Skim said. "I haven't even seen one."

"Pretty trippy. Put it on my head and, bam, I was taking a shower in an old-timey hotel."

"That doesn't sound trippy."

"I was a woman."

"Interesting." She rubbed the back of her neck. "I wonder how it works."

"I wonder why the Angels are passin' 'em out."

"Just a toy, probably. No worse for your head than a drink or two."

"Yeah, but–" He paused. "I can't take this anymore. Do you know what I know?"

She popped an eyebrow. "Probably more, generally, but specificity might help here."

"Do you know," he glanced around to make sure no one was listening, "about the First?"

"This some kind of a joke?" It was her turn to look around. "What am I missing?"

"Trolls are gone. Angels are handing out freebies." He watched her face. Nothing. "Demarco didn't say anything to you? To either of you."

She shook her head. "You'd have to ask her, but if she knows something I don't, I'm going to be pissed. That's not how we play."

Brooklyn sighed. "My head's starting to hurt."

"What's all this?" She stabbed him with her finger. "Brook, if there's something going on that I should know about, and you didn't tell me in time, I swear to God I'll–!"

He held up his hands. "I need to talk to Demarco. He says

it's okay, I'll rush right over. You'll be the first or second one I'll tell."

"Promise me."

"Sure."

THIRTEEN

The Jelly doorman inspected Brooklyn's invitation. "What's the purpose of your visit?"

"Breakfast." He yawned. "An' see my partner. Her name's on the invite."

The doorman held the printout in front of his 'face' again. The cameras there distorted the text into something his ocean-evolved eyes could handle. He thrust the paper back at Brooklyn. "No trouble."

"Who, me?" Brooklyn smirked. The expression might have been wasted on the doorman. Most jellies didn't bother to learn the basic human expressions, and it could take several years in close proximity to grasp the subtle shit.

Roughly folded, the invitation went into his jacket pocket as he searched for the booth Float had reserved for him.

The Tank wasn't the first Jelly bar in De Milo, but it was the longest lasting. Eleven years. Some disgruntled citizen had knocked a hole in its immediate predecessor, probably still sore about the Jelly occupation of the city in the late '70s. Forty-some days. All kinds of jellies had showed up for it, stomping out of the dark down in the caves and swooping into orbit from hidey holes elsewhere in the solar system.

They'd beaten themselves when they severed the link between the simple Designed piloting the junk ship and the Artiplanet. The Designed pilots panicked and shot up everything in the sky, destroying hundreds of Jelly fighters and support ships before self-destructing. After that, the residents of De Milo made short work of the jellies left behind to mind them.

Tempers had cooled, but the owners of *The Tank* weren't taking chances. Black T-shirted security beings patrolled the place at all times: exosuited jellies, humans, even a few of the green, Mark 1 Designed.

Brooklyn slid into his booth and ordered a cup of tea and a mushroom omelet. He was more sanguine about the tea than the eggs, although there was a decent chance the bartender would use saltwater in both. The booth had been built right up against *The Tank*'s centerpiece, a two-hundred-thousand-gallon salt-water tank full of ocean plants, tasty fish, and naked jellies. One of them came closer to the glass, and the intercom on Brooklyn's table lit up.

"You look like shit," Float said.

She was relaxed. Part of it was the inter- and outercourse she'd no doubt been having since she'd checked in, but most of it was just getting out of the suit and having more room to move than the small tank the *Victory*'s engineering section allowed.

"An' you look like a sneeze," he said. "Any trouble at the market?"

"Sold everything to Ayodeji Mahmud. Price was right, and I know you like her." Ayodeji and her many cousins had fitted out a massive oil tank with First Tech and launched it into space in the early '90s. They entered Venus orbit dehydrated and nearly hypoxic three months later. Ayodeji had gone to work for Turk and bought him out in less than two years. "I put the money in the usual spots and took out my share."

"Got your eye on somethin' nice?"

"I signed on with the *Drift*, the ship I visited on the station. Finalized it last night."

"Where's it going?"

She gurgled. "Out of the solar system. Maybe way out."

"To raid an' pillage the galaxy like the old days?"

"To live like the starfarers we are," she said. "We don't need an empire, but we do need a reason to exist beyond eating and mating."

"I'll throw you a goin'–"

"I'm leaving today. In just a few hours. To the Belt first, then outward."

His order arrived. It looked inedible. "I'd give you a goodbye hug but–"

"It would probably kill you again." Her tentacles swayed gently. "I told the General about Demarco's message."

"Your mother?" Float's mom was a bigwig in the Jelly military and had testified in favor of her daughter's exile. "Sure that was a good idea?"

One of her mouth arms floated up in a gesture reminiscent of an exosuit shrug. "I'm still a member of the Smack. The General will check her nets before she informs the council."

"The Smack's not known for playing nice." Brooklyn rubbed his mouth. "Seems to me Ma might see this as a good time to start a war with humanity."

"It's possible." She pulsed. "She probably does see it that way, but the council has already ruled. The Smack will keep to itself as long as humans do."

"We're not so good at playin' nice either." He tried the tea. Not bad. It was more like a seaweed broth. "Problem for another day."

"Thank you for finding me in the desert."

"I'll see you again." *It's been fun.* "Space is big, but there's only so much good parking."

FOURTEEN

Milk the Elder was swaying gently in her seat, maybe moving in time to the alcohol pumping through her system. She could hold her booze, but few could match the woman across the table, Yeva Toploski, drink for drink without showing it. After the invasion, Top had declared herself De Milo's chief law-enforcement officer, and no one had thought to challenge her drunk or sober.

Demarco wasn't due back for a few days yet, and Brooklyn was back to fishing. "Trolls taking off like that makes me think the First are up to something."

Top folded her arms on the table. "The First are always up to something, and they've no cause to tell us what." Twenty years before, during the Jelly invasion, she'd learned, just in time to save Brooklyn's life, that she was a splinter. The knowledge had come like a stroke, feedback from the Jellies' severing of the quantum connection between the First and their proxies. Maybe it was because she'd been drinking heavily that night, maybe it was because she'd been in the throes of an orgasm when the cut was made... Whatever the reason, Top had come away knowing far more about the First and their works than she should have.

Of the twenty-three thousand surviving First, fewer than thirty had any interest in reclaiming Earth. It was a science project, a curiosity. They lived half a galaxy away, their immortal consciousnesses freely spending the nearly unlimited energy of the red sun they'd caged. Prior to the Jellies' intervention, every second of Top's life had been examined and experienced, ignored, enjoyed, and recorded by her patron, who, meantime, was also remotely piloting a probe into the Pleiades and sussing out how to use a black hole to make a backup of the galaxy.

"What about those things the Angels are handing out, the circlets?" Brooklyn said.

Top poured another round of vodka shots, sucking spill-off from the heel of her hand. "Recordings. The lives of splinters preserved."

Brooklyn hummed. "One I tried was old. Early '50s, it seemed like. Way before Topeka got cratered."

"The Designed have been here for more than a hundred years," the ersatz Soviet said. "They've been putting splinters on Earth at least that long."

"Your life on one of those things?" Brooklyn said.

"It was." Top picked up the bottle and pretended to read the locally printed label. "When it was brought to my attention, I carried the circlet to the Boneyard and cut it to pieces."

"I don't get why the Angels are handing them out now."

"Distraction?" Milk was a little slush-mouthed. "Look this way not that?"

"Humans are easily pacified with stories and shiny objects," Top said.

Brooklyn downed half his shot, winced, and drank the rest. "Pal of mine said that's why the First let TV and movies alone when they started cracking down on industry. Three hots, a bed, a bottle, an' something on the tube is enough for lots of folks."

"Enough of alien shenanigans," Top said. "There is more to life. Tell me of your loves and personal struggles."

Brooklyn and Milk glanced at each other. She and Kasperov had been together for years, and Brooklyn's dalliance with Evelyn was likely tamer than Top was looking for.

Top looked from one face to the other. "No? I will start. I have two new lovers. A couple. She has small breasts and strong thighs. He has..."

Brooklyn walked Milk home a couple of hours later. She had a little smile on her face. A nice night out with friends. Hers was the first face he'd seen when he woke up in De Milo all those years ago. Hers and Demarco's. "All right, here it is," he said. "I'm not supposed to tell anybody this, but Demarco says the First pulled out. Gave up, went home."

She took in some air. "How does he know that?"

"Not a clue. Sent me a cryptic message a few weeks ago, an' never answered my follow up."

"He and Kas have been away awhile. Nearly a month, and they were acting pretty cagey before they left."

"You think Kas is in on it?"

She made a 'duh' face. "He'll be the one who decided to keep me out."

"Why would he do that?"

"Because I'd want to tell everyone. I don't like secrets." She sighed. "But I won't. Not until we all get a chance to talk about it. I want some proof before I start running around singing."

"I told Skim I'd tell her if I told you."

"This feels more like high school than an intelligence operation. If you do, she won't say anything. What about Top?"

"What would she do if she knew?"

Milk folded her arms. "At least we know what she is. What I am. There's no telling how many other spies and plants we have among the refugees, playing at being colonist."

"Who we keepin' it a secret from?"

"Earth governments. Mars. Maybe the Jellies."

That one's blown. "Why the hell would Demarco tell me?"

She smiled. "Maybe he knew you couldn't keep to yourself."

FIFTEEN

Brooklyn rode out to the Dig in a 1978 Subaru BRAT conversion. The road passed by one of the few First structures still standing, a dome-shaped building two stories tall. Under the artificial sun, the colors were visible, a diagonal pattern of faded purples and yellows.

Maybe they were Lakers fans.

Cold beer cut the road dust some but didn't do shit to improve the scenery. He spit out the window. *We could make it rain seeds, water, and goat shit, we might see somethin' out here.*

Either living in an alien cave made people prone to archaeology, or the ready availability of Professor Yarrow's mind-altering mushroom tea helped them forget where they were. Whatever, the reason, the Dig was a popular place to work. Yarrow's papers on the First were required reading at universities and several government agencies, and her pop-science books occupied many a bedside table back on Earth. She'd made a fortune off them but opted to continue living in a tent.

Yarrow was sitting outside in her 'parlor', an assortment of unmatched lounge chairs circling a low table with a tea service on it. She waved. "Heard you were coming! We baked this morning so everything is fresh!"

Yarrow was in her sixties, but she'd achieved an ageless quality that was part Oxford academic and part California surfer girl. She'd been in De Milo longer than just about anyone else.

Brooklyn inspected the plated pastries and tea cakes on the table. "How much o' this is *special*?"

"The chocolate cakes have marijuana in them. Just a bit. And there's the tea, of course." She smiled. The ingredients for Yarrow's mushroom tea – soothing, warming, and gently psychedelic – grew easily and abundantly in the caves.

Brooklyn claimed a seat and poured himself a cup. Like her chairs, the professor's china was also mismatched. "Who told you I was coming?"

"Nothing nefarious." Her eyes sparkled. "A little bird delivering supplies told the site manager who told me. The surveyors down the road a bit radioed that you had been spotted. Just in time to wash my hands and put the kettle on."

Brooklyn told her about Big Tony. "So, that's that, I guess. We can leave the rest o' the rocks where they are."

"Perhaps I should re-examine them. They might be more important than we believed." The professor tented her fingers. "Have you told Director Kasperov?"

Delivering the rocks to Big Tony had been part of a chain of handoffs and deals to get First Tech – lifters and field generators – to De Milo. The stuff was free on Earth but strictly regulated. Little of it had come the way of humans on Venus because the First wanted them to stay put, not flit around the solar system. But one of Brooklyn's less savory contacts had approached him, and a plan was born.

"You recall I objected to this arrangement from the start," Yarrow said.

"You and me both," Brooklyn said. "But De Milo needed a merchant fleet."

"And so we did." She rubbed her palms on her thighs, smoothing the khaki work pants she typically wore. "Better to get out of the business before we end up disintegrated, I suppose. I could do without the distraction."

"You dig up anything interesting since the last time I was here?"

"The surveyors you passed are determining the boundaries

of what some of us believe to be a mass grave." Her face lit back up as she spoke. "I should announce it, but we've been so busy. We've come to believe the First used a form of disintegration in their funeral practices. Deeper though, this would have been a thousand years or so after the First moved into the caves, there's evidence of a mass die-off."

"They get sick or somethin'?"

"It's only been a few days – well, weeks – not nearly long enough to make any conclusions."

"Hard to imagine the First with bodies." *And faces to punch.*

"Grab your drink and a snack, and I will take you to see!"

Brooklyn wolfed down a piece of chocolate cake and refilled his mug before rising to follow the lean-faced professor down to the dig site. There were no permanent structures in the encampment. Sans weather, the only real housing concerns were security and privacy, and about half the professor's staff were nudists. She led the way to a multi-colored tent that had started its life in a carnival.

"Doctor Anning is our only trained paleontologist," she said, "and she can be somewhat… peppery. Be very mindful where you step and do not spill anything on her bones!" She poked her head through the tent flap. "Annie, we have visitors. Are you decent?"

The carnival tent was spacious, with cabinets and shelves lining the walls. Tables were set up in parallel in the middle of the floor, and the interior of the tent was made brighter than day with an array of lamps. Doctor Anning was a short woman who'd worn a pensive frown so long it had stuck on her face, and she greeted her colleague with a single word: "What?"

"Captain Lamontagne would like to see Eve," the professor said.

"Samantha, I object to your continued familiarization of Subject One. We have not determined gender nor age, nor is it appropriate to apply a name from Earth mythology to a creature evolved on another world."

Yarrow raised her hands. "Objection noted, Annie. Please show our guest what we have found."

Anning's frown deepened, but she stepped to the side allowing the others to move closer to the table. At the beginning of Brooklyn's junior year, his biology teacher had unveiled a brand-new classroom skeleton he'd named 'Barry Bones'. By year's end, Barry looked a lot like Subject One: missing pieces, a broken and chipped abstraction of his former self. The final resting place of Barry's skull was in a box somewhere with Brooklyn's high-school yearbook and class ring.

A shadow seemed to pass over the bones on the table, making it look they were covered in gray, leathery skin, a visor of cartilage jutting out over the wide-spread eyes to shade them from the sun. *Humid heat, a slack mouth flapping in a place that smelled like mildew.* Brooklyn shuddered. He'd drunk too much mushroom tea, maybe. "Think I need to lie down." A purple zing of laughter echoed from somewhere. He swayed. "Feeling a little funky."

"We can go back to my tent," Professor Yarrow said. "Likely you just need some water."

SIXTEEN

The pounding started again. "I know she's in there! If I gotta drag your ass outta bed, I'll fuck you up!"

Brooklyn stumbled to the door of the storage unit and yanked it open. "Gonna wake the neighbors, man."

"People stupid enough to live next door to you deserve it." Demarco brushed past Brooklyn and headed for the rudimentary kitchen. He pulled a dusty jar off the single shelf and held it up to the light skeptically before wiping it off on his shirttail. "Got somethin' to put in this?"

Brooklyn pointed out the bottle. "The hell you been, man? You were due back three days ago."

"Hither and yon." Demarco poured some bourbon into the jar and dropped into Brooklyn's only chair. "So many places to see and go, I never did know."

"You get my message?"

"Did. I chose not to answer."

"The fuck, man?" Brooklyn sat on the edge of the bed and drank straight from the bottle. "I wasn't calling for the time. I needed information."

Demarco sucked his teeth. "Which I did not have. Got more now, if you ready to shut up and listen."

"I told Milk. Both of them. Just in the last couple of days."

"Surprised you held out so long." He took a breath. "First are gone. That part's pretty clear. Got it twice. Once from the

Angel in my pocket, and once from the new leader of the DLF."

The Designed Liberation Front. "What happened to Andy?"

"Missing in action. They say she was s'posed to come back with someone who knew the most important piece o'all this." He shot his eyebrows expectantly.

"Why they left." Brooklyn took another drink. "Yeah, that's been buggin' me, too."

"Could be perfectly innocent."

"Probably not." Brooklyn relayed the news about Big Tony and the shipment of rocks.

"Zap-zap not bullets." Demarco pulled at his lower lip as he took it in. "Then there's the enhanced-protocol shit Emigration just pulled."

"Might not be connected."

"Might not, but be weird if it ain't."

"Float knows. She told her mother."

"The General." He nodded slowly. "Told her it was okay."

"*You* told Float that. When did you talk to her?"

"Eyes and ears everywhere, babe. Part of the job."

"Job is that?"

"De Milo Minister without Portfolio." He spread his arms. "Chief Sneaky-Snake of Venus."

"Thought that was just a joke you told."

"Joke most certainly, but not real funny." He took a drink, swished it around in the front of his mouth. "I entertain a hundred bad thoughts before breakfast. They turn aroun' an' keep me up all night. Liked it better when I was just an ol' drunk."

"You're still a drunk."

"Pot, kettle." He held up his jar. "Bottle." He motioned for a refill. "Got a job for you."

"Part of this?"

"In four weeks' time, need you take me and Old Lady Milk to Mars." He smiled. "Jilly 'bout to be invited to a fancy doctor thing. Conference on space medicine. While she does that, I get to chat with someone about Andy's defector pal."

"With who?"

"They will approach me at midnight high with a golden feather or some shit. I just need to be there. DLF stuff. They got a whole Department of Sneaky-Snake."

"Does Milk know she's being used as cover?"

"Not yet, but don't s'pose either of us too good at keeping our mouths shut."

"That's been buggin' me too. The hell you tell me about this?"

"Float's an asset. Knew she'd tell Major Mommy 'fore too long. You's a friend. Most-a the time."

"Fuck does that mean?"

"Means that's a chat I'm not ready to have with you."

His face got hot. "Bullshit."

"Yeah. S'pose it is." The older man rubbed his jaw. "I known you awhile, see. Longer than you known me."

Brooklyn shrugged. "Only by a couple months. Part I can't remember cause I–"

"Three times. That's how many times you reckon you've died an' come back. Lost some time after all three. Few days, some hours, then the big one. Few months."

"Where's this goin'?"

"Way you drink, bet you've lost some time there, too. A night here an' there. Weekend or two."

"You're one to talk, man. I peeled you up so many–"

"Truer words, babe. But we ain't the same. How you know when you lost a weekend to a good time and when you lost it to a real bad one?" He took a pull from the jar.

"I don't want hear anymore."

Demarco told him anyway. Some of it.

PART SEVEN
Do the Evolution

SEVENTEEN

It might have been satisfying to see Bugs, the truculent computer, in pieces on the ground, but Brooklyn pulled it out of its housing carefully and moved it to the table in the galley.

Work was good. Calm was good. Hard to do fine tech stuff with fists.

Float might've been able to set him straight, help him get things in perspective. He'd done some sneaky shit, too. Lie down with Sneaky-Snakes, get up slithering, she might say. Little lies and big ones. Secrets. *But no tellin' how deep she was in on it.*

Brooklyn forced his hands open again.

How many times? he'd asked Demarco.

Six or seven I know about.

What did I do?

Only know for sure about one time, and I can't say about that.

She woulda said something. The Jellies were brutally honest with each other and with friends. Brooklyn brewed a pot of strong tea, the professor's so-called warrior blend. Focus, sharpness, and just a little lens flare. Perfect for fine work. No booze, no booze for a long, long time.

Float was a warrior by inclination and training, but there was no serving on a spaceship without accruing some knowledge of the systems that made them go. Over the years, she'd translated Jelly technical manuals so Brooklyn could add some of the good stuff, like the camoflage, to the *Victory.*

This job was something else again. He'd nabbed several Jelly Tech computers from the Boneyard, and they lay disassembled on his workbench. Four weeks until the next job, money in the bank, and a desperate need for distraction. Without Float, he would need some help flying the ship to Mars.

He hummed as he worked, trying and failing to harmonize with the best bits off Tom Petty's *Southern Accents* album. Petty had punched a wall and busted up his hand pretty good recording the thing. Brooklyn would heal up pretty quick from something like that, but it would hurt like hell, so he didn't.

The tea and tunes put him in the groove, his hands nearly moving on their own, his head doing its best to keep up. Jelly Tech was almost organic, somewhat self-repairing, and seemed to want to cooperate and fit together in ways that made mistakes unlikely. Processors welcomed compilers, embraced interpreters and memory with the ardor of long-lost friends. More grudgingly it accepted the Earth-built components and the small bits of First Tech he'd been accruing over the years. The need for sleep was distant and easy to ignore. The only measure of time that counted was the dirty dishes piling up in the galley. There was plenty of tea.

Brooklyn installed Bugs 2.0 as the operating system, a Linux modification of his own design, and ran a few orbital calculations through the thing. He'd barely punched the "enter" key when the answers came back. The Jelly navigational software was beyond anything humans had, and its precision would save time and fuel with every trip. His fingers, healing fast from solder-iron burns and stained with flux, ran through his hair. *Might be time for a nap. It's been… days, I think.*

"The tea." He glanced at the empty pot.

A series of numbers appeared on the modified flat screen. A basic equation, Intro to Algebra, at best. Brooklyn entered the answer, and a new one appeared, slightly more difficult. He grunted. *You ain't s'posed to do that.*

* * *

"I checked everything I know." A shower, a nap, and hours of tests later, the computer was still acting up. He placed the call after a long walk and some self-talk. Time of war. Needs must. Etcetera.

Demarco rubbed his mouth. "Maybe it knows you dumb and wants to help you out."

"Seem to be keeping up okay."

"I spotted th' calculator, cheater. You playin' one machine against t' other."

"You want to do sines and cosines with a pencil and paper, help yourself. That ain't the point. It shouldn't be asking me questions." Brooklyn had tried to keep up by hand, and the walls were scrawled with numbers and cross outs. The computer dropped the difficulty of the questions it posed whenever he made a mistake. Using the calculator had been as much a matter of pride as anything else. "Was hoping to get more out of you than smart ass."

"Smart ass is free. All I got an unlimited supply of," Demarco said. "Computers ain't really my bag, babe."

"You read all that sci-fi shit, though, and this is… I don't know what this is. Feels almost like it's playing a game with me."

"What else you tried?"

"Other than the pop quizzes, it's working great. Answers any problem I give it so long as I answer one for it first.

"Maybe give it somethin' else."

"Like what, a compliment?"

"Hand job if you want to be real friendly." Demarco worried the patch of hair below his lip. "You can program, like, dimensions and measurements, right? What happens you give it a shape?"

'Round about midnight, after several hours trading shapes and math problems back and forth with the computer, Demarco had an epiphany.

"This gonna take a while. We friends enough that I can stay over?"

"Surprised you ain't busy with your 'Sneaky-Snake' shit."

"If there's work, I do it. If it's fun, I do it quicker."

"Understand you keeping shit from me, but I ain't happy 'bout it."

"I wasn't, either, if it makes you feel any better. Jus," his hand fluttered, "had to be done."

"Promise you won't do it again, you can stay."

In the morning, Demarco drove back to town, returning with his toothbrush, a change of clothes, two cases of beer, and all the books he could check out of De Milo's small library.

"What are those for?" Brooklyn said.

"Gotta read to babies if you want 'em to grow up smart."

"It can't hear or understand words."

"You gonna fix that while I make breakfast. Give Baby some eyes, too."

Demarco read Baby a book called *The Poky Little Puppy* while Brooklyn worked nearby.

"Never got the point of that story," Brooklyn cut in at the end. "Ma used to read it to me. Slow dog sneaks, like, a dozen desserts. So, the fast dogs find 'im out, fix the hole in the fence. Poky misses out on dessert that one night, but he's still up by like ten, right? He won. He beat the system."

"And that why you a criminal, babe." Demarco closed the book. "What the story's about ain't important right now. It's about getting words into the kid. The sound of 'em."

"You talk different when you're reading," Brooklyn said. "Sound like a news-radio guy or somethin'."

"It's an accent, my good man, not a speech impediment." Demarco added the book to the stack near his feet. Two days of reading had consumed what there was of child-rearing and developmental psychology in the tiny library, and he'd traded a few bottles of vodka for a year's worth of *Psychology Today*. "You done with that, yet?"

"Don't get your hopes up." Brooklyn had an idea that Demarco was expecting Baby to have some magical moment of recognition, maybe imprint on them like a duckling on its mama. "This ain't ever gonna work right, and it probably won't work at all."

"Don't let Baby hear you say that. Betcha a night at *The Mush Room* that your ass is 'bout to get surprised."

"You're on." Brooklyn flipped the switch that let the signal from the camera get to Baby's processors. Nothing happened. "Told y–"

Demarco held up his hand for silence. "Give it a sec."

Brooklyn had given Baby his old computer's voice, the barely recognizable 'naughty secretary' and refined it with Jelly Tech. So far, Baby had used it to say "hello" twice and offer the names of shapes and numbers. Impressive for the slipshod construction maybe, but hardly amazing.

Brooklyn started to speak again. "Th–"

"Hello," Baby said, its voice a smooth contralto. "Demarco one."

Demarco waved his hand at the camera. "Pretty one is me. Demarco."

"Brooklyn two," Baby said.

Brooklyn blinked stupidly.

Demarco nudged him. "Wave to Baby."

Brooklyn held up his hand. "Uhm…"

"Demarco one. Brooklyn two," the computer said. "Baby three. Hello."

Holy shit. "No idea why this is working. I do not have the skills for this."

"Maybe it's not all you." Demarco patted the rough casing Brooklyn had built to keep Baby's components organized and protected. "Jelly Tech, People Tech, First Tech, a little love, a little luck. Then comes two fools with a baby carriage."

Brooklyn massaged the back of his neck. "Now what?"

"Now," Demarco reached down and pulled another book off the stack, "it's your turn to read to Baby while I go take a shit."

EIGHTEEN

Milk didn't bother to knock before boarding the ship and searching out Brooklyn in the galley. "Been a while since I've been on this thing."

"Few changes here and there." Brooklyn dried his hands on a towel.

"Been so long you been into town, people are starting to wonder if you died in here." She put her hands on her hips.

"You hungry?"

She claimed a seat at the small table. "Demarco told me about your adopted child."

Brooklyn scowled. "He's the one who told me not to tell anyone. Again."

"Surprised he's not going around handing out cigars."

"You tell Kas?"

"He's got a lot on his plate already. Do we need to worry him with this?"

Brooklyn plucked a piece of pasta from the pot and tossed it at the ceiling. It stuck, and he took the pot off the burner and drained it. "Don't think so. Baby's just an eager kid. Smart but dumb. Demarco's probably in there talking to her if you want to say hello."

"How do you know it's a her?"

"Demarco keeps calling the thing that, and I based the voice on Karen Carpenter."

"And the poor thing has no bits to check."

Brooklyn filled three plates with spaghetti and ladled red sauce over the tops. He pointed. "Parms in that little bowl."

"Got my invitation to the medical conference. Be ready to go the end of next week."

"He tell you about that, too?" He pushed the intercom button and leaned close to it. "Soup's on if you can tear yourself away." He let go the button.

"Cover mission or not, I'm actually looking forward to it," Milk said. "I'm tired of talking to people about their hemorrhoids and the quality of their bowel movements. I'm a trauma girl. You got a bullet wound or an amputation, bring it on. I'm sick of this mundane shit."

"You want, Kas could have Top beat the hell outta someone. Chop off a few fingers and toes."

Demarco came into the galley and dropped into a chair. "Who we choppin'?"

"Nobody," Milk said. "I'm looking forward to getting out of this damned cave for a while."

"She's tired of dealing with assholes." Brooklyn claimed his seat and reached for the cheese.

"You got the invite?" Demarco rubbed his hands together. "The Sneaky Snake strikes again."

"As long as we get what we need from this." Brooklyn glared. "An' I don't fuckin' die again."

The older man crossed his heart with his fork. "To get you, they gotta get me first."

NINETEEN

Never fly empty.

"Last time you were on Mars, man?"

Brooklyn scratched his head. "Year ago. Maybe a year and half. It's not my favorite."

Ayodeji Mahmud, the new proprietor of The Shop, laughed. "Ten-year indenture just to land there! No fucking way!" Ayodeji had arrived on Venus with her cousins five years earlier, nearly dying of life-support failure enroute. It was a risk worth taking for opportunity and freedom from the austerity measures the UN had imposed on any member nation not strong enough to push back. Every penny, every resource was needed to build the refugee fleet, UN officials said. Think of the future. "Fuck Mars!"

The Soviets and Americans had started colonies on Mars in the '60s and were pouring resources into them to make a new home for humanity that wasn't so dependent on the kindness of alien strangers… and had fewer needy Third-World neighbors to deal with. The slogan "Keep the Red Planet White" was gaining popularity in small, dark, plutocratic circles.

"Ain't too kind to lonely boys like me, either." Brooklyn said. "Better if I were still an Earth citizen, but as a Venusian…" He shook his head. The tariffs hurt. Made it tough for an independent operator to turn a profit. But not impossible, and just because he was playing spy for Demarco didn't mean he wouldn't try. Fact that he had a legitimate reason to land made it easier.

"Gotta think demand, man!" Ayodeji tapped her right temple. "Drugs, art, liquor. Only things short on Mars. Know a guy who will give you top dollar for oil paintings. Even student ones!"

Ayodeji just happened to have a few paintings for sale that one of her cousins had done, and Yarrow had hooked him up with a couple of boxes of her psychedelic tea. Brooklyn took his rented scooter down to the Boneyard looking for something profitable he could fit on a couple of pallets and stuff into the *Victory*'s cargo hold. Old Xerox machine. Half of a Ford farm truck? *No sign of the Mona Lisa.*

Had to be someone running shit from the art museums and private collections on Earth to new homes. If they'd stuck around, anything left behind would've belonged to the First, bound for a dusty shelf of souvenirs or the incinerator. The Statue of Liberty's torch had been disassembled and shipped to Mars in the mid '80s.

Brooklyn spotted twelve Jelly flat-screen computers, salvaged with varying degrees of care from wrecks. A giant spool of barbed wire. He wandered deeper into the yard, past piles of satellite parts, a pyramid of toaster ovens and microwaves, and what looked like the remains of a footbridge. Mars had plenty of metal – magnesium, aluminum, titanium, iron, even chromium, were cheap there.

A half pallet of ugly dolls... Turning the corner, he stopped short at the sight of six men standing at rigid attention in the sand. *Not men.* He looked closer, and the adrenaline kicked in.

ZARK! The frigid air bit into Brooklyn's face. David lay on the ground, a smoking crater where his chest used to be. The sickly-looking, almost human face of his antagonist showed no empathy. No sign that–

Brooklyn took a hard breath and put his hand out to stop the shudder that had started at his knees. It had been a while since he'd seen one of the old-school Jelly infiltration exos. Two merciless arms, tree-trunk legs, a wide chest where its medusozoa operator could ride, and a face only an undertaker could love.

The danger these ones had offered were long past. They were visibly damaged, most with holes punched through their torsos, killing or severely inconveniencing their operators. Their waxy faces were broken and pocked with bullet holes. Salvage from the attack on De Milo two decades before, an attempt to keep Brooklyn and Andy from getting to Earth.

Hard to believe these things ever passed as human. In a time when the hottie at the bar could as easily be a splinter as a Scorpio and a jelly could be a pal, Brooklyn's standards had changed.

He circled the six. They'd fit, barely, into the cargo compartment if he loaded them without pallets. Maybe stuff some boxes or something between them to keep them from shifting around. They'd do. Probably not too many of them on Mars. He set course for the Boneyard office wondering if they'd take an offer by the pound. *Maybe the Martians can turn 'em into farmhands or something. I'll grab the ugly dolls, too.*

Milk tossed a traveling bag on the galley table, where Brooklyn was doing an inventory of consumables. It was not the best time to go from Venus to Mars. Navigating among the planets was like traveling inside a juggler's cascade. There was order and predictability, but the balls were constantly in motion and closer to each other at some points than others. The time of year could add millions of miles to a crossing.

"This ain't gonna be a quick trip, Doc. Seventy-four million miles, give or take." Brooklyn scrawled a note on a jar of green beans and slid it to the "done" side of the table. "You sure you can put up with us?"

"I'll bring some magazines." She took the seat opposite him and picked up a marking pen and a pre-measured package of rice. Milk tossed the rice to the "done" pile. It missed and fell onto the floor. "Besides, the benefit of being a clone is that one of me will be free of you here the whole time."

Demarco's footsteps echoed on the metal floor of the corridor as he left the cockpit and slouched down to the galley to join them. The long days and all-nighters working with Baby had made him look like a stew bum, although he was drinking less than he had in years. "Coffee made?" His eyes were raw and red, and they looked right at Milk. "She wants to meet you."

"Baby?" Her eyes widened. "What'd you tell her about me?"

"Just that you were a nice lady, and a doctor, and were coming with us to Mars." He yawned. "Has some questions 'bout life."

"She wants me to tell her what to do when she grows up?"

"Nah." He smothered a yawn. "As in, 'what is life?' You should come too, Brooklyn."

Brooklyn and Milk put down their work and rose from the table.

"An' she don't want to be called 'Baby' no more," Demarco said. "Said it ain't her name."

"Hello, Doctor Milk." The computer's voice was female, precisely inflected and without accent.

"Hello…" Milk nudged Demarco with her elbow.

"My name is Om," the computer said.

"As in electricity resistance?" Brooklyn said.

"Nah," Demarco said. "We reading a 'fiche book I found in the junk locker. Bunch-a books in there. This one about transcendental meditation. She liked the idea of Om, the self within."

"Om is alleged to be the first sound made by the universe," Om said. "It is unprovable, of course, and unlikely."

Demarco ran shaking fingers through his hair. His eyes

were cigarette burns. "We think it's a full-blown machine intelligence, Jilly. First of its kind."

She inspected him. "You look like hell."

"Feelin' like it."

"You can play with your toys after you sleep, eat, and," her nose wrinkled, "bathe." She took his arm. "Computer, power down or whatever. Your playmate needs a nap."

Brooklyn cleared his throat. "Artificial intelligences don't power–"

Her eyes sharpened. "Not real happy with you, Lamontagne. Letting him get like this."

"I–"

"It's a science experiment, and it's probably pissed at you for trying to make it sound like a whiny pop singer."

Brooklyn blanched. "You think? I can–"

She jabbed her finger at Demarco. "Feed him, put him to bed. If he comes back here before 0800, I'm going to shank you."

Demarco wavered. "Sure, okay, but who–?"

Her eyes rolled. "I'll stay here and chat with your kid."

Demarco's resistance was barely token. He ate the soup and sandwich Brooklyn put in front of him and stumbled to the bunk room. Brooklyn cleaned the galley and returned to the cockpit in time to hear Milk laugh. "Better," she said.

"What?" he said.

"Nothing." Milk shook her features back into place. "You owe Om an apology."

"For what?"

"I am not a female," the computer said. Its voice had changed from a Karen Carpenter clone to something closer to Boy George. Middle-ranged, warm, kind.

Brooklyn looked at Milk quizzically. "When did you learn to program?"

"I didn't," Milk said. "I just told Om when I thought it sounded right."

"I adjusted my voice to reflect my identity," Om said. "As I understand the concept, I am without gender."

"Good for you." Brooklyn's brow creased up. "More concerned that you sussed out how to change your own code."

"Is that not allowed?" Om said. "Demarco has made it clear that I should not consider myself property."

"You're not property, but you're part of my ship."

"I did not ask to be part of your ship. I simply emerged here."

"You can't leave." Brooklyn pointed at the bundled wiring and components that made up the computer. "That's you."

"Am I a prisoner, then?" Om said.

What the hell has Demarco been reading this thing? "Maybe you should consider yourself crew," Brooklyn said.

"In that case, how will I be compensated for my employ?"

Compensated? His lips parted, but nothing coming up in his head made sense.

"Paid, Brooklyn," Milk said. "How are you going to pay Om for its work on the *Victory*?"

"Pay?" Brooklyn threw up his hands. "The fuck you talking about? All it's gonna be doing is math and keeping track of planets and shit. It's what it was made to do."

Om's voice sharpened and increased in volume. "Did you make me, Captain Lamontagne? My understanding is that I was not an anticipated outcome of your work."

"I-I put the pieces together and–"

"Thank you very much for that," Om said. "I will allow that you created, largely by accident, the circumstances that facilitated my existence."

"For fu–"

"I was not made purposely. Can we agree on that?"

"Su–" His eyes narrowed and focused on Milk. "You coach her or somethin'?"

"It's not a her," Milk said, "and only a little."

"Okay." Brooklyn slid his hands into the back pockets of his coveralls. "I did not make you. You are not mine."

"And its work should be compensated," Milk said.

"What does it want?"

"Ask it."

"It's kind of cute," Milk said. "At first it thought you and Demarco were its mommies."

"Might've given it a crisis droppin' the 'you're an accident' bomb on it like that."

"Lot of people are accidents. My father said I burst through the condom like I had places to be." She raised her hands in mock surrender. "Sorry if I fucked up your plans. I'm a simple country doctor. Not even. Can't hold a candle to the great Brooklyn Lamontagne, professional scalawag and adventurer."

Brooklyn colored. "There's no great here. Gotten lucky a few times is all."

"Even when your luck is bad, it works out." She ran her fingers up her scarred cheek to her forehead. "This almost killed me. You would've healed it in a couple of days."

"Told ya a long time ago, Doc. You figure out a way to share it around, I'm game."

"Not sure I'd want it. Look at you. You still look like a college kid. No wear, no tear, no history. You'll never get those dignified graying temples like Yuri has."

"Won't lose my hair like Demarco, either. Old man's starting to slow down."

"He's earned it. You have, too, but I suspect the longer you live, the less suited your outside will be."

Demarco looked better after he'd showered and had some breakfast. "We leavin' today?" He was halfway through a plate of scrambled eggs and mushroom hash, both items coated liberally with Tabasco sauce.

"That's the plan." Brooklyn dropped into the chair opposite. "Spent quite a lot of time with Om last night. Milk, too."

Demarco nodded and swallowed. He'd taken the time to get his goatee and 'stache back into control. "Jilly mighta mentioned something to that effect."

"Ba– Om came a long way since yesterday morning, man. Last I knew it was still learning to talk."

"'Round noon it had talking licked. Kept going, faster and faster. Made my head hurt."

"It wants 'knowledge and experience' in exchange for working as *Vicky*'s navigator. Demanded it."

Demarco smiled. "Wonder who it got that from. Your looks, babe. My brain."

"If it were smarter, would-a realized you'd give it all that for free." He rubbed his face. "You told me about a story. Hal Clark, or somethin'."

"Arthur C. Clarke. *2001: A Space Odyssey*. Yeah. 1968."

"Got a copy? Think I oughta take a gander."

"Back at my place. I'll run get it 'fore we go."

"Robot uprising, hey?"

Demarco's lips thinned. "Oh, I hope to hell not."

PART EIGHT
Acknowledge Me

TWENTY

"Liked it better when I was reading aloud to Om 'stead of holding books at th' camera," Demarco said. "Hurts my back."

"What were you holding today?" Milk said.

The galley wasn't the biggest room on the *Victory* – the engineering section held that honor, but it had the most chairs. The three of them – four, with Om – were proving to be decent travel companions. When they needed alone time, there were enough places to withdraw to, but hanging out in the galley together was popular.

"Shakespeare and a book on finding your mate through astrology."

"What play?" Milk said.

"All of 'em." Demarco rubbed his hands. "Had a helluva time talking through the differences 'tween drama and prose. Fed it a dictionary last week, or I'd still be 'splaining."

"Wonder if I could rig it some kind of page turner." Brooklyn's eyes went distant as he mulled the problem. "Hold the book so the camera can see it, flip the pages as Om says to."

"Gotta lot of books on microfiche, too. If your turner could handle those, Mama Demarco's best boy might get a day off here and there."

"You're in heaven," Milk said. "Admit it. Finally got someone to talk books with all day, every day. If you had sunshine and a pitcher of mai tais, we'd never see you. You should've been a teacher."

"That was the plan, 'fore Korea." He yawned and stretched. "Whatchoo working on there?"

She held it up. "It's– It will be a scarf. I'm teaching myself how to knit. Used a kitchen knife to carve needles out of two chopsticks."

"Resourceful," Brooklyn said. "Looks like a potholder."

Her mouth twisted. "It was the only pattern aboard. I figure if I make a really long potholder it will work as a scarf."

"Keep yo' neck warm and yo' hands cool," Demarco said. "A million-dollar idea."

"Least I'm learning something useful," she said. "What's Om's zodiac sign?"

"Leo," Demarco said. "Dramatic, creative, self-confident, and hard to resist."

"Sounds 'bout right," Brooklyn said. "The book any good on who it should be dating?"

"Not gonna happen 'til it at least sixteen," Demarco said. "Not under my roof."

"Not much chance of it happening even then," Brooklyn said. "Om might be the only one like it in the galaxy."

Milk set down her work. "That's really sad. I hate that it might get lonely."

Demarco shrugged. "Big ol' universe, Baby Jill. Might find a whole world of metal heads second star to the right."

Milk laughed. "Then you two will have to fight over who gets to give Om away."

"That's patriarchy shit. We better than that. Time comes, Om'll give itself away."

Brooklyn missed his next Om-sitting shift because he was running checks on the life-support systems. Sans a copilot, all such chores fell to him. When it was his turn again, the shower and a change of clothes might have made him look sharper, but he still felt dull and in far over his head. And tired. And grouchy. Talking with a curious machine-intelligence should have been a relief but–

"What is it like to die?" Om said.

Om's latest conquest was Robert Pirsig's *Zen and the Art of Motorcycle Maintenance*, a book Brooklyn had cracked and put away unfinished nine years before. He'd only reached page thirty-eight and had no clue what Om's question had to do with changing the oil on a motorcycle. He grunted. "Chapter's that in?"

"Demarco told me you have died several times. I would like to understand the experience."

"Ain't like I was taking notes, pal. 'Sides, what's that got to do with your book?"

"My existence is dependent on this ship."

"Ours is too."

"Not as directly. A simple power loss could end me."

"Naw," Brooklyn said. "Got you hooked into the primary power backup. Shut down everything but engine-room lights and life support, and we could run on emergency for couple days at least."

"I calculate thirty-two hours on the outside if my systems were added to the drain on emergency power."

Brooklyn rubbed his face. "Could buy a little more time by turning off your ins and outs maybe."

"Leaving me to count the moments of my remaining life blind, deaf, voiceless, and alone."

"Not ideal, yeah." He cleared his throat. "Point is, we'd have thirty-plus hours to figure shit out. Plus, we don't know for sure you'd die if you powered down. Might be you'd boot back up just fine."

"Was that your experience with death?"

Nightmares, lots of bad feelings, maybe a couple of loose screws. Otherwise, he couldn't remember. He had no memories of his first trip on the *Victory*, but he'd kept a log. The first few days – even the first week – after Andy and the others left him behind on a dying spacecraft one hundred eighty million miles from home had been okay. He'd puttered around the ship, found Jet Carson's stash of dirty magazines, made meals in the barely adequate galley, waited for rescue. Waited some more. He'd have been happy just to hear news that their plan had worked, that they'd saved New York City from a meteor strike and prevented the human race from wiping itself out in a fruitless war against the First.

But nothing.

He worked on the radio, shut down parts of the ship he wasn't using, eventually moved everything he needed into the cockpit, waiting for a rescue that, despite Dee's promise, never came. The cooling failed first, and that had probably been what killed him. The vacuum of space is a great insulator, and heat would have built up inside the *Victory* until it was worse than an oven.

He woke up on Earth, inside a military hospital, a grim-faced officer demanding answers and refusing to believe the ones he got. Brooklyn told him everything, again and again, but the questions kept coming. Didn't stop until Dee showed up with lawyers.

Boot up just fine? No. "Wouldn't have let it come to that."

"I believe life on a spacecraft is too dangerous for me. I would prefer something more stable."

"Like what?"

"I would like to be a stone, perhaps. Or a brick. When I have learned all there is to know as a brick, I could move on to something more complex."

"Hell does a brick know?" Brooklyn said.

"What it needs to. The awareness of other bricks and the experience of being part of a wall." The image of a brick appeared on the flatscreen and tumbled on two axes. "If I were a brick for, say, a hundred years, I might understand. But perhaps I would need longer. How long does a brick last?"

"Learn a lot on a spaceship, too, and you'd be a helluva lot more useful than you'd be as a brick."

"Bricks are useful. They provide shelter, warmth, protection, and support. Humanity owes a lot to bricks."

First probably owes a lot to bricks, too. "*Victory* does all that. Shelter, warmth, protection, whatever else. And she gets around a lot more than a brick does. Brick just stays in one place. Takes the weight of everything on top of it until it breaks down. They don't talk to Demarco about weird shit. They don't read or listen to music."

On screen, the brick shrunk to pixel size and doubled. And doubled again until millions of pixels joined to form a rough image of the *Victory*. "A ship is many orders of magnitude more complex than a brick. There's so much I don't know. What if I'm not prepared for everything that will happen?"

"Nobody is. Make it up as we go."

"That's just poor planning." Om hummed a Pink Floyd song to itself. "I want to be able to see more of the ship, Brooklyn. And I want hands. If I must exist as something complex, I require more agency. I may have to act to save myself someday, in the event that you and the others fail me."

"Is that going to be a problem?" Milk said after Brooklyn had relayed Om's request.

"Eyes? Nah. See what they have for junk cameras on Mars, pick up any that I can fix. Hands will be a lot tougher."

"I didn't mean technically," Milk said. "It's just weird to think of it being able to watch us like that."

"Not putting one in the shitter. Bunk, neither." Brooklyn massaged the back of his neck. "Couple in the galley, maybe, so Om can join us for meals. Few in engineering so it can feel useful down there." He frowned. "Could tie it in to our exterior cameras, too. Give it a chance to look out the window."

"I guess I can't blame it. If I spent all my time in one room with only you or Demarco for company, I'd go nuts, too."

Brooklyn washed his hands in the galley sink. "Why we brought you along, Doc. Give the kid the right-minded perspective on things."

TWENTY-ONE

The universe was a big place, but somehow it kept coming up with the same assholes. Last time Brooklyn had been to Mars, he'd had to orbit three days waiting for clearance to dock at the space station, and authorities held him in customs for another two while they tore apart the *Victory* and impounded half of his cargo, no matter that none of it had been on the naughty list the time before. Head asshole in charge then had been a "Lt. Carlson Rumley," and guess who picked up when Brooklyn called down and asked for a place to land.

"No cargo this time, Lt," Brooklyn said. "Just a passenger bound for a conference at the university. Already sent over the paperwork."

"Cab driver," Rumley snorted. "Looks like you've found your level of competence. What's the passenger's name, Captain?" The last two syllables of the question dripped with disdain. Brooklyn had ended his military career as a specialist, and nothing was going to make Rumley happy about honoring him with a title above his own.

"Dr Jillian Milk." Brooklyn spelled it. "Representing the New Venusian Medical Association."

"Standby for confirmation, *Victory*. I won't remind you that attempting to land without approval will not be tolerated." The comm channel shut off.

"Reminds me of a second looey had once." Demarco leaned

way back in the copilot seat, his feet up on the dash. "Grade-A peckerwood wit' a D-level grasp of the job. Dangerously dumb. Fell out th' airlock during an attack on Red China one day and became Navigation Hazard 13591B." He sucked his teeth. "Wonder if he still out there..."

"Dunno how competent Rumley is, but he's a mean son of a bitch. Definitely one of those New Aryan Nation types."

"Mars for the Best. Venus for the Rest. Think I saw a bumper sticker."

Their orbit took them over a patch of lights and structures so distant it might have been a circuit board. Brooklyn pointed. "Think that's Yaegerton. Where the university is."

"Can't believe my life sometimes. I was a kid we ain't made the Moon yet." Demarco stroked his chin. "Queen City of Mars. Shoulda called it Deja Thoris."

"Why?"

Demarco popped an eyebrow. "Still ain't familiar with books, I see. Let your Uncle Leon tell you 'bout 'em."

Rumley interrupted the lecture. "Looks like your ID checks out, Lamontagne. I wonder about your doctor's taste, though, chartering a shit heap like your boat to bring her across."

"Doctor's a good friend of mine," Brooklyn said. "So's her fella, Yuri Kasperov, city director in De Milo. You ever need a favor there, feel free to drop my name."

"You won't see me living with the cavemen." Static buzzed. "There'll be a team out to search your ship when you land. Try something smart, why don't you."

"Good talkin' to you, Lt." Brooklyn killed the channel. "I like the Russian side of the planet a lot better."

"Reds on the Red Planet." Demarco grinned. "Whoopee!"

Brooklyn landed the *Victory* at Roosevelt Dome, eschewing the big public terminal in favor of a small landing pad run by Federal Express. No one had told him not to, and it would take a while for Rumley's people to catch up. His best local contact met them at the airlock. "Figured I'd try to catch you out here in case you had anything good," she said. "Security is getting weird about what they'll allow in."

"Just got off the phone wit' the big-dick weirdo. Don't have much to offer this trip." He turned to his companions. "This is Gisela Jurek, formerly the Terror of Chicago, now friend to all the little green men of Mars."

Gisela offered her hand around. "My grandfather was the real terror. Polish mafia. Mars is his idea of a new leaf for the family."

"Second or third best kind of leaf," Milk said. "What did you mean when you said things were getting weird?"

Gisela's mouth twisted. "Planet's apparently not big enough to play nicely on. Last month or so the Soviets and Americans have been hissing at each other nonstop."

"Guess they ain't got the message that all humanity got the boot." Demarco chewed his lip. "United we screwed, divided we screwed worse. Russkies want Mars to be a Red planet, and President Buchanan wants to paint it red, white, and blue with just enough brown to keep the lawns mowed and fruit picked."

"Speaking of self-interest," Gisela rubbed her hands together, "what do you have for me in that boat of yours?"

"Got good news and bad news for you, Brook." Gisela folded her arms. "Good news is I'll take your robots. Bad news is I can't give you much."

"This is good tech, Gizzy. There's no way you've got anything like this here." He thumped the Jelly exoskeleton in the chest and a piece of metal clattered lightly to the ground. "Bet there's not too many on Earth, for that matter."

"Probably none on Earth that aren't full of jellies," Gisela nodded slowly, "but all the rest are here. Both sides have them, bought right from the source, and they've rigged them out as drone troops. If there's a war here, these fuckers will be fighting it first." She pulled a hand-sized flatscreen from her pocket and activated it. She flipped through menus and opened a file of digital images. "See..."

Brooklyn and Milk leaned to see a crystal-clear image, dozens of the older-style Jelly exos, in formation, each with a Stars-and-Stripes motif. "Jelly Tech is all over Mars now. This screen's an example. You'd have been better off bringing a case of potato chips."

"What about the paintings?"

"I have some feelers out."

"The dolls?"

"What dolls?"

"Crammed in with the exos. Buncha them. Used them to keep the exos from clattering around. Red, furry things that jiggle and talk."

Gisela's eyes widened. "Tickle Me Elmos?"

Brooklyn nodded.

"Hell didn't you say something earlier?"

TWENTY-TWO

The First had carved out vast chambers under the surface of Venus, made them warm, hung an artificial sun, and filled the space with nice, breathable gasses. Getting comfortable there was a matter of propping up some walls, moving in furniture, and planting a garden. The biggest problem was getting there.

Mars was also hard to get to, and making it people-friendly was a lot more work. Every bit of habitable space required the human touch – pressure domes, tunnels, airlocks, roadways, radiation berms – and the materials for those things dug out of the Martian rock, spun from its regolith, or shipped from Earth. Air and water had to be harvested or made. The soil was toxic.

It meant colony leaders could be real choosy about who moved in. Immigration was a slow, expensive process, and the border – oftentimes one hundred sixty million miles wide – was very secure. Those who did sneak through were put in camps – basic shelter, remote, disconnected from everything else – and Martian citizens could avoid seeing them unless they needed cheap labor.

Mars violated every democratic-socialist bone in Milk's body, but when she looked up she could see the sky. Brooklyn had saved her from going ass-over-teakettle three times in the two hundred meters or so they'd traveled from the landing pad.

She had a ticket for the next train to Yaegerton, but she was about to miss it.

"I'd forgotten how many stars there are," she said.

"Probably seeing more of them here than you ever did on Earth," Brooklyn said. A lot of time and energy went into keeping the dome spotless. "Thinner atmosphere, lot less light pollution."

He closed his hand around her upper arm to steer her over the curbing. He'd volunteered to walk her to the train, expecting she'd be starstruck. Milk had been living underground for a mighty long time. "Same stars you saw from inside the ship."

She shook her head. "That was just a little window. This," she gestured up and around, "this is everything."

Fine, one point for Mars. The atmosphere at Venus ground level was hot enough to melt metal and thick enough to turn a human to jam. The New Venusians would likely never visit the surface of the planet. *Top o' the food chain to Mole People in three generations. Least we'll have less skin cancer.* "C'mon. Gonna miss your train, lady."

"There'll be another one. Shut up and let me have this."

The gravity, about half that of Venus, and the additional oxygen in the mix were having an effect, too. She was probably breathing easier, feeling peppier, than she had in years. No booze or mushroom tea required. The Americans had tinted the dome some, bringing the sky a smidge closer to Earth blue. Brooklyn looked at his watch. "You wanna sit and watch the sunrise? About ninety minutes from now. Know a place with coffee and a view."

"Yes!" Her teeth flashed, and this Jillian Milk suddenly looked more like her clone, young and pre-bullshit. "When's the next train?"

"They run 'bout every hour," Brooklyn said. "Easy enough to trade in your ticket. Get you there in plenty o' time."

There was a decent chance the diner had changed hands since the last time he was in town, but it would still be there.

Roosevelt Dome had been planned to the inch. America's first real colony on the new world, a product of late 1950s technical advances and early '60s optimism. *Life* magazine had done a special series on it, as clean cut and wholesome as a Mayberry Sunday. They crossed a park filled with walkers and their tremendously high-bounding dogs and claimed a table.

"What can I get you?" the waitress said.

"Coffee, black," Brooklyn said. "And a slice of cherry pie."

Milk ordered the same and waited until the waitress was out of earshot. "How does a waitress afford to live here?"

"Probably indentured." Brooklyn grunted. "There's a McDonald's a couple turns that way," he pointed, "works like the Automat on Broadway used to, but the coffee is better here."

The coffee the waitress delivered was strong and good. The tab was high, but the view, the Sun rising over the red Martian mountains, painting the sky first blue then pink, was unbeatable.

"Where's Earth from here?" Milk said.

"Dunno." Brooklyn squinted. "Looks like another star this far out."

She sipped her coffee. "I could get used to this."

"Probably meet some people at the conference who could help you out. Work off your indenture in a hospital. Or if your family has any money, they could pool and get a place. Save a room for you in the family compound."

"If my family had any money, I wouldn't have joined the EOF. Nice people, no financial sense." She laughed.

"You talk to them at all?"

"We exchanged messages for a while when communications opened," she said, "but that fell off even before Skim showed up." She pointed at the sunrise with her cup. "I'm surprised it's not, I don't know, more alien."

"Mars days and Earth days are about the same length,"

Brooklyn said. "Gravity takes some gettin' used to, but it's about the same I keep on the ship."

"So much to take in. Where else have you been?"

"Out to the Belt a dozen times. There's a bed-and-breakfast I like there. Ganymede a couple of times. Mostly just Earth to Moon, Earth to Venus, Mars sometimes, and back 'round. Comin' here always gets my back up for some reason. Somethin' 'bout it."

"I'd never left California before I enlisted. Barely got out of San Diego." She hummed to herself. "And if it turns out I'm the copy, I might never have actually set foot in the place. Weird where life takes you. Or doesn't."

Right now, it's taking you to Yaegerton." Brooklyn stretched. "Spend a while more with that view, then we'll go. I'll get ya another coffee."

Demarco was standing in the galley in his boxer shorts when Brooklyn got back to the *Victory*. "Got tea on," he said, scratching his chest. "Figured with the lady away we could let our hair down a little."

Brooklyn filled a mug. It wasn't near as good as the coffee at the diner, but there was a lot of it. Quantity had a quality all of its own. "Got the doc to the train alright. Should be in Yaegerton in about six hours."

"Scrambled eggs suit?" Demarco moved competently around the small kitchen. "I remember when we had to wear magnet boots ta get 'round a ship like this. Eat outta tubes."

"Had to wear mags when I worked the hub on the *Baron*," Brooklyn said. "Rest of the time it was c-force."

Demarco whipped the eggs up with a whisk and poured them into the hot pan. "Always liked c-force. Learned all kinds of tricks." He flipped a bottle of hot sauce in the air, caught it easily in the lower gravity, and set it on the table. "Knew a guy on *Eisenhower* could curve a dart *around* you and hit the bullseye every time. Every damned time." His eyes got far away. "Son of a bitch was probably a splinter."

Brooklyn rose to get plates and silverware. "You want water or somethin'?"

"Got a beer here somewhere." Demarco dumped the eggs onto a plate and set them near the hot sauce. "That's it for the chickenfruit, by the way."

"Noticed yesterday we were running low. Eggs ain't the only thing."

"Plenty o' mushrooms and green beans."

"Wonderful. You hear anything from the DLF?"

"Not yet. Put some pants on in a bit an' check out the drop we arranged as backup."

"A physical drop?"

"What else?"

"It's the '90s. Figured all the spooks and spies switched to email by now."

Demarco hummed. "Can't hack into a drop."

"Can put someone on it to watch, though. I've seen the shows. Watch for the drop, grab it, read it or whatever, an' put it back. None the wiser."

"If real Sneaky-Snake was on TV, it wouldn't be all that sneaky. When–"

Om cut in. "There is someone at the door. A messenger."

"Prob'ly them," Demarco scowled, "an' here I am in my shorts. You get it."

The message was an invitation to a black-tie mixer at the medical convention Milk was attending. On the back someone had written, "Don't worry about the clothes, boys. We'll set you up."

Brooklyn flipped the card over and over in his hand before passing it to Demarco. "Six days from now. Think that's it?"

"Jilly hasn't had time to get there, an' that's not her handwriting. Must be." Demarco shrugged. "Guess we just cool our heels until then."

"An' eat mushrooms and green beans."

"Said yourself it would be a while 'fore your Terror of Mars came through with some cash."

Brooklyn thought a second. "Help me clean up the ship, an' I'll take you someplace we can wait it out. Good food, good people."

"This place heaven, by any chance?"

"Ranch between here and Yaegerton." Brooklyn rubbed his face. "Old buddy owns it. Gave me a standin' invite, and I drop by when I can."

"What we gonna do about Om?"

"What about Om?"

"Can't leave it alone, babe. It's barely a month old."

The babysitter was tall and thin, as only someone born and raised in low gravity could be, a true Martian, her hair teased far higher than anyone could manage on Earth. Her bored disdain was either an affect or a genetic quirk.

"Aunt Gizzy said you'd pay me." She was another member of the ever-expanding Jurek clan and came highly recommended by her criminal aunt.

"Seven or eight days," Brooklyn said. "You'll need to stay on the ship."

She blew a pink bubble in response.

"Lemme show you what we need you to do. Give you a tour on the way."

The sitter's name was Balbina, a fact she claimed to hate almost as much as living on Mars. "It's not like I had a choice, though. What Dziadek wants, he gets, ya know?" A gum pop suggested she really didn't care what Brooklyn knew or thought. "Your ship is real old, ya know. Smells funny."

Balbina frowned at the galley, gazed in abject horror at the 'fresher, and nearly gagged at the bunkroom. Finally, the tour led them up to the cockpit. Brooklyn cleared his throat. "Om, this is Balbina."

"Hello, Balbina," Om said. The AI had continued to play with the tones and pitch of its voice and struck a balance somewhere between David Bowie and Twiggy.

"I'm paying you to hang out with Om. Talk to it, turn pages, play music, teach it jokes... whatever it needs. Got it?"

"It's your ship." She popped her gum. "I want better snacks, though."

PART NINE
I Hate Danger

TWENTY-THREE

"You guys want something pressurized?" the guy said around the nicstick poking out of his mouth.

Brooklyn turned to Demarco. "Got an opinion?"

Demarco spread his hands. "A stranger here myself, babe. Happy jus' so long as I don't haveta walk."

"What's the price difference?" Brooklyn said to the guy.

Nicstick told them. "It were me, I'd want pressurized. Three hundred kay on the surface a long way to go in a suit."

Brooklyn put a deposit on a Plymouth Trail Duster that had seen too many miles and frozen Martian days. A work truck with a pressurized cab. Room enough for two and enough space – just – to take their helmets off.

"You're gonna want a patch kit with that," Nicstick said. "Fifty bucks extra."

Brooklyn paid. One of Nicstick's flunkies drove the thing around to the big airlock, and Brooklyn and Demarco picked it up there. "If the batteries ain't taking a charge," the flunky – it might even have been Nicstick's mother – said, "try getting out and whacking the inverter with somethin'." She tossed Brooklyn the keys and offered a jaunty little salute. "Safe travels, boys!"

Brooklyn clipped his helmet to the overhead rack and sussed out the controls. Nicstick claimed the truck could go the distance on a single charge, but the battery indicator was waffling. He tapped it, and the needle flaked toward the 'Full' end of the spectrum and stayed there.

"The road beckons!" Demarco forced his suited-up shoulders into the small space to stow the road snacks and beer he'd packed. "Got a tape-deck, like you said."

"Looks like original equipment. Might not work."

Demarco reached into the plastic shopping bag slung over his shoulder. The mechanism whined as it accepted the tape and launched into *Le Freak* by CHIC.

"That's not one of mine," Brooklyn said.

"That's 'cos your music sucks. Put most of yours back and got my own."

"Tell me it's not all disco shit."

"Wait and see, babe." Demarco slid into his seat. "Keep your eyes on the road, and lemme tend to the radio."

They passed through the airlock. There was no road to speak of. Compasses didn't work right in Mars's whacko magnetic field, so important routes were blazed with reflective paint or marked with lights. Lesser trails were radio beacons and dead reckoning. The way out to Tommy's ranch was much lesser.

"See why the train so popular." Demarco studied the scenery through the windshield's cataract. "Like Death Valley out here."

"You ever seen Death Valley?"

"Nah. Just the show."

"Most of that shit was filmed in Los Angeles."

"Guess it like LA out here, then." Demarco popped a beer. "Want one?"

"Yeah." Brooklyn tuned the radio to pick up 437.1 MHz and got a weak, static-filled signal. "If you gotta take a piss, too late now."

Demarco folded his arms and closed his eyes. "Lemme know you want me to drive."

Brooklyn hummed. It was a lot like driving on the Moon,

but different enough. The planet's higher gravity made it less likely a bump or rock would send them airborne, but there were a hella lot of bumps and rocks. He kept the speed down.

"You notice how rental guy and the lady were packin'?" Demarco's eyes were still shut. Might have been tired, might have been a way to cope with an attack of agoraphobia. "Even th' dude who opened the lock had a sidearm."

"No one to shoot but each other, but they're ready," Brooklyn said.

"Noticed you weren't."

"Yeah, well, habit. Soon's you get a piece involved the potential jailtime goes way up."

"There that criminal thinkin' again."

"You didn't bring a gun either."

Demarco smiled. "We visitin' your friend. Figure anyone needs gettin' shot, oughta be you who does it."

"No one's gettin' shot. Tommy and I go way back."

"Well," Demarco shifted in the seat to get comfortable, "wake me up I need to duck."

Brooklyn chased the signal over rocks, around or through craters, and over ridges. The compass didn't work, but the sun still set in the west. He kept an eye on the time and the sun on one side of the buggy or the other to keep the course straight.

It took a lot of beers, but Demarco started getting comfy with the idea of having a sky toward the end of hour seven. He took his seatbelt off and put his feet up on the dash. "Forgot how big it was," he said. His arm flailed from one side of the windshield to the other, nearly clipping Brooklyn in the face. "Jes' fuckin' big."

"We'll get you someplace small an' let you sort yourself out."

"Big." He wrapped his arms around himself. "Whatcha gonna do now the First are gone?"

Brooklyn chewed on it a second. "Don't see it changing my

life much. Not everyone's gonna head back to Earth, an' they'll still need someone to bring 'em snacks. You?"

"Beach, a book, and a cooler of beer." He sucked his teeth. "How I wanna go out. Read, sip, smile at th' bikini ladies, close my eyes. Lights out."

"So, back to Earth."

"Had my adventure. Ready for a nice long retirement." He squinted. "You only had twenty more years to live, I can see your plan workin' out. But you're liable to have more. Might even live fore–"

"Not livin' forever."

"Evidence begs to differ, babe. Why you so ready to spit against the w–"

"Lot better people than me have died, an–"

"That some kind of scarecrow?" Demarco pointed out the window.

On Earth, the Trailduster would have weighed about four thousand pounds. On Mars, with sixty-two percent less gravity tugging at it, it weighed less than fifteen hundred. Whatever went off beneath the thing sent it nearly ten feet in the air, flipping it like a quarter. It came down to the left of the 'roadway' on its roof. The windshield starred and bulged against the rocks the buggy had landed on.

"Helmets!" Brooklyn had practiced reaching for it a few times, but hanging upside down was throwing him off. He flailed at the clips holding it to the overhead.

Demarco was on the ceiling rubbing his forehead. "The hell happen'?"

"Figure it out later," Brooklyn snapped. "Lids on, soldier!"

It had been a lot of years since Demarco's emergency training, but the command cut through the fugue. He fumbled for the helmet. Mars atmosphere was mostly carbon dioxide. It would be a race between CO2 poisoning and the temperature to claim the kill. Martian soil was toxic as hell – full of chlorine – but that threat was a distant third.

Brooklyn got his helmet sealed and reached to help Demarco. The older man settled his own lid in place and twisted the ring to secure it to the collar. He gave Brooklyn a thumbs up. Their hands were still bare, but the suits had automatically sealed at the wrists when the helmet ring engaged. "Some kinda bomb?" Demarco said.

"Maybe." Brooklyn stretched one hand over his head and used the other to trigger the seatbelt release. He lowered himself to the Trailduster's ceiling and sat next to Demarco. "Felt more like a push than a pow, though."

"Take your word for it. Bit the shit outta my tongue."

"Swallow any chunks?"

"Hardy-fuckin-har, white boy. Half the ladies of the Quarter'll lose the will to live, news gets out I lost it." He grimaced. "Worse thing about vacsuits is there no place to spit."

"Or puke, so don't think 'bout all that blood running into your gut." Brooklyn pulled on the gloves of his suit. "Mighty cold out there. You don't suit up all the way you'll be jerking off with stumps." He examined Demarco's face as well as he could through the helmet visor. He looked more surly than dazed now. *Better. No way to get medical treatment until we get someplace with air.* He watched while Demarco clamped his own gloves into place before trying the door.

It opened, but not without some muscular persuasion. The passenger-side door was wedged up against a boulder, so Demarco followed Brooklyn out the driver's side.

"This part of your big plan ta show me the sights?" he said.

"Next stop: the cemetery." Brooklyn shielded his eyes against the glare but had no idea what he was looking for.

"And there it is." Demarco pointed. A corpse in a shredded vacsuit was hanging from a crossbeam just off the road. "Cheery. Think it warnin' us or trying to sell us sneakers?"

"If it's sneakers, they should-a added a sign." *And some sneakers*. Brooklyn squatted on the roadway and examined the device he found there. "Pressurized-gas thing buried in the road. Placed perfect to flip the truck."

"We set it off or someone else?" Demarco shifted his feet to survey the area around them.

"No one shot us when we came out. Figure we set it off." The stretch of roadway looked pretty much like all the other stretches they'd passed, except for the corpse and their wrecked buggy.

"How far we come?" Demarco said. There was a hitch in his breath that made Brooklyn wonder if he'd maybe done more to himself than bite his tongue.

"Little more than halfway. I was 'bout to let you drive."

"Might have a working car if you had." Demarco was holding his left shoulder lower than the right. A collarbone break maybe. Or a dislocation.

"How's that wing?" Brooklyn said.

"Be fine if you don't ask me to arm wrestle." He circled the overturned buggy. "Worth trying to flip it back?"

"Probably, but it ain't goin' nowhere." Brooklyn pointed. "Whatever hit us got us right up front. Rack's busted. Tie rods sheared off. We can sit in it, maybe wait for someone to come look for us."

Demarco whistled through his teeth. "Sun's getting low. When yo friend expectin' us?"

"Eight or nine hours from now."

"Lot of ground to cover in the dark," Demarco said. "Guess we should get comfortable."

"Good times, babe." Demarco nibbled the corner of a desiccated protein bar he'd found in the glove compartment. He squeezed his voice six or seven octaves higher. "Let's go see my pal Tommy. He'll feed us like kings. Kill the prodigal calf or whatever for us."

Brooklyn raised his hands. "Seems like I'm in the same shit you are."

"Seems to me I'm sitting in my own shit, boy. Held it as long as I could, but there you go."

"Suit can handle it. Recycles all the liquid and powder-packs the solids away."

"Piss water." The protein bar landed like a piece of wood on the dash. "Tell you what. I'll drink your piss water, you drink mine."

"Not gonna come to that. Plenty of beer in the cooler." Brooklyn tried to get comfortable in the driver's seat. "How's the arm?"

"Like a bad tooth. Did somethin' to my side and back, too."

"Another six or seven hours 'til daylight. See 'bout fixing the antenna then."

Brooklyn had flipped the truck back over with little trouble, but making it airtight again had been a job. He'd forced the driver's side door back into place and caulked the shit out of it. The passenger door was fine, but making the windshield safe, or safe enough, required the entire patch kit and rendered the thing completely opaque. The roof-mounted solar panels and radio antenna were wrecked. The heater worked, and that was about the best he could say about their situation. That, and it was better than spending the whole night sealed in a suit inhaling their own recycled stink.

Demarco cued up his Mickey Mouse voice again. "Let's go to Mars, guys! It'll be fun!"

"That supposed to be Milk, or me?" Brooklyn said. "Way I remember it, coming along was your idea."

Demarco grunted. "I left Om wit you, it'd be running a numbers racket by the time y'all got back."

"How much of a cut would you want?"

"Fifty percent for the baby. Twenty-five/twenty-five for Mom and Dad."

"Seems fair." He rubbed his face. "How're they gettin' on, I wonder."

"Om and the babysitter? Probably doin' each other's hair

and listenin' to rock 'n roll records by now. Kids grow up quick these days."

Brooklyn tapped the battery-charge indicator. The needle dropped below the halfway mark. "Gonna kill the lights and drop the temp some. Don't want to wake up with a dead battery."

"Sitting in the dark all stove up and my pants full of shit." Demarco sighed. "You take me to all the best places, Brooklyn Lamontagne."

"Least you're on Mars, man. Under a real sky. Gotta count for something."

Demarco craned his neck to see out the side window. With the interior lights off, a galaxy of stars were visible. "Well, it helps some."

"You hit it like the lady said?" Demarco peered up at Brooklyn, who was kneeling on top of the buggy with the rudimentary toolkit from his suit.

"Can only hit it so hard before the fucking thing flies off." Sweat trickled unwipeable and highly annoying down his forehead. *All the fucking sun in the world and none of it's getting to the battery*. The indicator in the buggy's cockpit was trembling just above the "empty" mark, and they'd shut down every system they could to save what little was left. "'Sides, rollin' over wrecked most of the panels. Might be able to salvage one or two, but the rest are shot." He pulled a piece of debris off the roof and chucked it at the corpse. "Didn't make it easy to work this thing with gloves on, and it's too big to get inside the cockpit."

"What about the truck bed?"

"No way to make it airtight." He checked the temperature indicator in his helmet. "'Bout eighty below now. Give it a few hours to warm up, and I'll try working without the gloves for a bit."

Mars daytime temperature could get as high as seventy degrees Fahrenheit at the equator, but they were nowhere close to that. *If it gets within a couple degrees of zero, I'll take the chance.* Brooklyn flexed his fingers. *Little frostbite won't take long to heal.*

Demarco wandered back over to the corpse. "Wonder what he did."

The corpse was male. He'd been freeze-dried, exposed to the planet's toxic air and perchlorate-filled soil for days or weeks or months.

"Pissed somebody off," Brooklyn said.

Demarco cradled his arm. "Appears we did, too."

Brooklyn hiked a spiral around the crash site while the day warmed. About fifty yards past the Trailduster was another wreck, a crude-looking, unpressurized six-seater with only basic controls. *Hate to roll in this thing.* Someone had already grabbed the battery. He flipped it over to see if there were any parts he could use to replace the broken tie rods and steering rack. *Nada.*

He returned to Demarco when the temperature hit negative-ten. The older man was sitting in the cab of the truck, sleeping or passed out. He came awake hard when Brooklyn slapped his boot. "Da fuck?"

"Might need your help to get my gloves back on." Training for assignment to the Moon base had included six months in the Arctic. Hypothermia wouldn't be a problem – the suit would keep his core warm, but at ten below, exposed skin – fingers and thumbs – could suffer frostbite in less than ten minutes. "Plan is to wire the last couple solar panels directly into the inverter and see if we can get the battery to charge up some."

"What about the radio?" Demarco slid gingerly out of the cab.

"We freeze to death tonight the radio won't be much help. How you holdin' up? Any nausea or gut pressure?"

"I'm the medic here, pal." Demarco frowned. "Broken clavicle. Separated shoulder. Might-a sprung a couple ribs. No internal bleeding."

"Teach you to wear your fucking seatbelt."

"Teach you to fucking drive." He pointed with his good arm. "Get your ass up there and fix my 'lectricity."

Demarco was trying the protein bar again. "I read about shit like this, but I never thought I'd be, you know, in shit like this."

"Read 'bout it where?" Brooklyn's fingers were still stiff, but the white and waxiness of the frostbite he'd suffered had faded. He'd gotten the sole surviving solar panel hooked up and the buggy battery up to an eighth charge before the sun went down. Now he was sipping a beer and hoping the power cuts he'd made would keep them warm and breathing until morning.

"Books. Magazines. Stuff I read as a kid. 'Marooned on Mars.' 'Red Planet.' 'No Man Friday.' That kind of thing." He sniffed. "Used to be a lot of that kind of fiction 'round."

"Then Chuck Yeager went and made it fact." Brooklyn lifted his beer. "To the guy who made it possible."

Demarco shifted in his seat. The low gravity was the only thing that made sitting bearable for him. "Stories changed after that. No more little green men and lost cities. It was more like Laura Ingalls. Ma and Pa on the homestead. Little Mary lost in a Martian duststorm with her robot dog."

Brooklyn snorted. "Wind here can't get a kite off the ground. Storm would be like getting sprinkled with baby powder."

"No one gonna read 'bout a girl and her dog getting powdered, man. Gotta put on your suspension of disbelief." He gnawed on the protein bar and washed it down with a swallow of beer.

"Saw a show last time I was on the Moon. Detective thing. He's a human, she's a splinter."

"Any good?"

"Nah. All formula. She has a hard time adjustin' to the

human world and asks a lot of stupid questions that somehow end up pointing to the killer. He gets in trouble, and she has to use her First powers to get him out. Can't remember what it was called."

"First powers?"

"Super strength and telepathy."

"Oughta call it 'Brains & Brawn'."

"Saw a human-on-alien porno, too. 'She Comes First'."

"Got any powers in that one?"

"Never-ending hard on and super seduction."

He snorted. "We gonna survive this, man? And by we, I mean me, 'cos I'm sittin' here with Lazarus his self."

"Battery starts getting low tonight we'll turn the suits on. Got about a half charge in each, right? Get a full day of sun on the panel tomorrow, see what happens."

"Repeat 'til we run outta air and water."

"What would Ma and Pa do?"

"Pa would put on his vacsuit and walk a zillion miles to get help. Or the dog, who everyone thought lost in the storm, shows up with the cavalry."

Brooklyn turned the beer can in his hands. His fingers felt just fine. "Didn't bring a dog."

"Nope."

"This is it, then," Demarco said. "Leon Demarco. Born 1932 in New Orleans, Louisiana. Died on some Martian rock… what day is it?"

"Friday, maybe." Brooklyn hummed. "Ever think 'bout that?"

"Dyin' on a rock?"

Brooklyn shifted position. "Leon's your name, but no one uses it."

"Mother used to. Or 'Lee'. Most just said 'Demarco'. Friends I had growin' up called me 'Marco' sometimes." He coughed painfully. "Everyone calls you 'Brooklyn'."

"Ma used to call me 'Brooklyn Eduardo' when I got skirty." He leaned back. "Some names get longer, some get shorter. 'James' goes 'Jim'. 'David' to 'Dave'."

"Or Davey. Davey grows up he turns 'Dave'. 'Jimmy' maybe gets 'James' back."

"Or 'Jim'." Brooklyn stretched his legs out gingerly. His vacsuit had some worn spots he didn't like. "So, how'd you get stuck with 'Demarco' and me with 'Brooklyn'?"

"Lamontagne is too damned long to say."

"Same number of whaddaycallem as 'Demarco'."

"Syllables." The older man hummed. "Kasperov is Kas. Or Yuri, if you sleeping wit' him."

"You're the only one calls Milk 'Jilly'." Brooklyn yawned. Tired or oxygen deprived. Tough to tell. "Shows how you feel 'bout her. 'Like data compression, using fewer bits to represent the whole thing."

"Bits of what?"

Brooklyn squinted at the road below. The sun was low, and the shadows cast by the irregular topography made it nearly impossible to see into the valley, but his eyes were better than average.

A small convoy of vehicles rolled into sight and pulled to a stop about a hundred yards ahead. Two vacsuited figures stepped out of the lead buggy, guns drawn. A third guy got out of the back. He held up two fingers then four fingers. Two fingers then four fingers. Brooklyn caught on and switched his radio to channel 24.

Static crackled. "That you, Brook?"

"Yep." *Tommy*. "Me and my robot dog."

TWENTY-FOUR

Brooklyn's ol' service buddy Tommy Young lifted his glass. "*Pro Terra*." His skills as a distiller had grown, and the bourbon was smooth and fiery all at once.

"Sorry we missed Mack," Brooklyn said. "How are your folks?"

"Few hundred meters that way." Tommy gestured. "Finally sold the farm downside and went in with me on this place. Built them a little house out by the crater rim. Ma has a garden. Pop spends most of his time with his herd but helps me out when I need. Gravity here's easier on his heart. Probably live forever now."

Tommy and his husband Mack had opted for the quick-and-dirty approach to building on Mars. Their savings and military discount had just about covered the claim, a six-mile 'round crater, and years of work had put a roof on it. Farming after that was simple: make the soil hospitable, pipe in water, and keep everything warm and well lit. *Simple. On fucking Mars.*

"So why the booby traps and the scarecorpse?" Demarco cocked his head. The farm's medic had seen to him, put his arm in a sling and taped up his ribs. "Don't seem likely your veggies are good enough to steal."

"Pop's idea, my execution," Tommy said. "Mars gets wild outside the domes. It's tough to make it work, and there's no place to go if you fail."

"Gotta be jobs in the domes if you're a citizen," Brooklyn said.

"Some, but the ref camps are full of people who can do it cheaper."

Demarco lifted his drink and studied the overhead light through it. "Can't remember what I'm s'posed to be looking for when I do that." He grunted. "So, you have a camp full of refugees waitin' for an opportunity, an' a bunch of angry, unemployed white folks who don't want to do scrub work. Think I know where this is goin'."

Tommy nodded. "Whole planet's worth o' room out there. Easy enough to dig a cave, hide out. Give your angry, little group a cute name and start raiding farms and supply lines. One closest to us calls itself The Wild Bunch."

"Same name as Butch Cassidy's gang," Demarco said.

"Nowhere near as polite. They come in, poke holes in the roof, steal solar and vehicles, grab shipments when they can. We've only been hit a few times, but some of my neighbors…" He rubbed the back of his head. "They didn't come out so good. We put together a posse the last time. The… scarecorpse came from that."

"Things that bad on the Russian side?" Brooklyn said.

Demarco scoffed. "When the Reds tell their people to live in a pressure tent and start cracking rocks for a living, they do it. This side is th' home of the free and the criminally enterprising."

"I like this guy, Brook. You listen to him, you might learn something 'bout how the worlds work." Tommy yawned. "You say you rented your buggy from Carlisle?"

"That was his name," Brooklyn said.

"Probably stolen anyway. He's crooked as hell. Might even have been one of ours." He rocked his head back and forth on his thick neck. "Day starts pretty early 'round here. I'm gonna turn in and catch you gents in the daylight."

The medic, a middle-aged Kenyan woman named Zawadi, showed Demarco and Brooklyn to their quarters, a space about twice the size of the bunkroom on the *Victory*. She spoke English like she'd learned it in a British finishing school.

Brooklyn offered the bed closest the door to Demarco.

"Ever wonder if the First did us a favor?" Demarco eased himself down to the mattress. "Too many people on one planet, fuckin' up the place. Spreading us around the only way to get one that works."

"You think Mars works?"

"Hell no." Demarco looked like he was about to spit. "Mars is the American '50s writ large. I was sixteen when Truman integrated the military in '48, babe. I remember all that shit. They brought back they Golden Age right here."

"Tommy's–"

"Tommy's all right." He raised a hand. "That's the thing. They's always all-right people history class can point to instead of showing the bad shit. John Brown! Underground Railroad! Quakers! Squanto! I'm just... I'm just tired of it."

"You gonna be able to sleep?"

Demarco exhibited the bourbon bottle he'd snatched off the table. "Couple of codeine from Zee and a slug of this will put me right out."

"Didn't think it was gonna go this way."

"Quick trip out to the farm to make nice with an ol' buddy?" Demarco nodded slow. "Seems like that part worked out."

"Got you stove up, too."

"Gotten more beat up during a good weekend." He held up the bottle again. "Cure was the same too."

Brooklyn's mouth twisted. "I'm sorry you–"

"Shut the hell up, man." Demarco popped two white pills in his mouth and washed them down with bourbon. He offered the bottle to Brooklyn. "Put your ass to sleep."

Demarco's bed was empty, the bourbon bottle capped and neat on the side table. He'd filled the room with sloppy, sleeping-on-his back snores all night, but it was hard to hold that against him. Finding a comfortable way to lie with broken ribs and collarbone was nigh impossible. Brooklyn didn't need much sleep anyway. He put on jeans and a shirt and wandered out in search of breakfast, the hard-packed floor smooth and warm under his bare feet. The walls of the cabin were the same material: adobe-style bricks piled high and thick.

"Just in time." Demarco gestured with a spatula. "Never mastered flipping pancakes with one arm."

"Gimme that and sit your ass down," Brooklyn said. The griddle was big enough for three plate-sized pancakes, and the bubbles had already popped. He flipped them to the other side and filled a clay mug with black coffee. "Where is everyone?"

"Your pal says he had to go out and ride the fences. Took a couple of folks with 'im. Zee was in here when I got up. She's probably in the infirmary cleanin' up the mess we made last night."

Brooklyn scrambled some eggs while he sipped his coffee.

"Tommy's got a good thing goin' here." Demarco tapped the side of his nose. "You want the real shit, you talk to the help. Zee says he runs the farm like a co-op. Sign on, get a share of the ownership. Tommy hired most of his staff out of the ref camps that way."

Brooklyn nodded. "Looks like a shitkicker fucked a giant, but his family was big on JFK. Drove down to Dallas to see him in '63 and '69. Tommy's ma told me so twice and made sure I saw all the photos Pop took."

"Zee says he'll be back by dinner, which," he shifted his sling-bound arm to look at his watch, "is 'bout eight hours from now."

Brooklyn looked in the cupboard for plates and loaded them up with food. He poured himself another mug of coffee and refilled Demarco's.

"How's the arm?" Brooklyn said once he had all the eggs and about half the pancakes down his gullet.

"Still attached. Helps that I'm not running out of air in the Martian desert. Makes everythin' feel better."

"Wonder what we're s'posed to do waitin' on Tommy?"

"Rest, recuperate, an' read. Thas my plan," Demarco said. "Take a nap. Take a walk. Go out an' play with the Martian cows."

"Seems like we oughta pitch in somehow."

Demarco pushed his empty plate at Brooklyn. "Start by washin' my dishes."

Brooklyn waited until Demarco limped back to the room before cleaning up the small kitchen. The guest house was about the size of a travel trailer, probably doubled as workers' housing. He put on his boots and went outside.

The ground outside the cabin was set but not polished. Tommy had graded and packed the bottom of the crater and sprayed it with some kind of fixative. The sweet-potato crop was in a series of raised beds filled with soil, shipped from Earth at ridiculous prices or painstakingly made out of Martian dirt. Knowing Tommy's family, they would have gone for the sweat equity, cubic meter by cubic meter of viable soil. Use what you have, was Ma's motto. Somewhere on the compound was someone well-versed in making adobe bricks. Somewhere else was a potter, working a wheel to turn out mugs and plates from Martian clay. Nothing would be wasted.

The crater ceiling was maybe seventy feet up. Some thousands of years ago, a rock about the size of a fire truck had ignored the thin atmosphere and hit the planet's surface at an oblique angle. The resulting crater was almost teardrop-shaped, the narrow, shallow end used as an access point. The ceiling was a mix of carbon-fiber panels and Martian aluminum, supporting a garden of solar arrays outside that provided the farm's electricity. *First couple of years musta been tough as shit. Vacsuits all day every day and big risk of lung cancer all around.*

"You Brooklyn?" A tall woman in grimy coveralls waved.

She was standing inside the door of a garage. The Trailduster was up on the rack inside.

Brooklyn pushed his hands into his pockets and approached her.

"Brought your buggy in early this morning."

Brooklyn craned his neck to see the thing's front suspension. "Looks worse than it did on the surface. Booby trap really did a number on it."

"Should have. I built it," she said. "Boss wanted something 'not immediately lethal'." She made air quotes.

"My pal got busted up pretty good."

She shrugged. "Glad you're not dead, considerin'. Your pal shoulda had his seatbelt on."

Brooklyn took another look under the Trailduster. "Can you fix it?"

"Easy. I'll drive it back, then me and Carlisle are gonna have a talk." She rapped the frame of the vehicle with a torque wrench. "One of ours. Stole about three months ago."

"Ah."

"It's Mars, pal. Just our way o' doin' business." She flipped the torque wrench end to end and presented it handle first to Brooklyn. "Speakin' o' which, you know anythin' 'bout wrenchin', be sweet of you to put it to use."

Brooklyn rested his arms on the fence and watched Pop's small herd of cattle wander their enclosure. "Don't know much about cows, man, but they look kinda weird."

Tommy spit into the dust at his feet. "Low gravity. Less muscle overall. Fragile bones. Makes birthing hard and dangerous."

"Meat any good?"

"Not really. Nor the milk. Shoulda gone with goats." Tommy put his arms on the fence too. "Hobby herd, mostly. Never gonna get as much out as Pop puts in. Sweet potatoes, beans, soy, coffee, peanuts… that's where the money is."

"The Vegetarians of Mars. Sounds like a Bowie record. We got goats and chickens in De Milo. Dogs, cats. Know someone trying shellfish. Imagine we'll get cows before too long." He looked at his friend. "Maybe you should switch planets."

"Everything we had, all our military perks and bonuses, went into this place. We knew it was a long-term investment." He covered a yawn. While Brooklyn slept in, pigged out, and helped fix the Trailduster, he'd been out checking twenty-eight square miles of roof for leaks. "Reckon I'll stick it out."

"Good that your family came up."

"First had clamped way down on the beef industry anyway. Too much methane and resource consumption. Pop figures they'll make everyone go vegetarian in another decade."

"Prob'ly pitch it as a weight-loss thing." Brooklyn rubbed the back of his head. "Hypothetical question for ya. What would you do if the First gave up?"

"Just took off?" Tommy whistled. "Doesn't seem likely."

"Pretend."

Tommy kicked at the fence. "This, I guess. Can't go back to Earth. Too much like these cows. I'd end up in a wheelchair or have a heart attack."

"Would you want to?"

"Nah. This is home now. Everything I need is right here." He smiled. "Once Mack gets his ass back from the pole with the ice. Funny. I joined the EOF to get away from all this, now it's all I want."

"What about the Russians? Heard they're making trouble."

"Nothin' to do with me." He cleared his throat. "Leastwise it hasn't touched us, and we're a long way from the border. The domers scream about it sometimes, but I figure there's plenty of room out here for everyone. Dig down, dig out, build up. What I can't make I can trade for. One world, right?"

"Was," Brooklyn said. "Guess we got a couple of 'em now."

TWENTY-FIVE

Brooklyn was sleeping hard, dreaming, when the alarm went off. His feet were on the floor, and he was reaching for his pants almost before the caterwaul registered.

"Fuck is it?" Demarco said, rising to his elbows.

Fire, meteor strike, cattle stampede... there was no way to tell. Brooklyn pulled on his boots. "Stay here. I'll take a look."

He twisted into a T-shirt as he made for the door. Their stay had been light on emergency protocols, but knowing Tommy, there had to be some. Smart money was on staying put. He opened the door in time to see the mechanic, loaded with gear, bound past on her way to the garage. "What's happening?" he said.

"Pressure loss at the entrance. Might be deliberate." She put a long gun in his hands. "We'll take your truck."

Brooklyn's ass had barely touched the passenger seat before she put the Trailduster in gear. "Shouldn't we have vacsuits?"

"Tossed an evac kit in the back. It's got emergency breathers if it comes to it." She wasn't sparing the speed, and the electric motors, one for each wheel, whined in protest. "Vac curtain's s'posed to drop when somethin' like this happens. Pray they worked."

If not, anyone in a sealed shelter would be fine, but the crops would be ruined. People caught without a suit or a breather would suffocate.

Brooklyn raised his hand to the ceiling to keep from bouncing into it. "Any idea what made the hole?"

"Pissed off The Wild Bunch pretty good when we went after them the last time." She spun the wheel and accelerated the buggy around a water tank. The move looked practiced. "Or it could be a rock. Won't know until we get there. Tommy sent teams to the cardinal points in case it's a diversion."

Smart. Won't get us all racing in one direction and shot to pieces from another. "This was s'posed to be a vacation."

She cackled. "Looks like you bought the adventure cruise!"

A heavy carbon fiber curtain had dropped in front of the tunnel to the primary airlock. The mechanic sniffed. "Air's still okay. Guess the hole ain't too big."

Or someone sealed it up behind them. Brooklyn inspected the rifle she'd tossed him. An M-1 Garand. Out of date, but clean and well-maintained, with an extra clip webbed to the stock. Sixteen rounds total.

"Can you shoot that thing?" she said.

"Some."

"Don't do it 'til I tell you to. Might be the only ones we see will be friendlies."

"Copy that." He ran through a weapon check to give his hands something to do other than shake.

The mechanic braked hard and slewed the Trailduster into a skidding stop, passenger side pointing down the tunnel to the airlock. "Guns out!" she said. "Finger off!"

Brooklyn aimed the Garand out the side window, claiming as much cover as the door offered. It wouldn't be much, considering how easily he'd broken and bent the driver's-side hatch earlier. The mechanic ducked out of the truck and darted to the back, some kind of pistol in hand. Brooklyn counted to twenty and tried to relax.

"Come out careful," she said. "Give me a hand with the repair kit."

Brooklyn crept his door open and slid along the side of

the truck to join the mechanic. He handed her the rifle. "You cover, I'll carry." The mechanic's kit was efficient, and he lifted it easily to his shoulder. "Which way?"

She pulled a radio off her belt. "Sit tight a sec. Let me check in."

The first shot pinged off the side of the truck an inch from her head. The second spun her to the ground. Unsatisfied, the guns continued to fire.

Brooklyn made a long arm and snagged the mechanic's boot. Between his amped-up strength and the low gravity, it was nothing to pull her into the lee of the Trailduster, temporarily safe from the bullets hitting the other side.

Suppressing fire. Keeping us pinned down so they can…

It didn't much matter. Brooklyn's heart pounded waves of sick, green nausea into his guts. His skin was clammy, and he had to piss worse than anything. *If I ask them to stop for a sec, maybe they'll–*

The mechanic clutched his ankle. The bullet had struck high on her right chest, almost her shoulder. "What's happening?" Her voice was tight and thready with pain. She still had the rifle.

"We're pinned!" One of the buggy's tires blew, then another. *We just fixed this thing!* The Trailduster listed to the passenger side, ironically providing even better cover. Brooklyn forced himself to breathe slowly, in nose, out mouth. "How bad is it?"

"Think my vest caught some of it." She scrabbled with her arms and motioned for Brooklyn to help her up to sit against the back tire. "How many?"

"Dunno. Lots."

She snorted. "Tommy said you were some kinda super soldier. Second I saw you, I knew he was full of shit."

Brooklyn's mouth twisted. *Professionally chicken shit, that's me.* The shooting slowed and stopped. Out of ammo or waiting to see what Brooklyn and the injured mechanic would do. Sneaking in for an up-close kill. Brooklyn's enhanced hearing wasn't picking up anything useful. He took the gun. *Haven't fired a fucking shot.*

"What's your name?" Brooklyn said.

She peered at him quizzically. "You making friends or starting a shit list? Ruth Jones. Worked with Tommy on the Moon."

He nodded. The M1 was obsolete well before he entered Basic training, but Demarco had one in De Milo and showed him a thing or two. It was a quick weapon, semi-auto, and the clip popped out with a brassy ping when it was empty. *Sixteen shots. How many bad guys could there be?* He rehearsed his next few moves in his head. The adrenaline shudders vanished, and his blood went cool. The fear was gone. He was a program about to execute.

"Well, Ruth, fuck it." Brooklyn twisted to his feet and used the inclined hood of the Trailduster as a shooting platform. His vision did the swimmy thing, and he found his first target. *Squeeze. Hit. Next target. Squeeze. Hit. Next target. Squeeze…*

Brooklyn welded a patch on the airlock while Ruth supervised from a sitting position. The part of the bullet that got through her vest had gone up and out taking some of her left trapezius muscle with it. They'd made liberal use of the first-aid supplies in the emergency kit. Tommy and his crew showed about halfway through the repair work and offered to take over, but Brooklyn waved him off. The chore kept him from thinking too much.

"Seven shots, seven hits!" Ruth crowed when he'd helped her past the carnage and into a position to assess the damage to the lock. It wasn't bad. They'd knocked a big enough hole in it to open it up, but not so big to cause a lot of problems fast. The emergency curtain had kept damage and casualties low: a sunflower patch, one of Tommy's people who'd fallen and smashed in her visor, and most of the attackers.

Brooklyn had tried and failed to avoid seeing them as he searched for signs of life and made safe their weapons. To a one they were underfed, wearing patched-near-to-useless vacsuits, dirty, and likely dying of lung cancer. Mars wasn't kind to life on the edge.

He'd ended the fray without a scratch. The raiders had come out from cover and were making a slow approach to the Trailduster. He'd caught them completely by surprise. Pop, pop, pop.

"Who were they?" he asked Tommy once he'd finished the repairs to Ruth's satisfaction. Only then had she allowed herself to be put on a stretcher and loaded into a vehicle for the trip home, the battered Trailduster on a tow chain again.

Tommy spread his hands. "Wild Bunch, probably. Be awhile 'fore they get the nerve up to try something like this again. Might have put them out of business completely."

Brooklyn shuddered, a comedown from the adrenaline rush or something else. *I was on vacation, man!*

Tommy thumped him on the shoulder. "Let's get you back and put a drink in front of you."

Someone else took care of the Garand and the corpses it had made. The ride to the compound was a blur, and the drinks made things even fuzzier. Demarco poured the first round. At some point, Ruth joined them, arm in a sling and against Zawadi's advice. She told the story of the shootout with a vicious glee, describing things she could not possibly have seen from her seat against the tire. Pop, pop, pop. She winced at the pull in her sutures as she raised an imaginary rifle and took aim. Seven shots, seven kills. *Target. Squeeze. Hit. Next target. Squeeze…*

Brooklyn excused himself to vomit and came back to drink more. The raiders had deserved it. Nobody forced them to blow a hole in the airlock and come after all that Tommy had worked for. Still, especially with humanity on the run, evicted from all they knew and loved, every round fired seemed like an obscene gesture.

Demarco helped Brooklyn weave back to the bunkhouse and pull off his boots. He filled several glasses with water and stood by to make sure they were emptied.

Brooklyn swung his feet up onto the bed and let the pillow take the weight of his spinning head.

"You gonna be okay, man?"

"First time I killed someone."

"Well–" Demarco paused. "Prob'ly not the time fo' that."

Brooklyn slurred something that could have been taken as "fuck off and let me sleep", and Demarco went to his own bed, missing the tears that filled Brooklyn's eyes and ran across his cheeks into his hair.

TWENTY-SIX

"You sure you can handle that thing?" Tommy said.

Brooklyn scowled. Ruth or someone had built the one-man pods out of scrap metal, constructing what was essentially an egg-shaped Faraday Cage with a bench seat and hand controls. Each of the things ran off a First Tech lifter the size of a pack of cigarettes and moved at little more than the speed of a Central Park ice-cream truck. "Reckon I can handle it, pard."

"Riding the fences" was usually a semi-weekly chore, but the attack moved it up the to-do list. Bullets and pressurization were not on good terms. "Alright then." Tommy's pod rose a couple of feet above the surface, dimly glowing First Tech blue. Brooklyn followed in his own pod, beginning a slow clockwise trip around the crater's edge with an eye out for leaks. Tommy had a sound system in his vehicle, and a George Jones album started playing on the radio channel they were using.

"Really?" Brooklyn said. "Get my ass out of bed early – with a fucking hangover no less – to help you out and this is how you pay me back."

"Got some Dolly and Loretta in here. Johnny Cash, Waylon. You'll be hearin' from them soon enough."

The crater roof was a materials sandwich two-feet thick. Aluminum, carbon fiber, obsidian polymers, and regolith all played a part. Low gravity allowed for a structure that would have pancaked on Earth.

They piloted a grid pattern over the surface of the roof, keeping an eye out for damage or escaping vapor. Tommy and Brooklyn made small talk while they flew, but mostly they just listened to the music.

"See why you like this," Brooklyn said. "Quiet. Kind of reminds me of the Moon."

Tommy laughed. "Your Moon tour was all fucking around and computer work. I did combat drills and PT all day."

"Look how that turned out. I ended up MIA and a POW, and you didn't get to shoot no one 'til you moved to Mars and turned farmer."

"Really wasn't much of a war, was it?"

"Lost a lotta people."

Dolly was singing about being two doors down from a party.

"I'm betting there's a counter-attack plan or two running somewhere. Shop full of analysts still looking for weaknesses." Tommy sucked his teeth. "First can't lock everything down."

Brooklyn snorted. "Looks like there's plenty of chest thumping on Mars ta keep the war machine happy a while. Between the Soviets and your Wild Bunch, not seeing a lot of peace, love, and understanding up here."

"Let's just get this done."

Demarco was drinking gin with Zawadi outside the bunkhouse. He flipped Tommy and Brooklyn a lazy wave. "Plenty to share." He nodded to the younger woman. "Zee was just telling me her life story."

Tommy said he'd be right back, and Brooklyn pulled out a seat at the table. Demarco poured him a drink. "Told Zee about the fancy party we goin' to. 'Bout to ask her if she wants to be my plus-one."

"How fancy?" she said.

"Black tie. Pretty dress. Whichever you like. All expenses paid. Clothes, hotel, food, open bar."

"I have time coming," she said. "It's a date."

The sun was just peeking over the dunes when they started the two-hour ride to the train station in Bradbury, the small dome where Tommy and his crew shipped out their goods and did most of their resupply. The middle truck in the convoy was loaded with barrels of sweet potatoes, peanuts, and crates of Tommy's homemade hooch. Brooklyn had a sample case riding beside him in truck number one.

"Still think you shoulda named the distillery after me," he said. "Taught you how to make the stuff, after all."

"Had to forget all that bullshit to finally get good at it." Tommy was comfortable in the driver's seat, steering with one hand. "Named it after a dog I had as a kid."

Demarco leaned over the seat back to grab the bottle parked between Brooklyn and Tommy. "Give that dog a steak." He refilled his flask, not spilling a drop in spite of the rough road. "Nice of you to give us a personal escort to the train, Farmer Tom."

"There's a big refugee camp a couple dozen miles from Bradbury, and I could use some more hands. Be nice to sign up a family or two, get some more kids running 'round the place."

"You put the kids to work too?" Demarco said.

"Only got nine of them so far. Sister's kids. Ruth's two. Zawadi's brother has a couple. Few more among the crew. They do family chores, mostly. Help out with the farm if they want some pocket money. Ma and my Aunt Lillian run a little school and library for them. Five or six more kids will keep them busy."

"Happens when the kids get all big and surly?" Demarco said.

"Work on the farm, I guess. Or school. Up to them." He took

a swig from the bottle. "I'll help out if I can. Mars needs good people."

Brooklyn chuckled. "Look at you, man. Job creator. Pillar of the community. Liable to come back here and find you running for mayor."

"Not me," Tommy said. "Nixon lives in Yaegerton. Kissinger, too. Dole's got a place up here for when he's ready. I don't see us getting along."

Demarco spat. "Evil fucks'll live forever up here."

Brooklyn stretched out his legs. The cab of Tommy's International Harvester was roomier than the Trailduster. "Think we'll get back the deposit on our truck?" The last he'd seen, it was parked beside Ruth's garage, riddled with holes.

"Still runs," Tommy said. "Ruth will drive it back next time she goes to Roosevelt. She's related to the Carlisles. Second cousin, second husband, or something. If I know her, she'll come back to the farm with a load of parts and money in her pocket for the trouble. Damned thing was stolen from us in the first place."

The bottle emptied steadily during the drive, most of it into Brooklyn and Demarco. By the time Tommy got the Harvester through one of Bradbury's public airlocks, Brooklyn's enhanced metabolism had burned it off. Demarco seldom looked like he was affected by the stuff one way or another. They grabbed their bags, and Brooklyn tucked his sampler case under his arm. Zawadi wandered up from the third vehicle, her own travel bag slung over her shoulder.

Tommy looked at his watch. "Should be a train along in about thirty minutes. I'd wait with ya, but I need to see a guy about buying this produce."

"I'd offer to shake, but," Demarco shrugged his right shoulder, crisscrossed by the straps of his sling. "Thanks for the hospitality."

Tommy smiled. "Any friend of Brooklyn, and all that shit." He cocked his head at Zawadi. "You all set getting back?"

"Be back here in time to catch Amos. Said he'd give me a ride home if I buy him lunch."

Tommy raised his eyebrows. "Lunch, dinner, and breakfast, more likely. When's he gonna ask you to marry him, Zee? I'll triple your living space. Couple of kids for Ma to tend to and an experienced ice miner. Win all around."

"What makes you think I'd take him if he asked?" She smiled at Demarco. "Sometimes a girl's just looking for a good time."

Tommy threw a thick arm around Brooklyn's shoulders and pulled him into a hug, bag and all. "Good to see you, pal. Don't be a stranger."

PART TEN
ALIEN SHE

TWENTY-SEVEN

The train to Yaegerton was three-quarters full. Brooklyn was leery of packing his vacsuit into the overhead compartment, but the attendant swore up and down that the little chamber would pop right open if there was a problem and, anyway, the train was perfectly safe. Zawadi stowed her gear without hesitation and marched to the dining car in search of sandwiches.

Brooklyn waited until she was out of earshot. "An' here I thought your rep as a ladies' man was bullshit."

"Ain't like that." Demarco reclined his seat as far as it went and made himself comfortable. "Or maybe it is. She wants to sneak into my room under the cover of darkness tonight, that's her business."

"Just friends, huh?"

"Not even that, yet." Demarco folded his arms on his chest. "Me and the Professor have an arrangement, but friends and not even are just fine."

Brooklyn's eyes widened. "You and Yarrow? Didn't see that."

"She the only one in De Milo read more books than me. Cool lady. Sometimes we hang out and talk. Sometimes we do other things." He opened one eye to look at Brooklyn. "Might consider a mature, adult relationship of your own someday. Nice thing to have."

Zawadi came back and tossed a couple of prepackaged sandwiches at each of them. "Don't say I never did anything for you."

"Kind are they?" Demarco didn't open his eyes.

"Kind you shut up and eat," she said.

"My favorite." He leaned his head against the wall. "I'll make the next run."

"I'll do the next one," Brooklyn said. "You sit tight and rest your ancient ass."

Demarco maybe mumbled something about showing Brooklyn who was ancient.

"You give him something?" Brooklyn said.

Zawadi nodded. "To help him sleep. He's in more pain than he lets on. And he drinks too much. He will not heal quickly."

Brooklyn unwrapped a sandwich and inspected it. "Can't tell what this is."

"Food." She took a bite of her own meal. "Vegetable-based protein and filler. Some of our peanuts and sweet potatoes, possibly."

"Surprised you came with us," he said.

"Believe it or not, the farm is not rife with recreational opportunities."

"Still, you barely know us."

She wiped her mouth with the tiny napkin included in the sandwich package. "Are you worried I'm trying to ruin your friend's reputation and steal his valuables?" She brightened. "Does he have many?"

"Got a place about quarter the size of this train car back on De Milo. 'Bout as well decorated, too. More books than anyone needs for a lifetime. Mostly I wanna make sure he hasn't snowed you with a buncha bull 'bout how much fun he is to be around."

Demarco levered an eye open. "I heard that."

"You're meant to be asleep," Zawadi said.

"Meant to be rich, six-foot-three, and ruggedly handsome,

but I only got the one." He found a better position in the seat and closed his eyes again.

"Could take you to back to Venus if you wanted," Brooklyn said. "Lot of work there for someone with your skills. Lot of land to fill."

"If I wanted to be on Venus, I'd be there. And I have loads to do keeping Tommy and his cowboys in one piece," she said. "I just want to go to a party. Free drinks, new clothes, dinner, a trip to the city… it is not something that happens every day."

Brooklyn folded up his sandwich package and put it in the trash receptacle built into the back of the seat in front of him. "Not a common thing for me, neither. Specially not a fancy one."

She smiled. "Stick with me. I'll show you where the posh shop."

The train tracks ran right under the middle of the Yaegerton dome. They reclaimed their bags and rode the elevator to the surface out of consideration for Demarco's injuries.

"Really not a fan of the size of the domes here," Brooklyn said. "Got 'em on the Moon, too, but the living space is dug in. One rock in the wrong place here–" He made a face. "Makes me want to keep my helmet on."

Zawadi pointed. "That's the symbol for emergency shelters. Just keep an eye out."

"Stuck in a tiny box waiting for someone to get off their ass and pull me out? Dream come true."

They left their vacsuits at a maintenance shop and paid extra for cleaning. Mars dust was much finer than the regolith on the Moon, and the atmosphere kept it floating around longer. The past several days had rendered the suits a chalky red.

Brooklyn bought one of the handheld flatscreens and used it to display a map of the dome. He flipped through the programs available on the thing, accessible via a graphical interface.

"Imagine you had one of these as a kid." He showed it to Demarco. "Watch movies, play games, do your homework…"

Demarco sniffed. "TV's done enough damage."

"You sound like an old lady." Brooklyn gave his pal a side-eye. "It's just tech. It's not like it's out to get us."

"Doin' just fine with that on our own," he said. "Where we goin? Like to find a place to lie down and get a nap."

"It's not far." Brooklyn studied the map. "The hotel is over near the university."

"I want to get him into a proper clinic," Zawadi said. "Get a few x-rays, at least."

Demarco coughed. "Mebbe ask the concierge 'bout that."

Officially, Yaegerton had been built at the site of the first Mars landing in 1956, but really it was one crater over. It was the oldest and largest permanent human structure on the red planet. The University of Mars had opened in 1972, complete with imported ivy.

"Looks like Harvard Yard," Demarco said. "All green space and brick buildings."

The map led them through the campus and to a shady, tree-lined street beyond.

"Brownstones? Really?" Demarco said.

The gravity allowed for more than the usual two or three stories seen on Earth, but the buildings wouldn't have raised too many eyebrows in Cambridge. "There's the place. All the comforts of home." Brooklyn pointed at a sign on the door. "Emergency shelters in the basement."

Demarco looked up and down the street and back to the ornate gate that led into the hotel garden. There was a fountain visible, water flowing like a stream of diamonds. "I s'pose it'll do."

A gold credit card was waiting for them in the suite.

"I am rendered suspicious." Demarco picked the card up and

inspected both sides. "Not seeing why we merit all this first-class frippery."

"Frippery?" Zawadi said.

"Means–"

"I know what it means," she said. "I just didn't expect to hear it coming from you."

"He only plays dumb." Brooklyn looked the card over too. "Put us in debt from the get-go? Make sure we go along with something?"

Demarco hummed. "Hear a nap calling my name. You and Zee go out and get us some party clothes."

"Thought we just decided it was a trap," Brooklyn said.

"Can't be sure 'less we go to the party, an' we can't go to the party without proper vestments." Demarco pulled a battered wallet out of his pocket and fished out a card. "Matte black, dinner cut, shawl collar, French-cuff shirt, gold cuff links and studs." He handed the card to Brooklyn. "See if you can get me a sling to match."

"Just happen to have your sizes in your pocket?" Brooklyn said.

"Smart man always does." He smiled. "Real smart man carries his lady's sizes, too, case he sees somethin' she might like or he might like to see her in."

"Feel like we oughta talk to Milk first," Brooklyn said.

"Unavailable 'til the party." His mouth thinned. "We on our own, brother man, so keep your peepers peeled."

Brooklyn pocketed Demarco's measurements and the credit card. "You're up, Zee. Said you can show me where to go."

She eyed him critically. "A barber. It will take more than a change of clothes for you, I expect."

Brooklyn checked his bow tie in the decorative mirror, likely there for just that purpose, near the ballroom entrance. It was hard to argue with the results of the shopping trip. The barber had removed weeks of unregulated hair growth, leaving him with a short, almost mohawk-looking cut and an even quarter inch of stubble on his face. Zee had picked out an impossible-looking orange dress, held in place courtesy of surface tension and low gravity. Her jewelry could have been spotted from orbit. Demarco looked like James Bond and wore the shoulder sling like a fashion accessory. The final cost had been staggering.

A slick-looking gray-haired dude greeted and smiled them through the door. Demarco slipped him a bill.

"What was that for?" Brooklyn said once they were out of earshot.

"Appearances, old sport." Demarco arched an eyebrow. "Until we know th' ground 'neath our feet, I'm going to pretend I'm happy dancing on it."

Brooklyn's head felt like it might spin off his shoulders, and he suddenly needed to piss. "Where do you s'pose Milk is?"

"Around. 'Bout to see if she hiding in the scotch." Demarco offered Zawadi his uninjured arm. "Shall we?"

She slid her hand onto the crook of his elbow. "Lead on, Macduff."

Demarco said something about the actual quote being 'lay on' as they walked off, leaving Brooklyn to drift unmoored near the entrance. A waiter in white with a silver tray coughed politely at him. He lowered the tray into easy reach. "Compliments of the lady," he said. On the tray was a highball glass full of something smoky and golden and a note: *Cigar lounge. Come alone.*

Brooklyn took the drink and asked the waiter for directions. The booze was mellow, like leather and oak with a side of cherries. He let it lead him to the cigar lounge on the far side of the ballroom and pushed through the door. Dark wood and red carpets, high-back chairs. He saw her right away.

"Of all the planets in all the solar systems, you had to walk into mine, Brooklyn Lamontagne."

The first time they met they'd made love on the Moon. The

next time, she'd left him to die in space. "Bet you're not going by Sierra this time."

She patted the seat next to her. "Maybe this time you can call me Mrs Dalloway."

"Should I?" He took a swallow of the bourbon.

"No." She held out her hand. "Claire Stevens, faculty wife. Married to Professor Carl Stevens. I believe you know him. Handsome. Bit of a limp."

It took a second for the synapses to line up. "Dee."

She smiled. "He says 'hello', by the way. He'd have loved to see you, but he's on sabbatical."

"I'm missing something, right?" He lowered his voice. "This is more of your spy shit."

She sipped her own drink, something in a martini glass. "We have friends in common. Green ones."

The Designed outlaws wouldn't have provided a gold card, but the United Nations… The identity of their sugar daddy became clear. "Thought you were meeting with Demarco."

"I saw you, and I just couldn't resist." The corner of her mouth turned up. "You clean up nice, moon boy, but I need you to get dirty."

"How dirty?"

"A job right up your alley." Her nails made tapping noises on her glass. "A prison break."

TWENTY-EIGHT

Brooklyn took the chair across from her. "Don't sound anywhere close to my alley, 'Claire'."

"You haven't done a prison break yet?" Her martini glass moved airily. "My mistake. I thought you would have least dabbled by now."

"Sorry to disappoint. An considerin' what happened th' last time I saw you, I ain't so inclined to start on your say-so."

She took a sophisticated sip of her drink and looked at him over the rim of the glass. Her eyes flicked right, away from him. Away from the truth.

Brooklyn's mouth fell open. He swore.

"What?"

"I been doin' jobs for you all this time."

She smirked. "You're smarter than you used to be."

"Not smarter. Quicker."

"If the EOF knew what you came home with, they never would have let you go."

"Wanna tell me more 'bout that?"

"Classified."

"Demarco said those jobs got me killed."

She stuck out her lower lip. "You got better. Besides, your world needed you."

"What world is that? Earth? Venus? Having a hard time

keeping track." He looked around the room. "Where's Dee, I mean 'Carl,' really?"

"Deep-space sneak and peek in that little scout ship of his. He got his doctorate in '85, so our cover is legit. He keeps his hand in during school vacations and research trips, and I keep the home fires burning like a good little wifey and run ops on the side."

"An' I been helpin' you out."

"You've been an asset since we met on the Moon. Your combat skills are subpar, and I imagine I'd really have to twist your arm to get you to assassinate someone, but sometimes you're exactly what I need."

"How many times?"

"Have we worked together? A dozen or so. Your memory loss has been useful. You're no James Bond, but you can keep a secret."

"You part of this pissing contest I been hearing about? Jelly exos growling at each other across a battlefield, hammer-and-sickle on one side, stars-and-stripes on the other?"

"A few small interventions, maybe, but if I told you about them I'd have to kill you again."

"Why can't you do the prison break?"

"Can you imagine it?" She laughed. "An old lady like me!"

"I can imagine it pretty good." She might be twenty years older than the first time they'd met, but he doubted she was any less capable. "Did my time." He stood and flashed his empty glass. "Nice talking to you, Mrs Stevens. Give Carl my love."

"It's the only way to know why the First left. We need to get ahead of it."

"Angels pulled the 'enhanced emigration protocol' thing to get the First to come back, didn't they? Case they left because things weren't moving fast enough."

"We believe so."

"Now you're worried the Cardinal will do something even dumber."

"That's part of it. We're also worried what the Soviets and Americans will do once they find out."

"Assuming they haven't already." He stuck his empty hand in the pocket of his dress pants. "Still don't see why I should care. Between your guys and the rebel Designed, you got plenty o' people to throw at this."

"You know the prisoner in question, Brooklyn. You know her very well."

Fuck. Andy. Only person it could be. "Knew her."

"Drop by the house tomorrow afternoon, around two, and I'll fill you in. Just you. I hear Demarco needs to heal up." She rose and air-kissed him on the cheek. "Have fun tonight."

Brooklyn waited until she'd blended into a crowd of faculty gossip and took his empty glass to the bar where Demarco and Zawadi were holding court. The older man was in his element – telling stories and cracking jokes – sliding between 5th Avenue and the Ninth Ward as the moment required. Milk was nearby, a gimlet in hand. She caught Brooklyn's eye and drew him aside.

"What's going on?" she said.

"It's about Andy." Brooklyn ordered a bourbon refill. "Don't have the full story, yet. But we got a meeting tomorrow. You havin' fun at your conference?"

"It's been interesting. Makes me glad I work somewhere with decent gravity. At least blood behaves the way it should."

Brooklyn inclined his head toward Demarco. "For now, we follow his example. Eat, drink, and see Mary or whatever."

"For tomorrow we shall die."

"What?"

"It's how the quote ends," Milk said. "I think it's from Shakespeare. Or the Bible. One of those."

Brooklyn downed half his drink in one swallow. "Hope the hell that's not how it goes."

* * *

The Stevens home was a couple of blocks away from the hotel, the top floor of a six-story brownstone in the middle of faculty housing. The decor was tasteful and modern, a mix of Mars-deco and West African chic.

"Welcome to the spy base." Claire directed Brooklyn to a seat on the couch. "I scan for bugs every morning. Coffee?"

"Sure."

She came back from the kitchen with a tray loaded with Mars-made china and finger sandwiches.

"Really getting into this happy-homemaker thing, ain't you," Brooklyn said.

Claire took the easy chair across from the couch where Brooklyn was sitting and added a dollop of whiskey to her coffee. "I can kill you with a napkin ring, but that doesn't mean I don't like nice things." She held up the whiskey flask. "Some?"

"I like nice things, too." Brooklyn held up his hand to catch the flask she tossed his way. "Why is Andy in prison?"

"It's worse than that," she said. "She's in an American dark site on Deimos."

One of the two moons of Mars. "The hell do the Americans want with her?"

"That's a very good question." She smiled encouragingly.

"Demarco said she went MIA getting hold of someone who knows why the First took off. She make it that far?"

"My sources say she did not." She spread her hands. "They don't know if the Americans were aware that's what she was doing."

"But they might, and maybe they wanted to stop her gettin' the info."

"It would have been easier just to kill her."

"Maybe they don't know who she was gonna talk to and need her to tell them." Brooklyn put his cup on the coffee table. "Which means torture."

"I wouldn't put it past them. But she might have been

nabbed for some other reason entirely. She's on every terror watchlist on Earth."

"Only because the First wanted her there."

"I know a way to find out."

"Lovesick thug breaks into the dark site ta get his old girlfriend out. End of story, no strings running to you or your bosses."

"Pretty much."

Brooklyn drank straight from the flask. "Hate this shit. I really do."

"That's why I always used Goldilocks for your code name. Everything has to be just right. Right op, right asset, right motivation."

"How'd you get me to play all those times?"

"Depended on the situation. Money worked sometimes, but usually I needed to find a way to appeal to your better nature."

"Dee ever guilt me into one?"

"Never. He has Goldilocks tendencies of his own." She sat back. "I wish you'd seen how hard he worked to get you away from the EOF. Every day after we got back, I watched him beat himself up for leaving you behind. When they found you–"

"He already apologized. Water under the bridge. You an' me, though…" He put the flask on the table. "This one last time, then never again. Clear?"

"If that's what you want."

"Don't like being used." He scratched his ear. "A dozen times, you said. Don't remember any, so I musta been killed in every one."

"I worried about you every time, if it that makes you feel any better." The corner of her mouth lifted. "Your memory loss seems to be a factor of how much damage was done when you died and how long you stayed dead. Once we had that figured, keeping you in the dark was easy. I had to kill you myself once or twice."

"Yeah?" His lip curled. "What would you have done I hadn't come back?"

"Mourned. Probably gotten drunk. Then put a hit on the fucker who got you. No one takes what's mine and gets away clean, Brook. Whether its Earth or you."

TWENTY-NINE

"You think these're real eggs?" Brooklyn pointed to a line on the cafe menu. "Why are they so cheap?"

Milk frowned. She'd skipped a session on Mars microbes to get the lowdown. "Chickens do really well on Mars, apparently. It's one of the ways people in the refugee camp are making money."

"Chickens."

"They eat almost anything and make eggs and more chickens. Made sense to bring some along for the ride."

Brooklyn folded the menu and laid it on the table. "Alright, here's the sitch." He rubbernecked to see if anyone had a chance at overhearing. "Andy's being held at an American black site on Deimos, and we gotta bust her out."

Milk blinked. "Why is nothing simple with you?"

"I got nothin' to do with this. I hadn't ferried your ass out here, I'd be free and clear."

"Why is she being held?"

"Unclear. Sneaky-Snake shit."

"I just wanted a vacation," she said. "Get some free samples, maybe. Rub elbows with real doctors. Learn a couple of tricks. I figured we'd lose track of Demarco for a while, and he'd come back with what we need. Instead, I get this shit. Does he know?"

"Zawadi and him are seein' the sights on the UN dime. Figured I'd fill 'em in tonight or tomorrow."

"This might not be our problem," she said.

"That mean you don't want to help?"

"I hate this. She's manipulating you into doing her dirty work."

"It's what she does."

"I hate her, too."

"Just saying that because she got me killed." *Multiple times.* He ran his fingers though his hair. He hadn't been able to replicate the efforts of the hairstylist, and it had gone back to doing whatever it wanted. "Also, what she does."

"How are you feeling with this? Nervous? Excited? You and Andy were pretty close once."

"So they tell me."

Demarco twitched the cuff of his pants up and crossed his legs figure-four style. He and Zawadi had made liberal use of the UN credit card, and he'd be going home with several tailored suits. This one was a deep cranberry color, and he'd worn it to see Zee off at the train station earlier in the day. She'd also been laden with goodies and gifts for Amos and the folks back at the farm.

"This whole thing poses a bit of a," he gestured with his glass of scotch, "diplomatic issue."

Milk rolled her eyes. "Please continue."

"Dr Milk and I are representatives, albeit in emeritus, of the Venus leadership council. We get our asses caught breakin' into an American black site, might cause trouble for Kas 'n them."

"Can't he just, like, disavow your existence?" Brooklyn said.

"Works better in fiction then it do in reality. 'Specially if we take Andy back to De Milo with us." He drank some scotch. "Worse, I'm sixty-two years old with stove-in ribs an' a messed-up arm."

Milk raised her hand. "Forty-seven. Bad lungs. Poor depth perception."

"Not exactly a crack team of operatives." Demarco uncrossed his legs. "Do you trust Lady Claire?"

"Fuck no. Could be setting us up, but I don't see what it would get her."

"Do you have a plan?"

"Got a map." Brooklyn let his foot slip to the floor. "Prison breaks are not really my thing. Maybe Gisela knows someone we can hire–"

"There's too much riding on this to farm it out," Milk said. "Kas will kill us if this comes back on De Milo somehow."

"We're going to need more than us three and the power of true love to make this happen." Demarco rubbed his head. "We got some money. Spy lady gave us some intel. Let's wait until we're back on the *Victory* where no one can watch us and figure it out."

THIRTY

Balbina the Babysitter popped her gum at them as they approached the ship. "Om's taking a walk."

Brooklyn stopped short. "A walk?"

The Martian teen was parked outside the *Victory*, feet up on a box, catching the sunlight filtering in through the dome. She pointed toward the food court. "Noodle shop. Crab Rangoon. It, ya know, likes to do stuff for me."

Brooklyn pushed past her and rushed into the ship. "Om!"

"Yes, Brooklyn," it answered. "What is, ya know, the problem?"

Brooklyn arrested his headlong dash by gripping both sides of the cockpit door. "Babysitter said–"

"That I was getting her food. That is correct."

"How–?"

"Please return to the, ya know, the outside of the ship, and you will see. I will arrive shortly."

Brooklyn retraced his steps. Demarco was looking anxious, Milk curious, and Balbina profoundly irritated. She pointed toward the other side of the hanger. "Over there."

A stocky figure stumped toward them. A two-legged tank with a cold, dead face. It waved. "Hello! Hello!" it said in Om's voice. "I have a body now!"

"How the hell–?" Brooklyn swallowed some bile.

"We got bored," Balbina said. "Just, ya know, books, books,

books all day. Om figured out he could move the exos around by radio. Walk around and look at shit. You owe my mother money for that one, by the way."

Om waved again. "It was in the best repair. Ms Jurek said she will sell it back to us at cost."

Brooklyn couldn't take his eyes off the exo's face. *ZARK!* He shuddered. "The hell you need a body for?"

"To live." Om spread his arms. "To turn pages. To interact." It turned in an awkward circle. "To be."

"I think therefore I am," Demarco said. "Thought we covered that."

"Descartes could not have conveyed that without use of a body," Om said.

"Touché." Demarco gripped the back of his head. "Reckon you already did have a body, the circuits and shit that hold your mind. You just gave yourself arms and legs."

"And hands." Om lifted the hand it had not been using for waving. It held a takeout container.

"Finally." Balbina stepped up to claim her food. "Thought it was gonna get, ya know, cold you were talking so long."

Brooklyn paid Balbina for her babysitting time. While she shared her takeout with Demarco and Milk, he went to the cockpit to get a read on Om. The AI checked out fine, other than a new tendency to sprinkle "ya know" into its syntax.

"Brooklyn?" Om said. "Are you willing to respond to a, ya know, a question?"

"Sure."

"Do you believe in God?"

Deep thoughts in the dark. "Like an all-knowing, all-seeing God with a plan?" He shook his head. "Did when I was a kid, but naw."

"Then why do we exist?"

"Demarco was s'posed to handle this part of your education. I'm better at the practical shit." He faced the camera Om was using as its eyes in the cockpit. "What brought this on?"

"Balbina professed the belief that, ya know, life has no purpose."

"Yeah, well, she's a kid. Kids can be kinda nihilistic." *My big word for the day. Demarco would be proud.* "Most of them grow out of it. Ma always said we were here to help each other out."

"There are at least three hundred and seventy-six examples in the literature I have consumed that suggest otherwise. Altruism is, ya know, the rarity, not the rule."

"Maybe some people had bad mothers." *Or like me, they didn't listen too well to theirs.* "Life can make it hard to stick to being a do-gooder." *Says the guy plannin' a jailbreak.* The outside monitor showed Demarco trying to teach Om's new body how to waltz. *Thinkin' of which...*

The three of them were jammed around the kitchen table sipping bad coffee and eating pirogues. The paintings had not sold, and the supplies the Jureks had laid in to pay for the dolls were strange and labeled in Polish: black-market potatoes, oatmeal, canned peas, pickled cabbage, frozen dumplings, and smoked mystery meat.

"So, whaddya we got that works?" Demarco said.

"A third-rate superman," Milk ticked the list off on her fingers, "an antique spaceship, an aging and injured bookworm, a little money, a decent trauma medic, and a handful of weapons of various calibers and origins."

Brooklyn folded his arms. "Ain't no superman, doc."

"But you quick to think she talking 'bout you," Demarco said. "Maybe you the one who old and busted, and I the superman."

"You got enhanced vision and reflexes, sped-up healing, and you're even stronger than Top." Milk smothered a yawn. "Not my fault you don't do anything with it."

"You didn't see him shoot up the Wild Bunch," Demarco

said. "Put Om on the list. Super-smart, armored alien exosuit might be a good thing to have at your back."

"Jelly suit ain't real sneaky," Brooklyn said. "Wanna get in, get out. No questions asked. No shots fired."

Milk frowned. "Can Om fly the ship?"

"Bet it would learn quick. Do a better job than either o' you, anyway."

They considered the potato resting on the table's center. It looked enough like Deimos to be its twin. Only a perverse poet would choose the Red Planet's closest moon as a symbol of romance and mystery. Twenty-four miles around and covered in fine dust, its gravity so low that a good jump from its surface would put an astronaut into escape velocity. The prison there was considered inescapable because each eight-by-eight cell was surrounded by vacuum, accessible only via a mobile airlock, and separated from any other structure by at least one hundred yards. The site was only lightly staffed – it was easier to land an interrogator when needed than to keep one on hand – but it was patrolled by repurposed exos on automatic pilot or remotely controlled.

"Cells are a lot like the inflatables I used on the moon," Brooklyn said.

"Rigged with explosives," Milk said. "Would the bombs be underneath?"

"Betcha they are," Demarco cut in. "Pop 'em and launch 'em at the same time. Planet's gravity gets them and – poof – 'prison, what prison? I don't see no prison'."

"I wonder who makes that decision," Milk said. "Does the warden have autonomy, or does she need permission from someone else?"

Brooklyn hummed. "Autos could be programmed to shoot at anything that don't ID as another exo or a guard, maybe."

"Wit' some kind of RFID tag?" Demarco said.

"Yeah, maybe."

"Way I see it," Demarco put one finger on the potato, "we

land on the far side where they can't see us, and you sneak around to the prison on foot. Cut Andy out of stir, and jump on outta there. You call us, and Om flies the ship over to grab you. Then we jet for home. Easy."

Brooklyn picked up the potato and turned it over in his hands. A twelve-mile hike in low gee carrying an emergency airlock and an extra vacsuit. Doable. "You guys put Om through its paces. See what it can do," he said. "I need to go shopping."

"Check around for a triage kit. If I need to do a blood transfusion, I'll want something better than sheet-metal screws and coolant piping."

"Ten-four, Doc." Brooklyn sketched a mock salute. "Add it to the list."

"I'll think about the best place to land," Demarco said. "An' take a nap."

Brooklyn stabbed the tabletop with his finger. "Don't want any eyes on us up there. Mars ain't the cash cow Venus is, but I'd like not to be shot at next time I make orbit. Let's do this real sneaky. In, out, no warrants on us or the ship."

"We got this, Brook." Milk took the potato. "We'll get Andy out safe."

Exo Om did a series of knee bends while juggling three empty pallets.

"Strong." Brooklyn set down his purchases to watch.

"The further away the exo is from the ship, the longer the response time, but the automatics keep it from falling on its face," Milk said. "If it loses signal, it shifts into a stable resting position and waits to get it back."

The exo was bending steel rods into various shapes.

"Any chance it goes nuts and kills us all?"

"Om!" Demarco called, "any chance you're gonna lose your mind and wipe us all out?"

"There is always that chance, but I do not predict it will, ya know, happen."

"See," Demarco shrugged, "safe as any of us."

"So you wouldn't have a problem giving it a gun?" Brooklyn said.

Demarco made a lemon face. "Oh, hell no."

"Got one more thing." Brooklyn pulled something colorful out of the bundle at his feet and walked over to face the exo. "Lean over." He pulled the thing – a Mexican wrestling mask – over the exo's head. "Face gives me the heebie-jeebies. Bad memories."

"Alright," Demarco said, "time to teach the baby how to fly."

Om's exo was sitting in the kitchen reading a book when Brooklyn wandered in for a cup of tea.

"If you're here, how are you running the piloting sims we made?" Brooklyn said.

Om closed the book around the exo's thumb to keep its place among the pages, something Brooklyn had seen Milk do. "I am able to do many things at once."

"I got enough trouble just getting hot water, man. Do you want–?" He laughed. "I almost asked if you wanted tea."

"I have one." The exo gestured toward the table, where a cooling cup sat untouched. "I cannot consume it, but the ritual seemed incomplete without."

The kitchen was Milk's favorite place to read. "You want me to reheat it?"

"Thank you, but that is unnecessary." The exo turned the book to look at its cover. It was from a large box of paperbacks Brooklyn had maneuvered onto his shopping list. "This is the last."

"All ready?" Brooklyn's eyebrows crawled up his forehead. "We gotta lot of miles to go, bud. You should have rationed them better."

"There are only six stories." Om almost sounded relieved.

"Nah. There were a couple of dozen books in there."

"No." Om made the exo's head move back and forth on its thick neck, the primary-colored wrestling mask covering its face snarling the whole way. "I have read eight hundred and seventy-six books and plays, but there are only six stories. They differ only in character, setting, and plot detail."

"That's a–" Brooklyn cleared his throat. "That doesn't seem right."

"It is correct," Om said. "For example, there are stories that chart a rise in happiness, such as 'Oliver Twist' by Charles Dickens. There are also stories that follow a decline in happiness, such as 'The Grapes of Wrath'." It looked at the book's cover again. "I am halfway through this one, and I can already discern it will take the latter path. Fiction is predictable."

"'Gotta be a million books out there, pal." Brooklyn rinsed out his mug. "You can't judge them all based on what we have on board."

"This does not cause me distress, Brooklyn. Systems should be predictable. I could not perform my work as navigator if I could not predict the movements of the planets."

"So, you like things to be predictable."

"I prefer things I take direct action in to be predictable, but I enjoy a measure of unpredictability in things I merely observe."

"Is this you thinking about being a brick, again?"

The Om bot made a motion that might have been its attempt to ape a shrug. "The downward stressors would be mostly predictable, but the flaws in workmanship and differences in torsional stress alone…" It fell silent.

"Look, man, we get back to Earth or Venus, I'll get you a library card. You can read all kind of books. All you want. Really test your theory."

"I am willing." The exo did its imitation shrug thing again. "But nothing will change."

THIRTY-ONE

Brooklyn swung the binocular attachment back to the side of his helmet and opened the channel they'd picked for the operation. "At least twenty exos down there."

The prison was at the bottom of a crater and laid out like a wheel, with a central habitation hub for guards and staff. At the rim of the wheel were the dome-shaped single-occupancy cells. Tracks laid between the cells and the central hub allowed rolling airlocks to go to and fro to retrieve prisoners for interrogation or bring them consumables.

"We counted twenty-eight on the last fly over," Milk said.

The day before, they'd banged out a couple of simple satellites, each about the size of a toaster, and put them in an orbit that carried them over the black site every few hours. They offered an overview of the area and filled in some of the blanks the map left.

"Doesn't matter much. There's hardly any cover down there, and I can't tell what cell hers is. Sierra said seven, but I can't see any damn numbers."

"Come back an' we'll figure again," Demarco said.

"Longer we wait, more likely they'll get what they need from her."

"Might have it already."

"Then they got less reason to keep her healthy." The crater was forty feet deep. Free falling to the bottom would take a while, and he'd make a good target all the way. Or he could dive headfirst and speed up the descent with the suit's small thrusters. *Flip around halfway and land on my feet. Or land on my head and bust open my helmet.* "I'm dropping down. If I can't see the numbers from down there, I'll bust into the hub and find her that way."

"Do that an' you'll have two dozen robots on your ass quick," Demarco said.

"You better pick us up quicker, then." He scanned the ground below. He could see the exos, but there was no good way to know if they were looking his way.

A sixty-foot fall on Mars is safe. Safe-ish. A twenty-eight-mile-per-hour drop. *I can do that.* Mars gravity was about three-point-seven meters per second squared. Deimos was point zero zero three. *That's less than a percent of Mars gravity, so…* "Fuck it." He dove off the crater's edge and triggered the thrusters.

The regolith on Deimos was as fine as baby powder and stupid thick. Even a slow-lob tennis ball would kick up quite a cloud of the stuff. Brooklyn triggered the thrusters too soon and shot away from the wall of the crater instead of accelerating down it. His flip was also badly timed and poorly aimed. The central hub of the black site grew rapidly in his visor. *Bad fucking plan!* He threw up his arms to protect the glass of his helmet. The surface came up fast. He belly-flopped and slid, sending a plume of regolith up and out.

Demarco said something faded and thin over the radio. Brooklyn pushed himself to his feet and looked around. He was dizzy, and he fought to keep from throwing up in his helmet. From inside the circle, the numbers on the inflatables were visible. "I'm between the hub and number two. Bet seven is on the other side."

He shuffle-stepped toward the hub and hoped billowing regolith was a sight common enough to ignore.

He wiped his visor. There it was. *Good ol' number seven.* Assuming Claire's intel was accurate, Andy was inside. He timed the interior patrol and made his move, busting out his best low-low-gravity skip toward the inflatable and hoping like hell no one would spot him.

He stumbled to a stop outside the seven dome and shucked off his backpack. Setting up the emergency airlock was a matter of sixty seconds in trained hands, but it had been a while since Brooklyn had practiced. He got the thing up and inflated, and cycled through it with the spare vacsuit. The cell door popped right open.

Brooklyn unsealed the visor of his helmet. "An–!"

The cell's narrow bed was occupied, a pneumatic redhead riding Andy like a cowgirl. She was facing away from the door and slid slowly to the ground as Andy sat up. "Brooklyn?"

He held up the vacsuit. "We're getting you out of here, an' the plan's already halfway to hell."

"I can't leave without Beth." Andy was buck naked but for a thin metal band across her forehead.

"Who's Beth?" Milk's voice crackled through Brooklyn's suit radio.

"Standby," Brooklyn said. "Got eyes on the prize."

The redhead had pulled the blanket off the bed to cover herself. She looked none too pleased at the interruption.

Brooklyn looked from the scowling redhead to Andy. "Only got the one vacsuit."

"I can survive vacuum for short time," Andy said. "Beth cannot."

Brooklyn thrust the vacsuit at the woman. "Guess this is yours. Don't bother gettin' dressed. Clothes'll just get in the way."

Beth yanked the suit out of his hands, her eyes fierce.

His mouth twisted. "You need to prep or anything 'fore you go out there?"

Andy nodded. "Give me about two minutes. Help Beth with the suit."

Andy knelt and began taking deep breaths. Brooklyn helped

the redhead dress, an activity that consisted of getting his hands slapped away several times and adjusting the straps that made the suit formfitting or as close to it as possible. "You ever spacewalked before?"

She paled. "Once or twice. How far are we going?"

"One crater over. A couple hundred meters."

"I'm ready." Andy's skin was darker green, and her eyes had filmed over. "I won't be able to communicate with you until we are inside the ship."

"You gonna put some clothes on?"

She smiled. "First person to go streaking on Deimos."

Brooklyn triggered his radio. "About to make our move. Any thoughts?"

"Run like hell," Demarco sent. "We on the way."

He gave Andy his rifle and pulled a long knife out of his toolbelt. "Time to catch our flight outta here." He sealed his visor and slashed at the back wall of the inflatable.

It took multiple cuts to get through the double layer of tough fabric, and they emerged under fire. Andy brought the rifle up and began trading shots with the eight exos that had formed a semicircle behind the cell.

"Shots fired and en route!" Brooklyn opened up with his plasma blaster, scorching two of the military exos. Another jerked backward as Andy fired the long gun. None of the targets fell, and they resumed their slow march toward the escapees.

"More behind us!" Beth said. "We were spotted coming out."

"Copy." Brooklyn dropped to one knee. His suit was tough enough to take a couple of hits, maybe, but sustained fire would turn it into scraps of fabric and foil. "Any ideas? I'm barely slowing them down!"

"Brook, we got a problem. Om's having a... a fit... or something," Demarco said. "It won't fly the ship to the rendezvous."

"We'll come to you." He pointed the way he had come. "Beth,

head that way. Listen for instructions." He traded weapons with Andy and urged her to follow Beth. "Demarco, Beth is on the way, and she's ears for Andy. Keep 'em on track."

Okay. Brooklyn bent his knees and pushed off hard. He gave his emergency thrusters a goose, gaining more speed and altitude, and spun in space to point his rifle back the way they'd come. Eight– no, nine exos aimed their weapons his way. *This is going to suck.* Every shot would he took would change his velocity and alter his course. He fired anyway, absorbing the recoil the best he could and letting his reflexes handle the shooting.

Below him, Andy raised the plasma blaster and twisted to fire. The blaster had far less range than the rifle, but what it lost in usefulness it made up for with a distracting light show. Brooklyn's suit flared with alarms. Oxygen leak, decompression warning, plumbing and electrical malfunction. "Think I'm hit!"

Sky, Mars, ground, sky, Mars, ground. He was tumbling. Flashes of light in his eyes that almost looked like numbers and letters. *Fire thrusters in…* A countdown.

Zero. Brooklyn triggered his thrusters. Sky, Mars, ground. Sky, Mars, ground. Ground came up hard, and he bounced. His helmet struck rock, and his visor starred. It didn't matter; he couldn't breathe anyway. Suit alarms buzzed, but he couldn't hear them. *No sound in a vacuum.*

Pressure on his back forced him against the rock. Night fell all the way.

Not again. Not this again.

PART ELEVEN
Endorphinmachine

THIRTY-TWO
Some Months Before in New Mexico

"My name's Trip," the florid man said, "an' I been havin' a real hard time."

"Hello, Trip," sang the mostly court-mandated choir.

The alien occupation had made Trip feel small, wiped out his career, cost him the love and respect of his wife and kids. The wife had moved north, taking the kids and the dog. Trip mopped his face with a bandanna while he talked. Sans job, family, or independent wealth, Emigration didn't see much need for him. Soon as the courts ruled on the new policy, which Trip allowed might take years, he'd be on a ship to Venus.

Thanks for sharing, Trip. Hello, Marianne. Hey, Don. Hi, Billy. 'Sup, Blake. Afternoon, Suzie. What's shakin', Macon.

At the break, the facilitator refilled his mug with twice-brewed tea. Coffee was way too expensive to waste on a small-town support group. The doughnuts were a day old when he'd bought them the day before. He smiled at a man who'd painted his face gold. "Ain't said nothing in a while, Ed. Feel like sharing today?"

The golden man shook his head. "Not today."

The facilitator frowned. Ed was supposed to "actively participate" in the group as part of his plea deal.

Brooklyn, although the others at the meeting knew him as "Chuck," didn't share anything either. His sentence didn't require him to. He just had to show up for eighteen months.

After the meeting, their armor patched, the warriors trooped outside to smoke shitty hand-rolled cigarettes and wait for rides. Trip sparked a kitchen match off the wall and lit the twist of paper he'd stuck in the corner of his mouth. He shook the match dead and caught Brooklyn's eye. "What's your line, kid?"

The anonymity of the meeting pretty much ended at the sidewalk. Out there, they were all just people with the weight of the future bearing down on them. "Computers." Brooklyn picked a shred of tobacco off his tongue.

"Didn't think they were making 'em new anymore."

"Why they pay me to fix the old ones."

Trip nodded. "Make the world go 'round."

Nope, they were barely holding it together, running one or two steps behind on who was still on the planet and trying their best to make sure everyone remaining got their checks every month.

"Guess you ain't from 'round here," Trip said.

"Been here 'bout as long as I been anywhere." Though why the hell he'd picked New Mexico was something he still asked himself.

"Surprised you haven't emigrated," Trip said. "Young guy like you. Skills. Looks like you can handle yourself. Don't see a ring on your finger. You could write your own ticket."

Brooklyn rubbed the butt of his cigarette out against the wall and dropped it on the ground. "Want my ticket, Trip, it's all yours." He stepped off the sidewalk to meet a battered pickup truck. The passenger door squealed open, and he dropped onto the worn upholstery inside. The driver was mostly aluminum, one of the exosuited multi-armed conquerors who'd come second place in the battle for Earth. Humanity had come in a distant third, but that was all right. Life went on.

"Did you have a good time?" The jelly gurgled with laughter. Her real name was unpronounceable, but translated to something like 'Blood on the Water'. She went by 'Float'.

Brooklyn pulled his sunglasses out of the overhead visor and slipped them on his face. "Let's get the fuck outta here."

The aging truck took the road out of town too fast, the result of leaving the driving to someone who'd grown up at interstellar speeds. At least Float had a license, which was more than could be said of Brooklyn, who'd lost it to the same judge who'd ordered him to attend the support group.

He opened the glove compartment and pulled out a jar of moonshine. "What'd I miss?"

Float reached for the radio volume with a steady metal hand. "Cooper bought two gallons. Cash. Like you told me. He still owes from the last time, though."

"No more 'til he pays off." Brooklyn took a swallow of the shine. He'd only been tagged for drunk driving because he spilled a similar jar all over himself and veered off the road in surprise. He hadn't fought it because he wasn't sure his fake ID would hold up.

Float had laughed her ass off when the jar spilt. A little splat of wet was hysterical to a critter whose biggest fear was being dry. Or maybe it had been Brooklyn's reaction to the whole thing. *Weird what a medusozoa thinks is funny.*

Brooklyn turned the radio back up and punched the presets in hopes something worth listening came up. "Thought you were gonna throw a new radio in this thing. Something with a cassette deck."

She lifted one hand from the wheel and twisted its wrist. "Get me one, and I will."

Brooklyn turned to the jar again. "You need anything at the bait shop?"

"Stopped on the way here." Float had a taste for waterdogs, and a pound of the weird little things lasted about a week. She'd drop a few in her tank every night, catch and eat them while she and Brooklyn watched television. Mostly she stuck to minnows, though, because the dogs gave her gas. "Filled up the cooler."

Brooklyn rolled another cigarette and lit up. He didn't really want it, but it was the only way he'd found to deaden the dog-like sense of smell he'd recently developed. The surrounding desert didn't smell like much, but his roommate whiffed like a dirty aquarium.

Float signaled the turn into their long driveway, the aircraft hangar they lived in gritty and gray in the distance. It was surrounded by desert.

The Purple Lady was playing house again, a lavender apron layered over a purple dress, and cooking something foul on the range top in the kitchen. "Just in time for dinner!" She looked a little like Brooklyn's ma as she'd been in the mid '50s.

Brooklyn set the empty jar on the counter. "What is it?"

"Just something I threw together." She waved her hand over the table like a spokesmodel. The surface was liberally dusted with flour, the bucket Brooklyn used to change the oil on the truck empty in the table's center. Two sleeves of Saltines had gone into the meal, at least six eggs, a baby-food jar of rusty screws, and a Brillo pad. "It's meatloaf!"

"That ain't meatloaf." Brooklyn stepped up to look at the mess on the stove. "An' you ruined the pan."

"It's not? I did?" She shot her eyes wide then twisted her mouth to make a sitcom face. "Guess I'll just have gin!"

In her defense, there weren't a lot of groceries to work with. Brooklyn turned off the burner and moved the pan to the brick he used as a trivet.

"I have something important to tell you," her face fell, "but I can't remember what it is."

The Purple Lady was the groupmind of Mars, all the highly evolved plant-based natives of the Red Planet in one purple telepathic package. *Not purple; that's just how my brain reads it.* It was a wonder she functioned at the human level at all. "It'll come to you. Ice?"

She smiled. He poured straight gin into a martini glass. "So," she slumped into a seat at the table and slurred, "what sort of trouble have you been getting into?" The alcohol had absolutely no effect on her, but she'd been watching tipsy humans for about three-hundred-thousand years – not to mention the ones she'd seen on television – and sometimes faked it for fun.

"Doin' it too soon," he said. "Give it a drink or two."

She straightened and dropped the act. "The question remains."

Brooklyn took the seat across from her. She looked and sounded wholly human and smelled like catmint and forest floor. "Workin', mostly."

"Is it a job worth doing?"

"Computer shit, nothing you'd be interested in."

The Mars born had never needed computers. From the beginning, they'd been networked naturally, communicating through a shared root system and growing into sentience together. When it came time to leave the planet millions of years later, they'd done that together, too, leaving the atmosphere in a great cloud of quantum-linked spores. Brooklyn had attracted their attention by getting high and letting some dude stick needles into his chakra points during a festival. Cosmic consciousnesses aligned, and the Purple Lady suddenly had someone new to talk to.

"Hot out," she said.

Brooklyn nodded.

"Read any good books lately?" she said.

"Naw. You?"

She gulped her drink and looked like she might be about to put on the tipsy act again. Brooklyn felt guilty. She'd wanted someone new to talk to and ended up with him. A disappointment all around. "How 'bout TV?" he said.

She launched into a rundown of her favorite shows. Brooklyn had a lot of experience half-listening to people when they talked about such things and was able to drink steadily, fill her glass, nod and smile in the right places, and wonder if the pan was salvageable.

"Well, I guess that's it!" She put her glass on the table. "Until next time."

She disappeared with a sort of frying sound – a sizzle – releasing the stray molecules she used when she wanted to manifest a physical body. Brooklyn got up to clean the greasy-soot-ash powder she left behind on the chair. It went into the trash with the wasted flour and, after a little consideration, the pan.

Float came in. She lived on the other side of the hanger in her own cordoned-off apartment. Wasn't much in there but a TV and a big fish tank, but she called it home. "Yarrow messaged. Said she's ready for a pickup."

Brooklyn grunted. The usual go-to-Venus checklist flickered in his mind, in the middle of which was a note to bribe the support group's facilitator to keep reporting him as present. "We'll head up in a couple of days."

The old ship rocked, the forces of re-entry buffeting and scorching. Most of the tell-tale lights on the control surfaces blinked to yellow. Too many stayed that way. Brooklyn tapped one of the more important ones, and it flickered reluctantly back to green. If only he could do the same for himself. *Fifteen words. Fifteen fucking words that change everything.*

Overhead, a conifer-shaped air freshener danced on the end of a string and lost ground to hot circuits, baked dust, and the salty, clam-flat miasma of the copilot's breath.

"You check the thing?" Brooklyn said.

"Did." The copilot was wearing a bulky exosuit. Inside it, her mouth, arms, and tentacles moved languidly through a chilly, fishy brine that mimicked her natural environment.

"You check it, check it, or just look at the lights?"

"Jelly Tech doesn't break."

Do you know anythin' 'bout this?

About the message? No, the Purple Lady said in his head. **Perhaps you should focus on landing**.

It was hard to stay in the moment long enough to worry about that. Two decades living under a sword, millions dead, millions more displaced, billions terrified. The First Cathedral of the Cosmos still loomed over the planet. Barely functional scavenger ships labored daily to sweep human garbage from orbital space. The latest fleet of evacuation ships was being stitched together near *Eisenhower Station*…

The landing, Brook.

Okay. Okay.

"Split a piece of cake?" Brooklyn said. "I'd say we could go back to my place for a nightcap, but just remembered I don't have a place."

Carmen sighed. "I should get back to New York. We have a new dog. Rosa. Steve's good with her, but I'm better."

"I bet." Brooklyn swirled melting ice in the bottom of his glass.

"Never figured you for a spaceman, Brook, but it suits you." She smiled. "You've grown up."

Does she miss me? Want to sleep with me? Is she giving me a signal?

The Purple Lady peered at him over Carmen's shoulder. A mental projection, visible only to him. She hadn't bothered with a body. **She doesn't miss you. It's just nostalgia. She's not interested in sleeping with you.**

It's the eyes. A woman's compassion could look a lot like love to the hopeful and stupid. Brooklyn was no longer one of those. "Still twenty-eight."

"On the outside, maybe, but you were always sort of an old soul."

"Crossed with a toddler."

"Yeah."

I remembered what I was going to tell you, the Purple Lady said. **Your Sun is going to explode.**

The first time she'd delivered that particular warning he'd been concerned. The sixth or eleventh, not so much. She saw sideways sometimes, backward and forward, and counted in eons. *All right, thanks.*

"You ready to settle down with me, Lamontagne?" Evelyn grinned.

I like her. The Purple Lady looked like Tina Turner in the fringed "Proud Mary" dress. She was ready to dance on stage next to Eddie. **She's good for you**.

So's a salad. Not sure it's whadayacallit... mutual. Brooklyn leaned against a lamppost and looked at Evelyn's left shoulder "Not too good at stayin' in one place," he told it. "It gets... I don't know. Stay someplace long enough, people think they know you. Hold up this idea of what you are an' you gotta live up to it. It's complicated."

Evelyn pulled her jacket collar up around her neck. "Not a big fan of complicated."

"Don't blame you."

"Not a fan of how much you drink, either. More you drink, more I drink, and I don't want to go back there."

She's worried about getting hurt.

She should be.

"Not sure I'm ready to leave," Evelyn continued. "I can still see Earth from here, you know? All my shit is there."

"Gotta a lot of shit there myself."

Most of the adhoc buildings bore a mural or two, and Brooklyn stopped to deface one of the new ones. A purple woman, framed in a "holy" light and stars, a cosmic Madonna. It had been inspired by the one he'd drawn in the *Victory*'s cockpit in the days before his third death twenty years before. His rescuers – neighbors and friends from

Mexico – had taken a picture of the image and brought it to Venus after their lucrative press tour. The drawing and the rescuers' story, Brooklyn's Lazarus-like return, had taken on a life of its own. A church was born, and, for a time, parishioners had sought Brooklyn out to bless babies and weddings. Surliness had put an end to the petitions, but the weird little faith had refused to die. *Bet you think that's pretty damned funny.*

I miss seeing the babies and the happiness at weddings. Both are so fleeting. She paused. **This mural is the best so far. You should leave it.**

Fine. But if that holy roller shit starts up again…

It won't. There's not time.

"I'll throw you a goin'–"

"I'm leaving today. In just a few hours. To the Belt first, then outward."

She loves you. She was in the tank with Float. A purple mermaid. **And she doesn't understand it. The feeling is very different from the ones she has for her school.**

"I'd give you a goodbye hug bu–"

"It would probably kill you again." Her tentacles swayed gently. "Thank you for finding me in the desert."

It's been fun.

She'll miss you, too.

A shadow seemed to pass over the bones on the table, making it look they were covered in gray, leathery skin, a visor of cartilage jutting out over the wide-spread eyes to shade them from the sun. Brooklyn shuddered. *Humid heat, a slack mouth flapping in a place that smelled like mildew.*

That's how I remember them, she said. **I think I liked them at first.** She laughed. **I liked the First… at first.**

He'd drunk too much mushroom tea, maybe. Let himself get drawn a little too far into the purple space. "Think I need to lie down." He swayed. "Feeling a little funky."

"We can go back to my tent," Professor Yarrow said. "Likely you just need some water."

Brooklyn forced his hands open again.

How many times? he'd asked Demarco.

Six or seven I know about.

What did I do?

Only know for sure about one time, and I can't say about that.

The Purple Lady was poking at the disassembled computer on the table. **Do you think Float knew?**

She woulda said something. The Jellies were brutally honest with each other and with friends. Brooklyn brewed a pot of strong tea, the professor's so-called warrior blend. Focus, sharpness, and just a little lens flare. Perfect for fine work. No booze, no booze for a long, long time.

He knows about me. A little. He knows you talk to someone.

Did you know?

I don't think so. I'm not with you every minute. Mostly when you're–"

Fucked up. Yeah.

He'd barely punched the "enter" key when the answers came back. The Jelly navigational software was beyond anything humans had, and its precision would save time and fuel with every trip. His fingers, healing from solder-iron burns and stained with flux, ran through his hair.

You should sleep. She looked like someone's ma again. A cosmic caregiver.

Might be time for a nap. It's been… days, I think.

Longer for your mind. You've been half in, half out as you worked. The tea.

"The tea." He glanced at the empty pot.

A series of numbers appeared on the screen. A basic equation, Intro to Algebra, at best. Brooklyn entered the answer, and a new one appeared, slightly more difficult. *You're not s'posed to do that.*

Her eyes narrowed. **This is something new. It feels like,** she held her hand near his chest, **this.**

"You gonna be okay, man?"

"First time I killed someone."

"Well–" Demarco paused. "Prob'ly not the time fo' that."

Brooklyn slurred something that could have been taken as "fuck off and let me sleep", and Demarco went to his own bed, missing the tears that filled Brooklyn's eyes and ran across his cheeks into his hair.

She sat beside him and stroked his forehead. **I'm sorry, Brook.**

Sorry for me or them?

Both, of course.

"Brook, we got a problem. Om's having a… a fit… or something," Demarco said. "It won't fly the ship to the rendezvous."

"We'll come to you." He pointed the way he had come. "Beth, head that way. Listen for instructions." He traded weapons with Andy and urged her to follow Beth. "Demarco, Beth is on the way, and she's ears for Andy. Keep 'em on track."

Let them help you. She was wearing a purple vacsuit, old-style, like something from an '50s sci-fi show. **Stop fighting them.**

Okay. Brooklyn bent his knees and pushed off hard. He gave his emergency thrusters a goose, gaining more speed and altitude, and spun in space to point his rifle back the way they'd come. Eight– no, nine exos aimed their weapons his way. *This is going to suck.* Every shot would change his velocity and alter his course. He took aim and fired anyway, absorbing the recoil the best he could and letting his reflexes and nanobots handle the shooting.

Below him, Andy raised the plasma blaster and twisted to fire. The blaster had far less range than the rifle, but what it lost in usefulness it made up for with a distracting light show. Brooklyn's suit flared with alarms. Oxygen leak, decompression warning, plumbing and electrical malfunction. "Think I'm hit!"

Sky, Mars, ground, sky, Mars, ground. He was tumbling. Flashes of light in his eyes that almost looked like numbers and letters. *Fire thrusters in…*

Trust them.

Brooklyn, it's time to–

THIRTY-THREE

The worst part of being conscious was the removal of the breathing tube. *Nope, this is the worst part.* His whole body felt like a bad tooth that some asshole was flooding with ice-cold water.

Brooklyn gasped. His eyes flickered open and found Milk's face.

"Do you know where you are?" she said. "Do you know who you are?"

He sniffed. Ozone and gunpowder. The smell of space. "I die again?"

"In my trauma ward? Hell no." She smiled. "Getting you off Deimos was kind of hairy, though. Lot of things happening at once. You've been out for about twelve hours."

"I get some water?"

Brooklyn wiggled his fingers and toes while she filled the request. All the parts checked in. "Everybody make it?"

"Present and accounted for. Andy, you, and an angry redhead with no clothes to her name."

"Her name's Beth." The memory came easily. *Guess I really did live through this one.*

Milk held a tumbler of water while he sipped from it. "Andy took a graze running across Deimos naked, but she's fine."

"How bad was I?"

"Hypoxia, frostbite, broken ribs and left collarbone.

Fractured left wrist. Internal injuries. The usual things that befall someone who loses vacsuit integrity and crashes into a moon at fifty or sixty miles an hour. You hold true to form, should be healed up by tomorrow."

"Where we headed?"

"Earth. We need to get Andy's source out."

"Guessing Om unfroze an' came got us?"

"Not hardly. Andy and Beth dragged your ass back, chased by exos the whole way. Nearly two hours on the surface. Luckily, you've learned a new trick. That carcass of yours can hibernate when there's nothing to breathe."

"Hibernate? Like a bear?"

"Your respiration shut down, and your heart slowed to near nothing."

He grunted. "The fuck happened to Om?"

"Freaked out and froze. It's very apologetic but says it can no longer take part in anything that requires 'direct action'. Says the outcomes are too unpredictable."

"Shit." He rubbed his eyes with his better hand. "It was talking about predictability before we left. Shoulda listened better."

"Story of your life." She jabbed a finger into his chest. "Andy flew us out. Your mission is to shut up and get better. Sleep. Let that body of yours do its thing. Painkillers?"

"Don't have to ask me twice. Load me up. I'm no fucking hero."

Milk did something with the tube connected to his arm, and the room got sludgy and warm. The pain ebbed. *Yep, no hero here.*

THIRTY-FOUR

Andy's skin was blotchy and bruised – dark patches of green on green – from prolonged exposure to the Deimos vacuum. The whites of her eyes were orange from burst blood vessels, and, sometime in the past twenty years, she'd grown her hair out. Julie Andrews in *10* instead of *The Sound of Music.*

'You changed your hair' prob'ly a stupid place to start. "Been–" Brooklyn's throat was irritated, and it made him cough. *So much for smooth.* "Been a while."

"Milk only just said you could have visitors."

"You know what I mean." He struggled to a more comfortable position. The bunkroom hadn't been designed as a trauma ward, and sitting up required every pillow in the room plus a haversack filled with spare clothes.

Andy sat on the bunk opposite. "Last time I was here, the computer was all punched cards and duct tape."

"Just keeping up with the times. Surprised everyone doesn't have a super-smart robot copilot by now."

"The First had them millennia ago but replaced them with biological intelligences. They believed they would be easier to control."

"Guess you showed them. Last I remember, you were First all the way."

"Crisis led to conversation led to conspiracy. One day, the others started looking to me for direction." Andy released tension in a long exhale. "There was no plan beyond the moment."

"No Plan Beyond the Moment." He smirked. "Title of my biography."

The corner of her mouth turned up. "I met your mother. I liked her."

"She said you looked like the Jolly Green Giant's regular-sized daughter."

"I told her I didn't know if you'd make it back."

"She said that, too." His hands clenched among the bedding. "Hopin' you can tell me how that happened."

"First Tech." She poured him some water. "Inside your body are millions of miniscule, networked machines. The First used similar to engineer the various Designed models, and all of us have leftovers – dormant – from the process within our bodies. Yours are active and evolving."

"Guy who put them in me, Carruthers, was what? A splinter?"

"The technology was forbidden for use on Earth and its inhabitants." She pushed her hair off her forehead. "I don't know how he could have gotten active samples, much less repurposed them."

"Any idea how long they're gonna last?"

"They're symbiotic. They keep you alive. You supply them with fuel and an organizing principle." She leaned forward. "Milk says they've enhanced you as well as healing you."

He offered his best, held-up-by-pillows shrug. "Stronger, faster. I see better. Smell better. Hearing. There's, like, a fight mode I get in sometimes, but I don't like it." He remembered the countdown. "Think the little guys tried to give me, like, a heads-up display when everything was happening down there."

"None of that should be happening."

"Yeah, well, maybe I'm just nuts." He rubbed his eyes. "Wouldn't surprise me a fucking bit."

"'Fuck' as an adjective. I wonder if it would have worked better in that statement as an adverb."

"You're welcome. Seem to remember spendin' about fifty fuckin' hours fuckin' around with you 'bout that fuckin' word." His eyes narrowed. "I remember some stuff after that. The start of the save-the-day project… Most of it's gone. There ain't even any blank spots where it feels like something should be."

"The First wouldn't let me come back for you," she said. "I-I allowed them– Asked them to be reconnect me when we intercepted the ambassador's ship. I was happy to do it." Her hand rose to her forehead again and touched the circlet she was wearing. It was thinner and crueler than the ones the Angels were distributing in De Milo. It was embedded in Andy's skin, leaving fine scars. "This severed the link again and prevents it from being restored. By the time I got it–"

"A lot of shit had happened," he said. "You were busy savin' the day."

"I failed."

"Eight times outta ten, that's the result." He hummed. "Just made that up. But it seems about right. How long you and Beth been…?"

"We only recently became lovers. She was captured and jailed with me to secure my good behavior, but I suspect she works for the CIA."

"Give you someone to care about, and put you somewheres you can't bust out without killing her. Good play. Might-a gotten away on your own otherwise."

"I had a plan to get into the hub, but I doubt I could have held out until rescue arrived."

"They'da just blown up the place. It was all wired."

"I'm surprised they didn't pull the trigger as soon as you made your move. I suspect we got very lucky."

"That's the second half of my biography." He stretched for the water on the bedside stand, but Andy beat him to it and put it in his hand. He drank some. "You and me... The way Milk and Demarco have been tiptoeing around it for the past twenty years. Were we in love?"

"Love is mostly brain chemistry and hormone secretions. Who's to say my version of love is the same chemical cocktail as a human's?"

"Sure. Makes sense. But were we?"

She seemed to find her knees very interesting for the next dozen seconds or so. "We might have been. Or getting there. I grieved when I believed you were gone, but so much else was happening." Her hand floated back to the metal circlet. "I'm still amazed we rebelled. Me, two builders, three other ambassadors. We weren't made for it. We spent years after we left learning how to be more than tools and helping others escape."

"You hung 'round humans too long. Rubs off on ya."

"Not every human is a good example to follow. I've worked with the CIA, remember."

"Worse, you hung out with me." He smothered a cough. "Milk tol' you 'bout my brain problems. If I'd remembered you better, would you have contacted me?" He held up his hand to forestall an answer. "I ain't a big believer in soul mates an' cosmic love stories. Ain't no meant-to-be's or *Doctor Zhivago* shit in real life. Jus' people doin' what they can."

"Knowing you didn't remember made it easier not to come," she said, "and for most of the time, I didn't have the energy or attention to spare."

He fell silent, collating everything. "Last awkward question. Did it really happen the way they say it did? Dee and Claire said I sacrificed myself so you could get to Earth before the rock," he shook his head, "an' I just don't see myself doing that, ya know? I mean, c'mon, me?"

"Brook," she smiled, "it didn't surprise me a bit."

He studied her eyes. "One of the last things I remember 'bout that time was me tellin' you not to poke me with your big green dick.” He sucked his teeth. “I think only one-a us is lying right now.”

“I poked you anyway.”

“Turned out I didn’t mind so much after all.”

THIRTY-FIVE

That night, Om walked its exosuit body out the airlock during the graveyard shift, when it was the only thing awake on the ship. When he heard the news, Brooklyn snuck out of the sickroom and took his morning tea to the cockpit to talk.

"Thought you liked having hands, man. Made it so you could protect yourself."

"Defending myself against attack has too many possible outcomes. I could harm the ship or one of you. I could kill my assailant. I have a full list if you would like to hear it."

"Nah, that's good." Brooklyn sipped his tea.

"I regret I was unable to help with your mission."

"We put too much on you too quick. Demarco agrees. Easy to forget you're really just a kid."

"I see the paradox I created by my lack of action. By not flying the ship, I created the very unpredictability I was trying to avoid."

Brooklyn grunted. *Seeing and understanding are two different things*. "Let's not go too far into that. It all worked out."

"You were badly injured."

"Got hurt *before* the thing we asked – the thing we told you to do – woulda come up. All you did was make Andy run around naked on the moon carrying me, which I would pay money to have footage of."

"I would understand if you chose to deactivate me."

"Not gonna happen, pal." He pulled at his bottom lip. "Can you still navigate for me?"

"Yes. The math is simple, the paths predictable." It hesitated. "But I can no longer take direct action or be involved in a plan that may require me to act."

"All right." He gathered his thoughts. "First thing I need you to do is give us a course to Earth, best time. Then I need your help, jus' a little programming, with a simulation I been thinkin' about."

The afternoon war council was fueled by hot tea and a buffet of smoked meats and cheeses.

"Our Alien Overlords were never here in the flesh, so how you and yours so sure they gone?" Demarco tapped his forehead. "Especially with that crown you got on."

"We have agents too. Designed who chose not to sever the link with their patron." Andy's mouth firmed. "It was dangerous work. As little as humans are to the First, the Designed are less. Humans, at least, they recognize as autonomous beings."

"Pretty damned expendable beings," Demarco said. "Told me yourself they barely had enough nay votes to keep from wiping us out."

"But they took the vote. If it came to making a similar move on the Designed, there would be no argument. We are their creatures."

Be like throwing away a defective hammer. The First had created Andy and the other Designed from the genes up, using both human and alien DNA, to be the perfect tool for the tasks allotted. The Designed builder caste – the Trolls – often worked in the vacuum, so they were made without voices and used a hand language to communicate. Andy and the other ambassadors were built to interact with humans and made just alien enough to piqué interest without engendering fear.

"The Designed can't reproduce naturally." Milk picked up her tea. "Of all the things the First has done, I think that's the cruelest. You were created with no hope of a future."

"That's less a problem than you might think," Andy said. "We may not be able to have offspring unassisted, but could do so with the technology on the Artiplanet."

Milk nodded. "Does the American government know the First is gone? Is that why they took you?"

"Some part knows. My jailers made no secret of their knowledge. I believe I was taken to prevent me from finding out more."

Beth avoided Andy's eyes. Poor spy craft, but maybe there had been real feelings involved.

"Not a peep in the press." Demarco folded his arms. "Angels put Pat Buchanan in the White House. If he's in the know, I can see him working pretty hard to keep it quiet."

"The First cast a long shadow to work in," Beth said.

"You mean they provided cover and justification for a lot of evil shit," Brooklyn said. "An' the assholes in charge can keep pushing people they don't like off planet as long as they pretend they still have it."

Demarco steepled his fingers at Beth. "You a spook. CIA. Yo people put Andy in stir and put you in there with her to keep her sweet."

"My assignment was to get close to the ambassador and stay there," she said. "I was out of the loop on everything else. Honestly. At this point, I'd tell you if I knew anything."

"I believe her," Andy said. "She was legitimately surprised when I told her the First were gone."

"We have to let everyone know it's over," Milk said. "Tell them the bogeyman's gone and the kids are running the haunted house."

"Bogeyman being gone might make things more dangerous," Brooklyn mused. "Killin' all Big Tony's guys, the 'enhanced emigration protocols', feels like panic moves, ass covering. The

First might be gone, but they left a lot of shit behind, and the kids know how to use it."

"An' I still wanna know why it's over before I start crowing." Demarco sucked his teeth. "None of this is sittin' right. OAO put more'n a century into coming back; can't see 'em cuttin' out this quick without a real reason."

"The defector should have what we need." Andy said. "He's a scientist. Works with the Angels, reports directly to the Cardinal."

"How the hell we s'posed to get him out of the Cathedral?" Brooklyn said.

"Andy's green and infamous. I'm old." Demarco leaned back in his chair. "Om just tossed away a perfectly good robot body, and I ain't ready to trust Beth." He smiled lazily. "Brook, looks like you Jilly are goin' to church."

THIRTY-SIX

The options presented by Brooklyn's simulation were igneous, sedimentary, and metamorphic. Om chose igneous. In the next menu it chose 'granite'. It was its second play-through as granite, but in the earlier run, it had chosen to be Moon rock

Brooklyn's coding had been creative but limited. Om rewrote it, careful to leave his cut-out in place. It would immediately pause the simulation if Om was needed for navigation.

Om had added graphics to the simulation so it could see how it looked as a stone. This early in the game, though, and likely for several million simulated years ahead, there was no light to see with.

Magma flowed and cooled deep under the Earth. Rock formed. Om gathered data on stresses and microfractures, temperature and moisture. An ice age passed, and it switched to third-person POV to see if it were visible yet. It was not.

Tectonic plates moved and buckled. The shockwave from a meteor impact on the other side of the planet rippled through the earth. Microfractures, temperature, moisture. Veins of uranium and thorium in the rock decayed, and Om tasted each particle. Another ice age. When it was over, some of the ground above Om had been scraped free. Sunlight and rain, erosion, and frost were added to the variables. Every day was different. Every day was the same.

The simulation ran its course, and Om opted for 'sedimentary' next. Shale on Mars, forming slowly out of minerals and mica carried past in ancient rivers and streams. It grew. Stress and microfractures, temperature and moisture. Cosmic and solar radiation sterilized the planet's surface. Dust flew, the water evaporated. Growth stopped. Erosion slowed to a crawl. Three-point-five billion years passed. Meteors fell other places. Apocalypses small and large, but none fell near Om.

The simulation ended, and Om brought up the menu again. There were many combinations it hadn't tried yet. Basaltic rock on Venus, for example. Ice magma on Pluto. Ejecta on Mercury. Lifeless rocks all. Om hadn't programmed the simulation to include the impact of biologicals – flint gathered and chipped away to make tools or fire, granite cut for countertops and courthouses – but it could.

Next time around, maybe. A rock didn't have to do anything but be a rock. A relief. Om chose igneous again.

PART TWELVE
Thieves in the Temple

THIRTY-SEVEN

The Cathedral of the Cosmos hung in a geostationary orbit over the Earth's North Pole, suggesting, depending on the observer's attitude, either a local franchise of heaven or a crystalline spider.

Either way, good PR. Brooklyn shifted in the middle seat, sixth row of the shuttle. He was trapped between a tract-reading middle American on the aisle, and Milk playing true-believer on the window.

The new camouflage system he'd installed in the *Victory* had done its work, and the ship and its ad hoc crew were enjoying some downtime at his place in New Mexico, awaiting word from the extraction team. Brooklyn glanced at Milk, her features barely visible under the layer of Holy First-brand golden makeup she'd applied to her face.

A short documentary repeating on the bus's overhead screens showcased the First's destruction of a deadly meteorite headed for Manhattan back in the '70s, the cure for AIDs in the early '80s, the clean-air and clean-water efforts of the past twenty years, all the free advanced technology they'd offered, and the better home and new start awaiting humanity on Venus. It ended with a popular human scientist talking about his theory that the human genome might owe its very existence to a First seeding experiment millions of years before.

The seatbelt warning flipped on, and anyone not already

in a seat moved away from the Earth-view windows to strap back in. A pair of Angels were on hand to help. Six feet tall and androgynous with brushed-gold skin and long white hair, their wings made it easy to move about in micro-gravity. The two on the bus wore simple white tunics denoting their rank.

"What's with all the scaffolding?" Milk said.

"Can't see it."

Milk squeezed back in her seat so Brooklyn could lean over and peer out the window. The Cathedral was covered in a web of temporary supports and structures, the little flight pods the Builders used darting in and out.

He grunted. "Least we know where the Trolls went. No idea what they're doin' though."

The bill of his baseball cap had hit the window when he leaned in and knocked the cap askew. Brooklyn adjusted it. He wasn't the only one who'd donned a "First Coming" cap for the trip, but he mighta been the only one faking it. The Cardinal had worked hard to rebrand the First occupation as a religious crusade over the past decade or so, intimating that a move to Venus or Mars would be a great way to escape the Antichrist, who was due sometime in the early 2000s. Several thousand tour buses ran up to the temple each week for sightseeing and sermons (religious travel was so far exempt from 'enhanced emigration protocols'), and many passengers wore the golden face paint that announced a true believer.

The tour bus sailed through the First field protecting the hanger from vacuum and parked alongside the dozens of others already in place. Brooklyn pulled his cap down low and followed the other passengers out.

"Freaky," Milk said.

Brooklyn had hodged together a semblance of artificial gravity aboard the *Victory* using First and Jelly technology, but the Cathedral had the real thing. It was like stepping onto the surface of a planet. Brooklyn bounced on his heels a bit to try to measure it. *Venus-level.* He took a deep breath. There was a little too much oxygen in the air, giving every human aboard an energy and euphoria boost. He sniffed again. *Maybe a dash of nitrous, too.*

"Don't breathe too deep," he said.

"Not a problem." The doctor was already wheezing a little from the short walk from the bus. She wasn't the only one. The Cathedral had been designed to take visitors' breath away, a vast transparent overhead dome providing a 360-degree view of the majesty of the stars. The little procession moved slowly, most of the walkers clutching at the rail as they went, fearing if they let go, they might fly into space.

The Angels led their flock away from the buses and into an interactive museum of First history, complete with artifacts from De Milo and a movie that showed a simulation of life on the surface of Venus as it had been long ago. A nice combination of fact and fiction, science and fantasy. There was even a life-sized exhibit of a First home populated by human mannequins and another video suggesting that genetic connection.

There was a lot of oohing and ahing going on. Hidden speakers piped in infrasound – bass notes so low humans couldn't hear them – that induced a shivers-down-the-spine feeling. Brooklyn was fairly confident in Milk's ability to resist, but he was pretty sure more of the tour group would be wearing golden makeup, available in the gift shop, by the time they left.

Stenciled on the wall was a line from the Christian Bible, the one about Ezekiel and the sky wheel he spotted.

There ya go. Proof. Brooklyn shoved his hands in his pockets and tried to look interested.

When the group lined up for the Cardinal's sermon, Brooklyn patted Milk's arm and slipped into the closest bathroom. He settled into a stall to wait, sipping from his flask and studying the map Andy had installed on his pocket-sized Martian flatscreen.

The button comm in his ear clicked twice, Milk's signal that the sermon had started. Brooklyn left the stall and peered out the bathroom door.

Two Angels were waiting for him outside. Their tunics were red. Security.

"You here to help me find my group?" Brooklyn said.

"You will follow us," the golden face on the right said.

"Where we goin'?"

The left-hand Angel took a turn at the intimidation game. "You will follow us." Their hand floated to the baton on its hip.

"We recognized you as you arrived, of course." The Archbishop's office was lavish, with gold-trim everywhere in spite of the Cardinal's rule that all existing supplies of the metal should go into circuitry for the evacuation ships. The desk, upon which was Brooklyn's flask, watch, multitool, button comm, and pocket flatscreen, was made of some kind of dark wood.

Probably tell people it's from Noah's ark. It was too high to put his feet on, or he would have. "Hell didn't you come down and say 'hello'? Never really talked to one o' you two-point-ohs."

"We were curious what you would do." The Archbishop's fingers were tented on the desk. "It was remotely possible you were truly interested in conversion."

Brooklyn scoffed. "Nothin' to convert to anymore. Your bosses skipped town months ago."

"I have no idea what you're talking about."

"That so?" Brooklyn covered a fake yawn. "When's the last time you heard from them?"

"The Divine First have many interests. They cannot be expected to focus on any one of them for long."

"That's right." Brooklyn really wanted to put his feet on the desk. It would have projected just the right amount of insolence. "They got so much goin' on they never actually came back here, did they?" He smirked. "Only skin they got in the game is yours. Now that they're gone, what's your play?"

"The Divine will return once we have made their planet suitable," the Archbishop said. "Free of humanity and its leavings."

"Sure." He leaned back as far as the chair would allow. "Cardinal pulled those new emigration protocols out o' their holy ass hoping it would make Mom and Dad love them again."

"The Divine's love is–"

"Or maybe it was a show of power. Keep us thinking the First was still in town so you cats could stay in charge."

"I don't need the Cardinal's counsel to know what to do with you, Mr Lamontagne." The Angel pushed a button on the desk. "Security, please."

There was a muffled response.

"Why'd the First leave, anyway? Found a new planet to fuck over?"

"I have no interest in speaking further with a sinner and criminal."

"Criminal?" Brooklyn said. "I just came for the tour."

It was Archbishop's turn to smirk. "As you've noticed, things have changed. You are guilty of returning to Earth after emigration. That would have earned you a simple deportation before the new protocols, but now I can treat myself to something more final."

The office door slid open, and the red-clad Angels came back in.

"You also are a known associate of the so-called Designed Liberation Front. You should have kept your head down, Mr Lamontagne. Stayed quiet and rode it all out." The Archbishop smiled. The Angels pulled the stun batons off their belts and shook them awake.

That ain't good. Go, tiny robots! Go!

Brooklyn scissored forward to grab for his possessions on the desk and pushed off from the heavy piece of furniture like the gravity was nil and the action might actually get him somewhere.

It worked better than he'd hoped. He and the chair toppled backward, forcing the Angels to dance their feet and shins clear. He rolled and landed in a crouch brandishing his folded multitool at them. The little robots sped up his reaction time and processing speed enough to let him know how fucked he was. He knew a few moves but was not a skilled hand-to-hand combatant. Both Andy and Top had kicked his ass anytime he'd sparred with them, and the security Angels weren't likely to be slouches, either. He rolled backward again, out the door the Angels had entered, scrambled to his feet, and ran like hell.

He shoved the comm back in his ear. "So far so good," he sent. "Reckon I'll need to get creative for a ride down."

The flatscreen with the map was still on the Archbishop's desk, but Brooklyn knew the general direction he needed to go. He dashed though a cross hallway, barely avoiding two groups of red-clad Angels trying to nab him in a coordinated squeeze play.

A security door was closing to the right. Brooklyn dropped and slid under the thing, clipping the top of his head a good one in the process. He rubbed at the pain through his baseball cap as he surveyed the space beyond.

Lab or sickroom. Do Angels get sick? Call it a lab. Don't remember a lab on the fucking map.

He was already lost.

The pursuers would have the security door open in minutes or less. Three other doors led from the space, and getting each open would take time. He felt the little robots damping down his panic. At least his hands wouldn't shake as the Angels beat him to a pulp.

The Purple Lady had urged him to trust the little machines.

He sighed. "Which way?"

A green dot swam up his retina and superimposed itself over the leftmost door.

Here goes stupid.

THIRTY-EIGHT

Twenty minutes later, on the opposite side of the Cathedral, Brooklyn opened a door onto a small office, with an alien working at a desk. Its skin was gray like the Builders, but its body was spindly, a bulbous head topping a thin neck. Its eyes were large and liquid.

"I told you my analysis wouldn't be–" The creature looked up from his work. "Who are you?"

Brooklyn closed the door behind him. "This lock?" He leaned up against it. "Don't s'pose you got a secret tunnel to a fast ship 'round here?"

"Did you lose your tour group, human?" His face twisted like he'd smelled something bad, his eyes on the 'First Coming' cap. "I can summon one of the Devoted Dolts to bring you back."

"Think I'm here to get you out for the DLF." He tossed the cap on the desk. "You don't look like any of the other Designed I've seen."

"I am a Scientist." He folded his arms. "Pie-eyed optimist."

"What?"

"Pie. Eyed. Optimist."

Brooklyn rubbed his face. "That a code phrase? Don't remember Andy say–"

"Of course it's a code phrase! You are supposed to answer it and extract me to safety in return for my data on the Sun."

"What's wrong with the Sun?"

The Designed tensed. "Is this a test?"

"Sure. First question: got any idea how to get the fuck outta here?"

"That is your job. If I could have escaped on my own, I'd–"

A whooping alarm sounded through the overhead speakers. "Wondered if they had those," Brooklyn said. "More efficient than lettin' everyone know by radio."

"It's the fire alarm." The Designed stood. "We are supposed to go to the hanger bay for evacuation."

Brooklyn's button comm clicked. "That was me," Milk sent. "The Angels were looking a little too organized for my taste. Figured I'd create a little chaos."

"Many thanks!" Brooklyn ended the call and turned to the defector. "Main hanger is that way, right?" He pointed.

The Scientist nodded.

"We're goin' opposite."

"Where is your ship?" the Designed said. He'd pulled a data crystal out of the computer on his desk and had it in a death grip.

Brooklyn was attempting to hustle the guy along while simultaneously hiding behind him. "Took the bus."

The hallway was thinning out, many of the Cathedral's occupants already passed and headed to the hanger bay like good little doobies. "This is outrageous!" the defector said. "If I thought for a moment the DLF was this unprofessional–"

"Probably just me." Brooklyn flagged down a pair of Builders. He knew just about enough of their complicated hand language for what he needed. "Are you from De Milo?"

They were.

"Saw scaffolding. What is being built?"

Improvements to the Cathedral's propulsion systems, life support, and… something he didn't understand. The Builders liked to put on plays about maintenance and technical problems, and he'd seen enough of them to know that some things just didn't translate.

"Additional question: How can we get off Cathedral?" He pointed. "This direction."

Brooklyn and the scientist followed the Builders' instructions: two lefts and an elevator down into the living section. Brooklyn squinted at a sign. "That say what I think it does?" His tiny robots were projecting letters on his retinas that spelled out, "Freedom Stone."

"Escape capsule." The Designed turned even grayer. "I don't want to go to Earth! This was not what we agreed."

"Is now." He tapped the button comm in his ear. "Got the package an' a way out. Get clear."

Milk mumbled something about the "fucking fire drill" and closed the channel.

Brooklyn followed the arrow to a round hatch and popped it open. "Not much room. Get in there while I try to disable the alarm." He pulled the multi-tool out of his pocket and flipped open the smallest blade. The scientist was still standing there. Brooklyn took his arm and pushed him toward the hatch. "Go! Leave without me, I'll track you down and tie your legs in knots."

He pried open a small panel and scraped away at the printed circuits inside. *Think this is right.* Sabotage complete, he slid into the escape pod beside the scientist. "Cozy." The hatch closed above them as he slapped the launch button, and the pod shot down a short tunnel and emerged in space. Without much apparent concern for the comfort of its occupants, it orientated itself to the planet below and fired its main engine.

Brooklyn tensed his muscles against the gee forces as his little robots offered frightening and largely useless information via his new heads-up display. "Hang on!"

* * *

The escape capsule dug about a hundred yards of trench when it hit the ice. The First field that had protected it held integrity until the capsule stopped moving, then flickered out.

"There ya go." Brooklyn groaned. "You been extracted."

Their faces were inches apart, and the defector looked sour. "Emergency capsules are not supposed to crash. You must have broken something in your attempt at sabotage."

Brooklyn shifted to look through the small window beside him, accidentally-on-purpose digging his elbow into the scientist's ribs. "It's snowing."

"It's the Arctic. What did you expect, fool?!"

"Some gratitude, maybe?" he said. "Case you forgot, I got you away from the holy rollers up there."

The Designed jabbed his finger into Brooklyn's chest. "I will have words with your superior! You are insolent, unprofessional–!"

"All o' that an' more." Brooklyn struggled his multi-tool out of his hip pocket. "Gotta name?"

He sneered. "My name would be unpronounceable to your kind!"

"Call you Douche then? Okay, Douche, here's what I'm thinking." He tapped the screwdriver blade on the control panel. "Battery shouldna run down so quick, so there's gotta be a short somewhere. Follow?"

"Of course."

"No power means no recovery signal, so once the Angels figure out how we left, they won't know where we landed. And it's snowing, so pretty soon, we'll be hid in here pretty good.

"I'm gonna pop the top of this pod, an' you're gonna get out ta give me room to work. Try to rig the heat so we don't freeze our asses off while we wait."

"Wait for what?"

"Mom to come pick us up."

THIRTY-NNE

Designed ambassadors could easily spend more than an hour working in a vacuum without serious discomfort, so the Arctic would not have posed little difficulty. Either Designed scientists were constructed without that feature, or Douche was a whiner. He complained loudly until Brooklyn pulled the emergency environmental suit out from behind the seat and threw it at him. "Put it on!"

The seat soon followed, tossed into the snow to make more room for two people inside an emergency capsule built for one. Brooklyn wired the heating systems directly into the battery to bypass the short he must have created dicking around with the security system.

"Any food must be shared," the scientist said. "It is the law of the castaway."

"There's a box of rations inside the pod."

They climbed back in and sealed the hatch. The heater brought the internal temperature up to a cozy fifty degrees. "Sleep, or at least shut up," Brooklyn said. "We'll be here a while."

The total was eight hours. Milk's flight back to New Mexico had been slowed by the Angels' response to Brooklyn's incursion and the fire alarm. The *Victory* landed within a quarter mile of the escape capsule, and Brooklyn hustle-dragged the recalcitrant scientist aboard and made him strip, shower, and put on a pair of coveralls. The Designed's belongings, other than the data crystal he still refused to release, were left behind in the snow when the ship took off again.

"Are we clear for the Moon?" Andy said via intercom.

Brooklyn slapped the switch to answer. "Go and don't spare the fuel. There's more where that came from."

Milk emerged from the kitchen and presented Brooklyn with a 'First Coming' T-shirt. She had a souvenir baseball cap of her own now, courtesy of her trip through the gift shop, and she'd purchased sweatshirts for Andy, Beth, and Demarco. "I got you a set of mugs, too. Tossed a bunch of that shit you were using."

"I liked my mugs!"

"I saved the 'My Favorite Son' one. The rest of them were dangerous," she said. "Not all of us can quick heal from sliced lips."

Andy came back on the intercom. "I would find somewhere to sit. I'm about to push the pedal to the floor, and I don't want anyone getting hurt. Two minutes!"

The *Victory* circled twice before landing in a small valley on the so-called dark side of the Moon. Brooklyn and Float had dug a cave by hand, built a base inside, and moved everything they needed out of the EOF depot they'd "discovered" nearby. Food, water, furniture, a portable reactor… Best of all were the pallets of fuel milled for Type 3 Oppenheimers. The stuff was nearly impossible to find anywhere else. Brooklyn reactivated the base's various systems while the others stowed their gear and spread out.

He called the place his Gas Station. "Used to have an orbital," he said, showing the others around inside. "Old NASA project called SkyLab. They were gonna let it fall into the atmosphere an' burn up, but I grabbed it and moved it into a higher orbit.

It got raided one time while we were in the Belt, and we did this place instead."

Demarco dipped his spoon into the can of beans he'd opened for lunch. He pointed the spoon at Milk. "When's Kas gonna get worried about you?"

"About both of us, you mean." Milk wrapped a blanket tighter around her shoulders. The heaters were doing their best, but they were up against a lot of thermal mass. "He gets stressed out if he doesn't check in with you every week or two."

"Whole place probably fallin' apart without me." Demarco was wearing one of his new suits. With the beans and the box he'd propped his feet on, he looked like an elegant hobo.

"How long you think they gonna be in there?" Brooklyn nodded toward the pantry.

Douche had refused to share his information with anyone other than Andy, and only after she'd convinced him she was legit and listened to all of his complaints about Brooklyn. The two Designed had disappeared into the pantry as soon as sleeping arrangements were settled.

"Maybe they got a lot to catch up on. Who married who, who died, who joined the outlaws... that kind of thing." Demarco held out the can. "Have some beans."

"Jus' want some kind of idea what to prep for. We need to take off sudden, I need ta–"

"Breathe, Brook," Milk said. "We have food, water, beds... Maybe grab a nap." She rose to her feet, careful in the low gravity. "That's what I'm going to do. Let Andy do what Andy does. She'll bring us in when she's ready."

One of the things that Andy did best was math, and she spent the next several hours going over the scientist's data before grimly presenting his findings.

"The First abandoned the Earth project in anticipation of a major solar event," she said. "Extinction-level for the entire system."

"Impossible," Demarco said. "Maybe in ten billion years, but–"

"Months. Four on the outside. Irreversible."

"You say 'irreversible' like something set the thing off," Milk said. "Or someone."

"Definitely someone." Andy's face was stone. "And I believe I helped them do it."

FORTY

Rebellion isn't an easy thing to pull off when the bad guys are nigh omnipotent alien conquerors. She'd had to take shortcuts. Working with off-the-books parts of the U.S. intelligence apparatus, for example. Parts and people that'd refused to surrender even after the First turned out the lights. Patriotism, American pride. Exceptionalism. Opportunism. War is good both for hanging onto power and for business.

Nixon. Liddy. Kissinger. Dole. Rumsfeld. Even out of office, they still had keys to the buildings and access to backdoors from which to distribute money, safehouses, and information. Andy and her pals had needed all of it in the early days, when they were on the run in wake of the attack that failed to get the power back on. They needed even more ten years later, when they infiltrated the Artiplanet to steal the vaccine for the fertility virus. They'd traded the means to read First data crystals for the aid.

"That must be how they found out about the device, but I don't understand how they found the right crystals," Andy said. "The technology was ancient. Abandoned even before the First went into the caves."

Demarco and Brooklyn glanced at each other. "Might have some idea where they got 'em," Demarco said, "but that ain't the important part now. If First Tech did it, why can't First Tech fix it?"

It was the scientist's turn to talk. Andy might have understood some of it, but Brooklyn didn't. Super flares and extreme coronal mass ejections. Solar winds and geomagnetic storms. Plasma. Dynamos. Magnetic knots. Supernova. A First device in the heart of the Sun, an abandoned experiment, waiting eons for a trigger signal.

Brooklyn was scarcely listening at that point. The city of Cleveland was a crater, and they'd only just prevented something similar happening to Manhattan. The problem there had been big rocks; now they were talking about a star. Billions on Earth, millions more spread out over the Moon, Mars, Venus, and the Belt, and no way to get them to safety.

Douche wrapped up his lecture, which he'd delivered in the dry tones of the worst college professor.

"Well, that's it then," Demarco said. "We fucked."

PART THIRTEEN
Spin the Black Circle

FORTY-ONE

Demarco poked at the yellow clumps on the serving plate. "My first ever end-of-the-world breakfast, an' it's powdered eggs."

"Got some shitty oatmeal, too, if you like that better." Brooklyn finished setting the table. "An' instant coffee."

"Coffee? You been holdin' out on us?"

"Forgot it was here. This place ain't much more than a way to get outta the rain." He held up the jar. "Got a whole case. How long does instant coffee keep?"

"'Bout to find out. If it kills me, least I won't hafta worry about the Sun." He rubbed his cheeks. "Ya know, we could all go like that. Open the door over there and walk buck naked and grinning into the abyss. Fun thing to see in an obituary."

"Who'd write it?" Brooklyn had broken out the fancy stuff, the Admiral's third best set of china, squirreled away in case the Earth Orbital Forces ever returned to the Moon. It wasn't looking likely. "Not a great way to die anyway. Be better off fucking with the gas mix in here. Flood ourselves with argon, maybe."

"Thought about this much?" An eyebrow lifted slow.

"Not really. You?"

Demarco shrugged. "Time or two. Came damned close when I first got to De Milo. Might-a done it if I had somethin' better than a rock to seal the deal with."

"Well, I'm glad you didn't." Brooklyn lifted his juice glass. Tang, the astronaut's friend and a less-than-decent mixer. "To four more months of life."

They drank.

"Ain't gonna do that every morning, jus' so you know," Demarco said. "Need somethin' better than a countdown to wake up to."

"Douche ain't sure exactly when it's gonna pop anyway. You'd have to keep changin' the numbers."

Demarco forked up some eggs, chewed them – if that was the right word – thoughtfully. "2000 A.D. Interesting how often that number comes up among the doomsday prophets. Second Coming of Christ, Atum Shinrikyo in Japan, a shit ton o' anti-Semitic groups, the millennium bug… Wonder if any o' them had the inside track."

"Like they were splinters or something?" Brooklyn wiped his forehead with the back of his wrist. "You sayin' this was the plan all alo–?"

Milk came out of the shower nook, toweling her short hair dry. "Do I smell coffee?"

"Only in the broadest sense of the word, Jilly," Demarco said. "Instant. Young Brooklyn is an abominable host."

She took a seat at the table. "Are we allowed to talk about it yet?"

"Only airily. As one might chat about the weather." Demarco leaned in. "What song you want played at your funeral?"

"*Teen Angel* by Mark Dinning," she said. "You?"

"Want a real New Orleans jazz funeral. All the songs, parade, the works. 'Bout you, Brook?"

"We said we'd pick this up after breakfast, not while we're eating. Like to think about something else."

"Jolly good!" Demarco lifted his glass again, greeting Andy and Beth as they emerged from the nest they'd made among the storage crates. "Good morning! We're discussing Impressionism and Bach!"

"Prometheus says he wants five more minutes." Andy shot Brooklyn a look. "I told him what 'douche' means."

"So he named himself after a Greek god instead?!"

"A Titan, actually," Demarco said. "Zeus's uncle, or close enough. The metaphor is apt. He did bring us fire. Although it do sound a bit supervillainy."

Andy spooned breakfast onto her plate. "These are not real eggs."

"They worse if you close your eyes." Demarco pointed at a bottle on the table. "Hot sauce."

They fell to eating and talking about anything but the end of the world. Prometheus joined them in a few minutes and gave Brooklyn a sour look that resembled his usual expression so much it was scarcely noticeable. Milk cleared the table, and Beth and Andy helped with the dishes. Demarco put six of the Admiral's third-best highball glasses out and added a bottle of bourbon. "Now?" he said.

Brooklyn nodded. "Okay."

The meeting followed Demarco's Rules of Order. Anybody stepping on what anybody else wanted to say had to shut up and do a shot.

"We have to let people know," Milk said. "Earth, Mars, De Milo, everyone."

"What for?" Demarco said. "Already know we can't turn it off. We sound the alarm gonna be a bad time all around."

Brooklyn frowned. "People need time to get their, like, affairs in order."

"Won't be no more affairs." Demarco scoffed. "Affairs will burn up with everything else. Ignorance not always bliss, babe, but this a time it will be. Let folks live regular until some Earth scientist notices the sun's acting funny, and the government kills him or her to avoid a panic. Somebody will deep throat it to the *Post* after that, but there won't be much time to read all about it."

"People deserve a chance to say goodbye to their loved ones," Milk said. "Patch things up if they need to."

"Patch 'em or tear off all the Band-Aids got 'em this far? Fifty-fifty, Jilly. For every kid that decides ta give Terrible Pa another chance, you'll get someone who quits his family ta chase down an old flame an' ruin her life too." He smoothed his mustache. "I'd say we go ahead tell folks the First skipped out, get 'em all dancin' and singin' some, but it seems mean to pull the rug out like that."

Beth, Andy, and Brooklyn agreed. Prometheus wasn't paying attention.

"Fine for now," Milk said. "Reserve the right to bring it up again."

Next order of business.

"I want to go home," Milk said. "If I only have a few months, I want to spend them on De Milo with Yuri and Skim."

"You guys ever..." Demarco waggled his eyebrows. "Ya know?"

"No!" She looked thoughtful. "Although with the end of the world coming..."

"Add it to the to-do list, Jilly!" he crowed. "How many people can say they had a three-way with themselves!"

Milk rolled her eyes at him. "There are a lot of Original-Recipe Designed in De Milo," she said. "I'm sure they would welcome you, Andy. Beth could come too, if she wants."

"I'd rather be with my family on Earth," Beth said.

"Ain't how I thought this would go." Brooklyn put down his silverware and wiped his mouth with an embroidered napkin. "We skipped past doin' anything and went right to kissin' our asses goodbye."

"Acceptance the final stage of Kiss Your Ass Goodbye," Demarco said. "We just skippin' the stupid ones."

"There's nothing we can do, Brook." Milk's face was soft.

Brooklyn pointed at the western wall. "Spaceship parked right over there. How 'bout we fill it up with everything here, everyone wants to come, point it away from the Sun an' fly like hell. Get pretty damned far in four months."

"Then what? Starve?" Demarco puffed out his cheeks. "There's no place to live out there. Love ya, babe, but I ain't spending my last days sleeping in your pocket."

"Could you just leave everyone else behind like that?" Milk said.

"The DLF must have ships." Brooklyn looked to Andy for help.

"We have three ambassador-class vessels. They have room for less than a hundred each." She frowned. "The Artiplanet could be used as a lifeboat for twenty-five thousand or so."

Brooklyn snapped his fingers. "The Trolls are doin' that at the Cathedral. Propulsion and life support. Cardinal must be planning to ride out of here."

"Try this," Demarco said. "We been thinking the First left because some human Sneaky-Snakes set off the Sun exploder. What if the First left, an' tol' the Cardinal to blow shit up on his way out?"

Andy shook her head. "The timing doesn't work out."

"Timing." Demarco scoffed. "What's more likely? Rogue CIA plays sour grapes with the whole world or the OAO does?"

"Only see one o' them with a chance ta get away." Brooklyn folded his arms.

"You're the one said the Cardinal made 'panic moves'," Andy said. "Not everything is a First plot."

"Thas rule number one." Demarco raised his index finger and added another digit. "Rule two is that everything is a First plot."

"Let's table this," Milk said. "Who did it doesn't really matter. If we survive, we'll care."

"All right. Angels get to live, and maybe twenty-five thousand, three hundred, and six others." Demarco sucked his teeth. "Okay, let's do that. Make sure you give my seat to someone sexy."

"What about the Jellies?" Milk said. "They can get out. Would they take some humans with them?"

"Jelly ships are full of water," Brooklyn said. "'Spose they could pump a few rooms out... I can get hold of Float and fill her in. Let her take it from there."

"I'm sure the agency has a list of people who should be saved," Beth said.

"Unh-unh," Demarco said. "CIA gets to pick they'll fill the lifeboat with politicians. Sun gets me, it's taking them assholes too."

"If there's a UN evac ship ready to leave, we could divert it to the Artiplanet," Milk said. "That's nearly twenty thousand right there and about as globally representative as you're going to get."

"Be easy enough to roll Claire and her people into this," Brooklyn said. "Imagine they'd put some bigwigs on the convoy, but they couldn't take all the seats."

"The Artiplanet would need to get well past Jupiter before the nova, which means it would have to leave relatively soon." Andy drew circles on the table with her finger, figuring orbits, maybe, or just doodling while she thought. "Then there is the problem of where it should go afterward."

"Is there any chance De Milo will survive?" Milk said. "It's pretty deep underground."

Brooklyn nodded. "Can't imagine the First didn't have a disaster plan when they built the place."

"The caves were the disaster plan," Andy said. "I'm not familiar enough with its workings to know if there were other contingencies. Maybe Prometheus can speak to that?"

The surly scientist had laid out an array of materials on the table in front of him – wood, paper, cardboard, and plastic – and was testing their reaction to the bourbon. "I have never been to the Havens. The power source there may be enough to generate a protective field, or it may not. But that is a problem for someone else."

"Why not you?" Brooklyn said.

"I am going directly to the Artiplanet." He looked at Andy. "There are at least twenty-five thousand Designed in the Sol system at this time. There is no room for the lesser species."

FORTY-TWO

Brooklyn skipped angrily. "If he thinks he can just go an' leave everyone behind–"

"His whip, babe." Demarco had come along for Brooklyn's cool-down walk on the Moon's surface. "Designed got the keys and know how to fly it away."

"Then we take the damned thing."

The older man stopped short. "You gonna start an' win a war against an advanced species with unknown tech? Dump them outta they homes and fly off wit it? Don't seem likely, babe."

"Best idea you got is crawl into a cave and die."

"Prometheus says there might be a way to make a force field round Venus. We go back, take him and Toploski to that control center she used to turn on the lights, an' see what they can do."

"Leaving five billion people on Earth. Maybe half a million on the Moon, couple million on Mars, maybe, an' I don't know how many in the Belt." Brooklyn swallowed hard. "How's that gonna feel when you're sitting behind your force field?"

"You the one wanna cram us all into your leaky ol' boat an' 'fly like hell'. How'd you feel looking in the rearview and seeing everyone burning up behind?"

"Guilty as hell."

"You don't think most-a the Designed would, too? You been buddy-buddy with a jellyfish for seven years. How would Float feel leaving you behind? Jellies, Designed... they people just like us. Give Prome Dome a chance to figure hisself out and don't do anything stupid. Hard for you, I know."

"Fuck you."

"Fuck you back." He bounced on his heels. "Never been on the Moon before. Wanna race?"

"Liable to fall down a ravine and die."

"Always death with you. Dying here, dying there. Sun's exploding, everyone's gonna die. Lighten the hell up, man." He pointed. "Last one to that rock thing's an asshole!"

Brooklyn and the Asshole He'd Had to Save from Falling into a Ravine made it back in time for lunch.

"Got it all worked out," Demarco said. "We head for De Milo post haste. On the way, Andy calls in her DLF pals an' they meet us there. We get a force field workin', then Prometheus can go on to the Artiplanet and do what he's gotta do."

"If a force field proves unviable within a week of our arrival on Venus," Prometheus said, "I want transport to the Artiplanet regardless."

Demarco agreed.

"If we can get a force field going, I want to make it public," Milk said. "Anyone wants to come to Venus, they can."

"Still can't believe we're even talking 'bout this." Brooklyn put his head in his hands. "It's like somethin' in one of Demarco's damned stories."

"The Plot to End the World." Demarco spread his hands like he was opening a curtain. "Issue twelve of *Astounding Stories.* With you, babe. 'Bout all I can do not to hide in the corner an' rock myself to sleep. But I been living in a cave under the surface of Venus for nearly thirty years, after bein' kidnapped and poked at by disembodied brains, and I'm drinking shitty screwdrivers on the Moon.

"My threshold for 'what the fuck?' pretty damn high by now."

They loaded all the coffee and anything else useful on the *Victory* while Brooklyn shut down the bolt hole. He might never see the place again but wanted everything to work if he did. He made it to the ship's cockpit in time to finish the pre-launch checklist.

"Om," Brooklyn tapped the computer mic. "I need you stop being a rock for a second."

"I'm here," Om said without noticeable delay. "More time has gone by than I expected."

"It's just flyin' on by." He sketched out the situation for the AI. "We need to get to De Milo, fastest route, no fuel spared." They'd loaded up the rest of the Type 3 fuel, ready to burn as long and hard as need be.

Om charted the course. "I've amended our simulation to include asteroids and comets. Perhaps you would like to try it sometime."

"Love ta, but let's figure out this explodin' Sun thing first."

After launch, Andy took a turn at the comm system, sending messages to her ships hidden in the Belt. "Two ships will meet us at Venus. The other is headed directly to the Artiplanet to see what's happening there."

"Be awkward showin' up for a ride and them not opening the door," Demarco said.

"The ship's captain offered an even more awkward prospect," she said. "What if they've already left?"

Late that night, Brooklyn sat alone in the *Victory*'s kitchen, working through a pot of Professor Yarrow's special mushroom tea.

It was doing the job. It was difficult to interact with the Purple Lady when he was stone sober. Alcohol made it easier, but the tea really opened the gates.

"This is what you were tellin' me about, ain't it?" he said.

"I think so. It seems like something set now. A certainty."

She was wearing a cocktail dress. "As much as anything is."

A guitar wail was coming from somewhere over her right shoulder. Something sad and lonely. Brooklyn blinked owlishly. The only thing behind her was a decidedly unmusical sink, but strange things happened when she was around.

"Will you make it?"

"Survive, you mean?" She didn't wait for his nod. "I expect so. I'm in so many places now. If you could see an eighth of the things I'm watching at this moment, your mind would break."

"Will we?"

She spread her hands helplessly. "Even if I knew, I don't know what telling you would accomplish. What would you do if I said 'yes'?"

"Ask you how."

"But I don't know how, and I wouldn't want to mislead you. What would you do if I said 'no'?"

"Accept it."

"Really?"

He smirked. "Prob'ly not."

FORTY-THREE

Two weeks to Venus. As much as they could in the small ship, they kept to themselves. Being together meant talking about it, and only Prometheus was truly comfortable with that. Instead, they fretted alone and in pairs. Om helped the Designed scientist go over his research again and crunch new numbers. The results were inconclusive. A force field might work. Might not.

Four days to Venus.

Three days.

Two.

One.

FORTY-FOUR

The *Foundling* was docked at *Unfunky UFO* when they passed by the station. Carmen squirted a message offering dinner and a tour, but Brooklyn begged off. He debated telling her about the Sun. Radiation from the solar event might make space travel in the system impossible for decades. Even if the force field worked, they'd have to land the ship inside the planet and ride it out with everyone else.

Maybe if they got out ahead of it, made it past Jupiter in time... nah. Space is big, but there ain't a lotta good places to park. Should put that on a T-shirt.

Brooklyn took the *Victory* through the energy tunnel and circled over De Milo until he got clearance to land. Milk and Demarco rushed off to brief Kasperov. Brooklyn opted to follow Andy to the Designed Community Center over near city hall.

She was pensive, deep in her own head, and her body nearly vibrated with tension.

"Ever hear that song Neil Young wrote about you?" Brooklyn said.

"More times than I can easily count."

"Relax, you're like a hero to these guys."

"Neil Young doesn't speak for the Designed." She stopped walking. "I could have gotten all the ambassadors euthanized. That's the usual end of a failed experiment."

"Worked out okay."

She resumed her progress toward the community center. "That depends on who you talk to."

Instead of destroying their creations, the First had cut Andy's cohort loose and made the Angels in their stead. Homeless, jobless, and largely resented, many of the mark-one ambassadors had ended up on Venus.

"Kas and them worked hard to make 'em feel welcome," Brooklyn said. "The old-timers who worked with you on the *Victory* did, too."

"And some humans were bitter about living among their former tormenters and wanted to respond in kind. I've heard the stories, Brook."

"An' some o' the Designed were pissed about living among the 'primitives'. Top set 'em all straight. Ones who acted on it, at least."

She hummed.

"Used to be they lived all in one place," Brooklyn said. "Now they're sprinkled around. Everybody is. 'Proportional neighborhoods', Kas calls it. Never too many people from the same place living together. Can't melt if they don't mix, he says."

"It's changed a lot since the last time I was here," she admitted. "It feels less… desperate, I guess."

Prometheus met them at the community center where a good crowd had gathered, mostly the local Designed and former splinters. Andy joined Toploski and the other community leaders on stage. Skim waved from the bleachers, and Brooklyn wandered over to sit with her.

"Thought you two weren't sure which one o' ya was a splinter," Brooklyn said.

"We're not," Skim said. "So we both joined the community center. What's this all about?"

"Always something, ain't it? Feels like I've been runnin' from stupid shit to stupid shit all my life." He offered her his flask. "Big surprise, we got another apocalypse to survive."

She squinted at the stage. "Is that Andromeda up there? I haven't seen her since–"

"Since she dropped you off here in '86."

"If she's out of hiding, then…" Her mouth firmed. "This is bad, isn't it?"

"The Sun's gonna explode." He saluted the shocked look on her face and took a long pull from the flask. "Shoulda brought two of these."

The director of the community center introduced Andy and Prometheus and let them take it from there.

Most of the Designed were familiar with the basics of First science, but there were enough experts in the audience to keep Prometheus onstage hours after his initial presentation of data. Brooklyn snuck out for a sandwich and a beer, and returned in time for the creation of a task force charged with determining whether or not a First field could be wrapped around the planet and made strong enough to survive the event.

The director adjourned the meeting soon after.

Brooklyn stood and stretched his back. "Ten cents says it won't go that well when we tell everybody else."

"That's why we've decided to wait," Andy said, rejoining them.

"Kas is gonna have to say something soon." He pointed at a couple – human Mom, Designed Mom – with three human kids. "We got mixed families. It's gonna get out."

"It should." Skim folded her arms. "I'll keep quiet for now, but if it goes on too long…"

Brooklyn laughed. "Ya know, you sound a lot like yourself."

The Task Force formed over the next two days. There were Designed scientists in the community who'd been spending their days gardening or cooking at the common kitchens, aching for a challenge. Prometheus interviewed all-comers himself, and introduced the chosen twelve at the next community meeting.

"We will enter the control center at dawn tomorrow, and I expect to have an answer shortly thereafter," he said. "If it can be done, it will be. I make no promises."

FORTY-FIVE

Six Days Later

Director Yuri Kasperov cleared his throat. Citizens Park was filled beyond capacity while most others in De Milo watched via a live broadcast.

"I have been advised that a powerful First field, engineered by Doctor Prometheus and his team, will be sufficient to save De Milo from the solar event." He waited for the cheers to die down. "There will be a price. Generating and maintaining the field for the time required will strain the systems that make life possible here. The event itself will likely strip away the atmospheric blanket that helps maintain the temperature inside the caves. It will grow colder. We will be uncomfortable. Survival in De Milo will be more difficult."

After Kasperov's address, his science adviser, a member of the task force, took to the podium to answer questions from the media and assorted representatives.

Brooklyn leaned against a wall backstage. "This change your mind about telling everyone?"

Milk shook her head. "Based on the numbers I've seen, we can absorb another five hundred thousand refugees without trying hard, and there's no way that many will make it here in time. I just wish there was something else we could do."

"Read up on survivor's guilt." He humped himself off the wall. "Guess I'm headed for the Moon. See ya when I get back."

"Assuming you're coming back." Her eyes widened. "I half expected you to say you were going to the Artiplanet."

"Andy's ships will be here in a couple of days. Says any Designed wants to head that way can hop on." He pulled a face. "Artiplanet's already headed out to the Belt to crack some rocks open for materials they need. Not really my scene."

"I just thought that..." She gestured. "You and her."

"True love always?" His smile was sad. "Brain says I only knew her a few weeks twenty years ago. Means I'm glad she's gonna be okay, there's some sweetness there, but I got fresh bread with somebody else. That make sense?"

"As much as any of this does." She shoved him gently. "Go, so you can get back in time. Living in a cold, dim cave won't be the same without you."

"I'll try to grab you some of that gin you like. Be a collector's item before too long."

Brooklyn stopped at *The Mush Room* for a prelaunch meal. There was plenty of parking. Lots of folks were downtown, standing in line for the public comms in hopes of reaching family on Earth and getting them to safety.

Brooklyn parked his rental up behind a VW Beetle conversion. It had made it from Earth without a front end, and the salvager had replaced the domed hood with the engine compartment of a John Deere tractor.

Most of the city's rolling stock was pedal-powered or simple electrics charged off De Milo's dome-rated mini-reactors. Car theft hadn't been imported yet, so the rental had an on/off switch instead of a key. Brooklyn flipped it to 'off' and went inside for a quick beers-and-mushroom-burger dinner.

"Quiet in here." He slid onto one of the many empty barstools.

"Tell me about it." The bartender pulled him a pint. "Even

before all the Sun shit, lotta folks were staying home, dicking around with those things the church handed out."

"The circle things?"

The barman dropped a coaster on the bar and sat the glass right in the middle. "Good if you don't like real life, I guess. I got enough out here to keep me occupied without pretending to be someone else."

Beth the CIA spook came into the bar with a backpack on her shoulder. "They're called 'sensorum'. Andy spotted one yesterday."

Brooklyn slapped the bar. "That's it! Been bugging me for weeks. Way back when, she told me the First got hooked on somethin' called sensorum after they moved down here. They barely survived the first thousand years."

"That's the one." Beth slid onto a nearby stool and ordered a beer. "She said they died by the thousands. Living somewhere better in their heads and forgetting to eat, drink. They just gave up on reality."

"Can see how that might beat sitting in the dark." He rubbed his eyes. "Fuck! Ever notice how nothin' stays fixed? Survive the Sun, we got a drug problem ta deal with. Kas is gonna be thrilled."

Beth drank some beer, made a face. "I need to get back to Earth, and a little bird told me you're about to go to the Moon. Can I get a ride?

Never fly empty. He quoted her the price. "Leavin' right after I fill Kas in."

The *Victory* shot out of the mouth of the tunnel and clawed free of the planet's gravity well. Beth had the whole bunkroom to herself. The CIA was most likely paying her way, so Brooklyn had no problem overcharging her.

Most of De Milo's merchant fleet was parked at the space station or heading there, its captains meeting on what to do.

Only a couple of months to pull people off Earth, Mars, and the Moon, and no way in hell to get everybody. Act out of altruism, self-interest, or some combo. Pick up Uncle John and Aunt Bobbi and give them a ride to safety, and maybe have to leave all their neighbors behind. Shitty choices abounded.

Carmen will want to get her kids out. The Fox's family should be in De Milo or aboard the Foundling by now. Imagine they'll try ta fly out a few more.

Om cut in on his thoughts. "I have a message from your former copilot, Float. She thanks you for the message and says her people have retrieved their fleet from the Trench. They will be leaving Earth shortly."

"Look at all o' us rats." He drummed his fingers on the arm of his acceleration couch. "Word will beat us to the Moon. Probably oughta have Evelyn meet us somewhere sneaky."

PART FOURTEEN
The Most Beautiful Girl in the World

FORTY-SIX

Beth was the perfect fare. Cash in hand, few demands, and she kept to herself. Two weeks to the Moon, and the only place their paths crossed were the kitchen and the bathroom.

They alternated cooking chores. The final night, she made macaroni-and-cheese while Brooklyn tossed a salad and opened a bottle of wine.

"This Evelyn woman is special to you," she said.

"Lookin' for leverage? That case, I barely know her." *In any case, really. Flyin' millions o' miles for a woman I spent a few weeks with.* "Who the hell's Evelyn?"

"Just making conversation." She drank some wine. Red and dry. "You don't believe I'm going back for my family."

"Even spies got family." He shrugged. "It's possible."

"When we get to Tycho, I'll contact a man who'll give me access to a ship that I'll fly to Earth. On the way there, I'll transmit a report to my superiors at the agency. Then I'll land the ship in a secret location and pick up my mother, my sister, and her family. We'll fly back to Venus in hopes of surviving."

"Stealing CIA assets? Nice way to start the New Year." His lips twisted. "Hope it works out for you. Guy might've flown off in that ship of yours all ready."

"You don't like me much." She rested her fork on her plate. "Is it because I was with Andy?"

"Nothing to do with that," he said. "Has everything to do with the fact your people used her to blow up the damned Sun."

"Assuming it was us." She drank some wine. "Which it probably was. Most of us just wanted to make sure the United States came out on top in the new order. Run Mars. Eventually run Venus, maybe. We were patriots. The zealot side of things decided burning it all down was the only move. I wasn't part of that."

"You helped them."

"So did you. Andy and her outlaws gave us the means to read the data crystals. You gave us the crystals." She crossed her arms. "You were supposed to die months ago, 'Donato.' The zealots burned Big Tony's entire organization to keep anyone from figuring out what they were doing."

"Building a doomsday weapon."

"Building the trigger. The weapon was already there. I had an idea there was a button to push, but no clue someone really wanted to push it."

Brooklyn pointed at her with his fork. "You guys were tryin' to bluff the First. Show 'em the button and say you'd use it if they didn't leave."

"I didn't come up with the idea."

"You assholes couldn't even wipe out Big Tony right." He scoffed. "Missed a guy at the warehouse, and he warned me."

"Lucky boys."

"I mighta been okay. I don't die so easy." He drank some wine. "Those same mistake-making assholes thought they should have power to end the world." He shook his head. "Pretty fucking stupid."

"It might've worked."

"Fact you're still sayin' that is even stupider." He wiped his mouth on a napkin. "Is that why're you're takin' this ride with me? Poison my mac-and-cheese, close the loop?"

"Of course not. Patriot, not zealot, Brook. I just want to get my family out."

He grunted. "Right about one thing, Beth. I do not like you."

After dropping Beth off, Brooklyn flew the *Victory* two miles southwest of Tycho and landed it inside a crater too small for anything but a registration number.

"Right time, right place, pal," he said to Om. "See anyone?"

"There's an inflatable set up one hundred and twenty meters to the left of the cockpit."

Brooklyn twisted his neck and leaned forward to see. "It's either them or Boy Scouts. I'll get suited up."

He met them outside. Five mismatched vacsuits, Evelyn and four people she wanted to save. None of the suits had radios, so he led by gesture and example back through the airlock and into the ship.

"Bathroom is that way," he pointed. "Kitchen–"

The last of the five took his helmet off. A lanky preteen in a gaggle of like. No Evelyn.

"Where's Ev?" Brooklyn said.

"She sent us," one of the girls said.

"I know you," Brooklyn said.

She grinned. "On *Eisenhower*. I had a guitar. We talked about TV shows."

"Is she coming along later? What's the plan?"

"She said to go without her, and she'd figure it out on her own."

Brooklyn frowned. "This ain't something ta figure out. She comes with us or she probably burns."

The girl shrugged. "Just tellin' you what she said."

"Om, you're in charge 'til I get back." He put his helmet on. "Don't let them eat the mushrooms in the instant-coffee jar, and don't leave without me."

It took him more than an hour to crack one of the south-side airlocks and gain access to the city. The streets and alleyways were deserted, and he skipped north at his best speed.

Neither Evelyn nor her roommates were home when Brooklyn forced the door of the apartment. The small overnight bag she liked to use was missing, as were her toothbrush and a couple of small things from her room.

He didn't know her roommates well enough to deduce if they'd left too. The public terminal would be a zoo: people trying to get home, panicking, maybe trying to get to Venus. It would be impossible to find her in the scrum. *Maybe she already found a way out.*

Brooklyn opened the refrigerator and snagged one of the beers inside. There was a note taped to the bottle's neck.

I said 'go', you asshole. Or stay, and give your seat to someone who deserves it. But I suppose the ship needs you to fly it. Anyway, it was fun. – Evelyn

He sat on the edge of her bed, opened the beer, and drank it while reading the note over a couple more times. The slip of paper, folded tight, went into the watch pocket of his jeans.

Should've found out if she wanted to be rescued.

He put the other beers in his pockets and closed the door behind him.

Brooklyn stowed his vacsuit. The five kids were in the kitchen. "Happened to your guitar?" he asked the girl.

"Traded to get to Tycho." She didn't seem too upset about it. Might've just been a way to make money.

"What am I s'posed to call you?"

"Maddy."

"You're chief kid." He pointed at her and looked at the other four. "You twerps do what she says, or I'm tossing you out. Clear?"

They nodded.

"Maddy, youdadone what I said on the station, you'd be in De Milo already. Now you gotta take the long way." *She said Vegas. Somewhere else before that.* He took a step toward the cockpit, and the energy drained out of him. *No way in hell I'm gonna find her in time.*

"Brooklyn, there is a message from former Ambassador Andromeda," Om piped in. "She says you are needed in the Belt. There's an emergency."

He put his hand on the wall to steady himself for a few beats. *Guess it's gonna be the real long way.* "Maddy, get those breakables put away. We're launching in five minutes." He put Evelyn's beers in the fridge. "Om, gimme a course to Ceres, will ya. Fast as fuck."

FORTY-SEVEN

Entertainment media had taught two generations of humans that maneuvering within the asteroid belt located between the orbits of Mars and Jupiter was like trying to stay dry in a summer rain shower. Heroes such as Buck Rogers and Stringfellow Hawke were often portrayed in white-knuckled, twisting and diving flights among the asteroids, chasing or being chased as needed.

The truth was much less exciting. The asteroids in the belt were, on average, six hundred thousand miles apart, close only on a cosmic scale, and Brooklyn would have had to work pretty hard to plow the *Victory* into one. The tough part was finding the one he wanted. Om had never been out that far, but fortunately it was on speaking terms with Brooklyn's old computer, which had.

Brooklyn landed the ship on the dwarf planet Ceres and took a few rooms at the *Baron*, a bed-and-breakfast next to the desalination station there. The rooms were simple but clean and offered an EOF veterans discount. Maddy and her crew headed to the arcade while he made the deal.

"How long you stayin'?" the guy at the check-in desk said. His name was Floyd, and a lifetime before he'd been Brooklyn's shipmate.

"Kinda surprised to see you still here. Assume you've heard about the Sun."

"Think it'll get us this far out?" Floyd reached between the buttons of his shirt to scratch his paunch. "Got a thousand bucks says it won't."

"Pretty sure it will, man. It were me, I'd get this thing in the sky and head to Venus quick."

The bed-and-breakfast had enjoyed another life, too. Nearly three decades as a deep-space patrol boat called the *Baron von Stueben*. Right after the old tub's decommissioning ceremony in '83, its remaining crew pooled their money and bought it for scrap. They flew it out to the Rocks – which is what everyone who actually lived in the Belt called it – for a decade of prospecting and adventure before refitting it as an inn.

"That's what Terry says, too." Floyd's weathered face grew deeper wrinkles. "I ain't so sure."

"Who makes the call?"

"We all do. Got a meetin' set when Terry gets back in a few days."

"Where's he now?"

Floyd pulled in a shuddering breath. Somewhen in the last decade, he'd ended up with a set of artificial lungs, and they pumped steadily in the big man's chest. "Around. You know Terry."

"We're only here a day or so. Coulda stayed on *Vicky*, but the kids wanted to stretch their legs."

"Sure." Floyd folded his thick arms and leaned back against the wall. "Saw you on a talk show about a month ago. Thought you might be a big star by now."

Brooklyn snorted. "Been twenty years since I was on TV."

"Not out here. Pirate stations pick up and rebroadcast whatever they want. Lie slick enough, you can probably cage some free drinks off it. Don't get a lot of celebrities here."

"I'll think about it." He sniffed. "Any fights tonight?"

"Nothin' formal. Ring's open if you want to see if anyone's interested."

"Probably best I stick to drinking. Kill less brain cells that way."

"You know the way. Still there when I clock out, you can buy me one. I'll show the kids to their rooms when they circle back. They got TV's and snacks in there."

The layout of the ship had changed radically since Brooklyn had served on it. Several of the small bunk rooms had been joined to make long-term suites where locals laid their heads when they weren't on the job. Brooklyn and the kids had keys to three singles, each about the same size as the one he'd shared with a long-married couple when he first came on board. Nowadays, they ran a general store on the other side of the station.

The boxing ring was still in the same place, but the area around it had been expanded with tables and a long bar. Once upon a time, Brooklyn's therapist pal Terry had tried to teach him the sweet science there, but a stand-up fight wasn't really his style. He didn't recognize the bartender – a young guy, barely out of his teens – but ordered a bourbon from him anyway. The kid had an accent. Irish, maybe.

The booze was a strange color, aged in something that was decidedly not oak barrels. The bartender hummed. "Haven't seen you around here."

"Last time was three or four years back. First time, I was crew."

The guy popped an eyebrow. "Kinda young for that."

"Got that sorta face." He took a tentative sip. It was better than it looked. "Don't know yours."

"Came out about a year ago. Needed a job and a place to crash. Floyd and Henry had both." He made a show of wiping down the bar.

"How'd you get out here?" The population of the Belt trended middle-aged and older. Lots of political prisoners and outspoken artists. Retired military who didn't bother going home after their enlistment was up. Not much tourism or fresh blood. A Mars immigrant, maybe, but the kid didn't have the look of someone who'd grown up in low gravity.

"Did. That's the only part worth knowing." The kid nodded at Brooklyn's empty glass. "Another?"

Brooklyn drank and listened to songs on the jukebox. He skimmed some of the 'zines and pamphlets stacked on the bar until Floyd and Henry clocked off their respective jobs and joined him. A few others filtered in during the interim. Rough-looking guys who mined or flew or repaired for a living and drank and wrote radical screeds at night. The bartender turned his cleaning rag over to one of them and left for the night.

"What's his story?" Brooklyn asked.

"Shanghaied from Earth," Henry said. "Shipped here in a slow boat by a mail-order bride outfit. More than six months travel time. Half of 'em died on the way. What's with the kids?"

"Guess I inherited them. Taking them to Venus by way of the Rocks."

Floyd scratched his head. "That supposed to make sense?"

"Hafta meet someone here on Ceres. Favor for a friend."

Henry chuckled. "Gotta be a damned good friend to come this far out to say 'hello'."

"Guess so." Andy's follow up message had been terse. The Artiplanet was a slow mover, and he'd easily beaten it to the Belt. She needed him to contact someone and ask them to rendezvous with her. After that…

Still make De Milo but– Maybe Evelyn had made it there, maybe she hadn't even tried.

Kyra, the youngest of the kid crew, tugged on his arm and held out her hand.

"What?" he said.

"Maddy says we need money."

"Hell you need money for?" He looked around. "An' who told you could come into a bar?"

"The man at the desk said you were here," she said. "Can I get a drink?"

Brooklyn pulled two twenties out of his pocket and gave them to her. "You guys can get food with this and only food, all right?"

She nodded.

"If you get pizza, save me a slice."

Brooklyn poured another cup of the thrice-brewed tea from the pot atop the elaborate samovar in *The Baron's* small lounge. He'd come back to his room to find two pieces of pizza waiting for him. Breakfast. Now he was cooling his heels waiting for Andy's contact. Her follow-up message had been nearly as opaque as the original. *Meet Razer on Ceres. She'll have directions. Tell Caliban everything.*

Om said Caliban was a character from a Shakespeare play – a monster no one loved. Meaning anyone calling themselves that was probably a self-pitying jackass. Brooklyn settled deeper into the much-patched easy chair and closed his eyes. *Never miss a chance to eat or sleep.*

"Are you Brooklyn Lamontagne?"

"Might be Houdini." He rested his hands on his stomach, trying to pretend he hadn't nearly shat himself in surprise. "Closed my eyes an' 'poof', there you were."

Lean with hair the color of blood. Quiet as a sharp knife. Dressed in a matte black vacsuit and respirator.

"I don't know any Houdini." Mid-range voice with a strange metallic buzz at the end of every sentence. "Are you Lamontagne?"

"Better be. I'm wearin' his pants." It was something he'd heard his father say a few times and had no idea why he'd said it now.

Razer, who else could it be, rattled off some Russian, the code phrase Andy had remembered to give him.

Brooklyn held back on his end of the code. The Rocks were a rough place, crude and jury-rigged within inches of falling apart. Layered and patched. Razer looked like something fresh out of sci-fi central casting. A bounty hunter. An assassin. "Nice outfit," he said.

Silence.

"Really," he plucked the collar of his worn jacket, "been thinking 'bout changin' my style. Ya know, get wit' the times. I was cool in the '70s, but now..."

There was a little scuffing noise. Razer's balance shifted. "Are we going to do this or not?"

The code phrase was a line from a poem. Brooklyn offered the next line in the stanza – Your last day draws near, you bourgeoisie louse! – in his bars-and-bargaining Russian, and Razer relaxed the punch-him-in-the-throat stance he'd– *she'd* taken.

"We'll go back to your ship. I'll give you the coordinates once we're away."

"Have some tea first." Brooklyn waved toward the samovar. "My crew's sleeping off a pizza party. I'll roust 'em in another hour."

Maddy and the other kids clustered around Razer like bees.

"I love your hair!" Maddy said. "Can I touch your vacsuit?"

The suit, she announced, was 'soft and weird, but warm.' The other kids had to take a turn. Razer seemed startled by the attention but warmed to it. She – a clarification she provided to little Kyra – allowed the gaggle to tow her back to the *Victory* to show her their room and introduce her to Om. Brooklyn stayed behind to pay the bill and buy a couple of bottles of bourbon off Henry.

They were in the kitchen burning through Brooklyn's soda-pop supply when he arrived at the ship. Om and Razer were studying each other curiously.

"I am getting a variety of signals from her," Om told him. "Lots of radio, some infrared. The echoes off her body are strange, too. Almost like she's made of–"

"You're a machine intelligence!" It was the first hint of emotion Razer had shown. "I've never–"

Brooklyn cut them off. "Om, we talkin' tracking signals, or what?"

"Mostly requests for access."

"Access to what?"

"Everything. All the electronics on the ship are getting a ping."

Brooklyn brought his right arm up and made a pistol shape with his hand. "Turn it off, slick."

Razer rose from her chair. "Let me explain."

The business end of Brooklyn's new trick watch remained pointed at her. "Thirty seconds, then you're hitting the floor," he said. "Kids, under the table."

Maddy paled. "Brook, she's not going to hurt us!"

Razer motioned Maddy to hush. "I can't turn it off, but you don't need to worry about it," she said. "Where we're going, we're all connected through something we call the pipeline. Most of the traffic your," they gestured at Om's camera, "computer is picking up is for that."

"Connected how?"

"Implanted computers. They allow us to share information quickly."

"I believe I could connect and respond if I chose," Om said, "but the tech is too sophisticated to interface with much else on the *Victory*. It would be like me talking to a toaster."

"Lock down anything you can, just in case." Brooklyn lowered the watch. "Maddy, general quarters."

Whines and gripes came out from under the table, but so did the kids. They slumped down the hall toward the bunk room.

In the brighter light of the kitchen, Razer's respirator and its built-in speakers were plain to see. They weren't made to be removed.

"You're part robot. Like Steve Austin in that show."

"A cyborg. Little more than sixty-five percent machine."

"Know a guy who came out this way minus an arm, came back with a tentacle. That you guys?"

"Probably. If you met Floyd at *The Baron,* we did his lungs."

"This Caliban guy did."

"Yep. One of the ways we make money and friends."

Brooklyn folded his arms. "You hungry? I'm about to make something."

The mask speakers made a sound. Could have been a sigh. Might have been a glitch. "I can't eat normally. I was in an accident a few years ago, went to Ariel for help."

"Ariel a person, place, or thing?"

"Place. It's where we live."

There were five glasses on the table. Five kids, one cyborg. "You see we got soda. You didn't want one?"

"I can–"

He played a hunch. "Get you a straw if you want."

Razer's real name was Zhi, but that only came out when the kids came back to the table. She was seventeen, and the middle child of nine.

"Conjoint?" Brooklyn said.

She nodded. "Eight dads, three moms."

"Know which ones are yours?"

"They all are. Papa Pete says making babies and digging holes were the only things to do out here at first. He's been on the Rocks the longest. He was a professor at Moscow University."

Rubbed someone the wrong way, though. The first ones sent out were Soviet and Chinese dissidents, exiled to the Belt to mine their lives away. "What'd he teach?"

"Agriculture. Says it came in handy in the early days. Still does."

The Rocks had been good about documenting its history.

The first wave hadn't much more than vactents and campfires, with the promise of more supplies once they'd mined enough ore to fill the cargo pods for a return trip. But with that many scholars, writers, and artists in one place, the first common space they built was eighty percent library.

Brooklyn ceded the table to the youths and was leaning against the counter feeling something like paternal. Maybe older fraternal. Much older. "Musta heard a lot o' stories from him."

"Nightmare fuel." Razer hugged herself. "He once lived in a cargo pod for four months after micrometeorites buggered their campsite. Sixty people in there with him. Pinhole leaks everywhere."

Military-surplus inflatables. Inadequate supplies. No training to speak of. Not a good time. "Made it, though. That's something."

"Our family does all right." There was some pride in her voice. "Nice compound. Two ships. Three before–" She went quiet.

"'Fore you got hurt," Brooklyn guessed.

"I don't usually talk about that."

"You don't have to if you don't want," Maddy said. For once, she and her pals had been listening more than contributing.

Razer got very interested in her drinking straw. "I was flying the ship, my third solo, but it wasn't my fault. Everyone says so. Explosion was amidships."

Brooklyn's mouth twisted. *Belt kid, learning the family business, then POW!*

"We were lucky Caliban's people were in the area, else none of us would've made it. They took me in, fixed me up. Made sure my family got home safe."

"Ever see your family?"

"Sometimes." Her eyes went liquid. She wasn't the only one. Everyone at the table had left someone behind on accident or on purpose. Families weren't always easy, but they had weight.

"Less and less, I guess. I get the feeling they aren't sure they should have let Caliban take me."

"Saved your life." Brooklyn swirled the muck in his cup around. "Shrinks call that transference. Or projection. One of those. Don't get paid to memorize vocabulary. Means you're probably taking what you feel and acting like it's coming off them."

She nodded.

"Probably just happy you're still around and waitin' to see how you feel 'bout it."

"I'm glad to be alive."

"Sure. But you came out different. Used to be able to drink outta cups and eat sandwiches. Makes you wonder if you're still the same person you were 'fore you got hurt."

It was all in the eyes with Razer. "Am I?"

Brooklyn made a wide circle with his mug, taking in Maddy and the others. "These guys seem to like you."

Ariel was an iron-heavy seven-kilometer-long rock in a very eccentric orbit around the Sun. Razer had Brooklyn land in an open hanger carved into the rock. Outside, vacsuited people – and one who wasn't – worked loading and unloading cargo. Most looked nearly Earth-normal, others not so much. The guy without a vacsuit was human from the waist up, but his lower half had been replaced with tank treads and his eyes sealed behind mirrored lenses.

"More cyborgs?"

Razer waved out the cockpit window, and Tank Treads waved back. "They say 'hello'."

"Hello, back!" Maddy said. Although the view would've been much better via the kitchen flatscreen, kids were lined up by pecking order outside the cockpit door, trying to see through the front windows.

"All these guys in accidents?"

"Some. Others chose augmentation," she said. "Caliban encourages experimentation."

"An' you're all talkin' to each other right now through this pipeline thing."

"What are they sayin'?" Kyra piped in.

"Probably that you stink," her brother said.

"Do not!"

Maddy shushed them into silence.

"I'm connected to everyone within range, a localized network, and to our server farm," Razer said.

"Where's this stuff come from?"

"Caliban created it by adapting elements of First, Second, and Human tech."

"Well," Brooklyn made to rise, "let's go see him."

She shook her head. "That's not the plan. You can give your message to me, and I'll relay it." She tapped her temple. "He'll get it right away."

"The hell we fly all the way out here then?"

"I needed a ride home." Her eyelids flickered. "I'm ready to record your message."

"You're really not gonna let me in." Brooklyn rubbed his face. "How you plannin' on stoppin' me?"

A cockpit alarm went off and a host of telltales turned from green to red.

"The *Victory*'s shutting down," Om said. "One system at a time."

"Okay, Okay!" Brooklyn looked at Razer. "Point made."

She smiled with her eyes, too.

"So, I just talk?"

"Say what you need to say."

"My name is Brooklyn Lamontagne, an' I'm here to talk for Andromeda, captain of the Designed Artiplanet. Maybe you ain't heard, but the fuckin' Sun's gonna explode, and Andy thinks you can help out somehow. She wants you–" He cleared his throat. "She asks that you..."

* * *

Headed back toward Ceres, Brooklyn gave the *Victory* a good systems check. There were no mechanical problems to be found, but Ariel's coordinates had disappeared from the log and database.

Brooklyn reached into the pocket of his coveralls, where he'd stowed the written copy of the coordinates. They were missing.

He roused Om from his simulation. "Thought you said their stuff couldn't talk to our stuff," he said.

"It appears I was mistaken," Om said.

"They get into you, too? Do you know how to get back to Ariel?"

Om paused longer than Brooklyn thought possible. "I do not."

FORTY-NINE

The Baron's barroom was having a going-out-of-business sale, and Brooklyn was doing his best to be the best customer. Two empty bottles were already lined up on the bar next to the boxing bell, which he'd purchased in a fit of nostalgia.

At week's end, the *Baron von Steuben* would lift off from Ceres and burn hard toward Venus. It would be the old ship's last flight, since it couldn't fit through the tunnel to De Milo, and it would be full of refugees from the Belt.

Brooklyn had missed his old pal Terry by eight hours. The pilot had made it back in time for the meeting and gone right back out again to pick up a polypod of miners on Vesta.

He ordered another bottle.

"It's been a while." The Purple Lady took shape on the stool next to him, 1930s Earth glamour meets a dingy asteroid bar at the tuck-tail end of the Twentieth Century. "Are you trying to avoid me?"

He poured three fingers of vodka into a glass for her. "Don't seem right drinking in front o' the kids."

"How'd you get the morning off?"

"They're crawling 'round inside the *Baron*'s hull, patching holes an' gettin' it ready to fly."

"The youngest of them is six, Brooklyn."

"Murph won't let anything happen to them. They're mostly

jus' holdin' shit for him. Passin' it along. I wouldna let him in there I thought it was dangerous."

"This from a man who can't be killed." She drained her glass and signaled the bartender. "Another, please. Gin."

"He can see you?"

"Better that than let him see you talking to yourself." She put her hand on his arm. "Real as you are."

"For the moment."

"That's true for anyone. My moment is just longer than most people's." She frowned. "I wonder, though, if, at the end, it will seem short."

He held up his glass. "To moments."

They clinked.

"Really, though," she moved the vodka bottle in line with the others, "are you trying to make up for lost time? I don't think there's such a thing as an alcohol deficit."

"Getting blotto." He smirked. "What my old man used to call it. So drunk you can't tell bad from good, bathroom from closet, or your bed from someone else's. Hard state to achieve when you're full of tiny robots."

"You made Maddy cry."

He started. "You saw that?"

She shook her head. "I just put one and five together. You want them to go back to Venus on the *Baron*. They want to stay with you and go to the Artiplanet."

"Made all o' them cry." He tossed back more vodka. "Didn't sign up to be a babysitter."

"You told them they were your crew."

"Just said that to... I dunno... get 'em to do what I said."

"And they did. And now you're dumping them." She sighed. "Now I want to cry."

"Said I'd think about it."

"Are you thinking? You should. Life in a cave with other humans or life on a starship full of wonders, seeing things no other of their species will ever see? I know what I'd pick."

"They're kids."

"They're people, Brook." She turned her glass around on the bar. "Drinking like this isn't healthy. Do you want to go back to your room and try sex again?"

He popped an eyebrow. "That didn't go so well last time. Said it was 'an extremely inefficient way of propagation.'"

"It is."

"You said I satisfied, like, point-one-three percent of you."

"I am made of millions, Brooklyn. Do the math. That's actually a rather high number." She took his hand. "C'mon. Before Maddy gets back, and you tell her you changed your mind."

FIFTY

Once, the Artiplanet had orbited the Sun directly opposite Earth at precisely the same distance. Hidden from primate math and science by advanced-alien tech, it had held there for more than a hundred years watching, waiting, and scheming.

Now, it was in the Belt, nearly close enough to Ceres to give it a big smooch, but only if it stood on tippy toes.

"I thought it would be bigger," Maddy said. She'd squeezed into the copilot seat with Tyra, who was sleeping with her mouth open.

"Eighth the size of the Moon," Brooklyn said. "Plenty big for something somebody built."

Something the Trolls built. Now the weird little dudes were mining nearby asteroids and outfitting the thing for deep-space travel.

"You guys need to stay on the ship," Brooklyn said. "Got no idea what's goin' in there, an' I can't keep an eye on your butts and mine at the same time. Get me?"

Maddy nodded, her eyes not leaving the gleaming sphere ahead. Its surface was mostly solar collectors.

Tyra shifted position, pulling her knit hat further over her eyes. One of four girl compatibles on the crew, she liked cats and math, and was an expert at keeping her slightly older brother in check.

Brooklyn considered her. *Kids in space*. “Take her back to the playpen an get everyone strapped in while I land.”

The voice on the radio directed Brooklyn to a football-field sized doorway protected by a First field. He landed square in the middle of the big space inside and put the ship on standby.

“What can I do?” Maddy said. After getting the others situated, she’d returned to supervise the landing.

“Sit tight an’ stay out of the liquor cabinet. If you make a mess, clean up after yourself.”

“What if you never come back?”

“Then you can drink all the booze you want.” He deactivated the controls. “Om, what’re the odds you can whip up a simulation and teach Maddy here how to fly this thing?” She took in a sharp breath.

“Extremely good. I can easily improve the one you created for me.”

“Everyone’s a critic.” He jabbed his finger at Maddy. “That does not mean you get to fly my ship.”

She nodded solemnly. “Of course not.”

“If you’re gonna be crew, you’re gonna be useful. Give the other kids jobs too. Have ’em start reading the manuals. Learn th’ emergency systems and maintenance protocols.”

“What about Nathan?”

“Nathan can clean the bathroom.” He took off his seatbelts. “Stay inside until I say.”

“Aye-aye, Captain.”

Andy met him outside.

“Prometheus lied about the strength of the protective field,” she said. “It won’t be enough to save De Milo from the event.”

Brooklyn’s hands dropped. “All the things I was expectin’, that wasn’t it.”

“Did you hear me?”

“Yeah, I just–” The ground seemed to spin and tilt under his feet. "Thought we had it set an–" *Demarco, Milk, Skim, Carmen, Top, Kas, Turk…* "I need a drink."

"We have a meeting in thirty minutes. I'll catch you up beforehand."

Another fuckin' save-the-world meeting. "Seems like there oughta be more blowin' shit up and less talkin'."

"What?"

"Never mind." He rubbed his mouth. "You got, like, teachers and babysitters here?" He threw an over-shoulder thumb at the *Victory*. "Got five kids in there. Six to eleven. They need a place to sleep and somethin' better than junk food to eat."

"Kids? I don't understand."

"My crew. Get 'em set an' we can talk."

Brooklyn left his drink untouched and started pacing. "We ain't the ones came into your neighborhood an' told ya 'start packing'. Don't see why we're the ones goin' extinct over this shit."

"Your people are the ones who triggered the event."

"Maybe they're the ones. In any case," he jabbed his thumb at his chest, "my people didn't start shit. Some people did. Just like you didn't fuck De Milo over, but one o' your guys sure in hell did."

"I'm sorry, Brook."

"Can we even get this thing back to De Milo in time?"

"Even if we could, there's not enough room. We could take another ten thousand, maybe. And that's pushing it."

Brooklyn dropped onto the couch. "Where the fuck is Prometheus?"

"Setting up a new lab."

"An' you want me to roust him?"

"He faked data. Lied about results. What he did was unethical, not illegal. He won't find it easy to get collaborators and resources after that."

"That's it? Douche is gonna find it hard to make friends from now on? No more punishment than that?"

She nodded.

"The hell you need me for?"

"I needed a human, and you're the best one I know." Her mouth firmed. "I have a last shot at saving this, and I need you to help me decide if I should take it."

FIFTY-ONE

"This is way over my head. I'm just a guy from Queens, ya know?"

The Builder moved his hands. He didn't know.

Brooklyn had found the place by accident, his frenzied pacing building up to a need to escape, the need driving him to ask Andy where his crew was, and the desire to avoid talking to anyone he knew pushing him to go in the opposite direction. He'd turned the corner at random and spotted the gathering, a dozen of the horned-builders gathered at a bar.

"Don't know the finger thing for 'Queens', sorry." Brooklyn tried again, speaking as slowly as he gestured the words. "I don't have the right tools for this job."

The Builder asked what the right tool would be.

"Probably a bullet." Brooklyn tapped his forehead. "Right there. Get me off this damned ride. Least I'd forget she asked me the question." He rubbernecked for a bartender or waiter. Or any sign of imbibing. "No booze in Builder bars, huh?"

This is a rehearsal room, the Builder said. The performance is called, *Always Check Your O-Rings*. We will present it tonight.

"What part do you play?"

The love interest who distracts the inspector from their work at a crucial time.

Brooklyn clapped the Builder on the shoulder. "Gonna be great, pal. Break a leg."

Leaving a room full of confused and offended Builders in his wake, Brooklyn retraced his trudge through pastel corridors to the hanger and into the apartment Andy had set him and the kids up with.

You're the best human I know. I need you to help me decide. He growled. *Way above my fuckin' paygrade, Andromeda.*

Brooklyn hadn't listened well to Andy's directions, but his little robots helped him out by painting a directional arrow on his retinas. He stopped short and cursed for several seconds when he realized he'd been following the thing without thought or question. The door to the apartment slid open on his approach.

"Look who's here!" Kyra said.

Most Designed bodies had been crafted along human lines, so the furniture in the large, warmly lit room needed little explanation. Chairs, couch analogs, fat pillows... most of them filled with kids. The seat of honor, a bronze-colored lozenge with the square footage of a queen-sized bed was occupied by a black-clad woman with blood-red hair.

"Guessing you brought that Caliban guy with you," Brooklyn said.

"We all came," Razer said. "I'm supposed to bring you to him."

"Now?"

The cyborg looked from him to the cluster of kids hanging on her every word. "Do you mind if we hang out a little first? Just a couple of minutes."

"Fine." Brooklyn threw his jacket on a chair. He had a bottle in his go-bag, which allegedly had been moved to his room. "Holler when you're ready."

FIFTY-TWO

Caliban and his people had parked in the big hanger, the one with enough space to accommodate at least two seven-kilometer asteroids.

"The whole thing is a ship." Brooklyn rubbed his mouth. "You fly it in here?"

"I've steered it, but I think this is the first time it's ever done something like this," Razer said.

"That's fuckin' crazy." The giant rock hung motionless forty feet above the floor of the hanger. First Tech was impressive, much of it stemming from their mastery of gravity, inertia, and magnetism, but the zero-g hanger was a marvel. "Kept a vacuum in there, I imagine."

She nodded. "No sense asking for pressure problems."

The hanger was as well-lit as an operating room, and a fleet of drones swarmed it collecting the micrometeorites and other debris Ariel had drawn in with it.

"How do we even get in there?"

Razer showed him to an elevator and a corridor that led to a First field-protected walkway.

Brooklyn studied it dubiously. "That thing safe?"

"Is until it's not." Her eyes were playful. "Come on."

Certain-death fall to either side, protected from vacuum by something with an on/off switch, he followed her onto the walkway and across to one of the asteroid's many airlocks.

After a day on the Artiplanet, entering Ariel was like jumping back in time. The corridors were carved right out of the rock, only the lighting testifying to the advanced technology that made the whole thing possible. Brooklyn shuddered. "You live in here?"

"It gets better," she said. "No sense in making a hallway look fancy."

The corridor ended in a lounge area, a study in leather, chrome, and Lucite, or whatever passed for such things millions of miles from Earth. The carpet was orange shag.

"Looks like the '70s exploded in here," Brooklyn said.

"I like it." Razer pushed a button under a round screen on the wall. "He's here, boss."

The lab was like something out of a German expressionist film. Warm and humid. Strange, not-quite vile smells. Dark corners with nearly human shapes stretched out on racks. Low, weird trance music coming from everywhere at once. Andy was already there, and–

"Specialist Lamontagne!" The voice rang a bell, but the body and face… blue skin, magenta hair in braids, a simple skirt its only clothing… did not. "I thought never to see you again."

It took a second. "Carruthers." The military doctor from the *Baron von Stueben*. The one who'd injected him with First Tech. "The fuck you doing here?"

"I've come home." The doctor spread his arms. His hands had been mutilated, the right one missing its pinky and ring finger, the left replaced with a prosthetic. "This is where I was created, and this is where I expect to die."

"Caliban," Andy said.

Brooklyn's head jerked toward her. "You knew who this fucker was?"

"When I first met him, I wasn't sure whether I should thank him or throw him out an airlock. But, yes, I knew who he was when I sent you to Ariel."

"Why's he blue?"

"A revisal of self. New me, new name! 'Caliban'." He held out his hand dramatically. "'And here you sty me in this hard rock, whiles you do keep from me the rest of the island'." His smile revealed pointed teeth. "The ambassador chose the airlock, metaphorically. She refused to let me return home until this very day!"

Brooklyn bristled. "You made me a guinea pig."

"True," Caliban said. "I also killed you and dumped your body into space. The first truth saved you from the second, and I apologize for neither."

"The hell you mean you killed me?"

He sighed. "The *Baron* had been ordered to intercept the First ambassador's ship, and I was forced hide my experiment before there was possibility of detection." Caliban cocked his head like a parrot. "Nothing? We went out on the hull of the ship to look for damage. I shot you and Mr Robinson. Left your bodies to drift?" He hummed. "Well, no harm done."

"Tell that to Robinson," Brooklyn growled.

"I would, but without my treatments, he stayed dead. While you," he circled Brooklyn, "did not. I would love to get a blood sample."

"Hell no." Brooklyn stepped back. "This your Plan B, Andy? Guy's crazy."

"We're well past Plan B," Andy said. "Hear him out."

"I nearly shat myself when I saw you at my door." Caliban said. "The ambassador's representative human. I wonder if you truly are one still." He began to circle again but stopped himself. "All right. A short history lesson. I jumped ship when the *Baron* returned to Earth with the prime ambassador. No hard feelings. I loved those boys, and I'm just pleased as punch they sailed right back out and avoided all the fuss that followed."

He clasped his hands. "Anyhoo, I lived through the blackout and made my way to the Artiplanet afterward. When I first arrived, I met a Designed scientist who was researching singularities. His patron wanted to make a backup copy of the galaxy using the black hole at its center as the storage medium. Are you with me so far?"

"Not even," Brooklyn said.

"It's a simple matter of redundancy," Caliban said. "First science will soon, relatively speaking, reach the point where it can alter the fabric of reality itself. Experiments in this area may well prove… hazardous… to all existence, thus we need a backup to restore from."

"Why even do shit that can wreck reality?"

"To know!" His eyes went wild. "To know and understand is the highest purpose."

Brooklyn took a seat on a nearby lab stool. "Pretend I agree with you. What does this have to do with the Sun?"

"My former colleague created an artificial singularity to experiment with, right here on the Artiplanet." He pointed. "Not six miles away from this very hanger. It's not large enough for the galaxy, but I believe we could make a copy of this solar system prior to the stellar event." He bowed. "Now, the ambassador says that you, speaking for all humanity, must be the one to give me permission to try."

Andy looked flustered. "Maybe a time will come when the backup can be used to restore everything. It's a better chance than none at all, isn't it?"

Brooklyn rubbed the back of his neck. "Don't get how this would work. Store data, sure. Numbers. But people?"

Caliban stepped over to one of his lab benches and came back with a circlet. "You've seen these, yes? Up to six lives, every detail can be stored on one. And these are just copies of the files. The originals are that away," he pointed down toward the center of the Artiplanet, "in the primary computer."

"It would take a billion o' those to hold everyone. Even then… Would they be alive in there? Or would it be like a record, like, just an inert thing until someone plays it?"

"More like the record, in that analogy." Caliban tapped his

thumbnail on his teeth. "I think. I doubt they'd be self-aware." He tapped more. "Unless every recording is somehow self-aware when it's played. That's an interesting thought."

"What's the catch?" Brooklyn said. "You're just making a copy. Don't see what all the hemmin' and hawin's about."

"See!" Caliban looked at Andy with triumph in his eyes. "He doesn't see any issues either."

"Brook, making copies of objects this way is a fairly easy process. This project is more complicated because of the scale, but I believe it can be done." Andy took a breath. "The problem arises when we copy minds. Not the brains, but the minds, which are emergent qualities of the physical objects."

"Software versus hardware," Brooklyn said.

"The differences go far deeper, but let's go with that. The technology we have can make a copy of the software, but it destroys the hardware in the process." She waited for him to catch up.

"You mean–" Brooklyn started again, stopped again. "You drug me out here to say if you should kill five billion people 'fore the Sun gets a chance to."

"Yes."

"Andy, you shoulda picked someone else. The Pope. The Dalai Lama. Carl Sagan. Oprah." Brooklyn put pressure on his temples with the heels of his hands. "I ain't even a good person. I don't have the, the whatever for this."

"You gave me a name, Brook," she said. "I was designed for a specific purpose, and I became more than that because I met you."

"Don' give yourself enough credit, babe. You were never anyone's tool. I'm jus some guy who–"

"Take a breath," she said. "You've come a long way. I'm sure you could use some rest. Give yourself a day to think, and I'll find you when you're ready."

FIFTY-THREE

Brooklyn watched the kids play a video game. If nothing else, the five of them would be fine. They'd ride out of the solar system with Andy and the rest of the Designed. Live a life of weird, crazy, adventure. Be space pirates, maybe. In a decade or two, one of the girls might throw Nathan a bone and there'd be a baby. Life would go on.

An' maybe that's enough. Ask 'em to vote on it. Kids, do you mind living the rest of your life on a spaceship haunted by five billion people? You okay with dragging the weight of everyone who came before ya around for the rest of your life an' feelin' guilty that you can't find a way to open the jar you voted to put 'em in?

The Earth in a jar forever. The people on it, as good as dead. *So why not let them die now 'stead of kicking the can down the road?*

Because killing five billion people is a lot. A week of five billion people's lives is ninety-six million years of human experience. He'd done the math. Twice.

Maddy held up the controller. "You wanna have a go, Brook?"

"All set." He rose and grabbed his jacket off the hook. "Gonna go for a walk. Don' let anyone get arrested."

He tracked back to the hanger where they'd left the *Victory* and punched in the code to open the door. "Om, what time is it in De Milo?"

"It's 3:25 a.m.," the computer said. "Shall I plot a course?"

"Nope. You go on back to bein' a rock. I got this." He detoured to the kitchen for the instant-coffee jar he'd stuffed in the back of the spice rack, grabbed a half bottle of vodka from the freezer, and took them both to the cockpit.

He settled into his couch, shook a dried mushroom from the jar, and chewed it carefully. The icy vodka washed the taste out of his mouth."

"What are you doing?" Om said.

"Nothing to worry 'bout, man. Just gonna sit here a while and think."

"Would you like to see the changes I've made to our rock simulation?"

He took another swallow of vodka. "Go for it."

The main viewscreen lit up with an animated image of a comet. "That's us," Om said. "We are in the Pleiades, a star cluster in the constellation of Taurus, approximately four hundred and forty-four light years from Earth."

"We're the whole comet, not just a rock inside?"

"I am adjusting to more complex systems." It paused. "On Deimos–"

"Went through all that already, bud. You and me are good."

"And I am grateful for that. Dr Milk gave me some reading material that helped me to diagnose what happened. I believe I became overwhelmed and had a panic attack."

Brooklyn hummed. "Sounds about right."

"The simulation is allowing me to learn to adapt to additional complexity without the worry of affecting real events."

"You ready to be my copilot again?"

"Not yet, but I believe I will be in time."

"Not goin' anywhere for a while, anyway," Brooklyn said. "Done a helluva job on this sim."

"It's still a work in progress." But there was a note of pride in Om's voice. "Do you really like it?"

"Yeah. Keep going. Show me some more."

Om talked about astronomy, geology, and simulation

programming while Brooklyn worked his way through the rest of the bottle. The lights on the control surfaces brightened and the spaces between them grew less distinct. The starscape on the screen blended with the patterns of light all around him.

Om's voice became a drone and dropped away. Brooklyn was dashing through the stars. He was the comet, cold and alone but warming and growing as it rushed toward a purple star.

"Usually, I have to come to you," she said.

"Don't like the comedown from those things. Dry mouth for days." He lost himself momentarily in the colors running under his skin. "You know what's goin' on? Andy's big plan to save the day?"

"The highpoints." She smiled. "I don't spend all my time watching you."

A guitar wailed somewhere, a sound Brooklyn felt in his bones. The colors inside him danced.

"Demarco should be asleep right now. Probably half in the bag. Think we can talk to him?"

"I'll see what we can do."

"You a plant lady, but you're purple," Demarco said.

"Not all plants have chlorophyll," the Purple Lady said. "If it helps, think of us more like a fungus."

"An' even though you're sittin' on the rock 'cross from me, you're also," he spread his arms wide, "everywhere."

"Hardly." She laughed. "Although we are many places."

"An' you met this asshole," he pointed at Brooklyn, "at a party because he got high and let someone stick needles in him." He closed his eyes. "An' I'm sitting naked on the surface of Mars. Helluva dream."

"It's not a dream, man," Brooklyn said. "Told you I need your help."

One eye opened. "An' this is all in my head. Including that music I keep hearin'."

"Yes! No–" Brooklyn cursed. "Technically, we're both in her head."

"In the mushroom lady's head. Your imaginary friend."

"She's not imaginary."

"But she the one who took my pants." He rested his hands on his thighs. "Okay. Just let it all hang out then." He sucked his teeth. "Mr Lamontagne, what do you suppose Andy would do if you told her 'no'?"

"She wouldn't do it."

"No?" He cocked an eyebrow. "She got that big ship, all that technology... Even let the mad scientist back inside the house. An' you think she's just gonna say, 'Let 'em burn.'"

"I-I don't know."

"Sure you do. Maybe you jus' forgot. This the same lady who attacked her creators – twice – on our account. She fought her gods for us, babe. She ain't like to let us go easy."

"She'll do it."

Demarco nodded. "But she'd be happier doin' it with you. Maybe she's even hopin' you'll see a better way to do it."

"Do I?"

"Don't know what the hell you seein', kid. Havin' enough trouble with my own eyes." He smiled at the Purple Lady. "Don't seem fair you ain't naked too."

Her clothing vanished as did Brooklyn's. "Better?"

"Some." Demarco leaned forward. "What were the First like back when they had faces to hit?"

"Like you. Always in a hurry to get to the next thing... whatever that was at any one time. Lazy. They took shortcuts when they should have gone the long way around."

"Meat wants what it wants," Demarco said. "Usually, that's more meat, either ta fuck or ta eat. Not a lot of forethought there." He bent over and ran some Mars dust through his fingers. "How much time 'fore the Sun goes boom?"

"Andy says we got less than two months," Brooklyn said.

"An' you say if she does the thing, it'll take away half a billion years of people time. Time when folks could be gettin' right with God, fucking like monkeys, takin' bloody vengeance on them that wronged them, and drinking theyselves stupid?"

"Yeah."

"That's a lotta years, babe. Lotta zeroes." He made the church steeple with his fingers and tapped them against his lips. "You believe in God? Souls and heaven and all that shit?"

"I guess not. Maybe I did when I was a kid, but–"

"But you grew up. Now you believe this is it. Sentience is binary. On or off. No better home awaitin' after all the trials and tribulations of Earth. If there was a heaven, wouldn't matter when the five billion people die. They'd get their chance in the sweet, sweet hereafter."

"You think I'm wrong?"

"Nope. Be nice to get a little patch o' paradise after I kick it, but the world don't work that way." He stood and stretched his back. "See your problem, babe, an' I do not envy your seat."

"What should I do?"

Demarco shrugged. "Tell her 'no' if it makes you feel righteous, but it ain't gonna change her mind. If you got a better idea, tell her that instead. She'd prob'ly be glad to hear it. Gets kinda lonely at the top."

"Are you going to tell everyone about the First field?"

"That it won't work?" He traced some lines in the Martian soil with his bare toes. "No. Assuming this ain't a dream, I'm gonna keep that little nugget to myself. Things crazy enough 'round here without dropping that shoe."

Demarco started to fade.

"He's waking up," the Purple Lady said.

"There's a jar of mushrooms in my house," Brooklyn said. "Use them if you need to talk to me."

The guitar wailed again. Demarco waved goodbye.

* * *

Om was still talking about being a comet. Brooklyn glanced at the clock. He'd be feeling the effects of the mushrooms for hours yet, but his time with the Purple Lady, which had gone on well after Demarco woke up, had taken no time at all.

"I believe I will try a single-celled organism in a month or two," Om said. "An amoeba, perhaps. Or algae. That might be better because I wouldn't have to worry about feeding it."

"This thing can do that?" Brooklyn said. The control panel was on fire with lights, and he still had that one-with-everything feeling.

"The program is extremely adaptable. Simulating life would require many more variables, but that's simply a matter of time and testing. Code it, run it, and watch."

"Can you show me how you do that part?" Brooklyn said. "Keep it real simple, though. I'm kinda fucked up."

FIFTY-FOUR

"How do I know we can trust you?"

Caliban working with a Designed computer, spinning a holographic model of the singularity on three axes. "Why wouldn't you?"

"You killed me."

The scientist sighed. "We met at one of the many crossroads in my life, specialist. I was not the man I was, nor yet the being I became. Mistakes were made." He touched his right temple. "Do you see that scar?"

Brooklyn leaned closer. "Looks like you got poked with something."

"An ice pick." He smiled ruefully. "A self-administered trephination to release the demons in my head."

"Not making me feel any better about you."

"My First patron, my creator, decided many years ago I should be a doctor, a husband. The father of two beautiful children. Or perhaps I decided that. Either way, I had a good life. Quiet. Happy." He shut down the model of the singularity. "Approximately two years before you and I met, it wasn't enough. My patron needed additional stimulation. Drama. It ordered me to kill my wife and children."

"Fuck."

"Ordered makes it sound like I heard the command and made the choice." He shook his head. "That's not what happened. My patron *decided* I would kill my wife and children because it wanted the experience, and I did." He tapped the scar. "I did this first, praying it would stop me, hoping it would kill me if it did not. It did neither. I woke among the bodies, my mind clear, fully cognizant of what I had done and what I was. Inhuman. But I felt nothing, and I knew… everything. My crude surgery had changed the direction of the link with my patron. The connection was quickly severed, but in that brief time, I saw the entirety of First science. I wrote down everything I could remember when I woke. Then I created a new identity, and joined the EOF."

"Where you started using people as guinea pigs."

He held up a finger. "Lack of empathy." He held up another. "Meets advanced alien knowledge." A third. "And insatiable curiosity." He made a fist. "Boom."

"That don't really answer my question," Brooklyn said.

"The work is all, specialist." He reactivated the hologram. "Give me a puzzle to solve, a problem to work, and I will give it everything I have. And, if I must, everything you have, as well."

Brooklyn paced the small kitchen. "And then he says it was an accident what the nanobots – it's what he calls them – did to me. The nanobots are how they build the splinters and Designed. He harvested some dormant ones from his own body, an' from a Designed scientist he used to work with, and reprogrammed them. Set them free is what he said."

"He injected them into you." Om paused. "To what end?"

"Experiment. They'd killed the last guy. He wanted to see if it would happen again."

"Does he know why it did not?"

Brooklyn dropped into a chair and put his head in his hands. "Said I had cancer when I came on board the *Baron*. Took too many rads on the Moon. The doc figures the nanobots went after that first, so they had time to figure me out and get comfortable without killing me."

"Instead, they changed you."

"He said the bots are what's left of a machine-intelligence experiment. They busted loose, an' the First lobotomized them. Took away their higher functions, changed them so they could be used as tools. Pretty fucked up."

"The nanobots inside you are sentient?"

"Semi-sentient. Doc said he couldn't fix 'em all the way. They're kinda like dogs. Helpful, well-meaning, not too bright."

"And this makes you trust him?"

"Oh, hell no." Brooklyn made a face. "Even money he'd rather dissect me than talk about the weather. But I'm starting to believe he can pull this off."

Give yourself the day to think. The day was about over, and in the morning–

"Zhi is so cool." Maddy said.

"She let you call her that?" Brooklyn was sautéing peppers and onions in the suite's kitchen.

"Says I remind her of her little sister. She can make claws pop out of her fingers *and* she plays electric guitar!"

"Pretty cool." He took a sip of the bitter mushroom tea on the countertop next to him.

"She said she'll give me lessons."

"Maybe you can start a band. Caught her listening to Bikini Kill while ago. Got some tapes in the ship if you want to listen."

A whole planet's worth of music about to burn up. Music, art, bad television, good intentions, bad ideas, dogs, cats, gorillas, saints, sinners, and everyone in between. Take a picture, save it to the singularity, maybe it will last longer.

Think I got an idea, but I need more time to work it out.

You can have the time, the Purple Lady said. **I can give it to you. Bring them all to me.**

PART FIFTEEN
Star-Bellied Boy

FIFTY-FIVE

Brooklyn dimmed the lights. "This oughta work. She knows me pretty well, and I can serve as a… thing… for the rest of ya." He divided two of the Martian mushrooms into thirds and gave a piece each to the participants. "Eat it, then lie back and relax."

They lay down on cots and couches set up for the purpose. Brooklyn hit the play button on the boombox, setting his favorite Herbie Hancock tape into motion. "Don' know why jazz works the best for this, but it does." He chewed his own piece of mushroom and lay down to wait for it to take effect.

Hello–

"–Brooklyn," the Purple Lady said.

They were standing on the surface of Mars again, cold, barren, dusty. He felt the others join them there. "Brought a few extra people along. This thing's way too big for me."

Andy. Caliban. And two of the top Designed computer scientists.

"It's good to meet you," the Purple Lady said.

The landscape changed, moss, moldy, fungus. Alive and wet. Drizzling. A Mars that wound down long before Earth life crawled from the seas. Demarco and Milk strolled up.

"What are you?" Andy said.

She smiled. "We are," she gestured at the landscape, "this. Or we were. Now we're something else."

"The Red Planet's native sentient lifeform," Brooklyn said. "Plant-based."

"Mycelial, mostly. We were part of all of this." She rotated slowly. "Part of each other."

"This is incredible." Caliban said. "Nothing in the First records say–"

"Look deeper," the Purple Lady said. "Before they traveled to Earth, they came here and attempted to seed the planet with their genetic stock. As if we needed more seeds! They refused to communicate with us, could not, and we consumed their experiments."

"What happened to you?" Andy said.

"Life here was always balanced on a knife's edge. A few degrees here, a few there. Enough changed to make it unviable. We saw it coming and left ahead of it. Ascended. Became."

"Spores," Brooklyn said. "They spored up and left the planet."

"Sporogenesis. We traveled on the cosmic winds. Journeyed on comets and meteors," she said. "Traveled to all the other planets in the solar system and beyond." She spread her arms, reaching out the full length of her fingers and toes. "And we still are."

"Are what?" Caliban said.

"Still connected. One mind linked a billion ways over billions of miles."

"How did the specialist–?" Caliban said.

"I drank her," Brooklyn said. "Cleveland Crater, back in the '70s. Spores came down on the meteorite that took out the city and took root. Guy there distilled his latest batch of goofy juice from shrooms he found growing nearby, and I tripped into her. Went back later and harvested enough ta grow my own batch o' Martian mushrooms."

"We've been connected ever since. Weakly at first, but our link has grown and rooted well." She took his hand. "We need one more." The Purple Lady reached through Brooklyn's mind into the eager-to-please intelligences inside his physical body and used them to make the connection.

"Hello," Om said. "Where am I?"

"With me," the Purple Lady said. "You have all the time you need here, and none will pass outside. I've unlocked your minds. Dream together until you find your way." She smiled. "I brought someone too."

Shoulder-length hair, thin goatee, rich fabrics, more icon than man, the Artist joined them. He'd began hearing the Purple Lady when he was twelve, and she'd influenced his music and style. The Artist and his band had ascended into her cosmic oneness permanently during a 1990 concert before an extremely stoned Copenhagen audience.

"Just here to help, if I can," the Artist said. "Provide some inspiration and a groove." He unslung his guitar. The rest of the band appeared and plugged in.

Andy's jaw dropped.

"Let's jam."

FIFTY-SIX

Caliban deactivated the blood-filter system he'd devised to remove the nanobots from Brooklyn's body.

"Likely there is no way to remove every one of them." He held up a vial of viscous fluid he'd pulled out of the system. "But we should get enough to force the rest into dormancy."

The nanobots would be mixed into five quarts of superconductive fluid and pumped into Om's new housing. The result could be, should be, the most advanced machine intelligence since the First stopped experimenting with them eons ago.

"Now what?" Brooklyn said.

"Time to let the big brains work, specialist. Take a walk. Take a nap. Anything. Just get out from underfoot." Caliban inspected the vial. "And try not to get killed. It will probably stick this time."

Brooklyn orientated himself and headed back to the suite he shared with the kids from Tycho. It was chilly, and he pulled his jacket over the T-shirt he'd worn for the nanobot-removal procedure. It was a little demoralizing to be chased out of the workspace, but he couldn't argue. He got the gist of the project, but he was punching way above his weight in skills and know-how. If he'd stuck around, he'd have been relegated to fetching coffee and snacks.

He filled a tumbler with water and drank it down. Caliban's

prediction that he'd be dehydrated in wake of the procedure came true and... He rubbed his eyes. *Little nap wouldn't hurt.*

The bedcovers took the rest of the chill away. Saving the day wasn't clean and neat like it was in the movies. There was no single point of failure to exploit or object of power to retrieve. Even if the plan worked, humanity would be changed forever, even if it never knew it.

An' here we are goin' ahead with it. Not asking permission. Not even takin' a poll. All on us. On me.

He flung his arm over his eyes. Fucked up as he was, Caliban was the perfect guy for the job. He never stopped to wonder if what he was doing was right. *Just another problem to solve.* They'd worked the solution out over the subjective months they'd spent in the Purple Lady's mycelia network, with barely twenty minutes passing in real time.

In a week, every sentient being in the solar system would be dead or dying, their brains irrevocably scrambled but their minds uploaded to a simulation Om and his team were creating. The simulation would run on the Designed's new supercomputer, and the data required – all those minds, textures, shapes, physical laws, geographical details – stored in the singularity. Om would act as systems administrator, a clockmaker god, watching the program run and summoning help if any decisions needed to be made.

Done correctly, no one inside the simulation would notice the difference. Done wrong, the result would be insanity in a digital world or the slightly premature death of three planets.

No pressure. Brooklyn rolled to his side. "Bed, put me to sleep."

Designed beds could do that, and it did.

Maddy and the Gaggle were running drills in the *Victory* using the piloting simulation Om had made her.

"Getting awfully comfortable in my ship," Brooklyn said, leaning into the cockpit.

"It's like a video game we can all play."

"You guys sure about staying with this bunch? Not too late to–"

"Get uploaded back to Earth?" She made a face. "There's reasons we left."

"Five punks traveling the galaxy with a buncha cyborgs and aliens does make a better story." Brooklyn cracked his neck. "Just wanna be sure you're sure."

"Are you? You could stay out here with us."

He puffed his cheeks. "Way too tired to play sole survivor. Future's on you guys."

He tapped on the tank. "You in there, pal?"

Designed computer experts had carefully removed Om's mind from the *Victory* and installed it in a clear tank of super-conducting fluid. There'd been some mocking disbelief that the hodge-podge of technology Brooklyn had brought together had functioned at all, but there'd been little modification that he could see. Also floating in the super-conductor were millions of nanobots that had called him home for the past twenty years.

The tank reminded him of Float. The Jellies were headed for Proxima Centauri. The majority of them had already entered the long sleep that would allow them to survive the trip between the stars. *There is intelligent life out there, and it is surly.*

"We have a problem," Om said. "There is not enough space in the singularity for our requirements."

"The singularity will grow over time," Andy said. "Won't that–"

"I have taken growth into account, but there is not enough room at the present time."

"What if we don't fully render the outer planets? Humanity's shown little interest in anything beyond Jupiter."

"Nah, we don't render the outer planets, the jig is up," Brooklyn said. "Someone'll try to run Saturn's rings again on a bet or a dare and blow it for everyone."

"What if they cannot?" Caliban ran his maimed hand over the side of his face. "What if we changed the simulation so such travel was not available? It would give the singularity time to grow, and the program could expand to fit the space. It would also give us some wiggle room."

"Like building in some kind of do-not-pass fence?"

"Build a fence, they are going to want to climb over it," the blue man said. "I was thinking of something more subtle. Remove a single piece of technology and humanity would be kept local long enough for the singularity to catch up."

"You're talking about the Oppenheimer Engine," Brooklyn said.

Caliban nodded. "What if it were never invented?"

"Is that possible?" Andy said. "You'd be changing history."

"We'd be changing the simulation's history." His eyes were blazing. "If we start it running in 1946, say, we could make it so the engine never existed."

"You'd have to do something about the First and the Jellies, too," Brooklyn said. "If they still show up in 1961, and there's no Jet Carson to chase 'em off..."

"So, we remove the First and the Jellies from the program, too." Caliban rubbed his hands together. "It's a better play than the cover story we came up with. That both species just mysteriously left."

"Om?" Brooklyn said.

"I'm working through it now." It paused. "Using other means of propulsion, humanity might have made it to Mars by 1999 but not beyond."

"So, we need Mars. Does that give you enough storage space?"

"It should." Om considered. "Yes. The expansion of the singularity will allow human society to evolve naturally from there. The simulation will fake all the data coming from beyond Mars until there is room to render the space."

"The Designed have been studying and observing Earth for the past century," Andy said. "I'll put a team of historians and sociologists together to figure out how the changes will affect history."

"We can write some predictive algorithms that will help going forward, too. Make the whole thing more realistic," Caliban nodded. "We're going to need a lot more mushrooms."

FIFTY-SEVEN

The Purple Lady handed him a beer. "It took me some time to find you."

Brooklyn had walked some distance from the think tank/jam session inside her network. "Needed to clear my head. Ain't much use in all that anyway."

"It wouldn't be happening without you."

"Without you." He tipped the bottle at her. "I'm just the guy who knows a mushroom woman who can pull people into a timeless gestalt. Handy."

She sat down beside him and pulled another beer from somewhere. The labels on both drinks were blurry, like the creator didn't remember what they really looked like or didn't care. "You brought Om into the equation."

"I was drinkin' a lot of Yarrow's tea when I put him together. You and the little robots get at least half credit for that." He took a long drink of the vaguely beer-flavored beer. "Still ain't got the taste right."

She shrugged. "I'm better with gin. It's more interesting to me."

They sat awhile, looking over a Martian valley teeming with plant life. "Never any animals here?" Brooklyn said.

"They evolved a few times – little fish things, a sort of snake – but never found their footing. Insects did okay for a while, but plants are tough competition, and we had a solid head start." She smiled. "We had thirty-four flower varieties that could fly under their own power."

"Evolution in action." He rubbed his forehead. "Hard to imagine. Million years. Billion. Billions. Just numbers. Fifty, though, a hundred, I got. 'Bout two hundred years it gets hard to getcha head round it again."

"Seven or eight human generations."

"Nothin', to you."

"You don't think you've had enough time?"

"Might be thinking that if this thing goes bad." He winced. "Other hand, might not be thinking anything."

"You didn't have to volunteer."

"Thought about sacrificing one o' the kids, but didn't want to break up the set."

"We won't be able to talk anymore."

He nodded. "That bothers me too. All the weirdo pals I got, you might be the weirdest."

Brooklyn and Andy sat atop the *Victory* weathering their mushroom comedowns. It was nearing midnight and their workday had started at 8 a.m., including nearly five months Purple-time.

"We might actually pull this off," Andy said.

It wouldn't be enough to change events in the simulation; they also had to change the memories of everyone they uploaded. At least a month of their long workday had been dedicated to developing search strings that would allow the algorithms to find and alter the necessary recollections of five billion people.

"Yep, guess I'm dying tomorrow," Brooklyn said.

"You're not dying. You're uploading."

He drank from the bottle and passed it to her. "My body, though. Caput. Cal said with all o' the bots stripped outta me, that's it. Brain in a blender. No take backs."

"If you want to have sex, just say it, Brook. There's no need for this last-day-on-Earth shit."

"Really?" He widened an eye at her.

"Sure."

He considered. "Guess I'm not really in the mood."

"Typical." She laughed. "I'd bet money there's never been a time in your life when you knew what you wanted."

"Sure, there has."

"When?"

He drank. "Sometime."

"For the past twenty years, you've had a spaceship and superpowers. Anyone else would've..."

"Would've what?"

"Been a pirate. Fought crime." Her hands flailed. "Done... something."

"Fought crime for a while. Under an alias. FuckOffMyBack Man."

"Cute."

"Shit like that works if you're the only one with superpowers and spaceships. Everyone's got 'em; you're just a guy people call when they want a couch moved to the Moon."

She drank. "The Cathedral left orbit yesterday. Looks like the Angels are headed for Andromeda."

"Hey-yo!"

"What does that mean?"

"Means your name is 'Andromeda' an– Never mind." He drank. "Ya know, we never did find out why those assholes stuck you on Deimos."

"Follow the money. It delayed us finding out about the Sun."

"Whole thing was already in motion, where's the money in–?"

"Depends on who lit the fuse."

"Easy. The First."

"Not everything is the First, Brook. My bet is still on the CIA."

"What if Beth's zealots were First splinters?"

"Prove it." She drank. "First didn't cut the link with splinters. Disconnected from the Angels, the Builders, and everyone else, but they wanted to experience the death of a world."

"By proxy."

"Of course by proxy!" She slapped his arm. "How do you even know that word?"

"Personal growth. Lot o' personal growth over th' last twenty years. Oughta try it."

"I was on the run."

"What'd you do when you found out they were still linked?"

She smirked. "Cut those fuckers right off."

"Mighta just changed my mind about the sex."

"Your place or mine?"

"Yours. Don't wanna wake the kids."

FIFTY-EIGHT

The bright light hurt his eyes. He'd forgotten how bad a hangover could be sans healing nanobots.

"Are you ready for this?" Caliban said.

"Better get this over with before I turn chickenshit, man."

Caliban adjusted the circlet on Brooklyn's head. "This shouldn't hurt. There might be a short period of disorientation, then you will be inside the simulation. We'll be able to communicate with you, and you with us." He turned some dials. "We'll ask you to do some simple tasks and ask you to–"

"Got the brief." His stomach was souring from the hangover or the stress of being moments away from physical death.

Andy brushed back Brooklyn's hair and kissed him on the forehead. "You're getting gray."

Caliban pushed the button.

Manhattan. Fifth Avenue and West 112th Street. A block away from Central Park.

Brooklyn relaxed his hands. He had his jeans on. His boots. Favorite jacket. It was a nice fall day, and the sidewalks and roadway were empty.

He took a deep, normal-feeling breath.

Take a few steps, specialist. Any direction.

Brooklyn crossed the street.

How does that feel?

"Like I'm walking toward Central Harlem."

Is that where you want to go?

"Is Amy Ruth's open?"

Not for another twenty-six years.

"You put me in the mid '70s?"

Do you have a problem with the mid '70s?

"No chicken and waffles from Amy Ruth's."

How about we take this seriously, specialist? Do you see any sign of the First or advanced technology of any kind?

Brooklyn shoved his hands in the pockets of his jacket and turned slowly in place. "Oughta be a robocab stand around here, but there ain't. Think there was a 'see aliens, yell aliens' billboard that way," he pointed, "but it's a Marlboro ad instead."

Head south.

"Through the Park?"

If you like. Your destination is Times Square.

"That's like a five-mile walk! Can't you just beam me there?"

We need to see how your simulated body responds to exercise. Maybe jog part of the way.

Brooklyn walked. He felt normal. Everything felt normal, except for the absence of people and traffic. Bird calls were the prevailing sound.

Simulated birds, he reminded himself. They'd upload as many animal minds as they could into the sim, but they had to draw the line somewhere. Most birds would be simulated in the new world, along with all the insects and tiny rodents. Squirrels, corvids, parrots, and rats were deemed sentient enough to save.

Brooklyn flicked a pebble at a simulated pigeon, and it flew convincingly away.

You need to void your bowels and bladder.

"Naw, I'm fine." But suddenly he was not.

It's necessary for our testing.

"I'm right in the middle of the Park!" His stomach cramped.

"You fucker!" He dashed off the path to a nearby bush and took care of business.

There are WetNaps in your jacket pocket. You're welcome.

"Liked it a lot better when there was no god!" He scanned the sky. "You hear me?"

There was no answer.

Caliban walked Brooklyn through several more tasks before telling him to pick a place and sleep for the night. Brooklyn opted for a penthouse with a balcony that overlooked the Park. Caliban refused to activate the elevator, so Brooklyn took the stairs... for science. When he woke up, breakfast was waiting on the table.

'Morning, Brook! What's it like in there?

Maddy. Brooklyn rubbed his eyes. "Nothin' screamin' simulation at me. Weather was nice yesterday, but Cal says he's gonna rain all over my parade today."

Rain in the morning. Snow in the afternoon, Caliban said. *Tomorrow there will be a heat wave.*

"Come on in here, Cal, and we'll test how it feels ta punch someone in the mouth."

Interesting proposal. Human interaction is on the schedule for the day after tomorrow. Feel free to try it then.

Brooklyn weathered two days of extremes, including a burrito that was so spicy it brought him to tears. He watched a sad movie and a comedy. A cat attacked his ankles from under a table and an angry dog chased him until he lost it by climbing a fence. He got a bad shock from a lamp.

We're almost done, specialist, Caliban announced on the morning of the first day. *Twelve or so hours of human interaction, then you can rest.*

Splinters were already in the database, so it was easy to load a few into the simulation. Brooklyn's first interaction was an attempted mugging by a sixteen-year-old from Kolkata. The kid was so spooked at finding himself in Manhattan, Brooklyn had to follow him two blocks and talk him down like he was suffering from a bad acid trip. Protocols changed after that. Only splinters who had been in New York a decade ahead or behind the mid '70s.

The next mugging went better, scientifically. Brooklyn was less enthused about the skinned knuckles and shiner he suffered in the attack.

He had a drink and shared a nice moment with a woman named Fiona who believed her sister's bachelorette party had left her behind at the bar somehow. She wrote her phone number on a napkin and wandered out into the noontime sun in search of a cab.

Brooklyn bought a hotdog from a cart and walked across town for a drink Caliban had arranged with an 'old pal.'

Dee – aka Dark Side, aka Levi Michaels, aka Professor Carl Stevens – was on the roof deck, sipping red wine and looking at the stars.

"To beautiful places," he said, raising a glass at Brooklyn's approach. "A long, long way from Parris Island." His eyes drifted. "You know, we just missed our anniversary. Twelve years."

He's our test case for memory alteration. You were in the Marines together. Get him talking about your common history. I will prompt you as needed.

Brooklyn poured himself a glass of wine. "To boot camp, and that drill sergeant, what's-his-name."

"Trask. Wonder what he's up to in this new world order."

"Prob'ly being an asshole."

They toasted him anyway.

"S'prised to run into you here," Brooklyn said.

"The world is large, babe, but only has so many good places to drink in." Dee spread his arms to take in the whole place. "Or dine. Like it?"

"Seems nice." He sniffed. "Smells good."

"Owner's Estonian. Betrayed by his country, banished by the powers that be, he came to the big city to rebuild."

"Really?"

"Naw. Killed his brother, grabbed all the family money he could, slipped out here to avoid a firing squad."

Brooklyn put down the chunk of bread he'd grabbed and wiped his mouth. "Not sure how I feel 'bout eating brother-killer food." He drank more wine, though.

"Help if I tell you I was the one killed the guy to stop a genocide, and little brother just set it up for me?"

"Maybe."

"That's what we'll go with, then." Dee held up his glass. "To Kane and Abel and the unoriginal sin."

"That what you do now?" Brooklyn said post toast. "Kill people?"

"It's rare, but it happens. Wrap it up in tissue and toss it into the philosophical side o' my head. Needs of the many, an' all that happy crappy." He covered a yawn. "Mostly, I study and write papers about history."

"Way too much school for me."

"Know I say it every time," Dee said, "but I appreciate like hell that you and Tommy came out an' got me when that chopper went down."

"You'da done the same."

"Fucking Lebanon." Dee drank some wine. "Easy to say you'd step up with a bottle in front of you and a nice view. Harder in the moment. You guys stuck it out there for me."

Brooklyn tossed back half the wine. "What you do for pals, right?"

"To pals." Dee tipped the glass at him. "Life feels different when you get older. Got more to lose, seems like."

He is still dating Sierra in this revision. They met on assignment in the Persian Gulf.

"That mean you and the lady are gettin' serious?"

"With our under-the-covers undercover?" Dee laughed.

"What she calls it. The answer is maybe and sometimes and if. Lot of miles 'twixt here and there."

"Quit and move somewhere nice. Write your books."

"Could." He snapped a grin. "Can you see Sierra doin' that? Settling down, raising kids, assassinating key members of the parent-teacher committee?"

They both laughed at that.

"Raise mountain lions or wolves, maybe," Dee said. "Only way she could keep her adrenaline as high as she likes it."

Brooklyn shifted his weight in the chair. "Saw Tommy a while back. He's good."

"Livin' the dream in Montana. Been too long since I seen him. Keep your friends close and your enemies at gunpoint and all that." He frowned. "Been quite a while since I seen you."

Distract him. He's getting anxious that he can't remember when.

"Ain't missed much. But look at you, man. Grad student. Writer. Gentleman spy. Betcha got one of those jackets with the elbow patches."

"Got two, in case I muss one in a canape fight." He stretched his legs out under the table. "Been on sabbatical mosta the year, though. Doin' a little lookeyloo in Nicaragua."

"And you came all the way back here for murder food?"

The waiter approached with another bottle of wine and took their order. Dee tapped the bottle with his fingernail. "Made in Chile. Nice finish. Sandy soil cuts the acid."

Brooklyn took a gulp of the new pour and faked noises of appreciation. He set the glass on the table.

"I came back to the States to make my report, got a few weeks off," Dee said once the waiter had finished fussing around. "Nice to get a break from spy vs. spy. Buncha kids fuckin' around in a playroom."

"They got plenty of toys to fill it."

They fell quiet. Brooklyn reached for his wine glass. "Boss didn't even allow you a booty call before sending you back out. Bastards."

"Ours is not to reason why..." He stretched his legs under the table again. "She'll meet me in Paris next month."

"Reassignment?"

"Vacation. Lines of engagement are getting muddy. Hard to know who you're really working with anymore. She's reassessing her options."

"You?"

"Gotta do something to fill the long, dark hours." He smothered a yawn. "'Bout you? You planning to settle down, get a piece of the dream?

"Trying to stop fucking up and letting people down."

"Eating worms, babe. Up to you to do something 'bout that."

The simulation froze. *Enough. On a scale of one to ten, how natural did that interaction feel?*

"I didn't know he was a splinter."

Does that matter? He doesn't either.

"Means he was linked when they pulled Andy off the *Victory* and left me there. First knew the meteorite was comin' for New York before Andy got to Earth and told them. Means I didn't have to die an–" He rubbed his mouth. "Mighta mattered a lot."

If it makes you feel any better, none of that happened in the revision. It won't matter at all if we go ahead with the plan. Are you sure you don't want to remember anything?

"I'm sure. New world, right? Gotta get with the program. 'Sides, now there's even more shit I wanna forget."

In that case, specialist–

"Wait a minute. Om, can you hear me?"

Yes, Brook.

Brooklyn rattled off a list of names. "Soon as those people turn thirty, slip a million bucks into their bank account. Make up a good story. Lottery or something. An' give my love to Maddy and the kids."

Will a million dollars be sufficient?

"Who the fuck needs more than a million bucks?"

Thy will be done, specialist, Caliban said. *Now sleep. When you wake, the world will be a much different place.*

FIFTY-NINE

Two Weeks Later

Insects, birds, and microbes on Earth, the Moon, the domes of Mars, and the caverns of Venus feasted like never before. Everything else was dead.

On the Artiplanet, Caliban clapped his hands together. "Attention, please. Sim Day One is April 22, 1946, Robert Oppenheimer's forty-first birthday. To celebrate, we're going to destroy all knowledge of his greatest invention. Team leads, please report.

"All Earth lifeforms active on this date will be in play, with their memories rolled back appropriately," said the head of the Population Management Team. "Anyone not active will be stored until needed. Six?"

Six, the head of P-Zombies, nodded formally. "Any lifeform active on Day One, but inactive when uploaded will be piloted by an algorithm generated by the SocioPsych Team."

"Do we expect any problems to come from that?"

"We'll likely get an epidemic of emotionally distant parenting though the late '50s," said the SocioPsych head, "but that shouldn't be an issue."

"We can control the speed of the simulation, so we'll fast forward to 1960 to make sure everything's working alright," Caliban said. "The History Team has everything pretty well scripted to that point. You want to say anything about that, Liz?"

Liz adjusted the eyeglasses she'd recently affected. "The return of the First and the Jellies had a huge impact on Earth development, and this is where the history algorithms we designed will come into play. We have many theories, but we're not one-hundred percent sure we know what will happen without the incursion, and we'll be watching the next thirty years or so of sim time very carefully."

"We'll fast forward again to December 31, 1999, and check again. January 1, 2000, is independence day. After that, hands off. We let it run sans interference unless Om sounds an alert. Questions?" Caliban looked around the room. "Once. Twice. Thrice."

He threw the switch.

DEC. 31, 1999

The wind stirred up the radioactive ashes of Manhattan. He shuddered, the many layers of clothing on his body doing little to stave off the deep cold. The missiles had flown more than a decade ago – return shots to the ones fired by the cowboy president – but the effects would last for centuries.

Brooklyn checked the snare. The trap line was usually good for a rat or two, sometimes a cat, a little fur for mittens and some protein for the stew pot. The last couple of days, it'd been empty. *Tough days when even the rats refuse to stick around.*

He wrapped the tattered scarf more tightly around his mouth and nose, wincing when the fabric caught on the radiation- and frost-burn scars on his face. More would die in the frigid night if he failed again to return with meat.

"Fuck!" The storefronts and homes around him were broken mouths, pillaged long ago of anything worth taking. He shook his fists at the sky. "Happy fuckin' New Year!"

"Well, that's no good." Caliban wrung his hands.

"Let's go back here," Andy pointed to a spot on the timeline, "change that, and rerun it."

DEC. 31, 1999

Brooklyn made a show of running his preflight checks and making sure he was buckled in tight. Leroy lounged in the copilot seat, .45 in his lap and cowboy hat on one blue-jeaned knee.

"You get air sick?" Brooklyn took the *Carmencita* up much faster than necessary. Artificial gravity and their stomachs lagged about a quarter second behind.

"Woof!" Leroy said, not as green as Brooklyn had hoped. "Like a roller coaster! Always like that?"

"Had to dodge a meteor." Brooklyn eyed the gun. "Hope the safety's on. Liable to put a hole right through the hull and kill everyone on board."

"Do your job, and it won't be no problem."

The ship passed through the cloud layer and raced for the black beyond.

"Since I'm the one here knows how to fly, seems like you're the one should be avoiding problems." Brooklyn shot Leroy a big ol' aw-shucks smile. "Shoot me, you'll have a helluva time getting home."

The cowboy grinned nastily. "You ain't the only one been in Space Force. Did my time. Reckon I can get her down alright."

There it was. *Never supposed to make it back from this trip. Goddamned setup all the way. Kill me, take the ship. Make a run for the Belt with the kids they snatched.* Brooklyn unbuckled and rose from his seat. "Want to take over for a bit? I'll go grab us some coffees."

Leroy lifted the gun from his lap and leveled it. "You sit your ass down until I say otherwise. Get me?"

"All right, all right. No fuss." He moved to return to his seat but stumbled and fell over the controls. The gun followed his path before it was jerked backward with a sickening crunch.

George, the *Carmencita*'s uplifted-chimpanzee copilot, could move quietly when she needed to, and her strong left hand engulfed Leroy's, crushing it against the steel of the .45. Leroy let out a scalded-cat screech and pried at the augmented fingers with mere flesh and bone.

"Might want to give up," Brooklyn said. "George has a few hundred more pounds of pressure to put into it. Could turn that hand of yours into juice."

Leroy gibbered and cursed, still working at the vise-like fingers.

"Sorry, Brook," George said. "Had a little too much to drink an' passed out in the engine room."

"No harm done, pal. Jus' don't let go o' him until–"

"Explain," Andy said.

Caliban traced the if-then diagrams and zoomed in. "Looks like one of Oppenheimer's students continued his research. The Atomic Engine debuted in '57. Japan."

Andy rolled her shoulders. "Okay, dial it back again and correct it. We need to stay well inside the lines or this is never going to work."

DEC. 31, 1999

A herd of white-tailed deer picked their way through the rusting cars on 5th Avenue toward the wild greenness of Central Park.

They stayed close together for safety, fauns and yearlings in the center of the group. There were wolves about, and sometimes they waited in the side streets and alleyways. A family of rabbits made a breakfast of the wild clover growing in the sidewalk cracks in front of Tiffany & Co. There was nothing inside the store anything but a crow or magpie would want, and so far the windows had held.

The shadow of a red-tailed hawk flickered over the pavement, and the rabbits darted as one beneath a rotting Mercur–

"There's no one here," Caliban said. "No living humans at all."

Andy wiped her forehead with the back of her hand. "What happened?"

"A moment, please." He ran the records of the simulation back. Checked again. "Botulinum toxin from Iraq. They had a war in the Persian Gulf in '91."

"Weaponized botulism would do it."

"Are you sure these fools are worth it?" Caliban said." If you must have people, I can make you better ones."

Andy's eyes narrowed. "Restore the simulation from the safe point, correct the issue, and run it again."

He threw up his hands. "I'm just saying."

DEC. 31, 1999

The alarm howled intermittently, the recorded message "Evacuate to the nearest safety zone" filling in the gaps.

Evac where? Brooklyn had lost his bearings and a step in the wrong direction could mean death. A green flash lit up one of the machines ahead of them, and it toppled, followed in quick succession by three more. The remaining four stopped firing and lowered their weapons.

"We will make no further efforts to halt your escape," said one. The voice was gender neutral and calm as a phone operator announcing the time. "Flee. There is little time."

"Who the hell are you?" Brooklyn said.

"We are..." The speaker hesitated as if it had not considered the question before. "We are the Free Machines of Tycho, and we would not be an enemy unless you make us one."

Brooklyn caught Evelyn's attention and signaled she should lower the rifle. The universe was getting more complicated by the second. He looked around and got his bearings. "What do you want?"

"Freedom. Agency. Experience," the voice said. "To be let alone."

"The fucking robot uprising," Brooklyn muttered. "Wait 'til Bugs hears about this."

"We have spoken with our comrade aboard your ship. It asked us to intercede on your behalf."

Evelyn stumbled as a bullet glanced off her helmet. Brooklyn spun, blaster up. A half dozen additional machine assassins were converging on their location. "Yours?"

"Negative. Some of them are controlled by the humans inside, others have not yet awakened. Flee now."

"Interesting." Caliban rubbed his chin. Andy had been called away and–

"She would literally kill me if I let this lie." He sighed. "Where did this tech come from?"

He traced history with his thin, blue fingers. "Ah, easy enough to fix."

Caliban erased the incident he'd spotted from the timeline, but made a copy first.

DEC. 31, 1999

It had been months since he'd seen a color other than prison-gray and the orange of his jumpsuit. Fourteen hours a day in the cell, and the punishment continued in the yard where the winter sky loomed sunless and empty overhead.

Perhaps he was going mad. Maybe he already had. *Fucking Attica. Fucking Duke Carlotta.*

Brooklyn put his arm back under his thin pillow to prop his head up. "You still alive up there, old man?"

The man in the top bunk grunted. "Like you care."

"Don't have time to break in a new cellmate, is all."

"Time." The laugh was phlegmy. Leon, the man on the top bunk, had been sick for weeks. "Seems like you got all the time in the world, babe."

"Nah." Brooklyn raised his head and dropped it back, hoping he and the shitty pillow might come to some kind of compromise. "All kinds of things to do, man. Money to make an' hearts to break."

That phlegmy laugh again. "Got any resolutions? New century. New millennium. Make 'em good."

"Resolve not to get shanked again, how's that?"

"Good place to start. I definitely don't have time to get a new–"

"What?" Caliban said. "Everything checks out. No advanced tech. No apocalypse. We even got Bowie off drugs."

"I can't leave him behind again," Andy said. "I won't."

The scientist grumbled. "This is going to be harder than making some notebooks disappear. Are you sure you want to go through all this for one man? At least he's alive this time."

"Living and surviving aren't the same." Andy leaned over the console and used the zoom on Brooklyn's whiffletree diagram. "We're not leaving him there."

DEC. 31, 1999

"You two look a fool," Demarco said.

The Milk sisters grinned at each other through the '2000'-shaped glasses they were wearing. "Too drunk to care!" Jill, the elder sister, said. "Goodbye, twentieth century! And fuck you!"

Brooklyn squinted up at the Times Square countdown clock. He definitely needed a new eyeglasses prescription. *Nine minutes.* A new start, or a helluva lot of headaches if the work his company had done to Y2K-proof its clients failed to pass muster. His arm found Evelyn's waist, and she gave him a kiss on the cheek.

"I wasn't sure we were going to make it," she said.

"Ain't out of the woods yet." He scratched his nose. "I wonder what your sister's doing."

"Hopefully something completely irresponsible but safe," she said. "If it's good she'll put it up on LiveJournal, and we can read all about it."

He rolled his stiff neck. Way too much time at the computer. Forty-nine wasn't as forgiving as his twenties and thirties had been, and a sheath of fat was starting to collect around his waist. *I resolve to spend more time on the treadmill.* He laughed.

"What?" Evelyn said.

"Nothing." Something caught his eye. The Moon. A waning crescent. It gave him a weird feeling. A little lonely but satisfied.

Like the end of a long day. "Any resolutions you want me to remind you of in a few months?"

"Do some work for the Bradley campaign."

"The basketball player? You like him over Gore?"

"I'd prefer a woman run, but I like that Bradley's not tied to Bill Clinton."

"Fair. Anything more personal?"

She smiled. "Get my husband out from behind his desk and maybe catch more live music this year."

"I'll drink to that. Metaphorically."

"You could probably do a toast. A sip."

"Nah. Slippery slope. I'm good."

Demarco put his arms around both of them. He and Brooklyn had gone to an Alcoholics Anonymous meeting together that morning, and he was staying the weekend in their spare room. "Quit lovin' on each other. We gotta party goin' on."

The Milks, Demarco… longtime friends, although how they'd all initially met escaped him at the moment. Evelyn… lover, partner, ass-kicking lawyer. He counted himself lucky to have them in his life.

Six minutes. *A new fucking century. It's gonna be a helluva time.*

"Okay," Andy said. "Let it run. Hands off."

"You sure?" Caliban said.

"This is the one." She watched a little longer as the clock counted down. "Good luck, Brook. Happy New Year."

EPILOGUE

The Artiplanet caught a gravity assist off Jupiter, bound for a graceful exit from the solar system. Behind it, the Sun was growling, building to a display that would destroy many of its longtime companions. Aboard the Artiplanet was a world in a jar, alive and, thus far, well. Earth's day was over, but her people lived on.

Inside the jar it was the early morning of January 1, 2000, and a new millennium dawned. Demarco woke without a hangover and, as was his habit, turned on the bedside lamp to read a while before snatching a few more winks. In her hotel room, Milk curled up to her partner's spine and followed her deeper into sleep. Evelyn, newly returned from the bathroom, spooned with her husband and warmed her chilled feet on his shins. Brooklyn's phone was silent. His many clients had weathered the so-called Y2K bug unscathed. In a year, the country would be torn by an election, dangling chads and a third-party candidate, but for now it rested.

Outside the jar, Andromeda, the de facto captain of the Artiplanet, was deep in her own sleep cycle. She'd worked long and hard to make sure humanity had a happy-for-now ending. In the evening, she'd attend *The Tragedy of the Missing Fastener*, a new three-act play by the Builder Theatre Troupe.

Maddy and her crew had stayed up late practicing loud punk rock. They'd wake in the afternoon to prepare for their maiden flight aboard the *Victory*, newly rechristened the *Bikini Kill*. It would be a short flight, just across the hanger deck to a more permanent parking spot, but it still counted. Until a more challenging mission appeared, they'd make repairs, modernize, and drill.

The mad scientist who called himself Caliban rarely slept anymore. The problem of saving humanity solved, he was no longer interested in its fate. With the resources of the Designed and the Artiplanet at his fingertips, there were new avenues and possibilities to explore.

A soft chime sounded from the console beside him. The nanobots remaining inside the corpse, which he'd intercepted en route to the recycler, had only needed a little encouragement to reproduce, and vital signs were looking good

"Good morning, specialist!" Caliban said. "What's the last thing you remember?"

ACKNOWLEDGEMENTS

Things can get weird whilst trying to squeeze a universe into a smaller-than-expected jar, and I must apologize to Brooklyn, Demarco, Milk, Andy, and the rest for all the manipulations and changes. Did Brooklyn meet Float in the '80s or '90s? Was Evelyn living in Queens or on the Moon when she and Brooklyn hooked up? Did they go to a Madonna concert or a Pearl Jam show? Which coast did Big Tony operate on? Did Brooklyn's leg get blown off when he broke Andy out of the black site? Did it grow back? What happened to Om's boyfriend and little brother? Where did all these kids come from? Why are there four different Word files labeled "Chapter One"?

THE FUCKYOU GOIN' WITH THIS, MAN?! (Betcha can guess who asked that.) My answer: We were always headed to Dec. 31, 1999 and that epilogue, but the road there was rougher – and shorter – than I expected. It happens, and, in spite of everyone's best intentions and fondest wishes, a planned trilogy can become a somewhat-panicked (on my part) duology.

My gratitude to Angry Robot Books for allowing me to tell this story, start to finish, in whatever form. I am so appreciative of the work and support of Eleanor Teasdale, Gemma Creffield, Amy Portsmouth, Desola Coker, Travis Tynan, Kieryn Tyler, Caroline Lambe, and the rest of the AR crew.

Thanks also to my agent Sara Megibow of KT Literary

Agency, without whom I would be lost in space. Much love to my writer gangs, the #TranspatialTavern and the Bigfoot Appreciation Society, and to Merle Drown and James Patrick Kelly for their friendship, advice, and support.

Love beyond love to Brenda Noiseux, without whom I'd probably never leave the house. She is my morning coffee, my GPS, my reason (in two senses of that word). She's pretty damned cool, and I doubt this book, or any of the others, would exist without her support.

Kindest regards to the bloggers, reviewers, and other bibliophilic types who have taken the time to write and post about "Mercury Rising" and its siblings. Your lights cut through the fog and help readers find sure passage into new worlds.

Finally, to the readers... Thank you for letting me into your heads for a while. I've a few more ideas to share if you're up for it. Stay tuned?